THE TALKING DRUM

We gratefully acknowledge the support of the Canada Council for the Arts and
the Ontario Arts Council for our publishing program. We also acknowledge the
financial support of the Government of Canada through the Canada Book Fund.

The Talking Drum is a work of fiction. All the characters and situations por-
trayed in this book are fictitious and any resemblance to persons living or dead
is purely coincidental.

Cover design: Val Fullard

Library and Archives Canada Cataloguing in Publication

Title: The talking drum : a novel / Lisa Braxton.
Names: Braxton, Lisa, 1961– author.
Series: Inanna poetry & fiction series.
Description: Series statement: Inanna poetry & fiction series
Identifiers: Canadiana (print) 20200204246 | Canadiana (ebook)
20200204254 | ISBN 9781771337410 (softcover) | ISBN 9781771337427
(EPUB) | ISBN 9781771337434 (Kindle) | ISBN 9781771337441 (PDF)
Classification: LCC PS3602.R385 T35 2020 | DDC 813/.6—dc23

Printed and bound in Canada

Inanna Publications and Education Inc.
210 Founders College, York University
4700 Keele Street, Toronto, Ontario, Canada M3J 1P3
Telephone: (416) 736-5356 Fax: (416) 736-5765
Email: inanna.publications@inanna.ca Website: www.inanna.ca

THE TALKING DRUM

A NOVEL

LISA BRAXTON

inanna poetry & fiction series

INANNA PUBLICATIONS AND EDUCATION INC.
TORONTO, CANADA

For my parents

Civilization degrades the many to exalt the few.
—Amos Bronson Alcott

BELLPORT, MASSACHUSETTS, 1971

Bellport Gazette, Final Edition

Investigation into Rooming House Fire Continues

October 16, 1971. Bellport fire officials continue to investigate the cause of a four-alarm blaze that destroyed a three-story rooming house on Pleasant Avenue in the South End of Bellport, an area informally known as "Petite Africa." Six people suffered minor injuries. Seventeen residents of the house were displaced.

The early morning blaze sent fire officials scrambling for backup. Boston was among the fire departments that provided mutual aid. Crews worked for nearly five hours to get the fire under control. Flames could be seen for miles around coming out of the roof. Clouds of thick, grey smoke filled the sky.

Bellport Fire Chief Patrick O'Connell says the blaze appears to have started at the back of the building, where fire climbed the walls. When asked if the fire could be related to two others that have occurred in the past six months in the largely immigrant community, officials would not comment.

The city has plans to redevelop the area, taking most of the neighborhood and some surrounding blocks by eminent domain to build a sixty-four million, twelve thousand-seat civic center complex, luxury high-rise apartments, restaurants, marina, and off ramp from the North/South Expressway along the seaboard.

The project is scheduled for completion in February 1974.

Anyone with information on the fires is asked to contact the Bellport Police Detective Division.

CHAPTER 1: SIX MONTHS LATER

BEFORE SYDNEY STALLWORTH could reach for the handle, her husband, Malachi, was out of the car and opening the door for her. She stepped down, stumbled, regained her balance, and then spotted the nip bottle she had just stepped on. It skidded across the driveway like a hockey puck. She shuddered as she looked around, scanning the asphalt. Several others littered the driveway.

"What're these doing here?" Malachi growled as he scooped up the bottles and tossed them in the metal trash can leaning against the house.

"Sorry, man," his best friend Kwamé said as he slammed shut the driver's side door. "I had some of the fellas clean up around here. They must've had a little taste after they were done."

Sydney doubted that it was just a little taste. She pictured men loitering around the driveway, guzzling booze from bottles in brown paper bags.

"Smells like someone's having a barbecue," Kwamé said a little more loudly than necessary.

"Must be the neighbors," Malachi replied, relieved at the change of topic.

Sydney sniffed the air and caught the aroma of brown sugar, ketchup, and a couple of other ingredients mixed with a trace of sea water from the harbor.

"People barbecue all the time around here," Kwamé said and popped open the trunk. "They're good people. Friendly.

They'll invite you over, feed you."

Sydney reached into her camera bag for her 35-millimeter Konica, her favorite, and aimed it at the Victorian house. *Their house*, 133 Liberty Hill Boulevard, she had to remind herself. She wanted a record of her and Malachi's first moments in their new home, which would also be the location of their business. The pictures would go into a photo album she'd put together after she had assembled their wedding album and honeymoon pictures. She focused her shots tight on their dusty blue Queen Anne with its banana custard-color latticework, shutters, and railings.

Kwamé pulled the couple's luggage out of the trunk, and plopped the suitcases onto the pavement. "What the two of you do down there in Jamaica? Pack up half the island?"

Malachi laughed and squeezed Sydney's shoulders. "The Missus got a little carried away with the souvenirs, but that's all right."

"I'd never seen soapstone before," Sydney added.

"Hey! I feel you," Kwamé said. "My Aunt Marie used to go to Nassau a couple of times a year with a church group. Couldn't get enough of those soapstone sculptures. She got one in the shape of a turtle with two heads. She used to scare the mess out of us kids with that thing. After a while, she started using it as a doorstop." He slammed the trunk shut and looked up at the house.

"You've got fourteen rooms here: three floors, the basement, and the attic. I don't think the Greensteins used the attic except for storage. The basement is finished. You could always do something with that."

Malachi had told her stories about Greenstein's Furniture Store, which had operated on the first floor of the Victorian. Malachi and Kwamé, childhood friends, grew up in the apartment building across the street.

They looked odd side-by-side, the slightly built Kwamé, in his dashiki, bell-bottoms, and platform shoes, and the taller

Malachi, in his tweed jacket, khakis, and loafers. Kwamé never stopped talking, but he seemed insecure underneath the bravado. Sydney sensed that he was hiding something. She felt wary of him, but decided to reserve judgment.

She focused her lens on the two men and took a couple of frames as they laughed and talked. A moment later, Malachi took her hand and guided her through the side gate. Its rusted hinges squealed.

A bird house built like a gazebo hung from a maple tree in the front yard. Its colors matched the Victorian.

To their right, Sydney admired the flower garden, brilliant with color. She crouched down to take close-ups of the crocuses with their cup-shaped blooms of yellow, white, and lavender.

"Della planted those," Kwamé said, "to welcome you to the neighborhood." He gestured with an unlit cigarette he held between two fingers.

"Tell Della we say 'thank you'," Sydney said thinking back on the woman she'd met the day of the wedding. Della Tolliver, Kwamé's girlfriend, was an assistant librarian at the Liberty Hill Branch Library. She had a trim Afro a little shorter than Sydney's and an athletic build, with a tiny waist and curvy hips that Sydney envied.

Malachi led Sydney up the porch steps. Kwamé handed him a slip of paper with the code to the alarm system typed on it. "Be back after you two check the place out. I think you'll dig what we've done to clean it up."

Kwamé waved and then crossed the street to the apartment building where he lived with Della and her daughter, Jasmine. He unlocked the door to the record shop that he operated on the first floor and slipped inside.

Malachi turned the key in the wrought iron security door of the Victorian and opened it, unlocked the heavy wooden door behind it, and then twisted the large knob. Then he turned off the alarm system and went back onto the porch for the luggage. Sydney took a deep breath and stepped inside.

As she stood in the vestibule, a stream of light came through the stained-glass window. It cast a rich, warm glow on the sweeping, cherrywood staircase.

Sydney led the way into the front parlor. She pressed a button on the wall near the doorway. Nothing happened. Malachi flipped the switch next to it and a brass candelabra chandelier with glass bulbs brightened the room with a burst of light. They walked the perimeter of the room, Sydney running her hands along the cream-colored wainscoting, Malachi fiddling with the knobs on the cast iron radiators.

The focal point of the dining room was the cherrywood fireplace. Sydney moved closer to study the detail work in the wood. The heels of her platform shoes echoed on the hardwood floor. Over the mantle hung a large, silver framed rectangular mirror the width of the fireplace. She looked at Malachi's reflection smiling at her. At six foot four inches, he was a full seven inches taller than she was, but he appeared even taller because of his Afro, a massive crown of dark, tightly curled hair. She thought the thin lines forming at the corners of his eyes and the traces of grey in his sideburns made him look sexy.

As they climbed the stairs to the second floor, Sydney slid her hand up the freshly polished wood of the thick, curving banister. The wail of sirens pierced the air as they ventured into the old-fashioned kitchen. The tin ceiling was embossed with silver metal. The walk-in pantry had two white paneled doors that could be pushed apart to provide for a wide entry. Sydney spread her arms the length of the pantry and still had room left over. Just outside the pantry she came across a dumbwaiter, large enough to fit a small child.

When they got to the bathroom, Sydney's eyes were drawn to the claw-foot bathtub on a platform in the middle of the room. Malachi leaned over it and turned on the hot and cold faucets. As he ran his fingers under the water, he looked up at Sydney and winked. Her cheeks began to feel warm.

On their way down the stairs the sirens sounded closer.

When they got to the front porch, Kwamé was waiting there, along with Della. Jasmine, who looked to be about five years old, held tightly onto her mother's hand. They all turned to the sound of more sirens and watched a Bellport Fire Department truck roar down Liberty Hill Boulevard followed by another. Jasmine covered her ears.

Once the trucks were gone, Della leaned down to Jasmine. "Can you say 'hello' to Miss Sydney and Mr. Malachi?" Sydney had never been referred to that way, but she thought it was sweet, probably a Southern custom.

"No!" The child shouted. Sydney flinched. Jasmine frowned and buried her face in her mother's hip.

"She's been acting up today," Kwamé explained as Jasmine whimpered. Everyone focused on the child.

"The flowers are lovely and so is the bird house," Sydney said finally. "I can tell you put a lot of care into what you do."

"It wasn't much of nothing," Della replied, glancing down at her daughter, her hand resting on the little girl's head. "I see something I like and figure out how to do it. I like to lose myself in things. Come by sometime, and I'll show you my little workshop."

Della's accent was charming, relaxed and different from the New England accents Sydney heard all the time. She felt she could listen to the woman speak all day long. Jasmine pouted, tugged on her mother's sleeve. "I want to go home, now, Mommy."

"No, Jazzy," Della admonished, gripping her daughter's shoulders. "Please be nice to our friends."

Jasmine looked from Sydney to Malachi and scowled. She had the curly eyelashes and thick eyebrows of her mother. She let loose a scream as piercing as the sirens. "I don't like them, Mommy. I want to go home." Jasmine then punched her mother in the stomach with her little fist.

Kwamé grabbed the child by the hand and growled, "You listen to your mama."

The child pulled away from him and clung to Della. "She needs a little nap, that's all," Della explained, as she stepped off the porch. She smiled weakly and waved before tugging the child through the yard and back across the street.

Kwamé watched them until they got through the front door and then turned to Sydney and Malachi, his smile wide. "We still on for tomorrow?"

Malachi's face went blank. "What's tomorrow?"

Kwamé leaned against the porch railing. "Man, don't tell me you forgot. Lunch. I'm taking you and the Missus to The Stewed Oxtail."

Malachi ran his hand over the top of his thick hair. "Man, I've got so much on my mind. It must've gotten past me. I really don't remember. I have to go back on campus, clean out my office, pick up my last paycheck. I need to put up some notices that we're looking for a student intern."

Kwamé stroked his goatee. "Intern? What you need one of them for?"

"We want to hire an intern to work in the store for college credit."

"Man, I was looking forward to taking you out. Lunch was gonna be on me."

"I'm sorry, but you and Della will have to give us a rain check," Malachi said.

Kwamé shook his head and frowned with disappointment. "Della can't go. She found out she has to fill in at the library tomorrow."

They said nothing for a while. Then Malachi turned to Sydney, his gaze hopeful.

"What is it?" she asked.

"You can go."

Sydney thought he was joking. But Malachi's facial expression didn't change. "I can't go," she entreated in a low voice. "Not without you."

He put an arm around her shoulder. "Baby, of course you

can. Go and have a nice lunch with Kwamé. The man's an encyclopedia when it comes to Bellport. It'll be good for you to learn more about the city."

But she didn't know Kwamé that well and Sydney didn't care to be around him more than she had to. She looked at Kwamé willing him to say they should postpone lunch until all four of them were available, but he just stood there grinning, waiting for her response. Maybe it wouldn't be that bad, she thought. It was only lunch. "Okay," she said in a voice that was barely audible.

Kwamé gave Malachi the soul brother's handshake. They angled their hands up as they clasped and then went palm to palm, interlocking with their fingers tight together. "See you tomorrow," he said as he hugged Sydney a little too tightly. Then he got to the front of the yard and pimp-strolled across the street.

"Thank you for doing this, Syd," Malachi said. "He's a good brother. Let him school you on the neighborhood. It'll mean a lot to him."

"But I have no idea what I'll talk to him about."

Malachi laughed. "Don't worry, Kwamé knows how to keep a conversation going. He'll do all the talking. He'll talk you to death if you let him."

Seagulls circled overhead, cackling as Malachi plunked himself down on the top step of the porch and then pulled Sydney down onto the second step between his knees. "I've thought up a name for the business. You can veto it if you don't like it. I want to call it The Talking Drum Bookstore and Cultural Center."

She leaned back, resting her head on his chest and smiled. The name had a melodious feel. "I wouldn't think of vetoing it. I love it."

"Every time people see the name they'll think of our African ancestors pounding on the drums to celebrate births, marriages, a call to war," he said. "Our Talking Drum is going to break it down for people, teach them about politics, economics, the Black Arts Movement. Then after we've been around for a while, I'd like to move into the next phase. We'll expand on the cultural aspect. It'll be a research center with collections from famous black poets, writers, philosophers, and artists. Scholars will come from all over to do research. We'll be quoted in research papers. Who needs Whittington University? I'll start my own academy."

Malachi sounded like he was lecturing a room full of college students. But she remembered reading somewhere that most businesses failed within the first year. What had her mother said before the wedding? *He's an academic. What does he know about retail?*

"And you think it'll make money?" she asked.

He massaged her shoulders. "I wouldn't have bought the building if I didn't think it would. We'll corner the market. Where else in the area are black people going to find books written by black people, about black issues? Where else can black people meet to discuss what's going on?"

He shifted around to face her. "You're not having second thoughts, are you?"

She rarely saw Malachi look so serious. The last time was when his application for a full professor's position was denied. She squeezed his hand. "No. We're offering something that's hard to find in this area. The neighborhood's not *that* bad, and the house is lovely. I don't see why we wouldn't get a lot of customers."

She pushed her mother's words to the back of her mind. This was Malachi's dream. She would give him her full support.

Malachi folded his arms around Sydney. "What would you say is your favorite part of the house?"

"The bathtub," she answered without hesitation. "You know how much I like a good soak."

He chuckled. "You looked a little flustered when I started running the water."

She loved it when he teased her. "I was thinking that the tub was a nice size, that's all."

He nibbled at her earlobe. "A nice size for what?"

She laughed. "A nice size for us both to fit."

He stood up. "Then we should try it out."

"What do you mean?"

He got up and walked to the front door. When she didn't follow, he turned around. "Are you going to join me?"

Sydney loved his spontaneity. He held the door open for her. As she crossed the threshold, he gave her a playful smack on the rear end.

CHAPTER 2

FROM THE SECOND-FLOOR kitchen window, Della had a perfect view of the Victorian across the street. She watched Malachi and Sydney get up from the porch steps and head to the door. Kwamé had already crossed the street. He must be downstairs in the record shop.

Sydney resembled Diahann Carroll. She had the same complexion, and her teeth were perfectly straight like the actress's, too. Sydney had probably worn braces when she was a kid, a rich young missy like that—Della bet Mommy and Daddy could easily afford to get her braces. Della didn't realize how attractive Sydney was when she and Kwamé were at the wedding. Sydney's gown had a full skirt that concealed her shape. The fancy "up-do" and fake eyelashes made her look much older though she couldn't be more than twenty-three or twenty-four. Malachi must be around thirty-two, a year or two younger than Kwamé and her.

Sydney seemed devoted to Malachi. Maybe Kwamé would leave this one alone. The last thing she needed was another tramp to deal with.

She plugged in the electric skillet and scooped out a big chunk of Crisco shortening, plopping it into the pan. She tore the butcher shop paper from the pork chops she had left on the counter earlier to thaw.

She couldn't help but feel a bit distracted by Sydney's arrival. Della decided not to get too comfortable about her just yet.

Women could not be trusted. Della had learned that the hard way, a long time ago, when her husband was still alive.

Kwamé seemed to have a thing for blondes, but he could always switch up and go for a suburban black girl. Della would give Sydney a few weeks to unpack. Then she would invite her over for lunch. Perhaps Della would find out what she was dealing with.

Della could hear Jasmine whimpering in her room down the hall. The child was thrashing around on the bed, her hands balled into fists, muttering in her sleep. Jasmine had seen more in her young life than anybody, child or adult, should have to witness. If Della could roll back time she would have sent Jasmine to her mother's for the weekend the first time Jasmine's dad—her husband, Tucker—beat her. Many other beatings had followed and Jasmine had witnessed the horror of it all.

Della had grown up thinking that marriage was blessed by God. Hers certainly wasn't. After everything she had gone through with Tucker, she was done. She knew the church elders clucked behind her back because she was "shacking up," but she didn't care. She had to do what was best for her and her daughter, and her living arrangement was none of their business. She would never marry Kwamé, not only because of her bad experience with Tucker, but because she knew Kwamé would never be faithful.

Della unclenched Jasmine's fists and climbed into the twin bed with her. "It's okay, Jazzy. It's okay," she whispered, rocking the little girl until she calmed down and went back to sleep.

A moment later, Della heard Kwamé put his key in the lock. When she met up with him in the kitchen, she put a finger to pursed lips to let him know not to wake Jasmine.

"Been a long day, and I'm glad it's over," he exhaled. "Had some meetings before I went to the airport. Malachi and Sydney are settlin' into the house."

"That's fine," replied Della, "as long as you ain't settlin' into *her*."

Kwamé slumped into a chair at the kitchen table. "Woman, you need to stop that."

She stood over him, a hand on her hip. "No. *You* need to stop it. Don't take me for no damned fool, Kwamé. Don't think I don't know about all the little bitches you got coming in and out of the record shop. I know what you're doing when you hang that 'out to lunch' sign on the door. You're doing it right under my nose. I'm not blind and stupid. I've got people who tell me things."

He leaned back in his chair and stroked his goatee. "Who you going to believe, them or me?"

She went back to the counter and turned on the skillet. "Stop the bullshit or get out." She seasoned the chops and then shook flour onto a paper towel and dredged the meat with it. "She's a pretty little thing. I just don't want any mess out of you."

He got up from the kitchen table and grabbed her hips from behind. "But not as pretty as you. She don't have the curves you got." He pressed against her, so she could feel the bulge in his crotch.

"So what time should I meet y'all at The Stewed Oxtail tomorrow?" she asked.

He let go of her. "We're not doing that now."

She turned around. "Why not? I was going to take the afternoon off for that."

"The Professah has to go back to the university to pack up some things. Sydney has errands to run, to get the house together. You know how you women are."

"Just as well," she said, carefully placing the pork chops into the hot oil. "Library's got a book sale tomorrow, and Maggie is sick. If I don't go in, they'll be up a creek."

The meat sizzled and the hot grease began to pop. She lowered the heat. Kwamé had distracted her. "They don't know what they're getting themselves into, do they?"

Kwamé reached into the refrigerator for a beer. "What you mean?"

She laughed. "This neighborhood?"

"Now don't go getting all negative on me, Dell. Once they build that civic center, this place is gonna light up. We'll get restaurants, high-priced shops. We'll make a killing. Malachi and Sydney's bookstore, the record shop, Tovah's Bridal shop, Jake's Tavern—hell, your library will get more patrons."

"You've been telling yourself that, huh? It'll take a lot more than a civic center and a few shops to turn this neighborhood around. If I didn't have the tenants upstairs, I'd have to shut down Rhythm and Blues. I bet you can't even remember the last time you had a customer."

"Now why you got to go and say that?" He took a sip of beer and set it down forcefully on the counter. "You thought more about what we discussed?"

She knew he would get around to it. For weeks he'd been trying to convince her to take some equity out of the building, *her* building, and give him a loan to bring in a new line of inventory to create an electronics department.

"The answer is still no," she said. "Let's drop it. I'm done talking about that."

"Oh, come on, Dell."

She raised the lid on the chops and pushed them around with a fork to keep them from sticking to the skillet.

"I'm not pulling out my equity. That's my decision. I bought this place, and I'll do what I want with it. If I decide to pull some money out it would be to do some upgrades in the building, not throw money out the window."

"I have a right to that money, Dell."

She flipped the chops. "The hell you do."

"I help pay the taxes. I paid for the new water heater. I even kicked in money for that dishwasher so you'd stop complaining about standing at the sink all day."

She wiped her hands on a dish towel and turned around to face him. "Tucker's insurance money paid for this building. I'm not gonna waste my equity on your fantasy."

"So this building is a shrine to your dead husband."

"You shut the hell up!" she hissed.

They both heard a thud, like a hammer against the wall coming from down the hall. Della turned down the skillet and headed toward Jasmine's room. Kwamé went to the living room. "We ain't done talking about this, Dell," he shouted to an empty hallway. "Not even close."

CHAPTER 3

SIX BLOCKS AWAY and across the Bellport River Bridge in Petite Africa, Omar Bassari read the notice that his wife Natalie held inches from his nose. The Bassaris had to pay three months' back rent by the end of the month—including late fees—or be evicted.

"*Il est un idiot,*" Omar muttered as he returned his attention to the peanut paste he had cooking on the stove. "Fullerton does not care a fig about us."

Natalie flung the notice, along with the rest of the day's mail and her canvas book bag, onto the kitchen counter. An accounting textbook, *The Bellport Gazette,* and some sheet music slid out. She tugged at the sleeves of her goose-down jacket and hung it on a hook in the hallway. "I knew a rent strike was a bad idea," she fumed. "Why did you listen to those people?"

The Bassaris rented a cramped two-bedroom apartment in The Commonwealth Arms, a pre-World War I building on King Street, in the heart of Petite Africa, owned by white businessman James Fullerton. They'd moved there six months ago when a fire burned down their three-story rooming house on the corner of Pleasant and Garfield avenues five blocks away.

Omar's uncle Mustapha had found them their first apartment a year and a half ago when the couple moved to town after they both had dropped out of Howard University in Washington, D.C. After the fire, Mustapha stepped in again, negotiating a reduced price from Fullerton for the couple to live at The

Commonwealth Arms. This allowed Omar to cover most of the household expenses with the thirty to forty dollars a week he averaged from his drumming performances.

Natalie was studying to be an accountant but dreamed of acting in theater and film. She had white classmates at Bellport Community College who got experience and a little extra money doing bit parts in television commercials. But casting companies rarely chose black performers. So she settled for jobs doing voiceovers and singing jingles for radio. She barely made enough to pay for her college courses and private voice and acting classes. Little was left over for anything else.

The Commonwealth Arms was in worse shape than the other building they lived in. The plumbing periodically backed up. The oil heat worked off and on. To Omar, the building's problems were minor inconveniences. Growing up in Senegal, he knew nothing of utilities, landlords, rent, or groceries. He spent his childhood in the family *ker*, a compound of mud huts with thatched roofs. There was no plumbing, running water, or electricity. Pit toilets were kept at the far end of the *ker*. At sundown, villagers lit paraffin lamps or candles, or sat in the dark and told fables.

Once, Omar got workers to fix the boiler, but within days it broke down again. He went into Liberty Hill and bought fan heaters for the apartment. Natalie had to heat water on the electric stove for bathwater. She complained that they weren't living much better than villagers from his community.

Then one night, the elevator broke. Tenants got stuck between floors for hours. Natalie was forced to haul her books and groceries up six flights.

All of the tenants were fed up with the conditions. One night, they met in the stairwell to vent about the building's problems. They decided on a rent strike. They would not pay Fullerton until repairs were made. Natalie saw the strike as a waste of time. She thought there was no way Fullerton would budge and that she and Omar should simply pack up and move. Declaring "the jungle is stronger than the elephant," Omar overruled his wife. Today, all the tenants found eviction notices taped to their doors.

On the stove the peanut paste was beginning to bubble. With a long-handled wooden spoon, Omar scooped up the paste and folded it in with the beef cubes, broth, and tomato paste warming in another pot. Normally, Natalie wouldn't be home in time for dinner, but her appointment with the voice coach had been canceled. To mark the occasion, Omar used some of the tip money from his drum performances and went to Bamba's Africa Food Market down the street to get the ingredients for *mafé*, or groundnut stew, one of the few Senegalese dishes Natalie would eat. Being an American, Senegalese dishes were unfamiliar to her. Bamba Toukou was out of goat meat, so Omar was using beef as a substitute. He ordered half the amount the dish called for so he could also buy a jar of herbs he needed.

"We shall not let this man chase us from this building," Omar declared. "We have the right to be here and to have good services. He cannot possibly put all of us in the road."

Natalie glared at him. "The man has no heart. What does he care?"

She lifted the cover and peeked inside the pot, sniffed at the contents, and warmed her nose over the rising steam. Then she whipped around and marched down the hall toward the bedroom. The cowrie shells woven into her braids made light clicking sounds as they bounced against each other.

Omar was glad to have her home. Since the fire, she had scheduled more classes, more coaching, more voiceover jobs. He had gotten into the habit of leaving a plate in the oven at night for her. She came to bed when he was asleep and left in the morning before he was awake. She claimed that she was trying to make up for credits she lost when she dropped out of Howard, but he wondered if she was telling the truth. She never talked about the miscarriage. It had happened a few days after the fire. They had had little conversation about anything since then and they no longer touched each other in bed. But tonight would be different if his plan worked.

Omar added water to the stock pot to loosen the ingredients and get the stew to the proper consistency. He watched the pot a while, then put a lid on it and left the stew to simmer.

Natalie came back into the kitchen. "Where are we going to live?" She sounded exasperated. "We've only got a couple of weeks to find something else." She'd changed out of her college clothing—bell-bottom pants, a blouse with a bow, and wraparound sweater—and into a jogging outfit, dark pants with a white stripe running down the outside of the legs and a matching jacket that zipped. "If you would knock it off with that silly drumming and those daydreams about playing with the Duke Ellington Orchestra and get a job that paid something, we could move to a decent place."

Omar felt deflated. Natalie didn't believe in him and his dream. The day he reunited with his musical hero, she would shut her mouth. He poked around in the stew with the spoon. The mixture had gone from buttery to brothy. He covered it again, and then grabbed a dish towel to pull the lid off a sauce pan of couscous simmering on a back burner. He fluffed the couscous with the wooden spoon. The aroma of peanuts, tomato paste, and garlic filled the apartment. "You know I have no desire to get a regular job, not after the boot factory."

He'd worked the assembly line of the Nathaniel Hawthorne Boot Factory along the Bellport River when he and Natalie first moved to the city. Every day he feared his mind would rot. He ran the shoe eyelet machine and feared punching a hole in his finger instead of the fabric. The work was so boring. He was glad when the company shut down and moved out of the country. "I keep telling you that the drumming institute will give us the income to be comfortable."

Natalie smacked the counter with her palm as if she were killing a cockroach. "You have to stop that nonsense."

"That is why I do not tell you about it. You shall not listen."

"Am I talking to a child? You're not being rational, Omar, not you or your Uncle Mustapha."

Omar shook his head. "Uncle believes that the drumming institute will open, and uncle is a smart businessman."

Natalie cut her eyes at him, then picked up *The Bellport Gazette* from the counter and looked over the front page. He glanced over her shoulder. A photo showed Bellport Mayor Chauncey McShane standing next to architectural plans for an arena that was the centerpiece of the Harborview Redevelopment Project. The caption told of plans to take Petite Africa and surrounding blocks by eminent domain, meaning that the government could seize private property and claim it for public use. Omar visualized the day when the news story would come out about how Uncle Mustapha would go to court to stop the project.

"The city says we are a blighted community, a ghetto." Natalie declared. "Fullerton has nothing to lose by evicting us. He's going to coast until the city takes over the building. He'll make a fortune selling it to the city."

Omar wished Natalie had left the newspaper at school where she'd found it. She was not in the mood for love. Ever since the miscarriage she had been angry. Lately, Omar would reach for her and she would act as if she'd been stung by a wasp. She'd start to cry and smack him away.

They each relived the fire. Omar woke at least twice a night, listening for the crackling of burning wood. Natalie tossed for hours most nights and cried. She could doze only after checking the street below. The fire had killed her feelings for him, Omar thought.

He lowered the flame under the pot. He would add the herbs to the *mafé*. "We shall not go anywhere," he announced. "Uncle Mustapha shall file a lawsuit to stop the project. Fullerton shall rethink his ways. I know this."

"Your uncle is as delusional as you are," she muttered.

Omar was offended but swallowed his anger. "They have been talking about taking over this building, taking over Petite Africa, for years, and nothing has happened, *ma chère*. And do you know why?"

"No, I don't," she hissed through clenched teeth.

"Because the people of Petite Africa are protected by a force much greater than a city or government."

She rolled her eyes and plopped down onto a kitchen stool. "Will you stop with that?"

"Allah will not let the people of Petite Africa lose their homes. That is why these plans keep dragging on. It shall never happen. If they put a letter under my door or tape a sign to the building that the bulldozer is coming, I shall not believe it. Allah will stop the bulldozer."

He wiped his hands on a dish towel and took the newspaper from her. He scanned the top of the page. "They have been making stories like this for years. The city keeps having dialogue and taking votes. I do not believe the government would put us out of our home."

"You are a very naïve man." She moved closer to him, almost shouting in his face. "Don't you read what the papers are telling us? You can't trust the government. The government has been lying about Vietnam for years. Our soldiers are dying over there every day, many of them black like us. We shouldn't even be there."

"You are a cynical American." He pressed the foot lever on the trash can to lift the lid and toss in the newspaper. But the inside section slipped onto the floor. The headline at the top of the page was a follow-up story about the fire at their former apartment building. Natalie snatched the section before Omar could get it away from her. She twisted her mouth until she was smirking. "I see they still don't know what or who caused the fire."

"You do not need to read these things," he said and reached for the section.

She pulled the paper away from his grasp. "Everyone has moved on and forgotten about it, but I won't forget." Her eyes brimmed with tears.

He made an effort to speak to her gently. "Natalie, the fire did not cause your miscarriage. The doctor told us that."

"Maybe the doctor doesn't know what he's talking about." She balled up the newspaper and stuffed it into the trash can. Then she pulled two dinner plates from a cabinet and silverware from a drawer. Omar watched her until she left the kitchen to set the table. When he heard the plates slam onto the dinette table, he reached into the back of the cabinet over the stove. Natalie never ventured there. He pulled out a shoebox-size container and pushed aside guinea fowl feathers, horns of a pygmy goat, and a fertility statue to get to two baby-food size jars of herbs he'd bought for twenty dollars earlier in the day. He picked up one of the jars and read the label, which was made out of a thick piece of white bandaging tape. *Zepis*, the word for "herb" in French Creole, was scrawled in ink.

He held the jar close to his chest to muffle the scraping sound as he unscrewed the lid. As he'd been directed, he crushed herbs between his fingertips. When he thought he had enough, he sprinkled a little of it over the stew.

"What's that?"

He flinched, nearly dropping the jar. Natalie was right behind him. He didn't realize she had slipped back into the kitchen. She stood on tiptoes to see over his shoulders. Her breath warmed the back of his neck.

"That's not some African voodoo spice, is it? Some *mojo*? Some *juju*?" She snickered.

He had grown tired of the jabs she made at his culture and she knew it. "My people do not do voodoo, *ma chère*. You are talking about the West Indians." He screwed the lid back on the jar and set it on the counter. "It's just a blend of herbs, that's all."

"Then why are you so secretive about it?"

"There are no secrets. Uncle Mustapha put these herbs to-gether. It is a formula only he knows how to make."

That seemed to satisfy her. She went back down the hall to finish setting the table.

Omar took a deep breath. Once he heard the clanging of silverware against the table, he unscrewed the jar again and sprinkled more of the crushed herbs onto the stew. It was a homemade love potion, a combination of rosemary, violet, myrtle flower, clove, and some secret ingredients that the seller, Hallima Santafara, wouldn't reveal to him.

It will make your wife want to make love to you all night. She will not be able to control herself, she'd told him.

Half an hour later the stew was ready. Omar heaped a generous helping onto his wife's plate over a bed of couscous. He looked for traces of the herbs, relieved that they had dissolved into the sauce. Hallima said the herbs had to mix thoroughly with food once it was cooked for the potion to work. Then he fixed his plate.

He missed the nights early in their relationship, when he would leave their bed to turn off the lamp across the room and in a husky voice she would say, "Hurry back." Maybe they could recapture that tonight.

"Why did the voice coach cancel," he asked as they sat down at the table. He always referred to him that way. Omar knew his name but wanted to keep some distance from the man.

Natalie stared at a brown water stain in the corner of the ceiling. Finally, she answered, "He had something else he had to do."

Omar knew he was pushing her but kept going. He couldn't stop himself. He cleared his throat. "Does that upset you?"

"Nope." Her jaw was tight. "He rescheduled for next week."

Omar sucked in a breath. Months ago, he had accused her of booking more coaching sessions than she needed just to spend more time with the coach. Since that night, she shared little about her sessions. Now, he watched as Natalie turned herself and her plate at a slight angle away from him. He hated when she did that. She picked at her food, pushing the outer portions of the couscous untouched by the stew onto the edges of her plate. Eventually she stood up. Omar pushed his plate aside. "We need to get out of this hellhole," she blurted out. "I'm calling Mom and Dad. Once I tell them about these conditions, they'll give us money to get a better place."

Omar had always liked the Coopers: Josephine, a former Peace Corps volunteer, and her husband Walter, a Georgetown dentist. Omar got along well with the family. While in college, he spent his second Thanksgiving in the United States at their home. They didn't object to the romance, at least not at first. But they cut off Natalie's financial support when she got pregnant.

Omar felt ashamed that Natalie would ask her parents for money. "I shall go see Fullerton. I shall talk to him."

Slowly, she sat back down and stared at her half empty plate. "You'd better. I will *not* live under these conditions anymore."

He watched her chew the last bit of food and wondered if Hallima's potion would work. Hallima hadn't mentioned if the herbs could make an angry person want to make love.

"I will start the teapot," he offered as he went to a cabinet for a bag of green tea and mint leaves.

"I don't want any," she snapped. "I'm going to bed."

He quickly cleared the table and scrubbed the dinner pots. He would never tell his family that he cooked for his wife and served her plate. They would think he needed to come back home to Senegal to see the village *marabout,* a holy man, to get medicine for his affliction. He boiled the tea, steeped it, and then he added mint leaves. He could hear Natalie down the hall, zipping or unzipping something, then pushing hangers around in the bedroom closet and opening and shutting the bureau drawers. He hoped she was cleaning out their closet. It was so stuffed with Natalie's garments that his clothes were pushed to the back.

He quickly dried the pots, then added sugar to the tea and

poured it into tea glasses. Down the hall, he heard the whir of the fan heater.

He got to the bedroom doorway in time to see Natalie getting undressed. She had her back to him. All the lights were out except for the small lamp on the nightstand. She was naked from the waist up, crouching to step out of her pink satin panties. He took in the full view of her body. His erection pressed against his pants zipper. He didn't know if it was the potion or happening naturally. He looked away a moment hoping to calm his lust, afraid he would burst if he didn't. He loved her and her body, not only for pleasure, but for the promise of children to come. The doctor had told them the miscarriage shouldn't keep them from trying for another child.

Natalie slipped her nightgown over her head. He could see her silhouette. Was she trying to entice him? He stepped into the room and crept around the bed. He stood behind her, pressing himself against her, and placed his hands on her waist. He sniffed the back of her neck, becoming further aroused by the smell of the cocoa butter which she used daily. He lifted a long braid resting on her shoulder and fingered a cowrie shell, turning it over in his hand. He brushed his crotch up against her back and dreamed of their bodies wrapped around each other. She stiffened. Had he surprised her? He tried to turn her around to face him; she pulled in the other direction.

"No."

"No? Why not, *ma chère?* What is it? What is the matter?"

She stood still a moment, then reached down and yanked one of the pillows off the bed and tugged at the sheets until they were freed from the mattress.

"Do … do you want to change the sheets?" he asked.

She turned around to face him, her eyes narrowed, and shoved the pillow and sheets into his chest. She tried to push him toward the doorway. "You go see Fullerton in the morning and get this whole thing fixed. You're not welcome in our bed until you do."

Omar's erection went limp. He tossed the sheets and pillow onto the sofa bed in the living room and went back into the kitchen. He reached for his glass of tea and took a swallow. Mint tea was soothing when it was hot, but when it was cold it was painful. He spat it out in the sink.

CHAPTER 4

MALACHI REACHED for a slice of toast as Sydney reached for the ringing phone, but then ignored it. "You know that was your mother," he said when the phone had stopped ringing. "There's no point in putting her off. You should have talked to her and gotten it over with."

"I know, but I don't want to hear her reaction. I'll call her back later." Sydney added scrambled eggs to his plate of bacon and home fries.

Yesterday, when the couple flew into Logan Airport after their honeymoon, Kwamé was going to drop Sydney off at South Station so she could catch the train back to her hometown, Old Prescott. There she would have a few days at home before resuming law classes at nearby Whittington University. Then Kwamé and Malachi would drive on the expressway twenty miles north of Boston to Bellport. But when their plane landed, Sydney called her mother to say that she would be delaying her return to Old Prescott, and that she would be staying in Bellport with Malachi for a few days. Bernadine pressed her for the reason, but Sydney hurried her off the phone.

"She's your mother, Syd. She's not going away."

"I know."

He pushed the food around on his plate. "This is good, but more than I can eat. Why'd you fix so much? You know I only eat this much on weekends."

Sydney put the bag of potatoes back on the pantry shelf. "You've got a long ride ahead of you back to campus. I don't want you getting hungry."

"But I'd have to be a lumberjack to eat all of this."

She took another look at the dumbwaiter, just outside of the pantry. "How cute," she said.

"Apparently, back in the early 1900s, there were servants here cooking the meals in the basement," Malachi said. "They'd send food to the main floor and upstairs to the living quarters."

She slid the panel open on the dumbwaiter and fumbled with the pulley system for a while until she figured out how to work it. "I never tried one of these before."

Malachi picked up a slice of bacon. "Greenstein had his mother-in-law in the basement, the furniture store on the first floor, and his family up here on the second floor. I remember Greenstein telling me he'd have his wife send his mother-in-law's food down on that thing to keep her from coming upstairs."

"Sounds like she was a real joy to live with." She tugged on the levers to move the cabinet down the shaft and then up again. The pulley squealed like the brakes on an old subway car.

Malachi frowned. "Oil. Put that on the list."

Sydney jotted a note on a pad on the kitchen counter.

"Which reminds me of something else we need to take care of," he said, "the classified ad for the basement apartment. Can you look into that?"

"Sure. I'll call *The Bellport Gazette* this week."

"And don't forget *Inner City Voice*. It's run by a brother. Max Turner. We should support him." He scraped the crumbs from his plate into the trash can and put the plate into the sink.

"Another thing we need to do is hire Lawrence part-time," he said. Sydney sat down across from him.

Malachi met Lawrence Briggs fifteen years ago when Malachi was his first-grade Sunday School teacher at Nehemiah Baptist Church in Liberty Hill. Raised by his grandmother in a high-crime area of Liberty Hill, Lawrence had already served time in the juvenile detention center after his arrest for car theft. Malachi talked his grandmother into enrolling him into a reformatory school. Later, Lawrence did well enough to qualify for a scholarship at Whittington University.

"You think he's gotten himself together?"

"I do," he said. "I want to do what I can to make sure he stays on the right path."

Sydney thought they should wait. With a new marriage and a new business venture, why take on this new challenge? "Have you asked him if he's interested?" she asked.

"Haven't talked to him yet, but I'm sure he'll want to do it. Why wouldn't he?"

He pulled back the curtain over the kitchen sink. The sky was a gun-metal grey, thick with fog. "It'll probably take me twice as long to get there as it normally would," he said. "I'd better get down the road."

With so much on his mind, Sydney hoped he would forget about hiring Lawrence.

Malachi turned back to look at her before he left the kitchen. "You know how to turn on the alarm system, right?"

"Of course. You only spent an hour going over it with me."

"Because it's important."

"I know, Malachi." She hated when his voice took on a lecturing tone.

"When you leave for lunch turn it on and when you come back, put it in the 'ready' position. Remember, you'll be in here by yourself."

"I realize that. No lecture please."

After Sydney cleaned up the dishes she decided to take a look at the basement. They hadn't gone down there during the walk-through yesterday. She climbed down the stairs to the main floor and undid the bolt lock to the door leading to the basement. A wall-to-wall rust-colored shag carpet covered the basement's living room and bedroom floors. The kitchen and bathroom had green indoor/outdoor carpeting, the kind she'd seen on people's patios. Strands of translucent glass beads separated the living room from the hall leading to the bedroom and bathroom.

She tested the burners on the stove and the oven. They worked fine. The refrigerator was larger than the one on the second floor and appeared to be relatively new. She would ask Malachi to hire some men to move the appliance to their kitchen upstairs and the old-fashioned one from upstairs into the basement.

Back in the living room she noticed a telephone sitting on an end table. Malachi was right. She might as well talk to Bernadine and get it over with. She picked up the receiver and dialed her mother's number.

"*Who gets a PhD and then decides to quit when things get difficult? I think that's a red flag.*" Bernadine had made the remarks shortly after Sydney and Malachi had gotten engaged. His application for an associate professor position had just been denied. He told Sydney he had lost hope of becoming successful in academia. He wanted her to stay in law school, but he would leave the university to purchase the Victorian, reasoning that they would be better off financially if he invested in real estate rather than trying to work his way up in academia at another institution. But he wouldn't buy the property unless he had Sydney's approval.

"*Do you really want to start married life three hundred miles away from him? How will you concentrate on your studies? I don't know, Syd, it all seems too risky to me.*" Her mother was afraid she'd drop out of school. Sydney assured her mother that she wouldn't.

In Jamaica, with the wedding behind her, Sydney had had time to reflect. She realized how deeply unhappy she would be living on the other side of the state while Malachi stayed in Bellport. She wanted to be there to help him start the business. She knew it would bother her to look back and have not shared in fulfilling his dream. Sydney decided that she would take a leave of absence for a year and then decide at the end of that time whether or not to return to her studies.

The line was busy. Oh well. She'd tried.

Moments later she heard a familiar rattling noise and then the beep of a car horn. On tiptoes, she peeked out the narrow basement window. *Damn!* Through the fog she could make out a hazy outline of the older model dingy-blue Chevy Nova at the curb. Kwamé. She checked her watch. It was later than she realized. She hurried up the two flights of stairs to grab her purse, camera bag, and a light jacket, telling herself that she would keep lunch as brief as possible. Something about Kwamé's manner made her feel uneasy. She would eat quickly and then tell Kwamé she needed to get home to unpack boxes. It was a convenient excuse. Lunch would be awkward enough. She saw no reason to prolong it. Kwamé was standing on the sidewalk by the car wearing a green army field jacket. He opened the door for her.

"I didn't know you served in the military," she remarked as he put the car in gear.

"Two years. Mekong Delta."

"I'm surprised Malachi never mentioned it."

"Your husband was busy working on his dissertation when I was in 'Nam," Kwame said loudly over the rattling sound. "We didn't talk all the time back then. My battalion saw a lot of action. That's how I got this souvenir." He steered with one elbow and pulled back his opposite sleeve to reveal a long, thick raised scar that ran from his Rolex watch to his elbow.

"I'm afraid to ask how you got that," she said.

"I'll spare you the details."

She glanced at the Liberty Hill Boulevard street sign as they pulled from the curb.

"We call this Malcolm X Drive, although the name isn't official," he said. "The community is working on that."

The buildings they drove by were old but well-maintained. They rode past a tavern and an after-hours club, a bank, library, ice cream shop, funeral home, pawn shop, and a bridal salon. A man walking up the street looked into the car and thrust his fist in the air, giving the Black Power salute. Grey, metal security shields covered some storefronts.

"Are these black-owned businesses?" Sydney asked.

"Except for the library and the bank, they're either black-owned or managed," Kwamé answered. "I took the shortcut to get you home yesterday. But now I'll give you the grand tour. That is, if you're up to it."

"Sure," she said, hoping the tour would be a short one.

Men in dark suits and bowties stood on a street corner selling tabloid-size newspapers. She recognized them as members of the Nation of Islam. She'd seen them in downtown Trenton, New Jersey, when she was a teenager spending summers there with her cousin Jocelyn.

They turned up Independence Avenue and slowed down as a patrol car approached from the opposite direction. The officer nodded at Kwamé as he rolled past. "Officer Wilson Stribling—our first 'brother'—the first black police officer we've had patrolling Liberty Hill. We worked with the mayor to get him on the force, after we wore him down with picketing about Harborview," Kwamé said.

The car's rattling quieted but surged every time Kwamé slowed down or accelerated. The noise didn't seem to originate in the body of the car but from something under the hood. Based on what Malachi had told her, Kwamé was running all kinds of enterprises—a handyman business, a small moving and storage company, real estate investments, and community organizing. She didn't understand why he didn't buy a decent car or get this one repaired.

A quick turn up Atlantic Avenue brought them to the Bellport River Bridge. The car swayed on the metal suspension bridge. Instinctively, Sydney grabbed onto the door's armrest.

"You cool?" Kwamé asked as he glanced at her.

"Just fine." Sydney knew her voice was tight and that she

had responded a little too quickly. She tacked on a smile.

At the end of the bridge was a wooden sign on a utility pole with the words "Petite Africa" carved on it.

"Syd, this is the immigrant section the city wants to take for that project," Kwamé said. "Some of the property owners are holding out, trying to save a piece of the neighborhood. I don't know how much luck they're gonna have with that, though."

The streetscape was congested, reminding her of *National Geographic* footage of a village marketplace in an underdeveloped country. Putting aside the trip to Jamaica, she had never seen so many brown people in one place before. Women wore colorful head wraps. Men wore long shirts and loose pants. No one seemed to be in a rush to get anywhere. They walked slowly or stood around talking in clusters in front of rickety pushcarts and dilapidated hole-in-the-wall stores interspersed with aging, multistory houses. Most of the buildings were only a few feet apart.

"It doesn't seem fair to evict them and take the land," she said.

"It's progress. City's gotten millions in grant money to construct the arena project. Something had to be done. The city's been on life support for too long. Property taxes have gone through the roof since most of the factories high-tailed it overseas. With this development, the taxpayers will get some relief."

"But what's going to happen to the people who live here?" Sydney asked.

Kwamé pulled a pack of Viceroys from the glove compartment and tapped it on the dashboard. He pulled out a cigarette and pressed it against the car lighter. "Housing vouchers. The city's going to build projects. Or folks can get a moving allowance and move where they want."

They came to a three-story wood-frame house on the corner of Pleasant and Garfield avenues. The roof was caved in. Soot splotches stained the siding like an ill-planned splash art experiment.

"What happened here?" asked Sydney.

"Rooming house fire, six months ago." Kwamé slowed the car to a stop.

"Can we take a look?"

They got out of the car.

The first thing she noticed was the smell—scorched wood mixed with water, which surprised her because the fire had been so long ago. She stepped carefully across the muddy yard to the front steps.

Porch railings hung precariously on both sides of the steps. The backyard was visible from the front of the house because all of the windows were missing. A burnt-out van sat in the driveway next to a pile of charred wood. The trunks of two front yard trees as well as most of the branches had been burned.

"Did everybody get out?" she asked.

"They did," answered Kwamé. He looked at his watch. "Don't mean to rush you but..."

"Sorry about that," Sydney said, and got back in the car.

"It was so bad they had to call in the Boston Fire Department," Kwamé continued as he pulled away from the house. "I got the Neighborhood Improvement Association together to get them more blankets and food after the Bellport Rescue Society left. Some of the people are staying with family. The rest moved into an apartment building a few blocks over, The Commonwealth Arms."

She had read in the newspapers that the neighborhood had had two other big fires in the past year. "Do you think the fires were set?"

Kwamé stubbed out his cigarette, lit another, and cracked the window open to blow out the smoke. "Fire department isn't saying. But you've got a lot of possibilities here. The buildings are old, wood frame. Most of them were built at the turn of the century, and the electricity is shot. The heating systems are old. The other problem is that these are immigrants, from Africa and The West Indies. Until they can get on their feet, they're living on top of each other, eight or nine in a unit when they should only have four or five people. You've got too many people in one space cooking, smoking, running heaters. They're living in fire traps."

They made their way back across the bridge into Liberty Hill. Kwamé took Sydney down Elmwood Street, one block over from Liberty Hill Boulevard. The car rolled past abandoned buildings and storefronts. Men stood in clusters talking in front of limestone row houses. Streetlights were smashed. Sidewalks were littered with nip bottles and soda bottle caps. She could feel her stomach tighten. She glanced at her door. It was unlocked. She was annoyed at herself for not thinking of locking it when she first got in the car. She covered the knob with her fist, as if she was merely resting her hand on the door, and gently pressed down so there'd be minimal sound, hoping Kwamé wouldn't notice.

Kwamé laughed. "Ain't your kind of place. I can understand that. That's cool."

"It might take some getting used to." She tried to sound nonchalant.

"This neighborhood's blowing your mind, ain't it?" he said as if teasing her.

She stared out the window at another burned-out building. "I could tell yesterday. I saw you scowl in the rearview mirror."

She shifted in her seat. She hadn't known she was under Kwamé's surveillance yesterday as he drove Malachi and her home from the airport.

"I've been to your town before," he continued. "I used to work at a summer jobs' program. I caddied at The Old Prescott Country Club. The white man acts like you're invisible, unless he wants something."

Sydney wondered how her stepfather acted with the black caddies. Martin had been a member of the country club until he married her mother, Bernadine. Soon after the marriage, the club's board of directors asked him to resign. Sydney remembered the day after kindergarten when Martin came in after work and told her mother about the meeting of the club's board. Martin had said he didn't want to be bothered with a "bunch of cretins."

"What part of Old Prescott you grow up in?"

Sydney tried to think of a subtle way to change the subject but could come up with nothing. "It doesn't have sections. It's too small for that."

"I know it well." Kwamé began speaking in his version of a clipped, British accent, his voice rising half an octave. "White picket fences, rolling hills, landed gentry. Horse country, isn't it? Malachi tells me you were taking lessons. Which style? English or Western?"

Was he asking simply to show off his knowledge of riding styles? "English," she said.

"But then you stopped."

"Yes. I quit a few years ago."

"Why?" he asked, soldiering on, apparently unaware of her discomfort.

"My horse died. I didn't feel I could bond with another."

Kwamé was silent for a moment. She was glad. When he finally spoke again, he'd dropped the affectation. His voice took on a soothing tone. "My apologies. What did he die of?"

"*She* had an illness. A respiratory disease. It happens to horses sometimes."

They drove past a building with scaffolding on it. Sydney was surprised considering the dismal condition of everything else within eyesight.

"Pet clinic's going in there," Kwamé said. "That's all you need, one new business can start a comeback.... What the *fu*...?"

The car skidded and spun halfway around as Kwamé jammed the brakes. A figure had darted into the car's path. Kwamé threw his arm across Sydney to stop her from slamming into the dashboard. He had come within inches of mowing the person down. Through the foggy haze, Sydney could see a skinny teenager with an Afro pick sticking out of the top of his head.

Kwamé pounded his fist into the steering wheel. "*Carajo que lo que le pasa! Que imbecil!* Look at that idiot," he shouted, "Don't even make no sense."

The smell of burning rubber filled the car. Sydney's heart raced. Thank goodness Kwamé had quick reflexes. The kid smirked and walked up to the front passenger window of a brown Volkswagen bus double-parked up ahead. A fading bumper sticker on the back read "Make Love, Not War." The kid jammed his hands into the front pockets of his jeans and strolled back in front of the Nova. He stepped onto the sidewalk and disappeared behind a dumpster.

"You okay?" Kwamé looked at her, his eyes wide.

Her hands were shaking. "I'm fine. Just glad you saw him in time."

Kwamé stared at her a while. Then he put his hand on her thigh, just above the knee.

"Your husband would have my head if anything happened to you," he said in a hushed tone. She expected him to take his hand back. He didn't. She brushed it off her knee and then reached for the cross-strap on the seatbelt. Kwamé shifted his attention to the glove compartment and leaned over her to get another Viceroy. Cars went around them. Once he lit his cigarette, he turned the steering wheel hard to head them back in the right direction on Elmwood Street.

"Was that a drug transaction?" she asked after they'd gone a few more blocks.

He nodded. "That kid can't be no more than fourteen. If we can get the cash flow we want here in Liberty Hill with the redevelopment happening, we can open a rec center, get young bloods like him off the street."

They drove on.

Kwamé found a parking spot catty-corner from The Stewed Oxtail. Sydney didn't realize how the near-collision had affected her. Her knees buckled when she got out of the car. She steadied herself by holding onto the door frame.

The Stewed Oxtail was a loud place—Caribbean music, patrons talking loudly, metal spatulas banging against the griddle in the open kitchen behind the front counter. Some customers sat in groups of five and six at the small, square tables in the dining area. Others shouted orders from the counter.

"Pick a table," Kwamé said. "I'll get us a couple of specials."

She had no idea what "the special" was but nodded. After the car incident, she didn't have an appetite. People's heads popped up. They watched her walk through the dining area to an empty table by the window facing the street. Just her luck. It was wobbly. She spotted a couple of empty tables across the room but felt self-conscious with people noticing her. She sat down, her back to the window, facing the front counter. It was her first opportunity to take a really good look at Kwamé without him noticing. He was nice looking, his black Puerto Rican ancestry evident in the cinnamon-brown color of his complexion, his curly, auburn Afro and trim goatee.

A couple of men went up to him and clapped him on the back. After he placed the orders and was on his way back to Sydney, Kwamé waved at a woman on the other side of the room. He seemed to stand taller than a few moments before when he'd entered the restaurant. Sydney felt as if she were watching a politician working the room before an election.

"That's Tovah Bright," Kwamé stated as he sat down, "the owner of the bridal shop."

Sydney remembered on their ride into the neighborhood yesterday seeing the woman with a tape measure around her neck in the display window arranging a wedding gown on a faceless mannequin.

"The sister's been in business about two years," he continued. "Struggled some to get customers, but things should pick up for her once the redevelopment comes in."

Two police officers walked in. It was Officer Stribling and a white police officer. The white officer went to the front counter. Stribling strolled over to their table. She was surprised at how broad shouldered and tall he was, about six foot five she thought. She imagined that he was the kind of officer who lifted barbells in his spare time.

"Hey brother, what's happening?" Stribling said to Kwamé.

Kwamé stood up and gave him the soul brother's handshake. Then Kwamé introduced the officer to Sydney.

Stribling took a couple of exaggerated steps back. "I didn't know Dr. Mal jumped the broom. Good to meet you." He gave her a strong handshake. "What's he been up to? Teaching college kids, right?"

"Up until recently," Sydney answered. She told him about the plans for the bookstore.

Stribling grinned as he shook his head. "I knew Dr. Mal was going places. I knew he would make something of himself. I could tell even when we was kids."

"How's the gig?" Kwamé looked up and down at Stribling's uniform.

"Not bad. The neighborhood's respectful. They're glad I'm here."

"What about him?" Kwamé gestured toward the other officer.

"Robertson? I'm his new partner. He's showing me the ropes."

"He's not giving you any static, is he?"

"No, man, he's cool."

Kwamé raised an eyebrow. "And the rest of the department?"

"Not a problem so far. They don't know what to make of me, so they leave me alone."

Kwamé eased back in his chair. "That's good, man. That's what I like to hear, 'cause if they were giving you trouble down there at the station...."

Stribling held up both palms. "I know, man I know. And I appreciate that. I hear they need more detectives. I'm thinking I might one day go for that."

"I'm with you, man," said Kwamé.

"Don't get me wrong, patrolling is good. I don't mind chasing the bad guys, but I'd like to get involved in investigations.

That's where the real police work happens."

Kwamé turned to Sydney. "Your husband, Wilson, and me go way back."

"Remember Sunday school, man?" Stribling's eyes brightened.

Kwamé laughed. "Nehemiah Baptist Church," he said, turning to Sydney. "Strib here's mother taught our Sunday School class. We were always trying to sneak out before service started to get candy from the corner store."

"But Moms always found out," the officer added.

"I know man. Either she saw us trying to cut out, or one of the deacons tipped her off."

"Those were some good times, man," Stribling continued. He narrowed his eyes at Kwamé's army jacket. "What you wearing that for?"

"'Nam." Kwamé responded stiffly.

The officer opened his mouth to say something, glanced at Sydney, and then stopped.

Kwamé tugged at his goatee. "How's your mother doing?"

The officer exhaled heavily. "Moms is still the same. She's hanging in there though, holding her own by the grace of God. Thanks for asking."

Officer Robertson walked toward the door clutching a plastic cup with a straw in it.

"I'll catch you later," Stribling said.

He and Kwamé shook hands again. Then Stribling extended a hand to Sydney. "Nice meeting you, and tell Dr. Mal I'm gonna holler at him soon."

"He seems like a nice guy," Sydney said after the officers walked out the door.

"One of the best." Kwamé stubbed out his cigarette in the tin ashtray on the table. "Wilson was all set to go to college, but then his mother had a stroke. He decided to stay here to look after her, thinking he'd go to college later, but he never did."

"So he became a police officer?"

"Not at first. He did factory work for a while. Then when

folks in Liberty Hill got sick of the cops bashing their heads in, I led some protests, and we got some of our people to study for the police officer's exam. We had to put together study groups because the exam was rigged. Strib joined the study group, took the test, and passed. We're trying to get more of our people in the pipeline."

The waitress brought their orders: two plates of red snapper with plantains, Jamaican rice and peas, and collard greens. The waitress left and returned a few moments later with iced tea for Sydney and a cup of coffee for Kwamé.

He pulled back his sleeve. "You've been here now about twenty-four hours. You must have some questions about our fair city."

She wasn't sure if he had actually checked his Rolex or was looking for an excuse to show it off.

"Yes. Malachi said you know everything there is to know about Bellport."

"I'm your man. Ask me whatever you want." His eyes floated down to her cleavage.

She looked away. "I can see why the city declared Petite Africa a blighted community, but it looks no worse than what I'm seeing out here." She gestured toward the street.

He scooped rice onto his fork and spread it on top of the fish. "You're right. A while back, the city tried to declare Liberty Hill a blighted community. It fit the bill. The mayor was secretly talking to the developers about building the arena project here. I put together a committee of folks to protest the project. Our complaint was that the city was gonna go behind our backs and take our property without telling us what they were up to. We collected money, got an attorney, signed petitions. Then the newspapers got the story. City Hall was so embarrassed that they held a public hearing, which is what they should've done in the first place. We got four hundred people to show up at council chambers."

He took a bite of his fish.

"So the city backed off under pressure?" Sydney asked.

Kwamé shook his head. "The city was still gonna go through with it. The only thing that saved us was that one of the council members was doing payback on the mayor because the mayor didn't do snow removal on his street the year before. Anyway, this dude on council defends our cause. He defended us better than our attorney did. The press had a field day with it. And that's what got the city to back off of Liberty Hill."

Sydney cut the tail of the fish and then severed the head. As Kwamé had done, she spread rice on top of the fish. "So how did the project end up going to Petite Africa?"

"The developer was getting impatient. He was threatening to pull out of the project and take it to Jersey. And the mayor didn't want that embarrassment on his watch. In fact, he had grand plans for the Harborview Project to be part of his legacy. He wrote a letter to the planning commission recommending that the South End, Petite Africa, be the alternative site for the development. It's a land grab. The city declares Petite Africa a blighted community, with rundown homes, bad streets, lousy schools. The people get burned out. The city gets state and federal funding to rebuild it. The immigrants get pushed out and the white folks with their money move in."

"How much of a chance do the people there have of stopping it?"

He shook his head. "Slim to none. A lot of the people down there are immigrants. In some of their home countries, you do what you have to in order to stay away from the government, unless you want to get your head bashed in or blown off. The last thing you want is for the government to get in your face. So they're not that vocal and don't fight. Then you have the issue of split loyalties. They're all from different countries, mostly first generation. Their loyalty is to their home country, not to each other. So they don't want to unify. And there's a language barrier. Many of them learn English growing up, but the American accent is so different from what they heard coming along. They have a hard time understanding the language, not to mention, the laws, municipal statutes, and rules."

Sydney was enjoying the fish with the rice mixed in. She topped it off with a little plantain.

"Another factor working against them is the change in the makeup of city council," Kwamé continued. "That councilman I told you about who was getting back at the mayor lost re-election by the time the city was seriously looking at Petite Africa, so they didn't have him to advocate for them."

"That's a shame. I mean, I guess it's good for the economy to get this development, but it's not right to take those people's homes."

"There's a restaurant owner over there from some African county. Senegal, I think. Mustapha Mendy. He's the godfather of Petite Africa. At least that's what they call him. He's organized a committee of some of the other property owners and tenants on those blocks. They're fighting eminent domain. They hired an attorney like we did. They say they're not selling. They're trying to preserve at least a little bit of the neighborhood.

Kwamé wiped away flakes of rice that had landed in his goatee. "I went down there every so often to give them advice. I told them to be more strategic with the rallies and protests." He shook his head. "They showed me no respect. I can't worry about the immigrants anymore. More power to them."

Kwamé seemed to be involved in just about everything. She chased down her spicy greens with some iced tea.

"You know, that used to be our neighborhood," he continued.

"What do you mean?"

"When black folks first started coming here from the South, they moved to that area, and that's how it got its name."

"I thought it was because of the African immigrants."

He shook his head. "The label was put on us by the white folks. It wasn't no compliment. It goes back some fifty years. The men got jobs at the wharves and in the factories; the women worked mostly as domestics. By the early 1940s they were getting themselves together. The women went to secretarial school or community college, and the men worked up the ladder in the trades. There were a lot of Jews in Liberty Hill from Eastern Europe at the time. We had a little melting pot going—the Jews and the blacks. The blacks left Petite Africa and moved into Liberty Hill once they could afford it. The Jews moved to Brookline, Newton, Belmont. The Africans and West Indians moved into Petite Africa, replacing the black people. No other place would rent to them."

He raised his cup toward the waitress to get her to refresh his coffee. "You know how it is, once our people get a little something in their pocket, they think they have 'arrived.' They want to forget where they came from."

Sydney mulled this over for a while. She knew that her grand-parents on both sides of the family had moved from Virginia to Western Massachusetts at the turn of the century. They rarely went back south for visits. She recalled her grandmother on her mother's side talking about working hard to lose her southern accent because people made fun of her. Sydney wondered if there was a downside when people distanced themselves from their background.

Kwamé wiped his hands on his napkin and checked his nails. They were perfectly straight with a clear polish finish on them. Sydney suspected that he'd had them professionally buffed.

"We've had a serious problem with absentee landlords, slumlords," he said. "That's why the conditions around here are so bad. As it is now, Liberty Hill is isolated. You saw how it was when I drove you around. You have to deal with the one-way streets, dead ends, traffic patterns that make no sense, the potholes. Then there's the drug problems and car thefts we've been dealing with. But Harborview will change it all. When they build that arena and off ramp, this will be a new neighborhood. Once the construction's done, you'll see thou-sands of people going to the concerts and the sporting events. Police patrols will pick up. The foot traffic will spill over into

Liberty Hill. Having people like Tovah, like you and Malachi investing in Liberty Hill, revitalizing it, is critical to the future of this neighborhood."

Sydney finished her food. Then Kwamé reached across the table and squeezed her wrist. "So what do you think? You think you'll have enough to keep you busy around here?"

She was reminded of one of those dismal dates she had gone on early in college, when, at the end of the evening, the date grabbed her hand or accidentally brushed up against her in a desperate attempt to hold her attention.

She told Kwamé about their plans to rent the basement of the Victorian and to solicit potential tenants through classified ads. He pushed back his plate and pulled a toothpick from his pocket and stuck it in the side of his mouth. Tacky, she thought, but she was relieved he didn't start picking at his teeth.

"Max Turner's a buddy of mine," he said in reference to the newspaper editor. "Mention my name and he'll give you a good rate on that ad. He'll give you some freelance work, too." He pulled a pocket calendar out of his army jacket and jotted something down. Then he looked up at her, grinning. "I've been hearing that you're quite the writer."

She tried to suppress a smile. "Where did you hear that from? Malachi?"

He winked at her. "You're good. I've read your stuff. You should pursue your art more."

She stirred her tea. "Malachi must have shown you some of my clips."

He shook his head. "I came across your work independently. *Harambeé* is a widely read student publication, believe it or not."

She knew he was lying. There was no way that he had read a student publication and one that was on the other side of the state.

"Those reviews, I just wrote because half the staff quit. They couldn't get along with the editor. They needed someone to fill in."

"Which gave you an opportunity to shine." Kwamé snapped open a lighter, a silver Zippo with the name 'Jonathan' engraved on one side, and lit another Viceroy.

"Who's Jonathan?" she asked.

His brow creased as he flipped the lighter over on the engraved side to look at it. "That's what my momma named me. But nobody's called me that in years."

She had a hard time imagining some of the guys who hung around the street corners of Liberty Hill calling him "Jonathan."

Kwamé stuck the lighter back in his jacket pocket. "*Inner City Voice* is part of a national news service. You get published with them, and every black newspaper in the country gets it. How does that sound?"

The idea of writing for the newspaper excited her. Maybe the editor would be interested in her photography too. Why was Kwamé being so helpful? she wondered.

"Sure. I'm interested."

"I'll talk to Max."

When they got to the sidewalk, a man with matted, bushy hair, and a belly large enough to hold a dinner plate staggered in their direction. He had a mangy German shepherd on a leash and stopped to let it pee at a fire hydrant. Sydney tightened the grip on her purse and crossed the street toward the car. Behind her she heard Kwamé greet the man and slap hands with him. If she kept going, she figured Kwamé would cut the conversation short and catch up to her.

"This here's Percy," Kwamé shouted at Sydney. "Come on back. Let me introduce you."

Sydney wanted to go home. Kwamé seemed to know everyone, or at least acted as if he did. She found him exhausting. She resigned herself to not getting home anytime soon and crossed back to the other side of the street.

CHAPTER 5

SYDNEY TUNED the radio on the nightstand to the classical music station. She was pretty sure the station was playing Mozart. Sure enough, the announcer confirmed her guess—*Symphony No. 29* by the London Chamber Orchestra. She was delighted. She'd made a game of being able to identify works by classical composers.

She dragged boxes from the hallway into the bedroom and pulled back the flaps on one labeled "memorabilia."

It felt good to have time alone after her dreadful afternoon with Kwamé. He was creepy—the way he put his hand on her thigh in the car, squeezed her wrist, and winked at her as if she was some kind of a tart. It wasn't worth mentioning to Malachi, at least not yet. But if Kwamé went too far, she'd let Malachi know. She'd stood in front of The Stewed Oxtail for another fifteen minutes. Kwame introduced her to Tovah Bright of the bridal shop and some of the other business owners as they were leaving. He talked to Percy, who'd been out walking his German shepherd, Bridgette. Sydney learned that Percy was also a Vietnam vet. Unfortunately he'd returned home with a heroin addiction.

She was relieved when Kwamé finally dropped her off. Ever since she could remember, she needed time to herself. If she spent too much time around people, they sapped her energy. Growing up, she had playmates but enjoyed her own company better. She never minded playing with her dolls alone or opposing herself in a game of checkers.

The radio announcer mentioned the time—five-thirty—and then played a symphony that she recognized immediately: *Ave Maria,* by Franz Schubert. She wouldn't have much longer before Malachi returned. She wanted to empty as many boxes as she could to make way for more he'd be bringing from his old campus apartment.

Sydney pulled a framed eight-by-ten sepia-toned photograph of Malachi's grandparents—Pappa and Nunna, as he called them—from the box. It was taken around 1900 in Fayetteville, North Carolina. VeNorris Stallworth, Malachi's grandfather, dressed in his Sunday suit, had a hand resting on the back of a Queen Anne chair in which his wife, Mercedes, sat. She was wearing a knee-length, high-collared ivory dress, her hands folded in her lap, her legs demurely crossed at the ankles.

VeNorris, a sharecropper, picked tobacco. Mercedes, a domestic, washed laundry for white families on the weekends to earn extra money. Seeing no prospects in Jim Crow North Carolina, they eventually moved to Bellport and got assembly-line jobs at Bell Manufacturing. They brought their grandson, Malachi with them. His mother had died from a kidney disorder not long after she gave birth to Malachi. She had never disclosed who Malachi's father was.

Next Sydney pulled out a framed wedding portrait she and Malachi had taken on the grounds of Hamilton Estate Mansion in Old Prescott right after their ceremony. She was glad they'd had an autumn wedding. For the portrait, they'd posed on a bed of stunning burnt orange, purplish blue, and yellow leaves.

She still marveled that the two of them had gotten together. Growing up in Old Prescott, Sydney had been labeled a "white girl" by most of the black students she met on Whittington University's campus. They mimicked her "proper" diction and vocabulary. Most black guys avoided her. The few who asked her out on dates inevitably asked her why she spent so much time in the photo lab and why she liked to read so much. Malachi was one of the few black guys she felt comfortable with. The assistant professor in the sociology department was different from the others—refreshing. After one of their first dates, he asked if he could borrow some of her books. He didn't seem to mind her so-called "whiteness" and instead took her to cultural events and lectures. He played his favorite jazz albums for her—Miles Davis, Thelonious Monk, John Coltrane. He encouraged her photography.

He'd come to an exhibit at the university museum during her first semester at law school where some of her photography was featured. Malachi was one of the few visitors who seemed interested in talking to her about her work.

"You've got a good eye," he told her over coffee at the student center after the exhibit closed for the day. "Tell me about the other shows you've had."

She laughed. "I haven't had any. I'm only doing this one because my undergrad journalism professor asked me to."

He took off his horn-rimmed glasses and leaned across the table. "You're kidding me, right? You've got talent. People need to see your work." He arranged to have some of her photos published in *Harambeé*, the black student newspaper for which he served as faculty advisor. He also asked her to write articles and music reviews for the publication.

She instantly loved his easygoing manner. For the first eight months of their relationship she insisted on meeting only in public for their dates—at the movies, restaurants, coffee houses, concerts. He respected that she was traditional and agreed to wait until their wedding night to consummate their relationship.

She put the now-empty box with the other empty ones in the hallway. Soon, she heard the familiar sound of the engine of Malachi's Mustang as the car drove up Liberty Hill Boulevard and turned into the driveway. As she headed downstairs, the phone rang. She ignored it, curious to see what Malachi had decided to bring from the campus apartment and what he had decided to toss out. She stopped when she heard voices coming from the porch. Malachi wasn't alone. Hopefully it wasn't Kwamé. When Sydney got to the foyer, she was relieved to see Lawrence Briggs, Malachi's former student, whom she'd gotten to know over spaghetti dinners at Malachi's apartment.

"Miss Syd, what's happening?" Lawrence held out his hand to her. Sydney was surprised at how much he'd filled out since she'd last seen him. He was at least a couple of inches taller and his shoulders had broadened. He was dressed in his usual attire, a Celtics jersey over a white T-shirt, jeans with one leg rolled up, and black and white high-top Chuck Taylors. The right side of his hair was braided in corn rows, while the left was a curly Afro.

She brushed past his hand and stood on tiptoes to give him a quick hug. Even so, he had to bend slightly to reach her.

"I saw Professor Malachi at his old apartment trying to put all of this stuff in his car, and I told him I could help him out," Lawrence explained.

"You rode all the way here from the university?" Sydney asked. "You didn't have to do that."

Malachi walked in carrying a couple of large paintings. "Ronald Bridgewaters," he said, referring to the prominent black artist. Bridgewaters' works—oil paintings of vivid, swirling colors, focused on black American, West Indian, and South American themes and symbols—also hung in the Smithsonian Institution. It had taken years for Malachi to acquire works by Bridgewaters, which he had proudly displayed in his university office.

Lawrence shrugged. "It's okay. I'm gonna surprise my grandma."

"Did Lawrence tell you he's coming to work for us?" Malachi added, while catching his breath.

Lawrence laughed. "I hadn't gotten that far yet."

"On the way here I was telling Lawrence that we're looking for an intern, and he says he wants the job," Malachi said.

"But he's going to school, Malachi."

"Not a problem, Miss Syd." Lawrence followed Malachi back onto the porch. Sydney joined them. "I'll come out on weekends," he explained. "I can be here during the summers and spring break. I can always stay with my grandma. The class credit will help me finish my degree sooner, and the pay sounds good."

"Pay?" Sydney looked at Malachi. "I thought payment would be college credit."

"Oh, Syd, we should be able to afford it. We'll take a little something out of what we get for renting the basement."

"And when I have time," Lawrence continued. "I'll cut grass, make a few extra dollars that way, too."

The two men returned to the car and came back with several more items. Malachi carried a box of smaller Bridgewaters, and Lawrence had a a rolled-up area rug flopped over his shoulder. Sydney wished he had discussed the matter with her before offering Lawrence the internship. She wondered what else Malachi hadn't told her.

"I got a new mower, gas powered. It'll cut through anything," Lawrence said.

"That's good," responded Sydney. "You'll help keep the yards looking nice around here."

Malachi and Lawrence later carried in a large oval mirror with a white ceramic frame and finally, an oak dining room chair. Malachi was carrying the chair upstairs when the kitchen phone rang. Sydney ignored the phone and turned to Lawrence. "You must be hungry after that long ride."

Lawrence nodded. "I could eat something."

When they got to the kitchen, Malachi was holding out the phone with his hand over the mouthpiece. "It's your mother," he whispered. "Syd, baby, you have to talk to her."

"I know." She took the phone from him and swallowed hard.

CHAPTER 6

A SPRING IN THE sofa bed frame poked Omar in the side as he shifted around to check the time. He squinted to see the clock on the kitchen range. It was six-thirty and time to get up. Natalie was already gone. He had heard her tipping out the door a few minutes ago. As she left, she announced into the air that she was going to an accounting study session. Unusual, he thought. She had never had a session this early. He was about to question her, then changed his mind. He knew it would lead to an argument about the heat not working.

Their landlord, James Fullerton, lived north of Bellport along the shoreline. If Omar timed it right and caught the seven-fifteen crosstown bus, he could transfer to the express and arrive at the landlord's doorstep by nine thirty. Omar would be done in plenty of time to get back to Petite Africa to play drums for Uncle Mustapha's lunch crowd. Fullerton wasn't in his office on weekends, so Omar would have to go to his home.

He stepped into the shower and braced himself under the spray of ice-cold water. It was something he never got used to. Once he was done, he turned on his transistor radio. The weather forecast a pleasant day with no fog and the temperature reaching fifty degrees by midafternoon.

He thought about making it easy on himself and dressing for the restaurant in a *boubou*, a loose, light flowing robe and trousers popular in his country, and a thin sweater underneath. But he was afraid that Fullerton wouldn't take him seriously dressed that way. Whenever he left Petite Africa, his wardrobe drew stares from people not accustomed to West African fashion. American people on the street, including the black ones, would stare at him. Sometimes children giggled and pointed at him. But if he wore the white man's clothes he wouldn't have time to change before going to the restaurant. He'd have to pack an extra bag. In the end, he decided to wear the *boubou*.

He quickly ate *tapalapa*, leftover homemade Senegalese bread he had gotten from Uncle Mustapha's restaurant, and then went to the spare bedroom. It was where he kept his drums, repaired them, and practiced. He had arranged his instruments along the perimeter of the room according to type—*djembe, ashkikos, sabars, benbes, agogos, dundun,* and *caxixis*. On the wall he had hung one of the framed photographs he had gotten from Duke Ellington and on the fireplace mantle was the tall, earthen pot from his mother, Fama, that she had intended for The Duke to have. He had yet to give it to the musician all these years later.

He picked up drums, cowbells, shakers, and mallets and stuffed them into carrying bags, then locked the apartment door, walked to the elevator, and hit the button. He wished Natalie had an appreciation for drumming. If she could meet Fama, she would explain to Natalie the drum's importance in his life. Fama would tell Natalie how Omar crawled around their hut in Senegal when he was still a baby, patting upturned pots, and how once he was able to pull himself up to a standing position he'd grab hold of one of his father, Ibrahim's *tamas*, or talking drums, and play with it. With pride, Fama would tell Natalie that not long after Omar started forming words he would pat the head of Ibrahim's *djembe* with his little palms and say *sabar, sabar,*" the word for "drum" in Wolof. Then maybe Natalie would understand.

It took Omar a few moments of not hearing any movement in the shaft to remember that the elevator wasn't working this week. He bolted down the steps, squeezed past an abandoned sofa in the foyer, and out the front door.

Saturday was his favorite day in Petite Africa. Shop owners pulled their merchandise out of their stores and displayed it on racks and tables, converting sidewalks into a village market. People shopped as if they were in their home countries; American tourists who found their way to Petite Africa bought "exotic" gifts. Omar walked down his street, King Street, which was known as "Cape Verde Lane" among the locals. Eventually, he passed an open field where children were playing "catch your tail," by linking arms, and trying to catch the handkerchief of the opposing team. He liked seeing them playing this game as kids did all over West Africa.

He turned onto Clermont Street and watched Bamba Toukou pull his wooden food carts onto the sidewalk. His son, Bamba Junior, a thick, squat teenage version of his father, ambled out of the store with barrels of ice on each shoulder. The sound of ice crashing into the trays soon followed.

"Hey, drummer man," Bamba Senior called after Omar, "got some fresh white fish today, too much for me to sell. Tell your uncle I give him discount."

Omar waved. *Drummer man.* He loved the name. Most of the shop owners along Clermont Street had either been to performances of The Fulani Sound—what he and his best friend Khadim Adepo called themselves when they performed together at the local clubs—or danced to Omar's and Khadim's rhythms at street festivals.

He turned a corner onto Hancock Avenue, called "Togo Street" by the locals. Two blocks later, the air was filled with the sweet smell of dough and sugar. Junio Ortiz, owner of Ortiz Cakes and Pastry Shop, was rolling up the metal shield over the front door of his business, signaling that the ovens were hot and ready. Next door, Uncle Mustapha's goddaughter, Esmé Tavernier, owner of Esmé's Africa Wear Shop, was pulling clothes racks of her hand-dyed batik dresses, skirts, and *boubous* onto the sidewalk. She playfully blew a kiss to Omar.

When Omar got to the corner of Hancock and Wheeler Avenues, he slowed at Hallima's Salon. A dingy sandwich board on the sidewalk listed prices for braiding and hair-pressing services. There was no mention of how much it cost to buy her useless herbs. He wanted to go inside to demand his money back on the love potion but hesitated. Hallima was a feisty woman, loud enough to draw the attention of everyone on the street and big enough to fill the front doorway. She might try to humiliate him in front of her customers.

One block up he reached Garfield Avenue, known as "Petite Africa Boulevard," which was filled with shops on the ground level and box-like apartments on the top. He walked past Le Baobab Restaurant, his Uncle Mustapha's place. Even outside, Omar could detect the aroma of familiar spices and herbs and knew his uncle was preparing *yassa guinaar,* a grilled chicken dish, and *michoui,* marinated roast lamb shank, for the lunch crowd.

Normally during the early hours of the day in Petite Africa, Omar talked to the vendors to learn of news from home, but he knew he'd have no peace with Natalie if he used this morning for anything other than meeting with Fullerton. Omar checked his watch. He had four minutes to make the crosstown bus. He walked faster. The crosstown bus never lingered. He had to catch it.

With one block to go, he spotted the bus at the curb of Seaview Avenue and Garfield. He ran, but the bus pulled away, belching sooty smoke in his face. He leaned against the bus shelter to catch his breath. It would be another thirty minutes before the next bus. He thought it wouldn't be worth his time to wait for it. If he walked four blocks over, he could catch the local. He'd probably be a little late getting to the restaurant, but Uncle Mustapha would understand.

Except for cleaning women, the shelter was empty. They

wore white starched uniforms, white stockings, and white shoes with matching soles. Omar caught bits of their conversation as they chatted about housing vouchers and the new high-rise apartment buildings they would move into once the redevelopment project was completed.

Omar couldn't believe it. These people had accepted the demolition of Petite Africa as a reality. They thought the apartments the mayor had announced that they would be moved to were luxury accommodations.

He heard a car horn in the distance followed by the sound of screeching tires. All at once, the car pulled to the curb next to him. "*Naka mu demee? Naka mu demee?*"

It was a familiar voice shouting the Wolof greeting. It was Khadim in his yellow taxi. Omar was pleased to see him. It had been days since they'd talked. Khadim was one of the few people he could have a full conversation with in his native language. Whenever Omar talked to Uncle Mustapha, the old man switched from Wolof to English to French then back to Wolof all in one sentence. Omar wasn't sure if his uncle was being lazy or showing off his language skills.

"*Mu ngi dox!*" Omar shouted in response that he was doing well. Khadim popped the trunk. Omar dropped his sacks of instruments there and slid into the passenger seat.

"I am glad to see that you are fine, my friend," Khadim shouted in Wolof over the chatter of his two-way radio. "I have been telling everyone about our partnership. I can see my name on my classroom door. *Master Drummer Instructor Khadim Adepo.*"

Omar slowly turned in his seat to face him. "I advise you not to tell everyone yet. The drumming institute is only in the heads of me and uncle."

Khadim's brow creased. "It will still happen, yes?"

"If Uncle Mustapha can stop the plans of the city to take Petite Africa, then maybe we shall get the African Cultural building. Nothing is certain."

"I hope we get the building, my brother. It could help us get the attention we need for the recording contract."

Omar looked back at the bus stop. "Those people believe anything they are told. They are ready to be kicked out of their homes, and they are so happy about it."

"That is because they do not have the inside details like we do."

"It is so good that we have Benata."

Khadim's wife gave them regular updates on the status of the redevelopment project from conversations she overheard at her desk at Bellport City Hall while processing tax delinquencies.

"Benata tells me we will have success," announced Khadim. "She knows because the mood of the mayor has been bad lately. His secretary told Benata that he is running scared because of the protests of your uncle."

Omar relaxed in his seat. Uncle was putting pressure on city hall, just as he said he would.

Over the two-way radio the dispatcher asked Khadim to pick up a fare by the navy yard. Khadim told her he was taking a bathroom break.

"Natalie does not want to believe that Petite Africa will prevail," Omar shrugged. "She thinks we will soon be in the road."

Khadim shook his head. "She must have the faith."

Omar had always been careful when he brought up Natalie's name. Khadim had never commented on Omar's personal decisions, but Omar was fairly certain that his friend disapproved of his marriage to Natalie because she was not only an American woman, but a non-Muslim. He had heard Khadim speak disdainfully when referring to the "mixed marriages" between Muslims and non-Muslims and between black Africans and black Americans.

Khadim snapped off the radio. "*Fooy Dem*? What is your destination, my friend?"

Omar told him of his plans to talk to Fullerton and gave him directions.

"You are going way out there? You are lucky. I have been up since cock crow and have made plenty of money already today. I can take a few hours' break." Khadim turned the meter off and clicked on the "off-duty" sign. "But why don't you just move, my friend? I could find out if we have any vacancies in my building. It would be an easy move since I am just one block over."

"But your building is no better than ours. You tell me all the time about the rats."

Khadim shrugged. "We have rats, but we have heat and electricity."

"I will stay where I am."

Khadim put the taxi in gear and pulled from the curb. "Do you think he will fix all those things?"

"I do not know. All I can do is talk to him."

Omar wished his friend would just drive and not ask so many questions. He was not at ease around Khadim, who grew up in St. Louis, a large, industrial center of Senegal, whereas Omar grew up as a *fanna faana*, a rural Wolof who spoke a rustic dialect. The city folk tended to look down on people from the village and saw them as *muuhat*, ignorant of modern ways. Khadim claimed to be a devout Muslim. He prayed more than five times a day, gave alms to poor people, and never drank. During Ramadan he fasted and abstained from sex with Benata from dusk to dawn. Omar was technically a Muslim but never honored the traditions.

The two men spent many hours together rehearsing as The Fulani Sound. They performed at venues across the Bellport metropolitan area. Omar was both impressed and intimidated by Khadim's skill in playing the *tama*, the talking drum, with precision. Khadim had a unique ability to manipulate the drum to change its pitch, squeezing it enough to make his bicep flex and women in the audience scream in approval. That never happened when Omar played the *tama*. Khadim also played the *balafon*, similar to the American xylophone, and the African lute. Omar had never learned to play either instrument. Then there was Khadim's hair. His dreadlocks were long, past his waist. He'd swing his head left to right, sending his dreads in all directions. Women would come up after a set asking for an autograph, admiring his dreads and touching them. Sometimes they had lit cigarettes between their fingers. More than once Omar wished a customer would accidentally turn the lit end in just the right direction to burn up those dreads. There was no reason for Khadim to draw most of the attention when they performed.

Khadim mashed down on the horn to alert the driver ahead of them that the traffic light had turned green. "You should obtain that community lawyer Uncle Mustapha knows," he said.

"I shall talk to Fullerton first. Maybe I can solve this easily."

Khadim shook his head. "The ways of Fullerton are known all over Petite Africa. He has a hot head and so does his wife. I will take you there, but I think you should have a bodyguard."

"You are being dramatic, my friend. Idrissa went to see him once and came back in only one piece."

Khadim laughed. "Maybe he did not tell you the end of the fable. My friend Mamadou ended up in Bellport Hospital after he went to see Fullerton. He was there for three days. The wife messed him up."

From the passenger-side window Omar watched homes grow larger, with attached garages and circular drives. There were more properties further from the road, and some had low stone walls along the perimeter. Lawns were manicured. This was the kind of community where Natalie wanted them to move.

"There is something heavy on your mind, my brother?" Khadim asked when they got to a stop sign.

Omar hesitated, not wanting Khadim to harshly judge Natalie. But he had no one else he could confide in. He told Khadim about Natalie's overbooked schedule.

Khadim banged on the steering wheel. Omar flinched.

"I told you not to marry an American woman, and especially

not a black American woman," Khadim shouted. "You cannot trust any of them, but you especially cannot trust the black ones. They are selfish, spoiled, lazy, and they have no morals."

"I regret that I introduced the topic," said Omar.

"You know what she is doing, do you not?" Khadim turned and looked directly at Omar, waiting for a response. Omar wished his friend would keep his eyes on the road.

"She is doing the *boom boom* with that voice coach," Khadim continued. "She is pretending that she has these gigs around town and all these classes. I bet she has not set her toes on the college campus in months."

Omar tried to remain calm. "You do not know what you are talking about."

"The black American women do it all the time," Khadim said, rocking back and forth in his seat. "They will cheat on you every second. You should read *Black Confections.*" He reached under his seat and handed him a rolled-up copy of a magazine. The cover pictured a woman in a bra and panties made out of wrapped hard candy. "One of my customers left this in the taxi. The black American woman waits for her man to leave for work and then she brings her other man in the back door for the *boom boom.* She makes him go home just before her man returns from work. Every single issue I read, the same thing happens."

Omar tossed the magazine over his shoulder into the back seat. "You should give Bamba that magazine to wrap fish for his customers."

"It is all true, my friend. You can pick up a copy at the five-and-dime store. It is right in there."

They drove on.

"I know she is at the college," Omar offered after a few minutes. "I dropped her lunch to her there last week."

"You dropped her lunch there because you do not trust her. You wanted to make sure she was there."

Omar wondered if Khadim would have considered marrying an American woman if he had not met Benata. Years ago, when the Senegalese teenager was visiting her aunt in Petite Africa, Khadim was at a friend's house next door to the aunt and noticed Benata. After meeting the extended family, he convinced them to get Benata to stay in the United States longer than her tourist visa would allow by having her enroll in college and obtain a student visa. Then he married her and got her to apply for permanent residency.

"It is not too late to fix your problem," Khadim stated.

"I do not want to hear it."

"You should have more than one wife." Khadim thumped the dashboard with the palm of his other hand. "In fact, you should have three or four wives."

Omar seethed. Polygamy had caused so much pain in his family. His father had four wives; his mother, Fama, was the first. He would never forget the day he, his father, and the other drummers returned from Dakar after drumming for Duke Ellington outside Amity Arena at the Festival of the Black Arts. Fama and the other wives cooked a feast: calabashes full of couscous, succulent slabs of beef, monkey bread, fresh milk with honey, and gourds of wine. Later in the evening, Fama went to serve Ibrahim wine as he rested under a Baobab tree and accidentally spilled some on his *boubou*. Ibrahim roared with anger, and then reached up, grabbed Fama by the hair and smacked her across the face with the back of his hand. Fama fell to her knees and cried out. Laughing, the other wives rushed to her, dragged her along the ground, and kicked and slapped her.

"That is your answer to everything, but the last time I looked you only had one wife," Omar responded.

"That way," Khadim continued, ignoring the remark, "if one of them gets lazy you can get rid of her and not even shed a tear because you will have the other wives to take up the duties. Keep two at home and make two get a job. In no time you would have enough money to move to a better apartment."

Omar eyed his friend. "Or I would move to a jail cell because the last time I checked, that was against the law in the United States."

Khadim's hands were flailing. For a moment, Omar thought he'd have to grab the steering wheel from him to control the taxi. "Does not matter my friend. You can have the ceremonies at home. No one has to know about it. Eat coconuts while you have teeth."

Omar didn't respond. Khadim said nothing more on the topic. A little later, Khadim turned the radio on. The news announcer was talking about a march by women for abortion rights. "American women," Khadim muttered and snapped off the radio. "So you do not believe that Natalie is doing the *boom boom* with this vocal coach?"

"Do not know," Omar gritted his teeth.

"She has you—how do the Americans say—twisted around the big pinkie." Khadim held out his thumb and rotated it to demonstrate. Omar was so angry he wanted to snap it off.

"She has not given you a baby," Khadim continued. "You have given her enough time. I am telling you, get rid of her."

Khadim's words stung. Omar remained calm. "She wants to finish her studies. She is still grieving the other one—our boy."

Khadim slowed down and took a U-turn to get back to the road he missed. "Be alert, my friend. When she finishes school she might leave town with that voice man, move to New York, sign a recording contract, and then you will never see her again."

Omar was stunned at the thought.

"It happens all the time. You should watch *The Mike Douglas Show*. It is right on there. A famous singer—she is a black American—was talking about how the day she left her husband and moved in with her white agent, her career took off. She lives in a Hollywood mansion with him."

Omar wished he wasn't trapped in the taxi with Khadim. If only he hadn't missed the bus. He relaxed a bit when they rode down a wide tree-lined road. When it narrowed, they passed a granite sign with a boat anchor carved in it welcoming them to Swift Moore Estates. To their right was the entrance to a golf course and up ahead, a guard's station. Two cars were in front of them. Omar and Khadim watched as the guard picked up a phone to place a call, then apparently hit a switch to lift the metal arm so the first car in line could proceed.

"I knew Fullerton had money bulging in his pockets, but I did not expect this," Omar said, gesturing toward the guard's station.

"I do not know what to say, my brother. I have never had a fare in this neighborhood."

"We should back up and get out of here," said Omar.

"Your landlord will not let you get beyond the gate."

"I am afraid you are right."

But it was too late. By now, cars were lined up behind them. The metal security arm rose, and the car ahead of them went through. Omar could feel his stomach roiling. Khadim pulled up to the guard's station. A pale white man with a dusting of freckles around his nose, the guard was dressed in a red linen sports jacket and white linen pants. He glanced at the taxi and gave Omar and Khadim a hard look.

"I will tell him that we are lost and need to turn around," Khadim said to Omar. He rolled down his window.

The guard's scornful look gradually turned into a smile. "My favorite taxi driver, what brings you here?"

Khadim paused a few moments before responding. "You surprise me," he said, finally, reaching an arm out of the taxi to shake the man's hand. "By chance we meet again, my friend."

"I thought I'd never see you again. I have to thank you for what you did."

"We will thank Allah," Khadim added. "He put me in the right place."

The guard reached into his wallet, pulled out a business card, and handed it to Khadim. "I need to make this right. Get in contact with me. My wife wants to thank you, too. She doesn't know the real story. We'll keep that to ourselves."

When Khadim told him they were going to see Fullerton, the guard hit the button to lift the metal arm without calling ahead. Under an azure blue sky, they crept along the posted speed limit—ten miles per hour—past the golf course.

Omar was mystified. "Are you going to tell me what is going on, or do I have to figure out the riddle myself?"

Men in golf carts bounced over grass as green as the tart apples Omar liked to get from Bamba's market.

"Harold was on death's front step, and I saved him," Khadim said. "This was a year ago. He was in downtown Bellport late one night getting the *boom boom* in The Badlands."

Omar had heard that the section of the city was made infamous by prostitutes and drug dealers that roamed the area. "Why were you there?"

"I was dropping off a fare. Harold came staggering out of a house. He had both hands around his neck. Blood was spilling out like a fountain. A hooker sliced Harold in the neck with a razor. I told him I would call for an ambulance from my two-way radio, but he said he wanted to keep it hush-hush. He did not want his wife to have a clue. His father is a big shot on city council. I rushed him to Bellport General Hospital. The doctor said Harold would have bled to death if he had not gotten there as soon as he did." Khadim chortled. "He paid a high price for his *boom boom*."

"You never told me that before."

Khadim grinned. "Remember, it was hush-hush."

Khadim turned the taxi onto Sea Horse Drive, passing white picket fences and high hedges. The tires crunched over the white gravel of a circular drive. In the distance sat a pale yellow colonial-style house with grey shutters. A pair of ceramic lions flanked the landing like sentinels keeping watch.

"I will wait for you here and keep the motor running in case some bullets fly," Khadim offered, putting the taxi in park. "We may need to make a quick getaway."

"*Dieuredieuf*," Omar replied. "Thank you my friend. But I am not worried."

To take the most direct route to the front door, Omar bypassed the stone walkway and crossed the yard, stepping over the thick roots of an oak tree. He rang the bell. After what felt like a full minute, no one answered. Omar turned toward the foot of the driveway. Khadim was standing outside of the taxi, leaning against the driver's side door with his arms folded over his chest. Omar thought about ringing the bell again but instead banged on the door with his fist. The weathervane perched on top of the roof squeaked as it turned in the wind. Then a door opened slowly. A young blonde woman stood in the doorway with an unlit cigarette in her mouth. She was wearing a white tennis dress with the initial "F" on the lapel.

"I am here to see Mr. Fullerton." Omar said.

"He's not here." She spat out the words and then shut the door in his face.

Omar thought about knocking again. Then he heard her on the other side of the door talking to someone. He wondered who it was since she said Fullerton wasn't home.

Moments later, she opened the door again, smiling as if she'd been forced to do it. He was surprised at the change in her disposition. "You can come in and stand here on the doormat," she said, backing up enough to let him cross the threshold, "but don't come any further."

Omar entered the house. His feet sunk into the brush carpet of a brown and gold doormat with "Fullerton" printed on it. He could smell the lemon scent of the freshly polished and buffed hardwood floors. Skylights brought sunlight into the house. A sliding glass door led to a patio overlooking sailboats bobbing in the inlet. He looked around, puzzled that he didn't see anyone else there.

She looked from his sandals to his *boubou* and wrinkled her nose. "You got the notice, didn't you?"

CHAPTER 7

MAXWELL TURNER'S PHOTO was deceptive. He appeared to be a tall man in the photo that ran with his weekly column in *Inner City Voice*. However, Sydney had to look down at the newspaper executive to meet eyes with him as they stood in the doorway of his office in Downtown Bellport.

"K-man has been speaking very highly of you," he said. He pointed her to a high-backed leather chair facing his desk. He wore suspenders over a starched, white pinstriped shirt with the sleeves rolled up to the elbows. He looked like a miniature version of the newspaper executives she'd seen in the movies. Plaques, awards, and certificates lined his office walls. On a shelf behind his desk were a number of large, framed photographs. Cicely Tyson smiled from one of them. It was autographed, *Max, my hero.* He swiveled around in his chair, picking Cicely up. "Miss Tyson was passing through town a few years ago. *The Heart is a Lonely Hunter* had just come out. Did you see it?"

Sydney nodded and then tried to think of a response that would impress Turner enough to hire her as a freelancer.

"There were a lot of important messages—racial tensions, sensitivity to deaf people, class differences—those themes stay with me even now," she responded.

His eyes twinkled. "When it's a movie you don't forget, that's a sign it was a good story. Miss Tyson sat right there in the chair you're sitting in. We must've talked the whole afternoon.

A fine woman. One of the most down-to-earth people I've ever met." He put Cicely's picture back and picked up one of himself and another man holding a plaque. Max's Afro was much bushier in the picture than it was now.

"John Johnson," he said, handing it to her.

"I don't think I know him."

He laughed. "You ever heard of *Jet* magazine? *Ebony?*"

"Yes, of course."

"He's the publisher. I met John last year at the Publisher of the Year Awards. Good man." He put the picture back and beckoned her to hand over her portfolio. "How'd they treat you in classifieds?"

"Just fine. She said I would get a three-line ad that will run for the next four weeks." In Sydney's nervousness, she couldn't think of the name of the woman who had helped her.

"Mamie." Max grinned. "Don't know what I'd do without her. She does just about everything, even fills in when my secretary's out." He pushed his glasses up the bridge of his nose, and began to slowly flip through Sydney's collection of photos and the newspaper articles she'd written for *Harambeé* about sit-ins and protests by the Black Student Union. The BSU had staged marches on campus to protest the lack of a black studies program and later held sit-ins at the administration building to demand that more black entertainers and lecturers be booked on campus for student events. Sydney was proud of the work she had done capturing the raw emotions of the students. It was while she was volunteering with *Harambeé* that her interest in journalism began to rival her law studies.

Now, sitting across from Max, Sydney realized that she was wringing her hands. She forced herself to stop. "I don't know what Kwamé told you," she said, "but my experience has been limited to activities on campus."

He took his glasses off and pointed them in her direction. "Mrs. Stallworth..."

"Please," she interrupted, "call me Sydney."

"Yes. Sydney. "Don't shine your light under a bushel. It's not about your level of experience. It's about talent, and you have it. You've got a good eye. I see you can write, too."

"Thank you." She felt her cheeks growing warm from self-consciousness.

He went back to her portfolio, a smile creeping into the corners of his salt and pepper mustache. "K-man tells me that you're from Old Prescott."

"I lived there for most of my childhood." She didn't like much attention being put on her, so she decided to ask him a question. "So, you and Kwamé are good friends?"

He put the portfolio down. "Met through 'the movement.' K-man was always heading a protest, a picket, a demonstration, a sit-in, and I was always there with my reporter's notebook. He tipped me off to some of the best stories I've written for this newspaper. I started working the night beat here in 1966, the year I graduated college. I'd come in after my shift at Nutmeg Brewery. I actually did some stringer work for *The Boston Globe*, Kwamé's idea. I tried to get on with them full-time, but it didn't happen. Being black and militant didn't help, I guess. So I continued working for *Inner City Voice*. Never thought I'd work my way up to executive editor. Kwamé's a good brother, one of the best. He'd give you the shirt off his back." Max leaned back in his chair and folded his hands behind his head. "K-man tells me that you and your husband are opening up a bookstore in a few months."

"Yes. It'll be a cultural center, too. We'll invite in poets and writers to do readings. We hope that we can also have actors come in and perform scenes from plays."

"Anything we can do to raise the consciousness of our brothers and sisters is important," Max said. "Let me know if you want the paper to co-sponsor a writing contest."

"That's a great idea."

He gestured at the portfolio, frowning. "Do you think you'll have time for this and the bookstore?"

She caught herself slouching and sat up straight. "The Talking Drum will take up some time, but it's my husband's dream. I'd like to pursue what interests me."

He chuckled. "You sound like my wife. She used to work here, but after a while she wanted to leave to open up a catering business."

"How did that turn out?"

"She loved it. Did it for a while until we had our daughters—twins, teenagers now—and she hasn't returned to work since." He zipped up her portfolio and handed it back to her, smiling. "So what would you like to do for us?"

She hadn't prepared for that question. "Tell me what you need. I can do it all," she lied.

He leaned back in his chair and folded his hands over his chest. "Tell you what. I'll be down a reporter next week. One of them is going on vacation. Why don't you check out the police and fire department news conference next week about the fires in Petite Africa?" He got up and paced the room, punching his fist into the palm of his hand. "It's a hot story, excuse the pun. I think we've got a firebug on our hands. If this keeps going on, someone's gonna get killed. The briefing's gonna be at the old Nathaniel Hawthorne Boot Factory." Then, in a loud whisper, he added, "I think one of the land owners over there has something to do with it, but that's just my theory. I hope I'm wrong." He went to a filing cabinet and pulled out a folder of newspaper clippings of recent fires and handed them to her.

"This does sound like an important story," she said, flipping through the clippings. "We saw a fire truck race down our street toward Petite Africa the day my husband and I moved in."

"There you have it. Take some notes and talk to people afterwards. You'll be fine."

He walked her to the door. "Glad you came in. You'll start to get a feel for what's happening by covering the news conference.

Right now, the big stories around here are the redevelopment and the fires."

Sydney felt goose bumps. Max seemed like a person who was plugged into an outlet. It wasn't until she was on her way back to the car that she realized that she hadn't asked him about the pay.

CHAPTER 8

EVERY FEW BLOCKS Omar glanced at the map he had spread out on the passenger seat of the 1972 Lincoln Continental he steered toward the voice coach's house in Peabody. Uncle Mustapha had marked in dark blue the roads that he should take to get there.

"*Jarbaat*," Mustapha had said, using the Wolof word for nephew, the day Omar told him about his visit to Swift Moore Estates, "When the branches of trees in the forest are fighting, the roots are kissing."

Omar always hated it when his Uncle, like Khadim, spoke in Senegalese proverbs. They confused him. He had finished drumming for the lunchtime crowd at Le Baobab Restaurant and was sitting in a booth across from his uncle during the conversation.

"What are you saying, Uncle?"

"There is nothing more about Fullerton to do. Do not go back to his house. A Senegalese man has his pride. But there is something about your wife you can do."

Like Khadim, Uncle didn't approve of Omar's marriage to Natalie. He never called her by her name.

"You investigate. See whether she cheats with the voice coach. You must know." Mustapha knocked on the table with his knuckles to make sure Omar got the point.

Omar sipped his ginger beer. "She does not talk to me about that man."

Mustapha leaned across the table. "You are not needing to talk. You are catching her."

"I don't understand."

Mustapha threw up his hands and walked through the kitchen doors shaking his head. He came back a few moments later and dangled a set of car keys in Omar's face. "When next she has voice class?"

Omar told him.

"These keys are of one of my renters. He is here two months. He wants reduced rent so I tell him let me use the car. Next time you go pick up your wife from voice lesson. Early get there." He pointed a bony finger at him. "Find out what goes on. You are sleeping better then."

Now, with his hands on the steering wheel, he was grateful that Uncle allowed him to borrow the renter's car even though he had never driven a car as bulky as a Lincoln. It reminded him of a small bus. The front end was so long. He worried he would rear-end another car.

He was glad he took Uncle's advice and left early, so he could arrive long before Natalie's lesson was over. It was best that he know for sure whether or not Natalie was cheating.

He leaned across the seat in an attempt to smooth the creases in the map. When he got to the block that Uncle had marked with a big, blue star, he started checking the house numbers on the mailboxes by the side of the road. The homes were hidden behind tall hedges. He parked by the mailbox with the voice coach's name on it: "Kostopoulos." Omar walked carefully, his ankle still sore from twisting it weeks ago in Fullerton's front yard.

As he stepped onto the porch, his heart pounded. He pressed the doorbell. A speaker emitted classical music.

Standing at the door reminded him of the moment on Fullerton's landing when he was waiting for someone to answer. He was fairly sure he didn't have to worry about a police cruiser chasing him out of town, but he feared that coming to the voice coach's house could be unsettling for another reason. It could make clear what he already felt—that his marriage was falling apart.

No one answered. He squeezed the handle on the double doors and pushed slightly, just to test them. To his surprise, the doors opened. He stepped into a brightly lit foyer with a glass chandelier hanging high above his head. He thought about stepping back onto the porch to ring the bell again or calling out to someone but decided against it. He heard sound coming from the second floor. Giggling. It was Natalie. He was sure of it. Omar slowly climbed the sweeping, carpeted staircase, careful not to make a noise.

When he got to the second floor landing he stopped and listened, holding his breath. He heard a man's voice. The sound was to his right. His palm sweaty on the banister, he followed the sound all the way to the end of the hall to a large room with dark, hardwood floors. It wasn't a bedroom. He breathed easier. When he peeked in, he saw the voice coach, his dark, curly hair resting on his shoulders, sitting at a grand piano, facing away from the doorway.

Natalie was standing next to the coach, looking over his shoulder at some sheet music, her back also to the door. She was holding a glass of white wine. Another wine glass, half-filled, was on top of the piano. The voice coach leaned over to her and said something. In response, Natalie threw her head back and laughed harder than he'd ever heard her before. Her shoulders shook. He tried to think of what to do next. He stepped into the room. Then he took another step. An uneven floorboard creaked. Natalie stopped laughing and swung her head around. Her smile dissolved and twisted into a grimace.

The voice coach looked up at Natalie and then turned around on the piano bench toward Omar. "How did you get in here?" he shouted in staccato fashion in his heavy accent.

Natalie touched the man lightly on the arm and explained that Omar was her husband. "I'll talk to him," she said.

Omar was incensed. Natalie had an apologetic tone in her voice, as if Omar was a pest, a bug that had to be swept away.

"Why are you here?" she whispered loudly after she hurried to meet him in the doorway.

"I wanted to surprise you. Take you out for a dinner meal."

She rolled her eyes. "You're lying. When was the last time you took me out?" She looked back at the voice coach and raised a finger indicating that she'd be back momentarily. Omar followed her out of the room.

"I know why you're here," she snapped when they got to the curb. "You're spying on me. You have these ideas rolling around in your head." She pointed at her temples with her index fingers and rotated them. "What you need to be doing is finding us a better place to live."

He gestured toward the Lincoln. "I appear in this nice automobile, and you do not even appreciate it."

She folded her arms across her chest and looked the car up and down. "Where'd you get this from?"

"Uncle let me borrow it."

She smirked. "You think I'm gonna get in that thing? That gangster ride? You must be crazy."

Before he could respond, she turned on her heels, went back into the house, and slammed the door.

CHAPTER 9

THE FORMER Nathaniel Hawthorne Boot Factory, was on Atlantic Avenue on the banks of the Bellport River. It was a five-story brick and stone structure with a flat roof and a clock tower that chimed on the hour. The old building housed a daycare and provided space for artist studios and community meetings. The cafetorium was where the Liberty Hill Neighborhood Association met monthly. Today, city police and firefighters had the space for a briefing on the fires in Petite Africa.

When Sydney and Malachi arrived, the room was nearly full. Sydney noted a seating pattern based on people's attire. Petite Africa people sat left of the center aisle, and Liberty Hill people were on the right. Onstage were Mayor Chauncey McShane, Fire Chief Patrick O'Connell, and Police Chief Francis Tolerico. To their right was Petite Africa resident and restaurant owner Mustapha Mendy. Sydney had seen his picture in the newspapers. Mendy appeared to be in his late sixties, bony, with heavy bags under his eyes and grey, coiled hair and beard.

At the back of the room were tables filled with toiletries, blankets, stuffed animals, and canned goods. Sydney picked up a can of corned beef. "What is all of this for?"

"The Neighborhood Improvement Association's Relief Effort," Malachi replied. "Whenever there's a fire or we find out about a needy family, people go shopping or bring things from home. Then they come here and put together care packages."

"We should go through our things to see if we can donate anything."

Malachi grinned. "As stuffed as your closets are, I'm sure you'd find something."

Sydney playfully poked him in the side. "I could say the same for you."

She spotted Kwamé, dressed in a grey, pin-striped three-piece suit. He swaggered as he worked his way down the aisle, shaking people's hands and clapping men on the back. His smile broadened as he strolled over to them. "Glad you two could make it," he said.

Sydney told him about her assignment to report on the meeting for *Inner City Voice*.

"Cool. So that worked out for you," Kwamé said. "Max is good people."

"Looks like you've got a full house," Malachi stated, looking around.

Kwamé nodded, and puffed out his chest. "We did what we had to to get the word out. I've been telling the mayor for weeks he needed to have one of these. I said, 'Mayor, my man, we can't keep people in the dark. It's not fair to them. Lives are in jeopardy. They need to know what's going on'."

Sydney rolled her eyes. More big talk from Kwamé, she thought. She and Malachi found two chairs near the back of the room by the tables of donations. "I'm sure Kwamé's inflating his level of influence with the mayor or making up the story entirely," she said.

"Not now," Malachi whispered, tightness in his voice.

She pulled her camera out of its case. As she took out her reporter's notebook and a pencil, a hand grabbed her shoulder. It was Max sitting in the row behind her. "I didn't tell you I was going to show up because I didn't want you to get nervous," he said in a loud whisper. "Just pretend I'm not here. If you need anything, you'll know where to find me." He got up and took a seat near the front of the room. She appreciated that. This was a big story and she wanted to do a good job. He wouldn't be looking over her shoulder. But he'd be close enough that if she needed some guidance, he'd be right there to help.

Once the clock tower chimed at seven p.m., the mayor rose to the podium and gave brief remarks. He introduced Kwamé. While Kwamé strutted to the stage, people resumed their conversations. When he go to the podium and slammed the gavel five times, more than was necessary, people quieted down. He introduced the other men on the stage and then sat down. Chief O'Connell stepped up to the podium. He was a burly man with thick, white hair, gin-blossomed cheeks, and a mixed-grey handlebar mustache. For some reason, as he opened his mouth to speak, he focused on a spot near the ceiling. Sydney took notes in her own version of shorthand.

"We want to bring you up on what we got with the fire investigation," he said slowly in a Boston Irish accent, pronouncing "are" like "ah." "We got different kinds of fires here in Bellport. Some are accidental, caused by residents. Some are acts of God. The fire where lightning struck the cupola on the Ukrainian church two years ago is an example of that. Some were caused by bad wiring, and some were set. They were deliberate."

He paused, as if waiting for the crowd to react. Chief Tolerico joined him at the podium and cleared his throat. "We have an arsonist setting fires. Petite Africa is being targeted. It may be the work of one person. There may be several. Whoever is doing this, we'll catch them. That's why we put together a special arson squad. Personnel from Bellport Police and Fire, plus the state police will work together. We'll have helicopters and patrols covering the neighborhood. In the meantime, we want people to be careful, and Chief O'Connell will talk about that." Tolerico sat down.

"We want you to protect your homes," O'Connell stated. "First of all, lock your doors."

Snickers went up in the audience. O'Connell raised a palm to get people to quiet down. "Now I know that sounds obvious, but when our fire investigators come around, the residents are telling them that they leave their doors unlocked. A simple lock can keep an arsonist out. Dead bolts are good. Lock the windows, too."

A man in a Boston Celtics jersey stood up. "That's part of the problem. The people down there in Petite Africa don't believe in locking their doors, nothing personal, but they need to be told." Sydney made a mental note to talk to him after the briefing. The man looked around at the room. "I'm not passing judgment on anyone, but there's a difference in the way they do things down there."

The room filled with the low hum of conversation. "Oh, no. Here we go," Malachi muttered under his breath.

"This might be a better story than I thought," Sydney responded.

Kwamé came to the mike. "Y'all need to quiet down and let the chief respond."

O'Connell nodded a thank you to Kwamé. "There's no point going into who locks their doors and who doesn't. The point is, we want everyone to lock their doors. We also want people to install lights outside of their homes. Those of you who are renting, ask your landlord to do it. Floodlights near your doorway will discourage an arsonist."

Malachi leaned over and whispered in Sydney's ear, "We should get those lights for our place, too."

O'Connell turned around to say something to Mendy. The restaurant owner slowly stood up. People on both sides of the aisle clapped as he walked to the podium. A few whistled.

"To find people starting these fires, we must work with arson squad," Mendy stated in an accent Sydney could barely understand. "Criminals destroy our community. This community is, how do the Americans say, a place of incubation. Before we pioneer the rest of America we come to Petite Africa. Without the neighborhood, we lose this. We cannot let arsonist steal our launch pad." People applauded. Mendy waited for quiet before continuing. "I know that many in my neighborhood do not have money to pay for bolt lock and motion light. I have sponsor taking care of these things. See me after." Mendy sat back down.

"Arson is a crime of opportunity," O'Connell said, returning to the podium. "We need to remove piles of leaves, paper you don't need, bags of trash, anything an arsonist can use to start a fire."

A woman stood up on the Liberty Hill side of the aisle. "Petite Africa is a mess. If they haven't cleaned it up in all this time, what makes you think they'll start now? They live in filth down there."

A woman on the other side stood up. "What about the gangs?" Her accent sounded West Indian to Sydney. "The gangs from up on The Hill are coming down to Petite Africa. It's those gang members in Liberty Hill. They shoplift. They pick people's pockets. They steal cars. I bet they're setting the fires."

A man stood up on the Liberty Hill side. "And Petite Africa doesn't have gangs?" he shouted. "I know there are at least two Jamaican gangs over there."

People started yelling at each other, some of them jumping to their feet. Sydney trained her camera on the activity. Kwamé shot to the podium and slammed the gavel. "Blame won't fix this," he pleaded into the microphone. The crowd didn't give him much of a chance. If anything, they grew louder. Some shook their fists at each other and shouted across the room. Sydney thought the news conference might become a riot. Chief Tolerico grabbed the gavel from Kwamé and slammed it down so hard that the handle broke off in his hand. "Can we have order?" he shouted. Then he shouted, "Order!" again, and the people quieted down. He took out a handkerchief and wiped it across his sweaty brow.

"All right then," he continued. "We want everyone to notice their surroundings," he continued. "If you see someone who looks suspicious or see some suspicious activity, tell us. We've been working with the city on boarding up the vacant buildings, but sometimes squatters pry them open and move in. They start fires to stay warm. If you see anything like that, let us know. We need you to be our eyes and ears. We can't do this on our own."

After the fire and police chiefs fielded more questions, Mayor McShane directed people to a table in the lobby. "Take a flyer. It's got the arson hotline listed and some fire precautions everyone should take. Chief O'Connell, Chief Tolerico, and I will be giving regular updates on our investigation in the newspapers, on TV stations, the radio. If necessary, we'll meet here with you again in person."

After the meeting adjourned, Sydney looked around the room, deciding which residents to interview. The police and fire chiefs and Mendy were surrounded by residents who climbed onto the stage to talk with them. She would get fresh quotes from them after the crowd thinned. Max was in a conversation with Kwamé

"It's a shame," said Malachi as they stood up. "We do so much for Petite Africa. We do charity work. We collect food and clothing for the poor families. But still, we fight."

Sydney decided her husband had just given the perfect angle for her newspaper article.

CHAPTER 10

"**P**OOR WOMAN." Bernadine was standing at the second-floor picture window, looking down at the street and shaking her head. "She can't get her child under control."

"That's Della, mother," Sydney explained, carrying a tray of hors d'oeuvres into the living room. "You met her at the wedding."

"I thought she looked familiar. Does this happen all the time?"

"Pretty regularly." Sydney placed the tray of sliced French bread topped with tomatoes, basil, mozzarella cheese, and garlic on the coffee table in front of her stepfather, Martin. "Della takes Jasmine to a kindergarten at the end of the block. Sometimes she's fine. Sometimes she kicks and screams the whole way."

Bernadine pulled the blinds open wider to get a better look. "She's trying to get the child in the car, and the little girl is raising a fuss, kicking, punching her in the side."

"I wonder what's the problem," Martin mused.

"Temper tantrum," Bernadine answered. "Sydney had them all the time when she was two or three. Just about drove her father and me nuts."

Sydney thought about Della's invitation to come by to see her workshop. She didn't know if Della was being sincere or simply polite. She would hold off on following up. Besides, she didn't want to endure another one of Jasmine's explosive tantrums.

She exhaled as she went back to the kitchen for a pitcher of lemonade and drinking glasses. Bernadine and Martin had surprised her. They called her from a shopping trip they had taken to Filene's Basement in Boston's Downtown Crossing. They wanted to drop in to see her on their way home. She was on her own with them. Malachi had agreed to sponsor a Liberty Hill Little League team, and the new intern, Lawrence, had gone with him to watch the team practice. From there they planned to stop at the hardware store to buy a drill and handsaw for work Malachi wanted to do on the third floor.

"Nice place. Solid," Martin said as he wrapped his knuckles on the mantle. "Nice wood work too."

"Old buildings do have their charm," Bernadine said as she let go of the blinds and joined her husband on the couch. Her hair was perfectly coiffed as always, her high-heeled strappy taupe sandals complementing her periwinkle pant suit. She carefully picked up an hors d'oeuvre between long, lacquered fingernails.

Sydney thought her mother and stepfather looked odd together—Bernadine, whose skin color was deep toasted brown and Martin's, chalk white.

Sydney poured them both some lemonade. "Can I get you anything else?"

"No, we're fine," replied Martin.

Bernadine smoothed a lock of hair behind her ear and looked furtively at her husband. "We might as well get on with this."

"Can you sit?" Martin asked Sydney gently.

Sydney's mouth went dry. She sat on the edge of her chair opposite them and felt the urge to wring her hands, but she resisted.

"We want to know what's going on," Martin inquired.

"You're supposed to be back in class next week," Bernadine said, raising an eyebrow.

Sydney looked from Martin to Bernadine. "But Mother, we talked on the phone. Remember?" She hated it when her voice cracked. "You said it was fine that I wasn't going back to school."

When Sydney finally spoke to her mother the evening Malachi returned from campus with Lawrence, she had braced herself for her mother to argue with her about taking a year off from the university. She had expected Bernadine to insist that Sydney get back to campus immediately to resume her studies and to see Malachi on weekends. Bernadine listened to her daughter recite her plans, and had said, "If that's what you want to do, so be it." Then, a rushed "Goodbye. I will speak to you soon." And that was it.

It was strange that her mother hadn't ranted. Sydney began to think that she was finally getting through to her mother—that she was an adult, capable of making adult decisions. Now she realized nothing had changed.

"Of course it's not fine," snapped Bernadine. "It's not fine at all. I didn't want to talk to you about something that serious over the phone. That's why we're here."

Bernadine reached for another hors d'oeuvre, but then pulled her hand back. "I was afraid of this," she added curtly. "Once you married Malachi I knew you'd have second thoughts about being away from him—and law school."

"You're halfway through," Martin piped in. "You only have a year and a half to go. Surely you can hang on for the rest of it?"

"I've already talked to the dean," answered Sydney, forcing her voice to be calm. "They'll reserve my spot for another year."

The sound of hammering outside filled the silence in the room.

"I just mailed your tuition check for the next semester." Bernadine's voice was cracking.

Martin took his wife's hand and squeezed it. "I'll call Roger from Rotary. He works in the bursar's office. He'll take care of it before it's cashed." He looked at Sydney. "I don't know what to say. Ian said the other day that he's got an internship spot ready for you at the firm next summer."

Attorney Ian Hoffman was a partner at a small corporate firm in the Berkshires and Martin's squash partner.

"I'm sorry about that," Sydney said in a firm, quiet tone.

Martin waved his hand in the air. "I'm sure he'll be happy to have you there whenever you're ready."

"And after one year, you'll go back?" asked Bernadine.

"That's my plan, Mother."

Bernadine pulled a tissue from her purse and dabbed at the corners of her eyes. "You know what I'm thinking about," she said to Sydney, her voice shaky.

"I know, Mother," Sydney responded in a quiet voice. "I know." Sydney knew that part of the reason Bernadine wanted Sydney to finish law school had to do with Sydney's father. Bernadine was keeping her deceased husband's memory alive partly by encouraging her daughter to fulfill his dream of Sydney becoming a lawyer as he had been.

Bernadine took a long sip of lemonade. "I'm trying to look at the bright side. At least you're not quitting."

"It's just a one-year leave to help Malachi start the business," said Sydney. "Then I'll get back to the books."

Martin walked over to the picture window. "This is a rough neighborhood, you do realize that, don't you?"

For a moment, Sydney considered telling them how she really felt, how she clutched her purse every time she left the house by herself. How she rushed to the car to outrun robbers who might be hiding in the bushes. How she woke up in the middle of the night to the sounds of the house settling, fearing it was a burglar. How she felt fear even with Malachi in bed next to her assuring her that they were safe. How she was afraid all the time even though they had an alarm system.

She wanted Bernadine to reach out with both arms and let her cry on her shoulder. A hug from Martin would have been reassuring. They would never say they told her so. But in the end Sydney could only say, "Of course I know how the neighborhood is."

"A lot of illegal activity is going on in the streets," Bernadine said.

"On our drive up here we saw two men on motorcycles ride up to a car parked a few doors down from here," Martin said. "One handed a package through the driver's window of the car and then the passenger got out and hopped on the back of one of the motorcycles. The three of them took off down the street."

The hammering had stopped. Now someone was using a drill. "What's changed, Mother?"

Bernadine shifted in her seat. "What do you mean?"

"You didn't sound this concerned when we talked about the neighborhood on other occasions."

Bernadine looked at Martin and then back at Sydney. "Well, that's because we thought you weren't going to be here that often. You would be staying with us, Malachi would come out to visit, and I figured you'd come here to Bellport only on a few weekends when you had time off from school. I was concerned before, but now that you're going to be staying here full-time, I am even more worried."

"I picked up a newspaper on our way in," Martin said. "Somebody's on the loose setting fires."

"That's in Petite Africa," Sydney responded. "That's not here."

"That's less than ten minutes away," he continued. "Too close. What's to stop the arsonist from coming this way?"

"Martin's right," Bernadine added. "He could come to this neighborhood too."

Martin turned away from the window. "That's Malachi down there, him and a young man. They're getting something from the car."

The three of them got downstairs just as Malachi had resumed drilling holes near the top of the doorway. Lawrence stood by with a canvas bag full of tools and handed Malachi a lamp that Malachi screwed into the porch wall, aiming it toward the walkway.

"When I'm done, we'll be able to see anyone coming up here after dark," Malachi said as he tightened the screws on the floodlight. He installed another one at the far end of the porch by the stairs leading to the basement.

"And Miss Syd," Lawrence said, "You can put them on a timer so they'll go on and off when you want."

Sydney turned to Bernadine and Martin. "See? We're taking precautions."

CHAPTER 11

UNCLE MUSTAPHA POSTED the "closed" sign on the door of Le Baobab. It was eight o'clock. No customers had shown up for dinner. Omar was disappointed. He would get no pay and no leftover *mechoui*, the slow-roasted lamb shank with herbs, which Uncle had planned to prepare. But he had reason to feel relieved that Uncle was closing early. The old man had a heart condition. He should rest and not work so hard. He looked tired. Omar noticed his uncle shuffling around the restaurant lately instead of strolling from table to table and greeting customers as he usually did. The bags under his eyes seemed etched permanently on his face. He feared that the fight over eminent domain was wearing Uncle down and making his heart weaken.

As he was walking down Wheeler Avenue past Hallima's on his way home, Omar thought about the herbs and their failure to entice Natalie into bed with him. Then he tripped on the plastic sandwich board advertising that day's salon specials that had collapsed on the sidewalk. Through the display window he noticed that lights inside were still on. Hallima, in a flowered smock and matching pants, gripping a broom, was sweeping the back of the salon. He picked up the sandwich board and knocked on the display window. Hallima turned around and saw him. She frowned. "We are closed for the evening," she shouted.

He held up the sandwich board. Her eyes softened. The hinges on the door squealed as she opened it. "Thank you. My niece forgot to bring this in."

He held the sign just out of her reach. "We need to have dialogue."

She crossed thick arms over her chest. "About what?"

"The services you provide."

She looked him up and down, stopping at his head. "You can come back tomorrow when the barber is here, but I don't think you need a shape-up yet."

"I am not here for that. You sold me the *zepis*."

She looked behind her in the salon and then back at him. "Come in."

It was the first time he had entered the salon through the front door. Hallima's salon was the size of a small variety store, narrow and deep. Shampoo bowls and hair dryers were in a row on the left. Styling stations and a barber's chair were lined up on the right. Black, plastic styling capes hung on a coat tree. Light calypso-sounding music floated through the air, as did the smell of burned hair.

He stood in the waiting area. A small coffee table in front of the row of chairs had copies of *Ebony* and *Jet* magazines stacked on it, along with copies of Khadim's favorite, *Black Confections*.

A young woman, probably a teenager, sat in a styling chair holding an oversized mirror to her face and plucked at her eyebrows with a pair of tweezers. Hallima barked something at her in what Omar recognized as a Ghanaian dialect. Hallima waited until the teenager left and then turned back to Omar.

She put the sandwich board under the front counter. "I only sell the *zepis* at the back door. You are not to come to the front to buy it."

"Is it because you don't want everyone to know that the herbs that you sell are useless?"

Omar suspected that Hallima was a fraud. In his village, Fama and his father's other wives used herbs to entice Ibrahim.

The wives always seemed to get more frequent visits to their huts when they did this. Hallima's herbs had had no effect on Natalie.

She shoved a mirror, tweezers, and bottles of hair products into a lower cabinet of one of the styling stations. "I receive no complaints about the *zepis*. You are the first. Did you crumble them in the food like I said?"

He followed her into the far end of the store, where she was turning off the stereo. "I did everything you said."

She looked down at his crotch and smirked. "Maybe you do not have what it takes to satisfy a woman. The *zepis* can do nothing about that."

Omar could feel his face getting hot. He forced himself to remain composed. "I want return of my money. Twenty dollars I paid you."

She stood on tiptoes, reaching up for the metal cord to stop the ceiling fan. "You are wasting my time."

"I shall not leave until I get my money."

She went to the waiting area to tidy the stack of magazines. When she finished, she looked up at him. "Then I guess you will stay here all night."

They locked eyes. Finally, Hallima offered, "I will not give you your money back, but since you are not satisfied, I will give you another formula."

"What does that mean?"

She pulled a set of keys from the pocket of her smock and opened a box on a shelf underneath the cash register. She handed him a jar that looked much like the one he had already purchased.

"You think that I am a fool?" he asked.

"I sell this one for ten dollars more. It has all the herbs of the other one but also *maca* and *yohimbre*. You should have success with this."

"At what price do you think you will rip me off again?"

She held up her palm. "I am not charging you. It is on the

house. If you do not like it, I will return your twenty dollars."

When he got home, Natalie was in the bedroom with the door shut. He turned on the television in the living room. As he flipped channels, he stopped at the sight of Duke Ellington. The musician was on a variety show running his fingertips up and down the keyboard of a grand piano. Omar sat down on the couch. It was good to catch a glimpse of his musical hero. He went and got the framed photo of Ellington on the wall in the drum room and compared it to the man he saw on the TV screen. Ellington looked much older now. His eyes were baggy, like Uncle Mustapha's. His hair was grey and he needed a haircut. The hair at the back of his head had grown so long that it was curled into a strange-looking flip. Omar wished he could call the TV station to talk to Ellington, let him know about his struggles with his drumming career. He turned down the volume during a commercial break and lay down on the couch, facing away from the TV, his face pressed into the cushions.

Whenever he thought of Duke Ellington, he went back to the day in 1965 when Ibrahim had made the big announcement. "*Doom*," Ibrahim had said, using the Wolof word for child as a term of endearment for the eighteen-year-old. "A big celebration is coming to Dakar. Kings, emperors, and presidents from all over the world will come to The Festival of the Black Arts. Some of our lost African brothers in America will be there, too, including the great American composer Duke Ellington. He will perform his famous 'Satin Doll'."

Omar knew all about Ellington's music. Ibrahim had played his albums on the gramophone in their hut. Sometimes Ibrahim used his wind-up radio to listen to Ellington, Ella Fitzgerald, and Dizzy Gillespie.

In the months before the festival, Omar and the other drummers spent almost all of their time practicing. The longer Omar played, the more alive he felt. The drums had a language that made him feel peaceful. Ibrahim's wives sat in the courtyard and created outfits—lengths of cloth covered in strips of calf skin that the drummers could wrap around their hips, beaded and tasseled arm and shin bands, feathered headdresses, *boubous* of various colors. Just for Omar, Fama made an indigo *boubou* with gold trim and a matching cap.

Before the trip, Fama took Omar to see a *marabout*, a holy man, two villages away, who prescribed Omar a *gris gris* for good fortune. The *marabout* placed the amulet, containing writings from the Quran, around Omar's neck.

Months later at the festival, on the day that Ellington emerged from Amity Arena with President Leopold Senghor, Omar stroked the soft leather of the *gris gris* with a sense of satisfaction. He, his father, and the other drummers had performed every day since the festival opened, hoping to catch a glimpse of their country's president and the famed American musician. Senghor walked past Omar and the others with his bodyguards. Ellington stopped where Omar was drumming and stood so close to him that Omar could feel the sleeve of Ellington's suit jacket against his arm. A bright light went off in Omar's face. A man with Ellington had taken their picture. He watched the man tip the camera forward and let the burned flashbulb, now purplish and swollen, fall onto the ground. The man put more bulbs in the silver hood—one at a time—and took more pictures.

Now, all these years later, he still couldn't believe he'd had his picture taken with Duke Ellington or that the famed musician had talked to him after the drumming performance and told him that he had talent. Ellington secured for Omar a four-year scholarship to attend Howard University as a music major, and promised to showcase him at one of his performances once he graduated. Months later, a box arrived from the United States containing autographed photos from Ellington, a typed letter on university letterhead welcoming Omar to the graduating class of 1971, and a one-way ticket to America on a ship departing from Dakar. Ibrahim sat a distance from Fama and

Omar in Fama's hut as they looked over the contents of the box. Omar went to his father. "Papa," he said, "America is for you, not me. You are the one who listens to the American jazz musicians. If not for you, Papa, I would not even know about Duke Ellington."

"*Doom*," Ibrahim replied, "you are the one who shall go to America. In some years, you will become the drumming ambassador of the world. You will spread the true African culture to the world through drumming."

Drumming ambassador. The words had excited him. Sometimes he wished he could relive that day, when his future was wide open before him. He didn't want to leave his daydreams, but at that moment he heard Natalie opening the bedroom door and coming up the hall in heels that slapped the floor. Even now he could feel the jerking and jolting of the train that took Fama and him to the Port of Dakar that humid day in summer 1967.

With tears, Fama handed him two earthen pots she had baked in the kiln to take with him to America. "Give one to Mr. Ellington and the other to your Uncle Mustapha," she said in Wolof. Uncle Mustapha was her brother. He had gone to technical school in Dakar to learn how to run a hotel but now lived in the United States. Omar knew little of his uncle except that he operated a restaurant in a city called Bellport, somewhere north of New York City.

"My heart will cry out for you every night," Fama exclaimed when they got off the train. Her lips were trembling. "But your uncle will look out for you."

He promised his mother he would write letters. Fama relaxed, the creases in her aging face disappearing momentarily. "There is a lady in the marketplace, Ndeye, who reads and writes English," she said. "I will have her read your letters to me, and I will tell her words to write to you."

He was pretty sure he could remember the rest of the conversation with his mother, but Natalie's hand gripped his shoulder, distracting him. "The hot water's not working." she grumbled, her hands on her hips.

"Bu ... but ... I used the shower earlier," he sputtered into the couch cushion.

"I don't care," she snapped. "I just went in there to try to take a shower, and the water is ice cold."

Omar rolled over to face her. "But it has been working since I talked to Fullerton's wife. And I paid the back rent."

"It's not working now," she hissed and began pacing the floor. She stopped when she saw Duke Ellington on the screen. She smashed the power knob off with the side of her fist. "Idrissa moved out, you know."

He sat up. "Idrissa?"

"He and his sister. They're gone. I saw them this morning, packing their things in his sister's beat-up car. They said they're moving to Stamford, Connecticut. They have relatives there. The building's half-empty, Omar." She started shouting. "If you were a husband, you'd find us a place so we could move, too." She spun around and walked away. "I'm getting out of here."

"What does that mean?"

"I'm not staying here," she shouted from down the hall. "I'm going to Beverly's. She has a hot shower, and everything works. She said I can stay with her as long as I want."

He liked Beverly. He had met her once at a cocktail party she had invited them to in her downtown Bellport apartment. Natalie and Beverly had met in an acting class.

He followed her into the bedroom. She was zipping up her makeup case and had started on a small suitcase, tossing in sweaters, jeans, panties, bras, a lint brush, and nail polish remover. She zipped the suitcase and grabbed it and the makeup case.

He rushed to the bedroom door to block her path. "You shall not leave, *ma chère*. A wife shall not leave her husband if she values her marriage."

"You're one to talk. If you valued the marriage, if you were a grownup, you would have gotten us out of here." She brushed past him.

He followed her to the front door. "If you leave, I shall file for divorce."

She turned around and choked back a laugh. "Go ahead!"

After she left, he stood there, staring at the door. He didn't think she'd be gone long. Maybe after a few days she'd calm down and come back, especially if he got Fullerton to fix the heat again. He put the chain on the door and turned the television back on.

After a commercial for Maxwell House Coffee, Duke Ellington was back on, smiling at the camera as he performed. The musician would never believe the path Omar's life had taken since the day they had met in front of Amity Arena in Senegal. It seemed like a lifetime ago. Ellington would expect him to have a recording contract by now, to be touring nationally, not stuck in a rundown building in jeopardy of being torn down, with a cold wife who wanted to leave him, and a stalled career. No, Ellington wouldn't expect that at all.

CHAPTER 12

*F*IVE THOUSAND DOLLARS, *payable to the order of Sydney and Malachi Stallworth*.

Sydney sat at her desk in the guest bedroom on the second floor, looking over the check to the hum of the IBM Selectric typewriter. It was the high point of an exhausting afternoon. She'd sifted through rejection letters that had come in the mail from talent agents and then typed new ones, hoping that among the few well-known writers, poets, actors, or musicians left on her list, someone would agree to appear at the grand opening of The Talking Drum Bookstore and Cultural Center. She didn't have much time left. It was June, four months before the grand opening. Malachi fretted. He insisted that they try to get "a draw," an attraction that would bring in a good-sized crowd and favorable coverage in the local papers.

Bernadine's flowing, elegant script and Martin's co-signature were on the check. Sydney reread the note her mother enclosed. She and Martin wanted the money to be used to purchase inventory, fixtures, and supplies, it said.

The check meant more to Sydney than just money. Bernadine and Martin had been against her leaving school but had relented, ultimately respecting her wishes. She knew it had been hard for them to accept the fact that she was taking a break from her studies, especially for Bernadine.

A rumbling sound came from the stairway. It was either Malachi or Lawrence coming down the stairs. They'd been up on the third floor all day finishing renovations on Malachi's poker room.

Lawrence peaked in the doorway. "Miss Syd, can you come upstairs?"

She switched off the typewriter and tucked the check back into its envelope. "So I'm finally going to get to see it," she said. "Are women even allowed up there?"

Lawrence laughed. "Professor Mal and I have a little more work to do, but you'll get the general idea."

When they got upstairs, Lawrence turned the doorknob that led into the room they had been working on.

"Is a door really necessary?" Sydney asked.

Lawrence turned around and grinned. "Poker games can get pretty loud, Miss Syd. You'll be glad we put this in."

He let the door swing open and gestured for Sydney to enter. Malachi was smiling as she swept past him. It was a large room that looked nothing like she imagined. Long, narrow work tables lined the walls. A couple of wooden stools were tucked underneath one of the tables. Rows of trays and a cutting board were on top. What looked like a wardrobe, or standing closet, was against a wall. Sydney and Malachi stepped through a door at one end of the room that led to a much smaller room, which had a counter, a deep sink almost three-feet wide, more trays and a storage cabinet. Rubber mats covered much of the floor's carpeting.

"What do you think?" Malachi's eyes bore into her.

Sydney slowly led the way back into the larger room. She was clearly puzzled. "I don't know what to think."

"Lawrence," Malachi called over Sydney's shoulder. "Sydney, here, doesn't know what to think of all of this."

"Really?" Lawrence grinned. "Ain't that a shame? We put a lot of work into this."

Malachi turned to Sydney. "What did you think it was going to look like?"

Sydney knew they were having fun with her and decided to

go along with it. "Well, I thought I'd see cocktail glasses lined up on a long counter or bar, some shelves on the walls filled with wine and liquor bottles, a few ashtrays here and there, a poker table, maybe a couch or two, a small sink. This sink is way too big for a wet bar."

Lawrence reached into the wardrobe and pulled out three wine glasses and a bottle of Blue Nun. Malachi poured. "In honor of the occasion, we got a bottle of your favorite."

Sydney took a long sip. She liked Blue Nun's fruity flavor. It reminded her of white grape juice with a shot of liquor added. She walked over to the cutting board "If I didn't know any better, I'd think that you were building a photo lab."

Malachi and Lawrence slapped palms. "Bingo!" exclaimed Malachi.

"And that's the darkroom." Lawrence gestured with his glass toward the smaller room, a wide smile on his face.

She was puzzled. "But why would you do this?" she said to Malachi. "When was the last time you even snapped a picture?"

"Don't you see? It's for you, Miss Syd," Lawrence said.

Sydney walked around the room, speechless.

"I did some research before I started the work," Malachi continued. "The instructions say that a good darkroom has a wet side and a dry side."

"You read manuals?" she asked.

"Parts of manuals. And I relied on Lawrence. He has a lot of know-how when it comes to carpentry."

She smiled at Lawrence. "Thank you."

He took a slight bow.

She walked over to the trays on the counter. "These are my print trays?"

"Yes, baby, and take a look in here." He opened the double doors of the storage closet. The shelves held boxes of film, a photo enlarger, and a timer.

Tears welled up in her eyes. "When I first walked in, I assumed you got this to hang up your buddies' coats."

Malachi beamed. "Surprised?"

She carried the enlarger over to one of the work tables and placed it next to the cutting board. "I can't believe it. My own photo lab."

"I'm gonna get some rubber strips and put them over the doorway to block out the light," added Lawrence. "There's some heavy black paper we use in some of the plays on campus. I can get that to cover the windows."

The doorbell rang. "You expecting someone?" Malachi asked. She shook her head.

"I'll check it out," offered Lawrence.

"You don't have to do that," said Sydney.

"I gotta get going anyway. I have to cut grass for a couple of my customers in the neighborhood," Lawrence explained on his way out of the room.

Malachi took her in his arms. "After all of the sacrificing you've done for me, leaving school, coming here, I wanted to do something for you. I remember all those nights that you spent in the photo lab at Whittington, developing your own pictures. I can tell that you've been missing that."

She stood on tiptoes and gave him a peck on the lips. "My own darkroom in my own home. Thank you!"

"It'll be more than that." He crouched down at one of the storage cabinets along the perimeter of the room to pull out a large black case.

She undid the buckles. It was a light kit, which came with light stands, bulbs, reflectors, and umbrellas.

"This will be your studio," he said, gesturing with a sweeping motion around the room. "I know how much you enjoy taking portraits of people. You can do that right here. I'm going to have Lawrence make you some backdrops, curtains probably, get some chairs, a couch, maybe a mirror. You can let me know what else you need."

They left the floor and headed downstairs. When they got to the foyer, Sydney was surprised to see Kwamé there with a couple who appeared to be in their seventies. Lawrence was gone.

"Miss Sydney, how you be?" Kwamé stretched out his arms for a hug. She sidestepped him and stood next to Malachi. Kwamé gestured toward the couple. "This here's Inez and Willie Taylor, some old friends."

"Pleased to meet you," Willie said. He was a broad-chested man wearing a lightweight three-piece suit. A deep purple handkerchief was tucked in his top suit pocket. He tipped his hat, a derby, then removed his wife's sweater cape from around her shoulders. He placed his hat and the cape on the coat tree. Malachi looked around. "What happened to Lawrence?"

"Oh nothing, man," replied Kwamé. "Said he had to get to his grandmother's house."

"He told me he had to cut customers' grass," Sydney said.

"One of your students?" Kwamé ignored her remark.

"Yeah, man," Malachi said. "I've been knowing him for years."

"What a charming house you have," Inez said. She was not quite five feet tall, at least a foot and a half shorter than her husband. She reminded Sydney of a delicate bird as she moved about with her silver-handled cane. She spoke each word distinctly, much like her husband, as if she was demonstrating elocution. "Reminds me of my Aunt Harriet's place on the South Side of Chicago."

"That's where we're from," Willie added.

"We left there a long time ago." Inez waved her hand in the air dismissively. "We've lived all over the world, you know—Europe, China, the Western U.S., Africa."

"Traveling school teachers," Willie continued. "Retired a few years ago, settled in Darien, Connecticut."

Sydney didn't know that black people lived in Darien. The upscale bedroom community outside of New York City relied on property taxes to balance its budget, which priced most working-class and middle-class people out of the market.

Sydney's thoughts must have shown on her face.

"I know what you're thinking," Willie grinned. "There are a few of us down there." He chuckled.

Kwamé led the couple into what would be the bookstore's reading room. Sydney and Malachi started to follow them, but Kwamé held them back. "You ain't rented the basement yet, have you?" he asked in a low voice.

"No. Not yet," Malachi replied. He turned to Sydney. "Has anyone come by to see the unit yet?"

"I've gotten a few calls about it, but that's it.

"So it's still available?" Kwamé said.

"Yes, but…"

"Good."

"Why?" Malachi asked.

"The Taylors need a place."

"But didn't they just say they live in Connecticut?" Sydney asked, puzzled.

"She's got health problems," Kwamé added. "They want to be up here, not far from the hospitals in Boston. Connecticut's just too far away."

"Then why don't they move to Boston?" asked Sydney.

Kwamé stepped back from her and grinned. "Look at you, Mrs. Twenty Questions."

Sydney didn't care for his condescending tone.

"Yeah," said Malachi. "Why *don't* they get a place in Boston? We're twenty miles away and public transportation up here is unreliable."

"They know people around here. Is that enough of a reason?" Kwamé seemed defensive.

"That sounds good, man, real good," Malachi said. "We'll have them fill out an application, check their references."

Kwamé stroked his goatee. "References? I go way back with Willie and Inez. I can vouch for them."

"This is not your apartment, Kwamé," Sydney said. From the foyer she could see Willie flipping through a volume from

Collier's encyclopedia in the reading room from a set Malachi had ordered to sell in the bookstore. "We need to check them out. That's standard procedure."

Malachi looked at Sydney. "She's right. We need to check their backgrounds."

"Backgrounds? Professah, with all due respect we don't need you to do a dissertation on them. Just rent them the apartment."

"I hear you, man," Malachi answered after a moment, "but no background check, no apartment. Like Syd said, that's standard. Know what I'm saying?"

Kwamé waved him off. "No, I don't know what you're saying. They would be insulted."

They stood there saying nothing, and Malachi asked, "How do you know them?"

Sydney fumed. Malachi was about to cave into Kwamé. Why wouldn't he listen to her?

Kwamé's eyes brightened. "Willie used to run the state NAACP in Connecticut a few years back. Inez was recording secretary. When the city was gonna let the feds take Liberty Hill for redevelopment, Willie and Inez rallied the troops, bussed in two hundred protesters. Professah, you were…"

"I know, I know," Malachi interrupted. "I was in my ivory tower at Whittington University."

"We owe them, man," insisted Kwamé. "If not for them, there would be no more Liberty Hill."

Malachi nodded. "I see your point, brother."

"What are you saying?" asked Sydney, but neither man responded.

It occurred to Sydney that Kwamé had elbowed his way into the apartment deal. She was glad she had made it clear to him that he had overstepped his boundaries. She looked over at Malachi. He stared at the ceiling and scratched his head, rather than meet her eyes.

Kwamé smiled broadly. "Okay. Let's join them down the hall."

The two men clasped hands. Sydney was furious. Kwamé

led the way. Sydney let Malachi walk ahead of her to give her a little time to cool down. She was determined not to let this go. Kwamé was up to something. She was sure of it.

Inez was sitting in one of the high-backed chairs. Willie stood at a bookshelf, flipping through another volume of Collier's. Sydney sat in the chair next to Inez's, while Kwamé and Malachi sat at opposite ends of a couch across from the women.

"Why do you want to move to Liberty Hill?" Sydney asked in a business-like tone.

"We put the house on the market," Willie replied.

"It was just too big," Inez added.

"We're getting older," Willie continued. "Boston has the best hospitals around. If either of us gets sick, we could be at Beth Israel in twenty minutes.

"You can't beat the hospitals of Boston," Kwamé chimed in. "They're the best around."

"I had a stroke," Inez explained, tapping the top of her cane with her fingertips. "Happened a few years ago. I took early retirement from the school system. All I need is this cane to steady myself, and I get around just fine. But you never know."

"I don't know if the apartment would give you enough space. It's kind of small," Sydney said. Kwamé shot her a look. Sydney glared at him in response.

"The basement unit has over eight hundred square feet," Kwamé rebutted. "It'll be pretty roomy if it's just the two of you."

"Excuse me, but what about the stairs?" Sydney asked, ignoring Kwamé.

"The exercise will be good," Inez responded. "Walking up and down will keep my joints from getting stiff."

"Miss Sydney and my buddy here could really use the extra income from the rental as they get their business off the ground," Kwamé explained.

"Kwamé, we're not discussing personal matters here," Sydney interjected. "Malachi and I will handle this."

"Opening a small business can be risky," Willie said, looking around. "The key is to draw customers early in the game."

"That's what we're hoping to do," Malachi answered. He told them about their attempts to get a celebrity for the grand opening.

Inez smiled broadly. "Willie and I know some people. We might be able to contact a few."

Willie shut the encyclopedia volume and put it back on the shelf. "How about The Fierce Warriors?"

Malachi shook his head. "The godfathers of the spoken word? We'll never be able to get them. They'll charge more than we can pay."

Sydney first heard The Fierce Warriors at Malachi's apartment when they were dating. He had two of their albums. They were a group of poets and musicians that had come out of Howard University whose lyrics were about black nationalism and the civil rights movement. She thought about the check she'd gotten from Bernadine and Martin. She was sure they could afford to spend a portion of it to cover the band's expenses.

"When you have the inside track you don't have to worry about such things," Willie said with a sly grin.

Sydney doubted that they knew The Fierce Warriors. It was likely all talk, all bluster. But it couldn't hurt to have them try to help.

"I'll make some phone calls," Inez offered.

"A group like The Fierce Warriors could attract some deep thinkers to your bookstore," Willie added.

"That's what we want," Malachi responded. "We want to attract that crowd, people who will come here and discuss the affairs of the day, like a salon. They'd sit and read, have debates, and buy books, of course."

Malachi left the room, returning with a set of keys. He looked at Sydney. "Let's give the Taylors a tour of the basement apartment."

The Taylors, accompanied by Kwamé, walked ahead of them.

Sydney grabbed Malachi's arm. "No. You give the tour. I'm going up to the photo lab."

She was angry. Malachi was letting Kwamé manipulate him into signing a lease with these strangers. She trusted this couple about as much as she trusted Kwamé, which was not much. Something about them smelled crooked.

"Don't sign anything without me being present," she added. "I have a stake in this too, remember? We're partners."

"I know, Syd," Malachi responded. "I know."

Sydney could tell by the look on his face that he was only half listening to her.

CHAPTER 13

OMAR AND KHADIM ran up the gazebo stairs two at a time as the crowd at Petite Africa Green began to cheer. It was an unseasonably hot afternoon in July, almost one hundred degrees. The air was heavy and damp after a morning rainfall. To Omar it felt like a day during the Senegal rainy season. Bounding up the steps after them were an African lute player, a keyboardist, drummers, harpist, and dancers. As the musicians tuned their instruments, the dancers fanned out in front of them and began swaying to the rhythms.

Usually The Fulani Sound performed alone. But Uncle Mustapha, the other property owners, and tenants wanted the Green packed. They wanted to remind the people of the upcoming meeting of the Bellport Redevelopment Authority and the role they could play in demanding that the project be halted.

Uncle Mustapha grabbed a microphone and shouted, "*Salamalekum, ça va, hello,*" switching from Wolof to French to English. People thrust their fists in the air and responded in their native languages. Next, Mustapha described, as he had done so many times, how the Harborview Project would bulldoze their homes and community, leaving them virtually on the streets.

"How is your wife doing?" Khadim asked, scooting his stool close to Omar's. "Is she still on the run?"

Omar looked up from tuning his drum. Khadim wore the grin of a hyena, he thought. He promised himself he'd never share his problems with Khadim again.

"Her time away is temporary. She will return soon."

Khadim shook his head. "I do not know why you have not replaced her with a new one while she is gone. This is so easy, my brother. Just do it."

Omar's jaw tightened. "You sound like a parrot, my friend. You only have one topic of conversation, and you keep repeating it."

Khadim shrugged. "Women are everywhere." He nodded to the crowd. "At least fifty out there right now could replace your wife, a good African woman who would wash your back, cook, clean, do the *boom boom*. You might even find one who will give you a son. You are crazy, man. All you can think of is your spoiled wife. *A stick that has a long time in the water does not change into a crocodile.*"

Omar got off his stool. He punched Khadim in the shoulder. Knocked off balance, Khadim dropped his drum and jumped to his feet. He looked stunned. The rough mixture of sounds petered out as the musicians stopped warming up and turned toward the two. Unaware of the commotion, Uncle Mustapha continued speaking to the crowd.

"*Tejjil sa gemmin!*" Omar shouted, breathing heavily. "If you do not shut your mouth, I will shut it for you. We can go on the grass right now."

Khadim glared at him, raising his palms. "I think I plucked a nerve, and I did not mean to. I am only trying to give you advice, my brother." They stared at each other and eventually both sat back down. Omar resumed tuning his drum. He thought about Natalie. When was she coming back? It had been two weeks. He thought she would have at least called by now. He had Beverly's number but he could not lower himself to call.

"I can handle my wife myself. She is not your business." Omar growled and turned away from Khadim. Incredibly, his friend would not be deterred.

"They are like fruit that is falling from the tree, my friend,"

Khadim teased. "You do not have to look far. You need to start plucking."

Uncle Mustapha finished his remarks and turned to Omar to see if he and the others were ready. Omar nodded yes. Mustapha handed the microphone to the harpist and walked off the stage, the signal for the show to begin.

Omar set the pace with his *djembe*. Khadim placed his *tama*, or talking drum, under his arm, squeezing it to change the pitch as he struck the drumhead a mallet. With every squeeze, Khadim flexed his bicep. Omar braced himself, knowing what was coming. Women started screaming and shaking their hips. This only encouraged Khadim. He swung his head around and sent his dreadlocks flying.

In the distance, Omar noticed the crowd parting for Uncle Mustapha as he left Petite Africa Green. Uncle deserved to relax.

As had been rehearsed, the lute player left his instrument and circled the gazebo playing hand cymbals. Omar switched to the *dundun*, striking the drum with a stick. He strolled to the front of the gazebo and looked out at the crowd of mostly women. They were moving to the beat. Under their sweat-soaked blouses, he could see erect nipples. One woman wiggled her tongue at him as if she was licking a lollipop. Maybe Khadim was right. Omar had been overlooking the fruit that was dangling right in front of him, so easy to pluck. Natalie didn't want him, so why shouldn't he satisfy his lust?

Out of the corner of his eye, Omar saw Khadim approaching. Apparently his friend had gotten over their fight and wanted to have one of their drumming duels, a favorite with their audiences. Omar pounded out rhythms with his stick. Taking his cue, Khadim smacked the *tama* in frenzied syncopation. The dancers spun back and forth like human tops and twirled, jumping higher and higher.

CHAPTER 14

AUGUST 15, 1972

Mr. and Mrs. Stallworth:
  I have received your request from Willie Taylor for a performance by The Fierce Warriors at your grand opening. I'm sorry it has taken us so long to respond. We were out of the country for an extended period. The Warriors believe in the cause you are undertaking, launching a bookstore and cultural center in the black community. We are available the date of your event in October.
  The Fierce Warriors perform charitable concerts each year for organizations that cannot afford to pay the full cost. Since your business is just starting, we will give you that discount. See the enclosed contract. Please return it, duly signed, within ten days.
Yours in the struggle,
Hideki Baruka
Manager
The Fierce Warriors

Sydney gasped as she read the letter. Finally. They not only had a headliner for the grand opening, they had The Fierce Warriors. This was more than a dream. She was sure they would draw a crowd. She folded the letter and contract and put them away in the rolltop desk. If only she'd met the Taylors sooner, she wouldn't have spent all those weeks in fruitless calls to performers' agents. But the important thing was that she *had* met the Taylors, and they had been more than helpful. She reached for the phone to call her mother and tell her the news but stopped before she lifted the receiver. Bernadine had probably never heard of the group. She wished Malachi was home. He and Lawrence had left about an hour ago to purchase jerseys, sports equipment, and other supplies for the Liberty Hill Little League baseball team.

She paced the room. She wanted to tell someone. Inez Taylor wasn't downstairs in the apartment. She had seen her climb into a Buick twenty minutes ago.

Then Sydney heard the ice cream truck roll onto the block as it always did on Saturday afternoons. Its piercing jingle was annoying enough but it also reminded her of Kwamé, who had bragged that he was the one who convinced the mayor to bring the ice cream truck back to the neighborhood. From the window she saw a small gaggle of kids gather around the truck.

Beyond the truck she spotted Lawrence coming out of Kwamé's record shop. Apparently, the two were becoming friends. Lawrence would be excited about the news, but he'd be gone by the time she made it down the stairs.

Then she glanced at the apartment above the record shop and saw the curtain flutter. Kwamé's wife was home. Della would be thrilled about The Fierce Warriors coming to perform.

But she imagined their conversation might be awkward. She didn't know Della. They were little more than strangers. They hadn't spoken except for a few words they had exchanged at the wedding and the day Sydney and Malachi moved into the Victorian.

"We've been here four months, Syd. You should have talked to Della by now," Malachi had said to her the other day. "Knock on her door. Ask for a cup of sugar. Don't women do that all the time?"

Sydney didn't need a cup of sugar, but she had a half dozen

blueberry muffins she'd baked that she could use to break the ice with Della. Before she could talk herself out of it she was in the kitchen folding muffins into a cloth napkin. As she searched for a container to put them in, she heard squeaking. It sounded like a rusted wheel. She glanced at the clothesline in the backyard and figured the pulley was the cause of the noise. She dropped the muffins into a straw breadbasket that was given to her and Malachi as a wedding gift.

She crossed the street, the breadbasket swinging from her arm. When she reached the other side, she decided to stop in the record shop. She was sure Kwamé would consider her rude if she didn't at least say "hi." He might be hungry for a snack and welcome one of her muffins. Despite her misgivings about him, she thought it only right that she try to maintain at least a cordial relationship with her husband's best friend.

It was her first time inside the record shop. It was bright and spare with naked light bulbs hung from sections of the ceiling. Record albums, 45s, and cassettes filled rows of unpainted wooden bins in the middle of the room. Eight-track tapes were stacked in cubby holes along the walls. Edwin Starr's "War" poured from speakers mounted in opposite corners of the ceiling.

Rhythm and Blues seemed more like a museum about a record store than an actual business. It was noon and it was empty. Dust covered the front counter and the cash register. Faded album covers sat on display tables. She spotted Kwamé in the back of the store in his office doorway, his back to her. She walked toward him until she realized that he wasn't alone. She began backing away. But he caught a glimpse of her out of the corner of his eye. He swung around. A young white woman peered over his shoulder. Kwamé glared at Sydney through narrowed, angry eyes.

"Need something?" he asked, sounding irritated.

She shook her head. "No. I was on my way to see Della."

He pointed his index finger at the ceiling, slicing the air. "Up there."

Sydney felt uncomfortable, as if she had done something wrong. When she got back to the entrance of the record shop, she remembered she had meant to offer him a muffin. She glanced back. Both Kwamé and the woman were staring at her. Sydney hurried out the door and climbed the winding stairs to the second floor. When she got to the door, she stopped to catch her breath. She heard a television. Sydney knocked and waited. She knocked again. Then she banged the door with her fist. A few second later, she heard the floor boards creaking from inside. After a series of clicks from the bolt locks, the door opened as far as the chain would allow. Two brown eyes peered through the crack.

"Yeah?" a voice behind the eyes said.

"I ... I don't mean to disturb you."

"You ain't disturbing me."

Then Sydney heard someone running up the stairs behind her. A boy about ten years old was headed to the landing and stopped short when he saw Sydney. He looked from Sydney to the door.

"Hol' on," Della shouted and shut the door. She dislodged the chain to open the door. Della reached into her bra and pulled out some one-dollar bills. "Get me a carton of Kools," she told the boy. He grabbed the money and hurried down the stairs.

"I know it's been some time since we moved in. We've been so busy getting everything settled that I didn't have time to visit with you before. So, I thought it was time I dropped by to say 'hi,'" Sydney said.

"Well ain't that nice of you," Della replied in her southern lilt. She invited her in. The apartment door opened into the living room. The décor was simple, reminding Sydney of her grandmother's parlor. A mustard green sofa, covered in plastic, blended with the walls. A matching recliner on the wall opposite the sofa was stacked with neatly folded children's clothes. A framed, sepia-toned picture of Jesus Christ, with long hair and palms pressed together in prayer, hung on the wall behind the chair. Flanking it on each side were framed photos of Martin Luther King, Jr., and John F. Kennedy.

Della reached to turn off the television but paused at a news bulletin—another fire in Petite Africa. The reporter stated the fire had broken out in the kitchen of Ortiz Cakes and Pastry Shop. No one was hurt. The kitchen staff was able to put it out with fire extinguishers, but the kitchen was destroyed. Della snapped off the set.

"That was a close call," said Sydney.

"Those people can't seem to catch a break over there," Della added.

"But at least this one didn't involve the arsonist."

"Yes, we do have to count our blessings."

Sydney felt relieved that the fire gave them something to talk about, an ice breaker of sorts.

"Please excuse the place," Della said. She swept a bean-bag ashtray off the coffee table and two crumpled Viceroy cigarette packages, apparently Kwamé's. Sydney followed Della into the kitchen where she dumped the ashes and empty packages into a trash can.

"This is my little workshop," Della announced, nodding toward the pantry. The shelves were filled with miniature gazebos and bird houses of untreated wood, rows of vases, and small pots of paint and brushes.

Della waved Sydney to the Formica table. A lawn bag full of clothes sat in the chair opposite her.

"What you got there?" Della pointed at the basket. Sydney lifted the lid, smiling.

Della began to smile back, exposing front teeth that overlapped. She quickly put a hand over her mouth. "I didn't know you baked."

Sydney laughed. "I don't bake a lot, but blueberry muffins are one of my favorite things to make."

"Then we got something in common." She reached into the refrigerator for a pitcher and poured them glasses of iced tea.

Sydney asked her for sugar.

Della chuckled. "You don't need no sugar. It's already sweet. We serve it that way down south.

Sydney took a sip.

"What you think?"

"Delicious." Sydney almost choked after one gulp; it was so sweet. She put her glass down. "Really. I can come back later. I feel I've caught you in the middle of something." She gestured toward the bag of clothing.

Della waved her off. "Reverend Williams asks me every year to head the clothing drive. You can't say 'no' when the pastor comes calling." In Della's southern accent, "Williams" sounded like *Wee Yums*.

As they ate, Sydney handed Della the letter from The Fierce Warriors. "I'm pretty excited about this. Malachi doesn't know yet."

Della's eyes grew wide. "The Fierce Warriors are coming to little ol' Bellport? Ain't that something. Me and Kwamé saw them in New York once at The Blue Note."

"I was about to resign myself to not having anyone for the grand opening, so this is a pleasant surprise."

"There are about eight of them," Della continued. "Drummers, poets. They're all over the stage. The performances make you think. Thought music. That's what it's called. You've got to follow along real close to catch the meaning. That's why I had Kwamé buy me the album afterwards." She handed Sydney back the letter. "People should come from all around for this. Y'all might even get the papers to do a story."

Sydney told Della about the meeting with Max.

"Then you're way ahead of the game, working for *Inner City Voice*." Della took a sip of tea. "So what you think of Liberty Hill so far?"

Sydney tried to choose her words carefully. "Even though we've been in the house for months now, I'm still having a hard time getting used to the neighborhood, cars and trucks up

and down the street at all hours. Then there's Jake's Tavern."
Della smiled. "That is a rowdy place.

"Did you hear it last night?"

"Can't say I did."

"About three in the morning I had to pull the covers over my head to try to block out the noise from Jake's. It sounded like a fight, people scuffling and screaming. I shook Malachi awake, but he told me to go back to sleep, that it was always that way."

"Malachi is right," Della said. "Cops are called just about every night to break up a fight at Jake's."

"In Old Prescott," Sydney explained, "I could open my bedroom window to catch a breeze without hearing sirens or cars."

"When I was at your wedding, that was my first time in that part of the state. I could see that you grew up in a sheltered environment, nothing like Liberty Hill."

Sydney thought she heard resentment in Della's voice, but she wasn't sure. "Does the crime in the neighborhood concern you?" Sydney asked.

Della sniffed. "It's safe enough as long as you keep your wits about yourself and take care of whatever business you got before dark."

Sydney hesitated to ask the next question, but then decided to go ahead. "I also wonder about raising children here. Not that Malachi and I are ready for that, but maybe someday."

"I am very protective of my daughter," Della snapped, her jaw tight. "She's my number one priority."

Della had taken her remark the wrong way. "I didn't mean to imply that she wasn't."

"If I didn't think she was safe I'd take her right on out of here. Besides, I'm not interested in raising some suburban pseudo-black Barbie doll who's afraid to be around her own people."

"*Like you.*" Sydney could hear the rest of the sentence in

Della's voice. Sydney regretted asking the question and tried to think of something to say to ease the tension in the room.

"I'm sorry you couldn't join us for lunch that time," Sydney said.

Della was about to take a sip but put her glass down. "What you mean?"

"When Kwamé and I had lunch at The Stewed Oxtail right after Malachi and I first moved in."

Della's eyes shifted from left to right. Then she turned the corners of her mouth up, forcing a smile. "Oh yes, a few months back. I'm sure I had some things I had to do. Did you have a nice time?"

"Kwamé introduced me to some of the other business owners around here. I also met the new black police officer."

"Stribling? He's good people, really looks out for the neighborhood." Della folded the paper muffin cup into her napkin and leaned forward in her chair. "You didn't run into Kwamé on your way up here, did you?"

Sydney thought about her brief visit to the record shop. She wasn't sure how to respond. "I did."

Della carefully crossed her hands and made a steeple under her chin. "Was he alone?"

They locked eyes for a moment. "No need to answer," Della wiped crumbs off the table. "I know what Kwamé's up to."

"I'm sorry."

"Don't be. He thinks I'm stupid. He calls it politicking. He calls it being friendly. I call it alley catting."

"I don't know what to say."

Della narrowed her eyes. "I just want you to know that's the way my husband is."

Why would Della want her to know that? Then Sydney realized what Della was suggesting. She backed her chair away from the table and stood up. "I don't know what you're thinking, but I only went to lunch with Kwamé to be polite. I didn't want to go, but Malachi insisted. Sydney began stuffing the napkins she had packed back into the breadbasket with the rest of the muffins.

Della stood up. "Where you going?"

Sydney ignored her and retraced her path through the living room. When she opened the front door, the kid that Della had sent to the store was standing there with the carton of Kools. Sydney took the carton from him and turned around to toss them on Della's coffee table on her way out, but Della took them from her.

"I can see that coming over here was a mistake," Sydney said.

"No it wasn't. Wasn't no mistake at all." Della took the change from the boy and then handed him back a nickel. After he ran back down the stairs, she turned her attention to Sydney. "Please don't leave. Please."

Sydney hesitated then thought it would be easier to sit back down and give the conversation another chance than explaining later to Malachi what had happened.

Once they had settled back at the kitchen table, Della opened a pack of cigarettes and gestured for Sydney to take one. Sydney said no.

"You don't mind if I have one, do you?" Della asked.

Sydney shook her head.

They were both startled by the sound of something being slammed into a wall. Della went down the hall to investigate. "Just my little princess waking up," she said when she returned, her voice a half-octave higher.

Sydney wondered if Jasmine was having another tantrum.

"I have to apologize," Della said as she sat back down at the kitchen table. "Kwamé thinks of me as this country girl who didn't have much education, and now he thinks he's outgrown me. That's my problem. It has nothing to do with you."

Sydney wanted to get off the topic. "How's Jasmine doing?"

Della forced a smile on her face. "Jasmine is Jasmine. Despite his faults, Kwamé has been good to me. He convinced me to come up here and get away from the South with all of that separate but so-called equal business, encouraged me to buy this building, got me to invest in this property, and he's good to Jasmine."

Della flicked a lighter on the end of the cigarette and took a long drag. "Kwamé tells me you were in law school."

The sound of a second crash down the hall made Sydney flinch. Della rolled her eyes and left the kitchen. When she returned she seemed weary, sighing heavily as she sat back down. "Jazz had some static on the TV and wanted me to fix the rabbit ears. Now what were we talking about?"

"Law school."

"Oh yeah."

Sydney explained why she was taking the year off.

Della nodded. "You're right. Why go spending all that money if you're not sure that's what you want to do. Besides, you got to stay with your man, support his dream. Starting a business is hard. Believe me, I know. If a man starts to doubt himself, he needs his woman to turn to. If he doesn't feel good about himself, then he's no good to you or nobody else."

"I struggled with my decision."

Della picked up a gingham shirt out of the bag of clothing, folded it, and placed it back on top. "Here's another reason why you're doing the right thing. If you let Malachi live here by himself, some of these hussies around here would start shopping at the bookstore and not because they were looking for something to read, if you know what I mean."

Sydney shifted in her chair.

Della continued. "There are vultures out here just waiting. By you staying here for at least a year, you'll be sending them a message: He's off-limits, he's your man."

A door down the hall creaked open and moments later Jasmine ran into the room and climbed into Della's lap. She buried her face in her mother's chest. Della grabbed Jasmine by one of her Afro puffs. "Chile, look at this head. What you in there doing?"

Jasmine's shoulders hunched up and down as she tried to catch her breath between whimpers. "Casper went off," she whined. "Can't find Leo. He's not under the bed."

"That's Leo the Lion," Della explained to Sydney. "You pull a string and he talks." She brushed a thumb across Jasmine's hairline. "Well, now you got all the dust bunnies all over your head." Jasmine swatted at her mother's hand.

"I've been trying to comb this stuff near a week, and she won't let me," Della said.

"Cuz it hurts!" Jasmine shouted.

"She used to sit still for me, but not anymore. She's like a Mexican jumping bean. It seems the older she gets the more tender-headed she gets. I know what I'm gon' do," Della winked at Sydney. "I'm gonna shave it all off."

Jasmine stopped rubbing her eyes and stared at her mother a moment. Sydney held her breath. The child started grinning.

"You give me no choice, little girl."

"Then I'll ... then I'll run away," Jasmine giggled.

"What you know about running away?" Della asked, laughing as she led Jasmine back down the hall. When Della returned, Sydney stood up to leave. "I think I've taken up enough of your time."

"I'm glad you stopped by." Della walked her to the door. "I was going to college for a while, too," she added.

"Oh?"

"Was working on my bachelor's degree in Arkansas. Had to stop for personal reasons."

"You could always go back and finish."

Della exhaled. "You're right. Sometimes when I'm at the library I think that I should be a librarian instead of just an assistant." Her shoulders sank. "But I put all my money in this building, and then I'd have to find a sitter for Jasmine so I could take night classes.

"Kwamé could always babysit, couldn't he?"

"Nah. Kwamé's always out somewhere."

Sydney thought for a moment. "There are scholarships, and there are babysitters. Back when I was in high school I earned spending money babysitting."

Della's eyes brightened. "So you have experience babysitting. That's good to know. You've given me some things to think about."

Sydney was glad she had stopped by but hoped Della wasn't interpreting her remarks as an offer to babysit. She and Malachi had a lot of work ahead of them to prepare for the grand opening of The Talking Drum in two months, especially now that The Fierce Warriors were set to perform.

CHAPTER 15

TWELVE CANS of ready-to-heat lobster stew were lined up on the kitchen counter, Natalie's payment for doing voiceovers for soul station WCLL. The Young Turk, one of the station's on-air personalities, had told her about the job. The owner of the fledgling Harbor Islands Seafood Company couldn't afford to pay for radio spots but could give the station free cases of stew. Natalie had agreed to take the job with the payment of one case.

She spooned the contents of two cans into a saucepan. "Why don't you wash up? This shouldn't take but a minute," she stated.

Omar shut the refrigerator door after finding nothing to drink that he could wash the stew down with and went to the hall bathroom. Anything that took only a minute to cook couldn't be too tasty. But he thought it best to go along with it and eat the stew. After Natalie had come in with the case, he had slipped the new jar of herbs from Hallima into his pants pocket. Once heated, the stew would be thick enough for him to dissolve some of the herbs in Natalie's bowl without her detecting it. This *zepis* was probably as useless as the earlier batch, but he thought he'd give it a try. If nothing happened, he'd return to Hallima, this time for his money.

Natalie returned from Beverly's apartment two days after Omar performed with Khadim and the others at the rally. Beverly's boyfriend was moving in, forcing Natalie to move out. Omar didn't know why, but, by coincidence, the heat and electricity had worked consistently in their apartment since she'd returned. As he washed and dried his hands in the bathroom, he wondered how he would distract her so that he could crumble the potion into her bowl.

"Next time you must insist that the client pay you cash money," he said as he sat down at the table.

"It's all about exposure at this stage," she countered as she opened a carton of heavy cream. "Every time I do one of these gigs, I can add it to my demo reel," she added.

They had not argued once in the week since Natalie returned. They stayed out of each other's way and were polite on the rare occasion they did have to talk. Natalie spent much of her time, when she *was* home, cleaning out the bedroom closet, removing clothing she said she no longer wore, and giving it to the Neighborhood Improvement Association Relief Effort. Omar was relieved to have room for his things, like his *boubous*, without them getting wrinkled.

"They are giving me payment enough," she added. "People all over the country eat this stew. If the company gets good response from my commercials, they say they'll call me in again to cut a different version that could go national. It's called 'paying your dues.'"

He wanted to remind her that he knew about paying dues, like playing gigs at Le Baobab and the little clubs around town, but he figured that would start an argument. She would remind him that his priority should be to get a full-time job so they could move out of Petite Africa. So instead, he watched her pour the cream into the saucepan and stir it into the stew.

The stew began to bubble. The smell reminded him of raw fish left in the hot sun. Omar was sure that she was burning the bottom of the saucepan. He stayed quiet, rather than risk her accusing him of telling her what to do. He followed her into the breakfast nook. She was dressed for the hot weather in culottes and a tight, sheer blouse. He wanted to unfasten the hook on the lacy bra she was wearing, but knew that would invite a fight.

"Stop staring at me," Natalie demanded as she placed a bowl of stew in front of him.

"What do you mean, *ma chère?*"

"You're staring at my chest."

"You are my wife."

She sat down opposite him. He stuck his spoon in the yellowish-orange mixture. It was so thick the spoon would probably stand on its own if he took his hand away. He scooped up a spoonful and choked it down.

"What's wrong? You don't like it?" Natalie was sitting ramrod straight.

Omar tried to choose his words carefully. "I do like it. I would just like some pepper."

She looked at his bowl and then up at him. "It already has pepper in it. It's listed on the back of the can. You want more?"

He nodded.

"Is this something they do in your African village, use a lot of pepper?"

He ignored the remark and waited until she pushed her chair back and went into the pantry down the hall. He reached into his pocket for the jar of spices, undid the lid and crushed some of the herbs between his fingertips. But then he heard Natalie coming back up the hall. She returned more quickly than he anticipated. He hid the jar in his lap.

"Here," she plopped the pepper grinder down in front of him.

He slowly twisted the top of the grinder to sprinkle pepper into the stew. As he ate a spoonful, which didn't taste any better, he tried to think of another excuse to get her to leave the room. Then the phone rang.

"Can you get it?" she asked.

"No. It is usually a phone call for you."

She let her spoon drop into her bowl. "But I was standing up at the stove for the past half-hour. I'm tired."

They stared each other down. On the fourth ring, Omar went down the hall to answer it. At first, he heard silence on the other end. Then, a brusque, "Let me speak to my sister." Not *Hello Omar, hi brother-in-law,* or *hey buddy.* That's the way it used to be with Natalie's brother, Richard. Apparently Natalie had told him of the trouble between them.

Omar called up the hall to Natalie. When she took the receiver, Richard was shouting loud enough for Omar to hear him in a high-pitched voice say, "What are you still doing with that clown?"

Omar went back to the breakfast nook and unscrewed the jar of herbs. He could hear Natalie on the phone in a low tone to her brother. He grabbed a spoon and tried to fold the herbs into her bowl. But the stew was too thick. He stabbed at it repeatedly, trying to create an opening. Then he took a table knife and cut into a lobster chunk, figuring he could tuck some of the herbs there.

"What in the world?" Natalie was back, holding the phone away from her ear. She had stretched the cord all the way down the hall. The knife slipped out of Omar's hand and clattered onto the floor.

"What are you doing in my food, and what are you doing with *that*?" She pointed at the jar in his hand. Then she put the phone back to her ear. "Richard, I have to go." She rushed back into the kitchen and slammed the phone back on the receiver.

"It is nothing, *ma chère*," he said calmly when she returned.

"*Ma chère, ma chère*, my ass!" She grabbed at the jar. He held it out of her reach, circled around her and went back to the kitchen, thinking he would put the jar back in the cabinet with the other ones. She followed him, grabbed him by the shoulder to get him to turn around, and tried to wrestle it out of his hand, squeezing his wrist with one hand and trying to grab the jar with the other. He easily pulled away. She wouldn't retreat. He grabbed her in a bear hug to immobilize her. She wriggled free and stood glaring at him in the middle of the kitchen, breathing heavily. Then, all at once, she took all of her weight and pushed him hard in the chest with both palms, surprising him. He fell back against the refrigerator, and the jar flew out of his hand, hitting the wall and crashing on the floor. "What was in that?" she shouted. "What is that stuff? You trying to poison me?"

"Of course not. I want to make love to you," he confessed, out of breath. "The herbs shall put you in the proper mood."

"Huh?" She was still breathing hard.

She pointed a shaky finger at him. "You crazy African. You've got all these witchcraft ideas from your little village, and you think you're going to use them on me."

"It is time for us to make a baby."

Her hands rose to her hips. "What?"

"It has been a year and a half. I want to have a son."

She looked as if she would vomit. "I don't want to have a baby. I have a career now. I'm finally getting somewhere. I certainly don't want to have a baby with you. I can't even trust you. What kind of man slips drugs into his wife's food?"

"The herbs are not drugs."

"Don't play word games with me. That's exactly what they are. You stay away from me, Omar." She backed out of the kitchen. "You stay the hell away from me or I'll slip something in *your* food." She rushed down the hall and shut herself into the bedroom. He could hear her sobbing. After a while he entered the room. The worst she could do was tell him to get out or push him again. She was in the bed under the covers, fully clothed. He climbed in behind her. Gradually, he inched closer to her and put his arms around her. "What happened to us, *ma chère*," he whispered in her ear. "Please tell me: what happened?"

She sat up, pulling her knees under her chin. "Where did we go wrong?" she screamed. "There was the miscarriage, then the fire. Then we move here and we have no hot water. We have no elevator, no heat, your suspicions of my instructor, and I walk in on you sprinkling stuff in my food. It's more than I can take, Omar. I want normal, a normal husband and a nice home. That's what happened."

CHAPTER 16

SYDNEY TOOK A BREAK from stuffing flyers about the upcoming grand opening into envelopes she would mail to businesses and organizations, giving them a couple of weeks to have the flyers posted on bulletin boards before the big event. She grabbed her grandmother's quilt and headed downstairs to Inez's. Even though Bellport was having a string of hot September days, Inez had said she was cold. Old people like Inez were apt to be cold. Plus, the basement was always ten degrees cooler than the rest of the house.

On her way down, she stopped on the first floor in the parlor to watch Malachi lift a large box onto the front counter. It was much larger than others shipped to the bookstore.

"Can't believe it's here already," Malachi exclaimed. He sliced the packing tape and pulled out a thick, hardcover textbook layered with dust. Sydney read the gold lettering on the thick spine: *The African and Black American Experience*. She took the box cutter from Malachi and peeled the packing slip off the box. It was a three-volume set.

"What are we going to do with them?" she asked.

Malachi picked up one of the volumes and flipped to the back of the book. "Syd, you've got to look at these illustrations."

She was growing impatient with him. "There's no way we're going to be able to sell this."

This was her latest frustration with operating the business with Malachi. Malachi and Lawrence had barely gotten the fixtures and furniture in place for the bookstore when Malachi started ordering inventory. He'd bought the twenty-six-volume set of *Collier's Encyclopedias* without discussing it with her. She insisted that he send them back, but he had refused. Sydney fumed. They were supposed to be equal partners in the business, but it was becoming clear to her that they weren't.

Malachi grabbed a dust cloth and wiped each volume. Then he arranged them on a table near the cash register. "The right customer will come along, Syd, and besides, I'm just trying to help a brother."

Sydney slapped the counter. "What *brother*?"

"He came by a couple of weeks ago, selling these."

"You bought these from a traveling salesman? And you didn't talk to me, your wife and partner first?"

"You were out."

He rubbed the spine of a volume with the dust cloth. "The man was selling these to raise money to pay for his daughters' college."

"They always say that. He's a salesman."

She then looked around the store. They had more than enough books on the shelves for the grand opening next month. She could pick out a dozen books she knew no one would buy. "We don't have the money to waste on merchandise that won't sell, Malachi."

"I hate it when you talk to me like that."

"Like what?"

"Like I don't know what I'm doing."

You don't, she wanted to say.

She smoothed out a section of tassels on the quilt she had bundled under her arms. "I need to get this down to Inez."

Malachi looked closely at the quilt, a crocheted patchwork of blue, green, orange, and brown rectangles. "But Syd, that's a family heirloom. Didn't your grandmother make that for you?"

"I trust Inez. I know she'll take good care of it." She walked down the hall to the door leading to the basement. She heard

Malachi say, "Why don't you just give her a blanket. We've got plenty of them." She kept walking.

In the couple of months since the Taylors moved in, Sydney had been downstairs to Inez's apartment several times to play gin rummy, or listen to classical music with the woman. Sydney enjoyed Inez's regal manner, which gave no trace of her background, growing up poor on South Side Chicago. Inez told Sydney stories of her childhood, as well as the early years of her marriage to Willie.

Sydney knocked. As Willie opened the door and greeted her, she felt something brushing up against her ankles. She looked down. It was a kitten, an orange tabby, its coat random swirls of light and dark orange.

"I didn't know you had a kitten," Sydney said as she entered the apartment.

He folded up his copy of the *Wall Street Journal* and set it on the coffee table. "Her name is Pumpkin. I think she likes you."

The kitten looked up at Sydney with her big brown eyes, opened her mouth, and let out a chirp.

"You don't meow?" Sydney said to the kitten in a child-like voice.

"We haven't heard her meow yet," replied Willie. "She chirps a lot and yowls sometimes."

Sydney bent down to pet Pumpkin, rubbing her thumb just above the bridge of the kitten's nose where the pattern of her coat resembled the letter M. "When did you get her?"

"Willie found her coming out of the backyard," Inez said as she joined the two in the living room. She leaned heavily on her cane. "We thought she would go home, but when she never did, we took her in."

"We were taking a walk one day and saw her." Willie picked Pumpkin up and cradled her in his arms like a baby. The kitten snuggled Willie and started purring. "She's made herself right at home. She's our little buddy."

Sydney wondered if she should ask the Taylors for a pet

damage deposit. She'd ask Malachi what he thought. "Is she declawed?"

"No," Inez snapped. "But she's a good kitten. She has yet to dig her claws into anything around here."

Willie gestured for Sydney to sit on the couch. "So where's the good professor?" he asked. Sydney told him where to find Malachi.

"Good," he said, climbing the stairs. "We didn't finish our discussion the other day about that crook Nixon."

When Willie was gone, Inez took the quilt from her and laid it on the back of the couch. "Thank you, dear. Willie runs hot, but I run cold."

Inez put an album on the stereo, then went into the kitchen and came back rolling out a tea service on a serving cart on wheels. The cart was elegant, made of gold and brass with two tiers. Finger sandwiches were on plates on the lower tier. She parked it next to the sofa. "Willie got all of this for me when we were in Newcastle during our teaching days," she explained.

"It's lovely."

Inez poured their tea. "I hope you like Earl Grey."

"I love Earl Grey. It's nice to know someone who has an appreciation for teas like I do."

Both women laughed.

"And an appreciation for good music," Sydney added, listening to the classical music playing softly in the background. "Handel, isn't it?"

"Handel's *Water Music* always brightens up my day!" Inez's eyes lit up. "You like him too? He's one of my favorite composers. His music is lively but relaxing."

"I couldn't have said it better." Sydney had a couple of friends who liked classical music in general, but she never imagined knowing someone who had a fondness for Handel. What were the odds?

Inez handed Sydney a spoon for her tea. As Sydney took it,

Pumpkin leaped up and bumped it with her snout, knocking the spoon on the floor.

"Pumpkin, you behave!" Inez shouted. Pumpkin arched her back and ran behind the couch. "She's making me a liar. I told you she was so well behaved, and now see what she's doing."

"That's okay. "I'll just go into the kitchen and get another..."

"Oh, no dear, don't bother. I'll get it."

Sydney watched as Inez struggled to her feet, propelling herself with one hand pushing against the arm of the sofa while holding onto her cane with the other hand. She returned after what seemed like a long time with another spoon.

"I didn't mean to trouble you," Sydney said.

"That's quite all right. I need to get up and down more. Doctor's orders." She served Sydney from the plate of cucumber sandwiches. "I don't think I have ever thanked you properly for renting to Willie and me."

"You don't have to thank us. It's been our pleasure. You're great tenants. You're quiet. You pay on time."

The needle moved to the next selection on the album. "I bet you'll never guess who this is," Inez said.

Sydney listened for a few moments, but wasn't sure. "Give me a little while. I'm sure I'll get it."

They continued their game until Malachi called down the stairs for her to come into the foyer because she had guests. Sydney and Inez agreed to continue later.

When Sydney got upstairs she was surprised to see Della waiting for her with Jasmine at her side. "I heard about this hair place in Petite Africa," Della said and grabbed a thatch of her daughter's puffy hair in a mock attempt to tame it. Jasmine pulled away. "I hear the owner will know what to do with Jasmine's head. She'll know how to handle her if she acts up, too. Kwamé's car's in the shop. We're catching the bus."

Sydney wondered why Della had come over to tell her this.

"It's gonna hurt!" Jasmine screamed as she ran to the front door and tried to wrap her little hands around the knob. "I want to go home!" she wailed. Della pried the child's hands off the knob. Jasmine shrieked and banged her fists against the wainscoting. Malachi came to the foyer to see what was going on. Sydney shook her head, and stopped herself from reaching out to grab the child to shake some sense into her.

Della's eyes darted from Sydney to her daughter. "Chile, you're gonna mess up Miss Sydney and Dr. Malachi's house. You want that ice cream, don't you?"

Jasmine calmed down and nodded.

"Everything okay?" Malachi asked.

Della gave him a crooked smile. "I think we got things under control now."

Malachi grunted under his breath, left the foyer, then came back with his car keys and hurried out the door.

"You need to behave," Della told Jasmine in a hushed tone and then shifted her attention to Sydney. "I heard there's a restaurant over there that's got peanut ice cream, and Jazz loves anything with peanuts in it."

Sydney had no idea why Della had come to see her. She wanted to get back upstairs to finish stuffing flyers. "Well, you two have a great time."

Della pulled a tissue from her purse and wiped Jasmine's nose. "I know it's last minute and all, but I wish you'd go with me. Are you busy?"

Sydney was startled by the request. She wanted to say no, but then realized she could use the trip to hand out flyers in Petite Africa. She nodded in agreement and ran upstairs to get two of the boxes and her camera. She now made a point of having her camera with her whenever she left home. She was Max Turner's newest freelance photographer/writer. He had been pleased with her story on the news conference about the fires and she had been working for him ever since. When she went out, she wanted to be prepared in case she saw something Max might be interested in publishing in *Inner City Voice*.

"I wasn't interrupting nothing, was I?" Della asked as the

three of them walked through the front yard. Sydney told her about her visit with Inez.

"The Taylors are a cute old couple," Della said. "I saw them walking around the block, holding hands the other day."

"It's probably good for them, especially her," Sydney added, referring to Inez. "Walking must be like therapy for her after her stroke."

When the bus came, they found seats next to each other. Jasmine sat on her mother's lap, resting her head on her mother's shoulder. She soon began to doze.

A few minutes into the ride, the air conditioning system broke down, turning the bus into an oven on wheels. Sydney took off her sunglasses and wiped at rings of sweat that had formed under her eyes. She was relieved that Jasmine had fallen asleep. She was certain the child would have complained about the heat and given Della another punch.

"I'm sorry about this." Della fanned herself with her hand. "If Kwamé had been home we could have taken his car."

"It's not that bad," Sydney said, shuddering at the thought of riding in Kwamé's dilapidated car. She looked out the window as the bus passed a Vietnam War protest in front of City Hall. "So how did you two meet, you and Kwamé?"

Della let out a heavy sigh. "Kwamé came down to Arkansas with a group to help with a voter registration drive. He was the only one who ended up at my location. I was an office secretary for the Voter Education Project. I knew all of the people. Him being from the North with his accent and high-falutin' ways didn't appeal to folks at first. I got him into meetings with the right people, convinced them to give him a chance to coach people on how to act when they tried to register. Then some of the other girls in the office started staying late," she grinned, "the ol' hussies. They started coming around Kwamé. They wanted him." Della paused as the bus swayed crossing the Bellport River Bridge. Once they entered Petite Africa, she continued. "My husband was in and out of jail at the time. I didn't have a full-time job. The project didn't pay much. Somewhere along the line me and Kwamé started falling in love. Kwamé told me that if I got a divorce he would marry me." Della gripped the back of the seat in front of her as the bus stopped abruptly at a traffic light. "Turns out I didn't have to get no divorce. My husband was dead and gone before long. We never did get around to getting married, though, Kwamé and me. He brought me and Jasmine up here, and I bought the building we live in with my husband's life insurance policy. Kwamé felt fond of the building because he grew up there. It's where his aunt raised him when his mother wasn't up to it. For me it was an investment. Jazz was an itty-bitty little thing back then." Della caressed a tuft of Jasmine's puffy hair. "It's been good for Jazz; she needed stability in her life."

The bus let them off on Seaview Avenue, on Petite Africa's waterfront. Remarkably, Jasmine climbed off the bus without making a sound.

They walked along the concrete sea wall, spray from waves crashing against it. Seagulls swooped over the water, poking at dead fish with their beaks. A few blocks later they turned inland on King Street. In the distance Sydney could hear a man shouting, his voice distorted by an amplifier.

Sydney wiggled her nose to keep from sneezing. The pungent smell of spices hung in the stagnant air. It soon gave way to a powerful stench. Garbage bags littered the sidewalks. Stray dogs ripped at the bags, tearing at or discarding pieces of meat and bones. Pigeons poked at the trash with their beaks, taking turns with the dogs. Sydney turned away. They walked past a brick three-story building with particle-board tacked over the windows. Soot stained the siding. "I wonder if the fire here was set," Sydney said.

Della nodded. "That building caught fire a few months ago. I saw it on the news. They're saying it's suspicious."

As they continued, Sydney put her high school French to use to read the tattered awnings, signs, and window displays of the shops and cafés. Some buildings were vacant. Metal gates over the entrances were marked with graffiti.

Walking through the neighborhood, she was able to see much more than when Kwamé had driven her through the area on their tour.

She was fascinated by the way people were dressed. Women wore ornate scarves on their heads in geometric shapes. Men wore skull caps and long, blousy, colorful shirts and matching pants. Every so often a woman walked by wearing long, loose clothing covering her entire body, except for a slit for the eyes. Sydney snapped photos of the people and the neighborhood. She hoped Max would run the pictures for the features section of *Inner City Voice*. Maybe she would write a story to accompany the photos if she found some time to talk to people.

Sydney thought about the sense of community these people seemed to have, the camaraderie and interdependence. Redevelopment would bring progress and badly needed revenue to Bellport, but it would also cost the people their way of life. That, she thought, could be her angle for a story.

Conversation was loud. People gestured with their hands and arms in sweeping motions. She caught snippets in French. Some languages she didn't understand.

They came upon Bamba's Food Market on Clermont Street, where a stocky teenager was tossing a bucket of ice on a pushcart full of red snapper in front of the store. Four blocks later, they came upon a rally. At the center of a town green , a tall man who looked to be about seventy years old, stood in a gazebo badly in need of paint. He shouted into a microphone. Sydney soon realized it was Mustapha Mendy, the man she had seen at the fire and police department news conference a few months back. His dark suit looked to be a size too big. She thought he'd either lost some weight since buying it or he was shrinking due to old age. His voice crackled and sounded tinny through the small speaker. Pacing the gazebo floor, he bounced from French to English to some other language she guessed was African. People stood in a semi-circle, six to seven deep around the gazebo and held up signs and placards in French and English, thrusting them high in the air each time Mustapha raised his voice. One said *Sauver Nos Maisons!*, which Sydney translated to mean, "Save Our Homes." Another said, "No Damn Expressway Ramp" and "Petite Africa is not a Slum." One translation upset her—*Liberte Hill est un Traitre*, "Liberty Hill is a Traitor." People started to shake their fists and shout as Mustapha spoke louder and faster. Sydney took wide, medium, and close-ups with her Konica, focusing on the action around her. She zoomed in on Mendy's sweaty face with her telephoto lens, as he jabbed the air with his fist.

Then she trained the camera on Della and Jasmine standing near the front of the crowd. She would surprise Della with the photos later.

After three more blocks, they got to a sandwich board in front of Hallima Santafara Beauty Salon. *We Braid Beautiful Plaits for Half-Price* it read. Della went in first, grasping the rusty doorknob. The hinges let out an agonizing wail as she forced the door open.

Della spoke to the woman at the front counter, who then ushered Jasmine to a shampoo bowl. Sydney stepped over tufts of frizzy hair on the salon floor as she looked around for a water fountain. She found one in the waiting area. She pressed the metal lever, but the flow was so low she'd have to put her lips on the spigot to get a drink and she didn't feel it was sanitary to do so. She sat down in one of the waiting area's vinyl chairs, her moist blouse sticking to the back of the seat. A black-and-white television, its image flickering, was showing a soap opera, "The Edge of Night."

After her shampoo, Sydney watched a large woman in a boxy, floral pantsuit lead Jasmine to a swivel chair at a styling station. The other beauticians were all much younger, trimmer, and fashionably dressed in multi-colored tube tops under blouses that tied at the waist, close-fitting bell-bottom jeans, and platform shoes. Sydney got up and crossed the room, ducking to avoid the rickety ceiling fan, to sit closer to Della and Jasmine. Della introduced Sydney to the woman, Hallima Santafara.

Hallima squeezed behind the styling chair and draped a small black plastic cape around the child. She pulled a stiff bristle brush from a long glass tube of blue cleaning solution and dried it off on a paper towel. She scooped a dollop of lime-colored hair grease from a jar with her fingers and dabbed it on Jasmine's scalp.

Sydney marveled at how Hallima untangled Jasmine's knots without making her shed a tear. Her thick fingers moved quickly, creating neat squares of stylish braids. When Hallima was almost done, Sydney told Hallima about the flyers. The woman turned around and spoke in her African language to a young woman who was sweeping up tufts of hair around the barber's chair. After exchanging a few hushed words with Hallima, the young woman started a conversation with the shampoo girl in the same language. Sydney noticed the two clucking and narrowing their eyes at Della. Sydney glanced at Della who noticed the same thing.

Della looked at Hallima. "What they saying?"

Hallima frowned at her employees and shook her finger at them while speaking to them in their language in a scolding tone. Both women sighed heavily and went back to the work they were doing.

"Do they have a problem with us being here?" asked Sydney.

"If they do, we can leave," added Della. "I can finish Jasmine's head myself." She turned to Hallima. "I'll pay you for what you've done so far."

Hallima shook her head furiously. "No, no, no. Do not worry, ladies. Those are my nieces. They are rude. From the younger generation. You know how it is. Please accept my apology."

"What were they saying?" asked Sydney.

Hallima snapped blue and yellow barrettes at the ends of

Jasmine's braids. "Some of our people blame the Liberty Hill people for moving the demolition project to our neighborhood, but we know that you are not to blame."

Sydney thought about the *Liberte Hills est un Traitre* placard at the rally on the green. "I'm sorry I mentioned the flyers," she apologized.

"Please, please, Miss, leave your flyers here. We are happy to help you." Hallima untied the styling cape she'd put on Jasmine. "I am so sorry for your trouble." She turned to Della. "I will give you half-price discount for today's services."

"Well," Della smiled, "I can't argue with that."

Once the three of them were back on the street, Sydney had one box of flyers left. They headed in the direction of the restaurant. People gave them a wide berth on the sidewalk. Some swung around to glare at them as they passed by, especially the women.

"What is wrong with these people?" Sydney whispered to Della, wondering why they seemed so hostile.

"They must have the same disease as those hussies in the salon," Della whispered. She pulled a tissue out of her purse and dabbed at a trickle of sweat rolling down her neck. "They think we're in bed with the Harborview developers and the city."

"Why?"

"Remember what Hallima said? People here blame Liberty Hill for the Harborview Project."

"Is that it?"

I think they're also anti–black American in general."

"Why would that be? They're just as black as we are."

"Because our ancestors were slaves. They see themselves as different, better than us, even though some of them have slavery in their history too."

Sydney thought this over. "But if we had our heads wrapped up like they do, and we were wearing what they have on and didn't open our mouths, they wouldn't know the difference."

Della stopped abruptly and faced her. "But that's not the reality, is it?"

Sydney felt relief when they reached Garfield Avenue and saw Le Baobab Restaurant. She'd been thirsty for hours and was tired of dabbing at her sweaty brow. But, to her dismay, the door was locked. She and Della took turns peeking through the door's small, square window. The place was dark.

"Can I look, Mommy? Can I look?" Jasmine raised her arms so Della could lift her to the window. "Maybe they're hiding," Jasmine said.

Della chuckled. "I don't think they're hiding, honey. I think we got here too early."

Sydney looked up at the awning. Over the name of the restaurant was an illustration of a tree with spindly branches and a thick trunk. She wondered why anyone would name a restaurant after something so hideous looking. As they turned to leave, Mustapha Mendy approached, holding a large box with leafy vegetables in one arm. His white dress shirt was rumpled. Rivulets of sweat ran from his temples to his salt-and-pepper beard. With his free hand he held a suit jacket over his shoulder.

"*Mesdames*, your timing is perfect," he said rapidly, in an African accent. "We are just opening."

They followed him inside. "Are you sure you want to eat here?" Sydney whispered to Della. "They'll probably spit in our food."

Della laughed. "I think we'll be okay."

Quickly, Mustapha slipped through the kitchen's double doors ahead of them. When he returned to the dining area he flipped on a series of wall switches. Lights came on as well as a large metal ceiling fan. Within minutes, the stale, hot air had been pushed out.

Like Hallima's Salon, Le Baobab was shaped like a shoe box. It had plush seat cushions, freshly polished hardwood floors, and textured, copper-colored wallpaper on three walls, exposed brick on the fourth. White linens covered small tables in the center of the room. Booths lined the perimeter. Large gourds with animal carvings on them were placed on counters and tables throughout the dining room. A framed black-and-white photo of a deep, brown-skinned man wearing glasses hung behind the counter. Sydney read the caption that was printed in French. It was Léopold Sédar Senghor, the president of Senegal. A flag with green, yellow, and red panels and a green star in the center hung next to the photo. A photograph of athletes dashing toward a soccer ball hung on the other side of the flag. It was the Senegal National Football Team, according to the caption.

"*Olele! Olele!* Welcome! I say to you, welcome to my restaurant," Mustapha announced from the middle of the dining room. He wore a broad smile. In his hands he held a tray of drinks, one cup smaller than the others, with a straw in it. "My name is Mustapha Mendy, but all the people are calling me Uncle Mustapha, as you too, can." He gestured for Sydney to sit down in a booth where Della and Jasmine were already seated. Mustapha put the drinks on the table and handed each a menu printed with fancy, cursive lettering.

Sydney guzzled her drink without pausing to ask what she was drinking.

"What's that?" Jasmine pointed at her cup with an upturned nose.

"Ginger mango lemonade," Mustapha said with a touch of pride. "All little boys and girls in Senegal love it. Big and strong it makes them." He turned to Della and Sydney. "I know that you are newly to Le Baobab, but are you newly to Senegalese restaurant?"

They nodded.

He looked from one to the other and then took back the menus. "You have special treat from me. Do not worry about identifying the food you want. I bring for you what I think you like."

When he'd walked away, Jasmine picked up her cup with both hands, took a long sip through the straw, and then spat it back into the cup. "I don't like this, Mommy," Jasmine whined. "That's fine, honey," Della said softly. "You don't have to drink…"

"Don't like it!" Jasmine screeched loudly and glared at Della. She slammed the cup on the table. "I don't like this place, Mommy. I want to go home." She elbowed her mother in an attempt to push her way out of the booth.

Della glared at Jasmine. "We're not going anywhere, Jazz," she said in a low, but firm voice. "We're staying here, and the nice man is gonna bring us something to eat."

"Jasmine, my specialty is peanut butter cake," Sydney said, hoping to calm the girl. "Have you ever had that before?"

Jasmine shook her head.

"Well, if you behave, you can make one with me sometime."

"Okay," she whispered.

Sydney had no idea how to make a peanut butter cake, but she figured she could find a recipe in one of her cookbooks.

Della exhaled, letting her shoulders relax. Sydney now realized why Della had her come along. Jasmine was sometimes more than she could handle alone.

Lyrics in a foreign language floated from speakers mounted on the walls near the ceiling. Other diners, mostly white men and women in business suits, began to walk in, followed by a few Africans. A little boy and girl handed the new arrivals menus and led them to tables. They looked to be around six or seven and were dressed in African clothing, long loose-fitting print tops with matching billowy pants.

Mustapha returned with silverware and a white sheet of butcher-block paper as a placemat and crayons for Jasmine. "Can I move this someplace for you?" Mustapha pointed at the box of flyers.

"I actually wanted you to take a look," Sydney said.

He left the table and when he returned, he had a pair of

wire-rimmed reading glasses perched at the end of his nose. He reached into the box and read one of the flyers. "Is this business belonging to you?" he asked.

"It's mine and my husband's."

Mustapha stretched a bony hand across the table. "I must as one business owner to the other congratulate you. It is hard thing to run business. I wish you best of luck on this new adventure. How am I helping you?"

"I was hoping you could leave a stack of these at the front counter, but if you think people will be offended..."

He frowned. "Why think this?"

"No reason," Della answered quickly, then shook her head at Sydney.

He looked over his shoulder at the boy and girl across the room. "That is Kofi and Anamara, *mes petit-fils*, my grandchildren. They are twins. They are the star pupils for The Uncle Mustapha Culinary Institute. I instructing them on how to make meals, wait on customers, make the kitchen spic and span."

"That's good, gives them discipline," Della said.

"Keeps them far away from no good, gives them something to do after school while their mother Ansa is working still," Mustapha continued. "They collecting skills they use later." He called Kofi and Anamara over to the table.

"What's the language you're speaking?" Sydney asked.

"Wolof. That is our mother tongue. I do sometimes speaking to them in French, but I desire them to understand language of their ancestors."

"That must be what we heard you talking out there at the gazebo earlier," Della said.

His eyes widened. "You are there?"

"Only for a few minutes," Sydney answered. She told him of her freelance work for *Inner City Voice* and the pictures she took of him today and for the newspaper a few months ago.

"We want to remind city that if they try to take Le Baobab or the other businesses in neighborhood, they will have to answer to the people, to us. Everybody ignoring this neighborhood for long time. We move here from West Africa, from West Indies. We build it up. Now the city wants to destroy it."

Mustapha went to the front counter and returned with sheets of paper on a clipboard. He showed it to Sydney and Della. It was a stack of petitions written in English and French. It said that the city was threatening an injustice against Petite Africa residents by destroying the community and that it would cause a hardship to the recent immigrants just learning the American culture. Mustapha leafed through the stack.

"We include three hundred signatures, and we get more when we take them to City Hall. We stop condemnation and eminent domain." He told them that when members of the Petite Africa community addressed the Bellport Redevelopment Authority at a recent hearing, the authority took no action. So their next step would be to pack the city council meeting next week with people who would be displaced.

"Good luck," wished Della. "You have a nice restaurant. It would be a shame if the city took it."

His jaw went slack. "I spend years building reputation for Le Baobab. Now they want to put plaza for civic center here. I tell them 'no.' The people still need Petite Africa."

A customer across the room waved Mustapha over. The man gripped the table with both hands and rocked it to show how wobbly the legs were. Mustapha made his way over there slowly, crouched down and fiddled with the table's legs, and then made his way back.

"I know that man is real estate developer," he jeered through gritted teeth after returning to the table.

"How can you tell that?" Della asked.

"I know my customers. He is not regular, and he is wearing a jug of cologne. He is licking his chops but not for what is on the menu of Le Baobab, I am afraid. But he is buying most expensive thing on the menu, brochettes—and I am needing the money."

Sydney remembered seeing the dish of cubed filet mignon on skewers with yucca fries on the side listed on the menu.

"But he's checking the place out. That's rude," Della agreed.

"Even though this place is right now full," he made a sweeping motion across the dining room, "I have only one fraction of the customers of before. Long ago people line up outside the door. This talk about the city taking over Petite Africa wipes my customers away. Some of them already think we are closed. They are stopping coming 'round. If I do not have the tenants upstairs, I have not even a calabash of rice to eat.

"I struggle my whole life," Mustapha continued. "In Senegal I study to be hotel operator for two years. But I have no career prospect. That is before they build new university. I leave Senegal for better opportunity. But America say my skills not enough. I have to start over again at university. I get mad. I say no. America say I do not comprehend English enough. And when I speak English, when I come here first, people do not comprehend me."

Sydney could believe it. Trying to understand what he was saying did not get any easier for her the longer he talked.

"All I do is drive taxi. I saving my money—every Abraham Lincoln penny," he continued. "I get myself apartment. Then I start to cook food in my kitchen, food people in Petite Africa say remind them of home. Fresh food, lamb, fish, plantains, and yams—the way they like it. Not like in America. I learn to cook when I am little boy. I watch in my village in Senegal the women, and I remember from all those years before how to make meals. Then I get street cart; I get permit. My fellow cabbies like it because they stop and get provisions without getting out of cab and losing fare. I have four boys deliver dinners to neighborhood. Ladies in church sell my dinners. Shopkeeps in this block make regular stops for lunch here. They tell me I should open restaurant. I listening. Then I buy the building and rent out the apartments upstairs. I pay good money to fix building. My renters live in luxury."

Mustapha seemed to go into his own world as he told his story. His gestures became more animated, his eyes glassy. Sydney didn't feel he was looking at her and Della, but through them. He didn't 'come back' until Kofi and Anamara came to the table with steaming bowls on a tray. They noticed Jasmine but said nothing to her. She was busy coloring her placemat.

"*Soupi Kandja*," they said in unison.

"*Petit-fils*, tell our guests the ingredients," Mustapha commanded them.

"It has shrimp, oysters, fish, and rice," proclaimed Anamara proudly.

"What else?" he asked.

"It is kind of like your…" Kofi paused, screwing up his face, apparently trying to remember, "American gumbo."

"*Très bien, baah na*, very good," Mustapha cheered, clapping.

Sydney poked the soup with her spoon following what Della was doing. She identified crab claws, okra, and beef in addition to the ingredients the twins had mentioned. Sydney waited until her soup had cooled. She tasted a spoonful. It did remind her of gumbo but with a little more tang and oil. The shrimp was succulent.

She looked over at the other tables. Some of the couples ate from the same large bowl, sopping up their food with spongy bread.

"You're grandbabies are so cute," Della said to Mustapha.

"Because they resemble *grandpère*." Mustapha threw his head back and laughed loudly. He escorted the children to other customers' tables and then went back into the kitchen.

Sydney was tipping her bowl to scoop up the last of the soup when the front door opened, filling the restaurant with rays of late afternoon sunlight. Della and Jasmine turned around to see a man come in carrying several large sacks. Sydney thought he was handsome with his thick mustache and dark chocolate skin. A small gold hoop earring hung from one ear lobe. He looked to be in his mid- to late-twenties. His eyes were striking.

From a short distance, she was pretty sure they were green.

He was tall but not as tall as Malachi. His flowing robe ended at his shins and was in a bright shade of blue with gold stitching around the neck and cuffs. He wore matching baggy pants and a skull cap over close-cropped hair, a leather choker with a small pouch around his neck, and leather sandals. His clothing reminded her of outfits she had seen people wearing on her walk with Della and Jasmine earlier through Petite Africa, except that his garments looked newer and ironed.

He unzipped the sacks in the middle of the bandstand, and pulled out a drum about two feet tall with a bell attached to it. Another was a *djembe,* shaped like a goblet; the top half had a series of black chords criss-crossing each other. A third was shaped like a small barrel, reminding Sydney of the kind of drum she saw marching bands use at football game half-time shows. He opened a smaller sack and arranged a bell, wooden mallet, drumsticks, and rattler in front of the drums.

"Is he gonna play all those at the same time?" Della asked.

"I'm waiting to see that myself."

As Omar patted the *djembe*, Kofi and Anamara burst through the kitchen's double doors and ran up to him on the bandstand. He picked each of them up above his head and shook them until they giggled. Once he put them down, they grabbed the noisemakers, spreading them around the stage. They went from noisemakers to drums, apparently eager to play with all of the instruments.

Mustapha returned to the table with a platter of *poisson farci*, stuffed whole fish, fried plantains, and mixed vegetables. To Sydney's relief, he set down additional glasses of juice.

"We try *bissap* juice this time," Mustapha said, nodding toward Jasmine. "Little boys and girls in Senegal this, too, like."

Jasmine folded her arms across her chest and grimaced.

"Thanks," Della said, looking up at Mustapha. "You tried."

They watched as Omar tied the *djembe* around his waist using a thick cloth belt. He closed his eyes and started striking the face of the drum, alternating with his palms, fingers, and fingertips. Diners turned in their seats to watch him and began bopping their heads in time with the beat. He produced sounds that were high-pitched and sharp as well as low, deep, round, and full.

Then he leveled off, patting softly, and producing a sound low enough that diners could talk without shouting. Kofi and Anamara played along on the rattler and the bell. Sydney went to the stage with her camera. Without missing a beat, the drummer gave her a nod and a smile.

After finishing off the roll of film, Sydney rejoined Della and Jasmine. She tried the fish. It was delicious, flavored with a spice that gave it a sweet, intense taste.

Jasmine's eyes were focused on Kofi, Anamara, and Omar.

"You like the drumming, Jazz?" her mother asked.

"Yes, Mommy. Can I go watch?"

"Sure, sugar pie. I'll take you to the edge of where he's playing. But don't bother what the man's doing."

After they walked away, Mustapha sat down across from Sydney. A waitress, Marie Thérèse, brought the next course, *croquettes de poisson*, fish cakes.

A rapid drumbeat turned everyone's attention to the bandstand. "The drummer is talented," Sydney said.

Mustapha's eyes softened as he looked over at Omar. "He is my nephew. Samir, my wife, die some time before of the cancer. It is hard. I almost every night cry, I love her so much. My daughter Ansa has her own life with hubby and my grandbabies. But not long after I bury my wife, Omar, my nephew, move here from Washington, D.C. He help me not be sad. I don't know if without him I survive my grief."

Mustapha told her about his plans for the drumming institute and encouraged her to write about that for *Inner City Voice*. "In future we give to people of all ages the master classes. We attract the scholars in their ivory tower, people who have heavy pockets full of money who donate to us. We teach drumming, and we teach English to people who need lessons. We also tutor kids in school. Our drumming institute into the national spotlight bring Petite Africa. It is our hope."

"I had no idea that a project like this was going on here," Sydney said.

"Because Uncle Mustapha telling nephew to keep it hush-hush. We collecting names for people donating money."

"Good luck," Sydney said.

"If the city decide to toss away our lawsuit, our dream die. They knock down the African Cultural Center building we want to use for drumming institute. They take this building also."

Sydney looked around. "But wouldn't they have to pay you fair market value for this place?"

Mustapha chuckled. "What is fair market value? They pay me to get out of their way, then they build a gleaming cement jungle, and the price of everything goes up. If they destroy Petite Africa they are cutting off the blood supply to the brain of this community," he pointed at his temple. "Do you know how many people right here get their beginning in America in Petite Africa?"

As Sydney cut into her fish cake, Mustapha continued. "This community is the first step for many from Africa or The West Indies. Hundreds of people first coming through Petite Africa and staying here until they are ready to go to U.S. other parts."

Mustapha froze at the sound of a siren wailing. Then he looked toward the door. "It is just a police car."

"You thought it was another fire?"

Mustapha's brow creased. "It is not coincidence that insurance give some building owners more money than fair market value. But I think another reason is there for these fires." He leaned across the table. "Somebody wants to scare Africans and West Indians away. They do not want us here in Bellport. But that is not right. We are Americans like all the other Americans."

"I find it hard to believe that someone would try to chase you away with the fires."

"That is my belief," he shot back. He looked at his watch. "I must check to see if my other cook is late again. He did not show up on time yesterday."

She wondered why it was taking so long for Della and Jasmine to come back. She looked over at the bandstand. Della was talking to the drummer, laughing as if she was having a grand time.

"I told Jazz to stay on the edge and watch, but she don't listen very well," Della said after she returned to their booth.

Jasmine was striking a medium-sized drum with the mallet while Anamara played a cowbell and Kofi danced around. Jasmine was playing in perfect rhythm. Customers put their forks down and clapped.

"What were you and the drummer talking about?" Sydney asked.

Della's eyes twinkled. "His name's Omar. He's a funny man." She began on her fish cake as the drumming continued. When she was done, Mustapha returned with bowls of caramel bananas, peanut ice cream, and a slice of coconut cake.

"Dessert is always free for first-time customers," he said, smiling.

"I can go up and get Jasmine if she's disturbing your nephew," Della offered.

Mustapha shook his head, "No, she is fine. The child is natural talent. Let her play."

Della took a bowl of ice cream. "Maybe I best get Jasmine anyway before her ice cream melts."

"Please, I think the child is finding some new friends," Mustapha explained, nodding toward Kofi and Anamara. "I put away her ice cream for now."

Sydney watched Della dip her spoon into her ice cream. Jasmine wasn't the only one who found friendship, she thought. Della had only talked to Omar for a few moments. But this was the first time Sydney had seen such joy on Della's face.

CHAPTER 17

FIVE SUITCASES were lined up by the front door. Down the street, Natalie's brother, Richard, had parked his apple green Gremlin with a trailer hitched to it. That morning Richard had driven up from Washington, D.C., to move Natalie back to their parents' house. It was a rescue mission.

"Do you want me to help?" Omar asked, peeking through the doorway of the drum room. Richard and Natalie were removing the legs from her desk. "No man," Richard answered without looking up.

Omar didn't want to be there during the packing. He wished he could be on another planet. But he knew that if he left, he'd wish he had stayed. This could be the last time he would see Natalie. A few days after they wrestled over the jar of herbs, she shocked him with her announcement that she was leaving for good. Omar told Uncle Mustapha, who offered to loan them money to move to a nice apartment in a different section of Bellport. But Natalie said, no. She wanted a divorce. Upon hearing that word, Omar felt so low he could have cried.

Sulking, Omar walked into the living room. He pulled a flyer from the drawer of one of the end tables and sat on the couch. He'd read it at least twenty times. It helped take his mind off Natalie abandoning him.

One of the Americans from Liberty Hill had given a box of flyers to Uncle Mustapha. Omar had watched as Uncle placed a stack of the flyers at the front counter and taped one to the side of the cash register.

It was just before the other American, Della, walked up to the bandstand with her daughter Jasmine. The child had natural ability on the drums. It was unusual for a child so young to keep the beat that long, especially with no training. She had great coordination and technique usually only seen in children twice her age. If he and Uncle opened their drumming institute, he would see that she got a scholarship. Her talent should not be wasted.

"Do you want this?" Natalie stood in the doorway, holding in her hand their wedding album, a white, three-ring binder of cardboard pages with a sticky sheen and plastic cover sheets that held the pictures in place.

The question struck Omar like a blow to the chest. He understood that she wanted to move on with her life, but why would she want to throw the album away? It was as if she wanted to rid herself of any reminders of their marriage and time together.

"No, *ma chère*, you keep it."

She hesitated, as if his response surprised her. She spun around and left the room.

He studied the flyer again, making a mental note of the grand opening. He hoped that Khadim hadn't gotten a copy from Uncle in the stack left at the cash register. This was a solo project, not a Fulani Sound project. The grand opening might be his break, his chance to launch his drumming career. If so, Natalie would wish she had stayed.

After Natalie and Richard came back into the unit after putting the remaining boxes of her things in the trailer, Omar picked up the last two suitcases to take them to the car.

"No, Omar," Natalie said softly. "We'll do it."

"We don't need your help," Richard added.

"But I want to help," said Omar. "The elevator is not working. I know that you two are tired."

Richard exhaled. "Okay then."

The three of them walked half a block to where the Gremlin was parked. Omar was aware of a deep emptiness inside of him. This must be how people felt when packing up the belongings of a loved one who had died, Omar thought. He deposited the suitcases in the backseat and watched as Richard shifted the car into gear and he and Natalie drove away.

CHAPTER 18

USING TONGS, Sydney grasped the corner of exposed photographic paper and shook it in the tray of developer until the image of Uncle Mustapha became clear. He was standing in the middle of the gazebo at Petite Africa Green, with his fist thrust in the air. She had two more rolls to develop. After publishing one of her photos from the rally she and Della and Jasmine had stumbled onto, Max wanted more shots to fill a two-page feature on urban renewal for an upcoming issue of *Inner City Voice*. He assigned her to write a story to accompany her photos.

She loved the hours alone in the darkroom, seeing how her camera technique, using various filters, lighting, and shutter speeds, conveyed visual stories. As she worked, her mind drifted back to her conversation with Uncle Mustapha. She was disturbed by suspicions that property owners would burn down their own buildings for the insurance money, endangering not only people's homes, but their lives.

"Syd, you in there?"

The Neighborhood Improvement Association meeting must have finally ended. She told Malachi to wait while she squeegeed the front and back of the picture and hung it to dry. Then she removed her black rubber gloves and opened the darkroom door.

"Sorry I missed dinner," Malachi said.

"It's all right. I've been up here for hours and haven't eaten yet myself. The food's still warm in the oven."

He sighed deeply. "I thought that meeting would go on all night. Kwamé really needs to limit public comment to two minutes or less."

"Anything interesting happen?"

"We're trying to get property from the city before the mayor gets too distracted with the redevelopment project. I figure if we can get a large enough parcel, we can build the recreation center, and a couple of baseball fields. We can use the rec center as the home of the little league team. We can start having annual banquets, that sort of thing."

"You'll probably get more kids involved," Sydney said.

He paused for a moment. "And there's something else."

"What?"

"Kwamé wants me to run for vice president."

"Of the Neighborhood Improvement Association? Were you going to talk to me about it?"

"Of course. I wouldn't say yes without you." He leaned over to kiss her on the cheek. She crossed her arms and shifted away from him.

"But you said yes to the Taylors without me agreeing on it. You stood there and let Kwamé shove the Taylors down our throats. You never did get their references."

He exhaled. "I was wrong, Sydney, and I'm sorry. I've learned. We'll discuss the board decision and if you're not comfortable with it, I won't take it."

"I don't understand you. You want to open a business, sponsor a little league team, and now be vice president of a neighborhood association. What's next? Mayor?"

He said nothing.

"Why did you let Kwamé force the Taylors on us?"

"I wouldn't put it that way, Syd. He saw an opportunity for both the Taylors and us to get what we wanted. They needed a place, and we needed tenants. And it's working out, isn't it? They're paying on time, they're quiet, they're not damaging the place, you get on well with Inez. And they helped us get

The Fierce Warriors to agree to perform at our opening."

"Yes, all that is true. But that's not the point. Kwamé bullied us into renting to them. He rolled right over us, and maybe he's doing that again to you right now with this neighborhood association thing."

Malachi sighed. "You've got a point. Kwamé can come off like he's the boss man sometimes."

"Why is he like that? Why do you let him get away with it? He's so pushy and he talks all the time."

Malachi sighed. "It's how he is. Kwamé grew up poor. His mom had him wearing handouts from Goodwill. She never had food in the house. He never had a nice pair of sneakers, or decent clothes. He didn't have a lot growing up. There was no stability in his life. Half the time his mother didn't feel like raising him, so she sent him to her sister's. He grew up thinking that he had to get his, since no one else was going to look out for him. He and I lost touch while I was working on my PhD. Word on the street was that he did a tour in 'Nam. That must have done a number on him too. A lot of brothers got messed up over there."

"Well, he's your buddy, so I am going to try for your sake. But we're going to have to keep him in check."

"Baby, he helped me find this house and process the paperwork."

"Agreed, but Kwamé's not your business partner. I am. We both have a lot riding on this. I'd have been a lot happier renting to people with a background check. We're lucky that they've turned out to be pretty great, so I'll let this go for now."

Malachi looked around the darkroom at the photos from Petite Africa that Sydney had hung using twine and clothespins. "These are really good."

"You think so?"

"You should mat some of these and put them downstairs. We can do an art exhibit in the bookstore."

She laughed. "You're just trying to butter me up for something else you want me to go along with."

"Not true. I mean it, Syd. You've really got an eye for the camera."

CHAPTER 19

"WHAT WE DOING here, Dell?" Kwamé let the menu of Le Baobab's specials drop onto the table. "Anything we need to talk about we can talk about at home."

Della wished he would lower his voice. She scanned the room to see if they were drawing the attention of other customers, but no one seemed to notice. She leaned across the table and spoke softly, hoping he would follow her example. "We can't talk at home because you're never there. Besides, I can't remember the last time you took me out."

He lit a Viceroy. "We could have stayed in the neighborhood. Jake's restaurant isn't bad. I need to talk to him about something anyway. Or we could have gone to The Bell Tower."

It had been years since Kwamé had taken Della to the upscale steakhouse on the top floor of downtown Bellport's main financial building. The rotating restaurant had windows on all sides, from which patrons could see the sailboats moored in the harbor.

"Only reason you'd take me to The Bell Tower would be to see your political cronies. I'd end up eating by myself while you worked the room, as usual. At least here, you don't know nobody."

Since the first time Della visited Le Baobab, with Sydney and Jasmine, she had wanted to come back. She wanted to hear more of Omar's drumming, try Le Baobab's famous *mafé*, lamb stew, and chat with Uncle Mustapha. Waitress Marie

Thérèse had told her that Mustapha was down the street at the mosque for evening prayer and wouldn't be returning. At least Omar was there. He and Khadim were setting up their drums for the night's performance.

"Know what you want to order?" she asked.

"Nothing." Kwamé was staring at the drummers. They were tightening the ropes on their drums and patting them softly, to check the sound. Della thought Kwamé was enjoying watching The Fulani Sound warm up, until he turned back around to face her, scowling.

"You got me here, so what you want to talk about?"

"Can't we enjoy a night out, listen to some music?"

He took a long drag on the cigarette. "*Mierda*, Dell. You got something on your mind, you might as well come out with it."

She hated when he used his Spanish profanity. "I want to go back to college."

His eyebrows gathered in a knot. "What for?"

"I'm halfway to my bachelor's degree. If I finish, I can go for my MLS."

He blew out smoke. "What's that?"

"Master of Library Science."

"What you need that for? You're already working at the library."

She didn't know if Kwamé was dense or being difficult. She decided that it was both. "I know, but with the MLS, I can be a librarian, not just a library assistant."

A loud volley of slaps on the drums signaled that The Fulani Sound was beginning its performance. Omar and Khadim stood at opposite ends of the stage performing a drumming duel. Khadim seemed to be the showman, flinging his head back and forth to send his dreadlocks flying around, reminding her of an amusement park swing ride. He squeezed a little drum under his arm as his biceps flexed. Omar had his drum strapped to his waist and played an intricate set of beats. In the end, the audience clapped the loudest for Omar, declaring him the winner.

"Where you get an idea like that from?" Kwamé stared at Della, paying no attention to the show.

"I was talking to Sydney and..."

He flicked his cigarette over an ashtray. "Sydney? What she know about anything, walking around with that silver spoon jammed in her mouth?"

"You didn't feel that way a few months ago when you two were sitting all cozy in The Stewed Oxtail."

His eyes widened, but he said nothing.

"Thought I didn't know about that, didn't you?"

"Oh Dell, she wanted to learn about the city, the history of Liberty Hill, that kind of thing. I just wanted to spare you from being bored. And, anyway, that was a long time ago."

"Uh huh. You think I'm stupid."

They sat there in silence.

"How much?" Kwamé snapped. Omar and Khadim began their next number.

"What?"

"How much is this schooling you want gonna cost?" he shouted over the drumbeat, drawing looks from the next table.

Marie Thérèse brought Della a glass of *bouye* juice and Kwamé a scotch and soda. She brought two glasses of water too. The drummers lowered their volume and continued to play. "I have the money for the classes," Della declared. "I just need you to spend more time at home, babysitting Jazz.

He stubbed out his unfinished cigarette, pressing it into the ashtray hard enough to drive a hole through it. "When you need me to babysit?"

"Most of the classes are at night."

"Can't do it with the hours I keep at the record shop. I need to be open most evenings." He swirled his drink and took a sip.

"She could sit in the office and play."

He choked on his drink. He put it on the table and grabbed

a glass of water and downed it to stop the coughing. "And what if she has one of them fits? You expect me to leave my customers and try to control that kid while she's wailing and crying?"

She got up and went to his side of the booth and forced him over. She moved close so that she could talk directly into his ear. "You're full of shit! That's not the reason you don't want Jasmine in the store."

"You need to watch yourself, Dell!" he hissed in a guttural tone.

"Why you need to keep the store open all those hours anyway? You're not making any money. You don't have any customers. The place is like a ghost town."

He elbowed her to get up. Della returned to her side of the table. "You have no business talking to me like that, Dell. What do you expect me to do? Close up just to take care of Jasmine?"

They turned to watch the drummers for a while.

"Dell, the times I don't stay open late, I'm at community meetings, or seeing the mayor."

"You've been meeting with the mayor at three in the morning?" *Or the mayor's blonde assistant?* That's what she wanted to say, but stopped herself. She knew the conversation would deteriorate if she pushed the subject of his female friends. She checked her watch. Jasmine was with Sydney and Malachi. They agreed to watch her until nine o'clock. It was already eight.

"Why should I do this for you when you haven't done what I want?" Kwamé tucked a toothpick into the corner of his mouth.

"I told you, I'm not comfortable with it. That property is all I've got. Every cent I got from Tucker's insurance policy I put in that building.

He sipped his drink. "You keep saying that."

"We're not even married, Kwamé. Your name is not on the deed. I want to keep it that way."

He shrugged. "Then let's get hitched. Let's make it legal."

"So you can get at the equity? No thanks."

He leaned across the table, closer to her face. "I have a right to have my name on the deed. Who's been helping you with the mortgage? Who got you that new furnace when the other one broke down? How about the washing machine and dryer in the basement that everybody in the building uses? I've been putting my money in this property, and what am I getting for it? A bunch of nothing."

Della took a sip of her juice. "You operate the record shop rent free. Now you want to throw more of my money at it."

Marie Thérèse returned. Kwamé waved her off.

"If you knew anything about running a business," he said, "you'd know that these days you need to do more than just sell records. You need to sell everything people need for entertainment—record players, stereos, tape recorders, microphones, Super 8 cameras, projectors."

"What about the time you bought all those reel-to-reel tape machines? You sold a couple, and then you couldn't give them away. You got stuck with three boxes of them. People weren't even buying them anymore. They'd moved on to cassettes."

"Those machines weren't a mistake. We just got into the market late. It happens." He finished his drink and slammed his empty glass on the table. He tossed the car keys on the table. "I'm tired of yapping about the same thing over and over and getting nowhere. I'm outta here."

Della was stunned. "Where are you going?"

He slid across the bench and stood up. "For a walk. If I get tired I'll catch a cab. You can drive the car home when you're ready."

As she watched Kwamé leave, she could feel the tears coming. She didn't count on Kwamé being so surly and responding so critically about the idea of her going back to school. Not only did he try to deflate her, he had focused on what *he* wanted—the loan. Della looked around. The restaurant was packed. She put a twenty-dollar bill on the table and rushed to the bathroom where no one could see her crying.

Kwamé would not let go of having his name put on the deed, but she would never agree to it, no matter how difficult he became. After what she went through with Tucker, she vowed that she would never let a man have control over any part of her life again.

She'd married Tucker because she'd gotten pregnant with Jasmine. She knew that he had other women, but she thought providing a father for her child was the right thing to do. If she had known that Tucker would pull a gun on her, kick her around, and beat her she would never have married him. She would have had Jasmine on her own. There were times when he was so loud when he was beating her that Jasmine woke up in the middle of the night, ran to Della screaming her head off and tried to punch Tucker in the legs with her fists to defend Della.

In some ways, it was a relief when Tucker pulled a knife on a cop and the cop shot and killed him. She didn't have to deal with the abuse anymore.

But Jasmine was scarred. Della regretted that her daughter had been exposed to Tucker's abusive behavior. She knew that her little girl relived the abuse in her nightmares.

Della left the bathroom stall, looked in the mirror and dabbed at her tears, careful not to smudge her eyeliner. She smoked a cigarette, which helped calm her down. When she sat back down at the booth, the twenty-dollar bill was still there. This puzzled her. She was surprised to see Marie Thérèse approaching the table, holding a small round tray with a glass of white wine on it.

"I didn't order that," Della said.

"From Omar," Marie Thérèse said as she placed the glass in front of her.

Della looked over at the bandstand. Without missing a beat as he patted the drum, Omar smiled at her and then winked.

CHAPTER 20

SYDNEY POURED lavender eucalyptus bath salts into the tub, which turned the water a purplish pink. She'd already been lolling in the clawfoot tub for about twenty minutes and decided she'd stay there until either her fingertips began to shrivel like raisins or the votive candles she had lit burned all the way down. She could feel herself beginning to doze and welcomed it because she had slept little the night before. Malachi kept her up tossing and muttering as if he was holding a conversation. Once he rolled on top of her, hugged her and then flipped to the other side. Sydney thought he had jitters about the grand opening next week, although he had not openly shared with her any of his concerns about starting a business. Sydney had a few anxious moments herself.

She sank lower in the tub, letting the water lap at her shoulder blades to relieve a tightness that had been building there for days.

When the water had begun to cool she reached for the hot water nozzle and cranked it to full blast, kept it there until her skin stung. She ran an index finger down the headlines on the cover of an old issue of *Look* magazine she'd propped up in the bathtub caddy. Industrialist Howard Hughes was pictured in 1939, along with a frightening artist's illustration of how he looked last year in 1971. Sydney decided to skip that story and instead read the piece about how Warren Beatty and Julie Christie were "together at last" as the headline read. She didn't know if that meant that there was a romance or they were making a movie. She flipped pages. It was a shame that *Look* has ceased publication last year. She'd try to be careful not to get the pages wet. It could become a collector's item someday.

As she got to the article on Warren and Julie, who were in fact just making a movie together, the warmth of the water lulled her into a daydream. After a while she heard familiar footsteps. As Malachi came through the door, she opened her mouth to ask him not to turn the ceiling light on, but before she could form the words she realized she didn't need to. Clutching an 8-track player/radio under his arm like a football, Malachi walked across the checkerboard floor to the far end of the bathroom. He plugged the radio into the outlet and twisted the dial, stopping at the local soul station, WCLL, "Cool Radio." The deejay was playing The Temptations' song, "Just My Imagination." Malachi left the room momentarily and returned holding a bottle of Blue Nun and two wine glasses.

He poured the wine and handed her a glass. Sydney took a sip and closed her eyes. "This is the right music for the mood I'm in. I just want to relax."

Moments later, water sloshed around in the tub as a now undressed Malachi climbed in. Bathed in candlelight, the sight of his body, taut and sculpted from his college track-and-field days, always got her attention.

He settled into the opposite end of the tub, facing her, then raised one of her feet and caressed it with a soapy washcloth all the while keeping his eyes on her. After massaging the balls of each foot and rinsing them, he placed her toes in his mouth, one-by-one, massaging each one with his tongue. His touch tickled her, making her twist in the water until she splashed some over the sides.

"I'm not playing the radio for the music," he mumbled, one of her toes in his mouth.

She lifted herself up slightly. "Then why'd you bring it in here?"

Malachi switched to her other foot. But this time, he sucked on her heel. "They're supposed to start making announcements about the grand opening."

She giggled as he licked the arch of her foot. "I love it that we're getting free advertising."

"I went down to the station yesterday and talked to The Young Turk. Kwamé put in a good word for us. We'll get some free commercials about The Talking Drum if we agree to keep his station coming out of the speakers during business hours." He tipped his glass so that wine trickled into the space between her first and second toes. Then he licked the trail.

"Shouldn't we wait until we see how the grand opening goes before celebrating?" she asked.

He sat up. "Baby, it's an achievement that we got this far. I'm having my celebration now. The Young Turk said he'll mention us two or three times a day until the grand opening ends."

The news came on—a bulletin—FBI agents linked the Watergate break-in to the Nixon re-election. After a series of other news bulletins, the program went to a commercial break for Schlitz Malt Liquor and Ultra Sheen Hair Care Products.

After that came the raspy voiced Young Turk. *"Listen up, y'all. A revolution is coming to Bellport. We've never seen anything like this in the community, and I don't think we ever will again—a bookstore in Liberty Hill."*

"He's talking about us," Sydney said, raising herself to a sitting position.

Malachi raised a palm to shush her.

Next, The Young Turk gave his listeners The Talking Drum address and invited everyone to come hear The Fierce Warriors. Then he went onto a commercial promoting Mister W's, a men's clothing store.

Sydney grabbed the washcloth floating in the water. She wrung it out and draped it over the side of the tub. "This grand opening is going to be a hit."

"Baby, people are going to talk about it for months." He

drew her close, planting kisses on her cheeks, the tip of her nose, and both ear lobes. Sydney shut her eyes and focused on the sensual feel of his full lips and the tickle of his mustache.

"Do you think Kwamé was being honest with us when he said he thought we could make a profit with this place?" she asked.

"I do. He's a smart businessman. He wouldn't steer us wrong, Syd."

"But he's not doing much business at his place. Della told me he barely gets any customers."

"Every business goes through a slump. What Kwamé's been saying about the extra foot traffic we'll get is true."

"I hope so."

"And on top of that, Lawrence has some ideas for discussion groups we can host in the bookstore's lecture hall. We could pull in young people, high school and college students."

"You think that'll bring in money?"

"He shrugged. They may not spend a lot on books, but they like to read, so we should get some sales from it. Lawrence thinks we should open a snack bar for the groups that meet, serve coffee, sodas, fruit, cookies, that kind of thing. We can mark up the price enough to make a few dollars that way."

Another news bulletin came on the radio station—another house fire in Petite Africa. Sydney and Malachi sat motionless, listening. The fire was considered suspicious. There were no injuries, but three families lost everything except the clothing they wore, fleeing the building. Witnesses said they saw a car leave the back of the house minutes before the blaze started. The announcer stated that this was the fifth fire in the past two months in Petite Africa that appeared to be suspicious and that the frequency of the fires had increased.

"They must be scared to death," Sydney said. "Uncle Mustapha, Hallima, I wonder how they can sleep at night with those fires so close."

"I'm not surprised that the pace is picking up considering that the groundbreaking is scheduled for April. That's only six months away. If this is part of an insurance scam, then there's not much time left for the crooks to put in their claims.

Malachi climbed out of the tub and put an 8-track tape into the player, the Stylistics' "Betcha By Golly Wow."

"I should call Max," Sydney said. "He might want me to report on this, talk to people, take some photos."

He climbed back in. "If Max wants you over there, he'll call you. We're not going to have many moments like this for a while. Let's enjoy them while we can." He moved behind her and soaped her back to calm her down. "Baby, let's not worry about what's going on over there right now. He kissed the back of her neck and teased her earlobe with his tongue. "We've got our hands full with the bookstore. We've got a lot of work ahead of us."

CHAPTER 21

OMAR STOOD on Liberty Hill Boulevard with his back to Rhythm and Blues Record Shop. He focused his bleary eyes on the activity at the bookstore across the street. A man was painting a slogan in gold on the inside of the large display window. So far it read, *All Power to the....*" It had been a tiring night. He had performed solo at an after-hours club in downtown Bellport and got home just before sunrise. Since Natalie moved out a month ago, he'd had plenty of time to perform. He'd begun filling more of his time with bookings. He set them up himself. He felt it made sense for him to book gigs without including Khadim. Omar had ambitions for where he wanted to go with his music, whereas Khadim was content to be a small-town drummer.

He felt the prickle of goose bumps on his arms. Since it was Indian summer, he didn't anticipate the day being so breezy or cool.

He knew it would be much more pleasant for him inside the bookstore, but he decided to linger outside just in case Della came out of the apartment building. When they talked on the phone a few days ago, she said that this would be about the time she'd be leaving home for her classes at Bellport Community College.

The evening a few weeks ago at Le Baobab, they had talked for more than an hour after his performance. Della was the first person he felt comfortable sharing his feelings with about

Natalie deserting him. Della understood his broken heart. Della let him talk without interruption and at one point rubbed the back of his hand and, in her Arkansas drawl, whispered Bible verses to lift his low spirits.

He'd learned enough about Della to know that she too had had troubles with her boyfriend, Kwamé.

"*People.*" That was the final word of the slogan. "*All Power to the People.*" Omar watched the man come outside to admire his work. He then went over to the speakers to position them at proper angles. The announcer on the soul station was introducing a selection by The Fierce Warriors, "Time to Agitate." It amazed him how accepting the country had become of African drumming since he first came to the United States. Now, few people mocked it as "jungle music," as some of his classmates had at Howard.

"Omar?"

He turned around. It was Della. She was coming out of the door next to the record shop.

"I thought that was you," she said, smiling.

He liked the way her clothes fit her, the fabric of her blouse clinging to her large breasts and hips. He eyed her cleavage, then looked away, hoping she hadn't noticed.

"What're you doing here?" she asked. "Did you just come out of the record shop?"

"I saw the advertisement about the grand opening and thought I would go."

"But why are you over here? The grand opening's over there." She gestured in the direction of the porch. "I see Malachi's putting the finishing touches on the display window. That's nice."

Omar was mildly flustered. He didn't want her to know he'd been standing there hoping to run into her. "I am here to get air. I know it will be stuffy inside with so many people."

She stepped closer to him. "Malachi and Sydney might get a packed house. I know a lot of people are gonna come see The Fierce Warriors. I wish I could go, but I've got a class to get to." She reached into her satchel, pulled a file folder halfway out, looked at a sheet of paper, and then put it back. "But my daughter will be there."

He smiled, thinking about the impromptu jam session he'd had with Jasmine, Kofi, and Anamara at Le Baobab. "Your daughter is a natural talent. Most children her age cannot keep up with the beat that well."

Della's eyes twinkled. "I couldn't believe it when she walked up to you to watch you play. I held my breath when you let her get on the drums. I thought she would try it for a minute and then start acting up, but she actually liked it. The drumming calmed her down. If we didn't have no other tenants in the building, I'd get her a drum set and let her play all day."

He told her about the drumming institute he and Mustapha wanted to open.

"That is exactly what we need in Bellport. The kids around here have dancing school and basketball, but don't get to play instruments. You will get your drumming institute. You are a natural teacher. I saw how patient you were with your little cousins and Jasmine. You have a real gift."

During all his time with Natalie, she had never appreciated his ambition and talent. She referred to "the art of drumming," in a derisive tone. She saw it as an obstacle to his earning "real money," as she called it.

"If we can keep the city from taking the building, Uncle and I will open the institute. Jasmine will be our first student."

"No," she pointed at his chest. "Even if the building is taken, you must open your institute. Don't let what's going on in Petite Africa stop you. Kids will benefit from this. You can find another building in Bellport if you have to."

"You are very enthusiastic," he said.

She looked at her watch. "I have to get downtown. But I wanted to thank you again for sending that glass of wine over to my table and talking to me."

"You do not have to thank me."

"I was having a really hard time. You made me feel better."

He couldn't help smiling. "I enjoyed our talk, and our talks since that talk."

She seemed to become shy, glancing away from him to look at the sidewalk. "Me, too," she said finally.

He called after her as she turned to walk down the street. "Will you come back?"

She turned around, a smile forming on her face.

"To my uncle's restaurant, I am performing for the dinner crowd tomorrow."

She slowly nodded. "Maybe. I'll try."

As Della walked away, Omar thought about what he had wanted to tell her: that he was the one who had founded The Fierce Warriors when he was a freshman at Howard University and he was also the one who had come up with their original name, The Wolof Warriors, after his tribal affiliation. Also, that he taught the group members to drum, including classmate Henry Nims, who he wrote lyrics with, and that he helped Henry choose his stage name, Hideki Baruka.

But now would not have been the right time to tell Della those things. He would wait until he got to know her better, *if* he got to know her better.

Omar touched the hardened leather pouch around his neck, the *gris gris* the *marabout* had given him in Senegal years ago. He breathed out heavily. The leather was as stiff as a dried gourd but still intact. If things went as he hoped, he would soon be joining The Fierce Warriors. He corrected himself—actually *reuniting* with what was originally *his* group and getting the recording contract that was rightfully his.

Omar reached into his pants pocket and unfolded the crumpled leaflet about the grand opening. He checked his watch. It was well past noon. The place seemed large, but more and more people kept going in.

It was time he got on with what he came to do—reunite not only with The Fierce Warriors but also with Hideki. He looked again at the lettering on the large display window. *All Power to the People.* He held onto that thought as he stepped off the curb.

CHAPTER 22

"AUNTIE SYD, you can come to my tea party?"

"Yes, Jasmine. As soon as I'm done taking these pictures."

Dressed in a hot pink tutu and bright blue tights, the child pretended to pour tea from her plastic teapot into the large, black case for Sydney's light kit. "I want you to play now."

"Be patient, dear," said Bernadine. She was seated on a stool in a stylish pale orange pantsuit, her eyes facing the camera and body turned away slightly as Sydney had instructed. "Let your Auntie Syd finish what she's doing."

Jasmine looked up and squinted at the bright studio lights and then ran into the darkroom.

"You need to stay out here with us," Sydney shouted. "There are chemicals in there that can make you very, very sick."

"Okay," Jasmine responded in a faint voice.

Sydney had her mother posed in front of a cobalt blue drape, one of many backdrops that Lawrence had fashioned out of curtains for her.

Bernadine and Martin had arrived two hours earlier for the grand opening. Sydney offered to take some headshots her mother could use for the directory her social club was putting together. Sydney enjoyed having this time with Bernadine. With the hours she'd be putting in preparing the bookstore with Malachi, and writing freelance articles and taking photos for Max, she knew she'd scarcely have moments like this in the future. "I just need a few more shots, and I'll have enough for a package," Sydney said, peering through the view finder.

She admired her mother's ability to style her hair so that every strand was in the right place. With her regular clients, she had to tamp down, spray, or tuck away stray hairs from view.

"Does she want to come to the tea party?" Jasmine pointed at Bernadine as she skipped across the room to where Sydney stood.

"I wouldn't miss it for anything," Bernadine responded without moving an inch. "Just give us a few more minutes, dear."

Jasmine dragged an old tablecloth across the room that Sydney had let her play with and spread it out. "How come there's black paper on the windows?"

"Because we're in a photo studio," replied Sydney. "We have to keep sunlight out." She adjusted the height of the camera to photograph her mother from a different angle for the last few shots.

"Why do we have to keep the sun out?"

"So we can have the lighting the way we want it for the pictures." Sydney clicked off the studio lights, folded up the reflector, and took it, along with the camera, into the darkroom. Bernadine followed her.

"You're really patient with her," Bernadine said in a low voice so Jasmine wouldn't hear.

"Haven't had a problem with her. Maybe because I make peanut butter treats with her when I babysit—peanut butter cake, peanut butter cookies. I've never seen a child who loves peanuts so much."

Sydney had been babysitting Jasmine since Della decided to take classes at Bellport Community College.

Bernadine smiled. "Don't sell yourself short. You have a way with children."

Sydney put the reflector in a cabinet under the sink and popped out the roll of film, stacking it with others on the counter. She reloaded the camera with a roll of thirty-six exposures for The Fierce Warriors' performance. Max had assigned her to take some shots. "But I worry about her. She grinds her teeth. She was doing that last night when I went in to check on her."

"Obviously something's bothering the poor child. Della's never said what it was?"

"Not really. She did say she had a traumatic marriage and her husband died, but nothing more."

"I'm sure you being there for Della, babysitting Jasmine, means a lot to her. You're a good friend. You encouraged her to go back to school."

"I remember how much it meant to you when Mrs. Rusnak babysat me so you could go to school."

"Oh yes, Mrs. Rusnak." Bernadine smiled and looked off in the distance. "What a sweet lady. If not for her, I wouldn't be where I am today. I wouldn't have met Martin. We wouldn't have our beautiful home. I couldn't have afforded to send you to Whittington University."

"So I realize how important it is to be there for someone who needs a babysitter so she can go to school."

When they left the darkroom, they found Jasmine with her cups and saucers arranged on the tablecloth on the floor for a tea party.

"What on earth is that?" Bernadine wrinkled her nose in reaction to a high-pitched squealing sound. "Sounds like somebody's dying."

"It must be the clothesline out back. I need to get Malachi to take it down."

"Nearly scared me to death," Bernadine exclaimed. She went to the back window. I don't think it's the clothesline. It sounds like it's coming from inside the house."

"It's a witch!" shouted Jasmine. "A wicked witch."

"I've gotten so used to it that I don't even notice it anymore," Sydney said.

"Is the witch gonna put a spell on us?" asked Jasmine.

"Don't worry about it dear," replied Bernadine in a soothing voice. "I'm sure we'll be okay."

They all got on the floor in a cross-legged sitting position. Jasmine handed them their teacups. "Auntie Syd, what's a grand open?" she asked, while pretending to fill their cups with tea.

"A grand *opening*. It's a celebration that people have when a business opens for the first time. It's a big party."

"A party?" Jasmine's eyes grew wide. "Like my tea party?"

"Kind of," Bernadine answered.

"Can I go?"

"Yes, you can go," Sydney agreed.

"Will there be cake?"

"Yes, there will be cake."

"Ooh! And ice cream?"

"And ice cream," Bernadine replied.

"Peanut ice cream?"

"You have to go to Petite Africa for that," Sydney said.

The three of them 'sipped' their tea and 'munched' on cookies. After a while, Jasmine asked, "Will other boys and girls be there?"

Sydney glanced at her mother.

Bernadine laughed. "There's nothing more precious than a child who has a lot of questions, Sydney. This is good practice for you."

"Point taken." Sydney placed her teacup on her saucer. "Remember Uncle Mustapha?"

Jasmine nodded.

"He promised that he would bring his grandchildren, Kofi and Anamara, as soon as the doors open, so you'll see them in a little while."

"Will Mommy be there?"

"No," Sydney responded. "Your mommy has tests to take at school."

"I have tests, too."

"You're in school already?" Bernadine teased.

Jasmine nodded. "Kindergarten."

"So you know how important this is to your mommy," Bernadine asked.

"Why is Mommy's test so long? Is it really big?"

"Your mother is studying for something very important," Sydney responded. "It takes months and months to study for all the tests, and then she has a big test at the end."

Sydney glanced at her watch. "We need to change your clothes, Jasmine."

"I can do it all by myself," the child announced.

"Good!" Bernadine exclaimed. "Now go on and get ready so we can all go downstairs."

Sydney haphazardly stacked the saucers and cups on the tablecloth while Jasmine ran down the hall.

Bernadine looked at her watch. "Martin said he'd come up before long, but that was more than half an hour ago."

"He probably got into a conversation with Malachi and Kwamé."

Bernadine chuckled. "Politics, I'm sure. We should be able to stay for a few hours. We'll definitely stay long enough to hear The Fierce Warriors' performance."

Sydney stopped what she was doing. "You know about The Fierce Warriors?"

Her mother pursed her lips. "Of course. I've seen them on TV. Your father has a couple of their albums. We don't live under a rock, you know."

Sydney put the tea set back in its box.

"I've been telling all of my friends how you worked so hard to book them," Bernadine continued.

"I can't take all the credit. The Taylors helped."

Bernadine folded the tablecloth and took it into the kitchen. "They sound like interesting people, world travelers, rubbing elbows with famous people."

"And they taught at the École Bilingual International sometime in the mid-sixties."

Bernadine slowly came out of the pantry staring at Sydney. "What a coincidence. That's the same school that Guy was teaching mathematics at back then."

Sydney had forgotten that her stepbrother taught there. "Maybe they all know each other."

"Could be. We'll have to ask."

Bernadine walked back through the living room to the window facing the street. "I'm proud of you. You know that, don't you?"

Sydney joined her. "Thank you, Mother, but what's brought this on?"

"Moving to the other side of the state to live in a city like Bellport, postponing your career plans for your husband's dream. You've made some tough decisions, mature decisions."

Sydney blinked back tears. "It means so much to hear that from you."

Bernadine sighed. "I did the same thing for your father when we first got married. I worked while he went to law school."

"I didn't know that."

"I guess we never talked about it. After you came along and he started his career, we didn't look back on that time much. But it was all worth it."

When they got to the first floor, Jasmine joined Kwamé in the reading room, where he was handing stacks of leaflets about the opening to some of Malachi's former students to give to passersby on the street. Sydney and Bernadine found Martin and Malachi at the large display window looking over a slogan Malachi had painted in gold using stencils.

In the hallway, Lawrence stood guard over the Ronald Bridgewaters paintings hanging on the walls.

Bernadine turned to Sydney. "Are you sure you should even have this artwork out here like this? They're part of Malachi's collection, aren't they?"

"I know, but Malachi insisted. He says displaying artwork is all part of this being a cultural center."

"You have nothing to worry about, Miss Syd," said Lawrence. "We're working in shifts, me and Kwamé—I mean—Mr. Rodriguez. Nobody's gonna walk out with this art. I'll go run the cash register when he relieves me."

Lawrence excused himself for a moment and came back with flyers about an upcoming healthy eating seminar the bookstore would be hosting on the uses of sweet potatoes. He handed them to Sydney. "If you wouldn't mind helping me hand these out to the customers. My grandmother says she can't wait to do this for y'all."

Sydney and Bernadine returned to the foyer. The first customers came through the front gate and onto the porch. Many of the women, wearing African clothes—long, loose-fitting print tops and matching skirts—held up their skirts as they climbed the stairs to avoid tripping.

Uncle Mustapha has been true to his word about passing the word along, Sydney thought.

The customers seemed thrilled to see African masks and the paintings on display and ran their fingertips over them. Sydney was relieved that Lawrence was watching everyone closely.

She glanced toward the front door as Willie came in. She had never seen him look so tired. His shoulders sagged. She stepped forward to greet him, introducing him to Bernadine.

"Had to take Inez to the doctors this morning," he explained.

"Is she all right?" asked Sydney.

Willie shrugged. "Headaches. She'll be fine. She gets bad ones sometimes. Because of the stroke, I'm careful. I took her for an exam. She's downstairs resting."

"I hope all this activity up here won't disturb her," Bernadine said.

"She'll be fine. Pumpkin's down there with her," he replied. "The little kitty helps her nerves."

"Sydney tells me that you and your wife used to teach in Paris, at the École Bilingual International?" Bernadine inquired.

He gave her a blank look. "Yes," he answered, finally.

Bernadine looked at him quizzically, as if expecting him to say more. When he didn't, she continued.

"My husband's son, my stepson, taught there around the time you were there. His name is Guy Doucette."

Willie's eyes darted left to right. "I've got to get downstairs to Inez. It was nice meeting you." He shook Bernadine's hand, and then quickly turned on his heels. As he left, the women watched as he got swallowed up in the crowd.

Bernadine turned toward Sydney. "That was odd, don't you think?"

"Maybe he didn't hear what you said with all of the people. He's got a sick wife on his mind."

"No. I think he heard me," Bernadine said.

She left Sydney to find Martin. Sydney figured she could hand out some of Lawrence's leaflets but could not remember where she put them. She walked down the hall to find Lawrence. She was surprised not to see him at his "post," guarding the artwork, but in the lecture hall unzipping his duffel bag. She watched him curiously as he grabbed the three-volumes of *The African and Black American Experience* off the shelf. She identified them by the gold lettering on the spine. What was Lawrence doing? Maybe Malachi was letting him borrow them for some reason. But she couldn't imagine why. It was an expensive set. Sydney shook her head as she backed out of the room and went back to the foyer.

In a moment, Malachi joined Sydney there. "Baby, this is going better than I thought," he said, surveying the scene. "I'm going to have one of my students take a notebook around and get the addresses of everybody here so we can create a mailing list."

"Good idea," Sydney agreed. "We've got some notebooks in the supply room."

She led the way down the hall. They stopped at the sound of the familiar greeting in Wolof.

"*Olelele! Olelele!*" Uncle Mustapha shouted as he came

down the hall trailed by Kofi and Anamara. "Is little Jasmine here?" he asked.

Sydney told him where to find her.

He looked down at his grandchildren and nodded. They rushed passed him into the crowd. Sydney and Malachi motioned Mustapha to the supply room doorway where they could talk away from the noise.

"So how are the emotions on this first day in business?" Mustapha asked.

"I was feeling nervous until I saw all of the people from Petite Africa coming in," Sydney said.

He held up his hand to interject. "Uncle Mustapha cannot take the full credit, only part," he said. "I tell my customers if they coming to Talking Drum grand opening and they spend money here, they can bring receipt to Le Baobab and get ten percent discount on next meal."

"Sir, thank you," said Malachi. "That's gracious of you."

Mustapha's eyes twinkled. "I want hubby-and-wife team to be success. I giving you friendship I do not find when I first open Le Baobab."

Malachi extended his hand to Mustapha. "We appreciate it."

"I aspire to stay whole day but cannot."

"Why? What time do you have to open the restaurant?" Sydney asked.

He folded his arms across his chest. "Le Baobab not open today. Tonight is city council hearing. The community must organize plans for the meeting. We have more signatures on petitions, another five hundred."

Sydney had read in the paper about tonight's planned public hearing before city council. The hearing would allow residents to state their objections to the city's plan to take Petite Africa properties by eminent domain.

"When will council make a final decision?" Malachi asked.

"Any day. They do not tell us."

Malachi left to find Lawrence to put him on the cash register. Sydney walked back to the foyer. She was shocked at who she saw walking into the bookstore. It was Percy, Kwamé's friend, wearing a foul-smelling snorkel jacket with brown and green stains. "What brings you here?" she asked, barely able to muster a polite tone.

"How y'all doing today?" He offered Sydney his dirty, bloated hand for a greeting. She swallowed hard and gently shook it. "K-man was telling me all about the grand opening. Told me I should come. Well, here I am."

She quickly turned toward the room behind her. "I don't see Kwamé at the moment. I think he's pretty busy back there. You can come back to catch him later."

"No, that's all right. I'll just walk around and have a look. I'll find him," he said. He stood taller than most of the other guests and was as wide as the hallway.

"Where's your dog?" she called after him.

He turned and smiled, exposing brown teeth. "Bridgette? I tied her up on the fence out there. She's okay. She don't bite."

Sydney looked outside to see Bridgette's leash looped through the front gate as if she were guarding the event. The animal would scare off customers. Where was Malachi? They'd have to get Percy and that mangy dog out of here, she thought.

As Sydney went looking for him, she stopped at the lecture hall. Strange. There was Willie talking with an elderly couple, pointing to some photos he had taken out of his wallet. But only minutes earlier he had told her he had to get downstairs to Inez. There was no way he could have checked on her, come back upstairs, worked his way through the crowd, and found a seat in the reading room. It was impossible. Even for a young person. She decided not to waste time trying to figure it out. The Taylors could take care of themselves.

CHAPTER 23

OMAR HEARD the blare of a car horn as he stepped off the curb. The car was speeding in his direction. He jumped back onto the sidewalk. The tires screeched as the taxi came to a sudden stop. It was Khadim wearing sunglasses. He rolled down the window.

Naka my demee? Naka my demee? "What are you doing here in Liberty Hill, my friend, hiding from me?" Khadim shouted over the fuzzy squawking of the two-way radio.

Omar couldn't believe his bad luck. Khadim was to know nothing of his venture at the bookstore. "I should ask you the same thing," Omar said. "I do not remember you having taxi fares in this neighborhood."

"I am taking the shortcut to City Hall."

"Why do you go there?"

"You still have not answered my question."

They locked eyes.

"I want to pick up some African drumming albums." Omar gestured at the record shop behind him.

Khadim flipped his sunglasses to the top of his head. "African drummer needs to buy albums of African drummers?"

Khadim's attention shifted to the crackling sound of the two-way radio. He grabbed the loudspeaker/microphone and pressed it to his lips, speaking into it too low for Omar to hear. "I have a pick up down at the Harbor," Khadim stated. "I have bad news to tell you," he added, turning back to Omar. "My landlord says the city is taking my building."

Khadim's news stunned Omar. "I thought the owner of your building was in that lawsuit with Uncle Mustapha and the other building owners?"

Khadim shrugged. "I guess he dropped out. He said I can get housing vouchers. I go to City Hall after I pick up this fare. We talk about this later." He put his sunglasses back on and sped off.

Omar watched the taxi turn the corner. Across the street at the bookstore, two college-age men came down the porch stairs as Uncle Mustapha approached with Kofi and Anamara trailing him. One of them tried to hand Uncle a flyer, but he brushed it aside and climbed the stairs to the porch with his grandkids close behind. He hoped Uncle Mustapha and the other residents fighting the action wouldn't get discouraged by this latest news. Omar was surprised that Mustapha's shirt was wrinkled and untucked, its tail fluttering behind him. That wasn't like Uncle. He was always meticulous about his appearance. He ironed his shirts and never left home without checking his ensemble in a full-length mirror. His upcoming rally at City Hall probably had him too preoccupied to think about ironing his clothes.

He crossed the street. Sam Cooke's voice came from the porch speakers. Omar smiled to himself. He'd grown up listening to Cooke on Ibrahim's gramophone.

He wished that he had worn shoes instead of sandals as he stepped into the foyer. The high heel of a fat woman's shoe stabbed his foot like a knitting needle. She wobbled off balance, bumping her rear end up against him.

"Well, hello," she purred as she turned around to look him up and down. He smiled and sidestepped her.

The crowd was so thick that he was forced to float with it into one of the rooms. A small, gold-plated sign over the doorway indicated that it was the reading room. Over the hum of conversation, he heard children playing. He looked down.

It was Kofi, Anamara, and Jasmine tearing through the room as if they were on a playground.

He looked around. He hadn't seen so many books in one place since being in the college library at Howard. They were divided into categories like *Slavery, Reconstruction, Black Nationalism, White Supremacy* and were wedged into bookcases six feet tall, placed so close together that he had to walk sideways to make his way down the narrow aisles.

His stomach tightened at a tap on the shoulder, anticipating that it was Hideki. But it was Sydney, the friend of Della's. She handed him a flyer about a healthy eating class scheduled in a few weeks. It said people could learn about forty different ways to prepare yams. "Is this a tale?" he asked her.

"It's true," replied Sydney, smiling. "The lady who teaches the class says she has enough recipes to write a cookbook if she wants."

"Then she knows more than the women of my village. I wonder if she will make yam pottage and sweet potato fritters."

"You'll have to come back for the class to find out," she said with a wink and walked away.

Omar watched Sydney go over to Jasmine, Kofi, and Anamara and wag a finger at them. He looked at his watch. He needed to hurry if he was going to talk to Hideki before The Fierce Warriors' backyard performance. But he didn't know how to find them. He approached Sydney in the hallway.

"The Fierce Warriors are old friends of yours?" she was smiling. "As good as you play, you should be part of the group."

"That is more true than you know," he said.

Sydney led him to the landing in the attic. Omar could feel his heart rate pick up as he knocked on the door. He tried to calm himself, not wanting to appear nervous.

"Hideki! My brother!" Omar said, trying to sound casual, as his old friend opened the door.

Hideki stared blankly at Omar.

"It is me, Omar." He spoke a little louder than he intended.

"I know." Hideki responded in a dry, flat tone.

Omar expected his old friend to open the door wider to let him in, but Hideki folded his arms across his chest and blocked the doorway. Was Hideki joking with him? Omar walked past him into the living room. It was empty except for a couch and recliner. Another doorway led to a kitchen.

"How long has it been?" Hideki turned around, joining Omar but leaving the door open.

"I have lost track," Omar responded.

A voice coming from the stairwell said, "Hey, man, you all right up there?"

"Yeah, man, it's cool," Hideki responded to Malachi, who reached the landing.

"Just checking." Malachi gave Omar a stern look.

"Not a problem, Dr. Mal," Hideki responded.

Malachi went back down the stairs.

"I haven't seen you in years." Hideki sat down on the couch. "You caught me off guard."

"I did not mean to startle you." Omar didn't know whether to sit down or leave. From the kitchen he could hear the other members of the group. He waited but Hideki didn't call them in to announce him. His old friend looked at his watch, then at the kitchen doorway. "We need to get downstairs and warm up a little on the stage before we play," he said. "You're welcome to join us there before we get started. We'll be down in a few minutes."

Before Omar could respond, Hideki ushered him out the door.

Later, with the customers streaming into the yard, Omar waited for The Fierce Warriors to appear. He began to wonder if Hideki had delayed their entrance, hoping that Omar would give up and go away. Then, one-by-one the band members mounted the stage—his other old friends Shaka Tabur and Baba Lumumba shook Omar's hand. There were several new members that Omar didn't know who joined the others onstage.

Hideki beckoned Omar to follow him up to the stage. Hideki walked to the far end, sat on a stool, and began tuning his drum. "You cross my mind when I come through Massachusetts, but I had forgotten what city you moved to." Hideki's voice was still flat. Omar had hoped for a reunion warmer than this.

"How's the drumming going, man?" Hideki asked as he did a mike check. "You were on your way somewhere when you left Howard."

Omar stiffened at the question. "I get bookings. I stay occupied."

Hideki snickered. "I thought you and your uncle were going to start some kind of drumming school. I thought you were going to get a recording contract. I expected to see your name in lights somewhere. What happened?"

Omar didn't know if this was a question or a slight. "I see your celebrity has grown like a bush fire."

Hideki chuckled. "Man, you crack me up with that African stuff you talk. I had forgotten about that."

Omar began to feel awkward. He thought it was odd that Hideki had not introduced him to the newer members of the band. They were ten feet away, testing their drums, doing mike checks. Omar thought about introducing himself but decided it was only proper that Hideki handle introductions. "Will you be in town for a while?"

"Nah, man. We're leaving right after this, heading to New York City. Got a couple of gigs uptown. That'll be the end of our tour."

"Too bad we will not have more time to talk."

Hideki stopped in mid-motion, the ropes of the drum in his hands. "Really?" he snapped. "Talk about what?"

Omar was jarred by Hideki's instant switch in mood.

"The Fierce Warriors have been to Bellport before, and we didn't hear from you," Hideki continued. "We were out in Worcester last year. I'm sure you knew about it. What you want, man? You must want something. If you didn't, you wouldn't be here."

"I was going to tell you later, after you perform, but since you ask me, I shall tell you. I have a business proposition."

Hideki said nothing, moved upstage, and continued tightening the ropes to tune his drum.

Omar followed him. "I want you to settle your debt."

Hideki stopped what he was doing. "What debt?"

"I wrote half the songs The Fierce Warriors perform and recorded with ABC records. I am willing to negotiate."

Hideki stood up and motioned Omar to come with him to a corner of the stage. He spoke in a loud whisper. "We wrote those songs together, all of us," he said. "We were just a bunch of kids drumming." He stabbed Omar's chest with his finger. "I don't owe you nothing."

Omar brushed Hideki's finger aside. "I want what you are obligated to give me."

"That's ridiculous, man, you got nothing in writing. You can talk to my attorney."

Hideki walked back to where he'd left his drum. Omar followed. "You didn't even know what a drum was until you begged me for lessons," Omar exclaimed. "You thought all of us Africans were savages until I educated you out of your ignorance."

Hideki's chest was rising and falling fast as he patted the drum head to check the sound. Omar was pleased to see that his words had affected him.

"*You* are the savage," Hideki growled. "You took my woman. You had no respect. I thought we were 'brothers.'"

Omar was stunned. Hideki was still angry because Natalie left him for Omar. Omar assumed Hideki would have dismissed the incident long ago, like so many men from his country would have. "You are the one who had no respect," Omar responded. "She knew all about the others."

Hideki grimaced. "That has nothing to do with anything."

Baba Lumumba yelled, "Hideki, man, we got to get ready."

Hideki glared at Omar. "I don't have time for this."

As Hideki walked away, Omar stepped in front of him. "I do not have time either. I have no time for your lies," he countered. "You are a thief. You stole my music."

In the next moment, someone grabbed Omar from behind by the shoulders.

"Time to go," Malachi boomed, forcefully walking Omar off the stage, through the back yard and onto the back porch. Mustapha stepped into their path as they came through the kitchen.

"He is with me," Mustapha explained to Malachi. After a pause, Malachi released him.

Uncle Mustapha took Omar's arm, and the two snaked their way through the bookstore to the front door. Omar knew better than to try to resist his uncle. Growing up, he had heard stories about what a legendary wrestler Mustapha had been at amateur competitions in Dakar. Omar was sure that, despite his years, Uncle still had all the moves. Once they were outside the gate, Mustapha flung Omar against the chain-link fence, setting him free. Omar lost his balance and fell on the sidewalk as a mangy German shepherd on a leash looped around the front gate barked at him ferociously. Omar was relieved that the dog was far enough away that it couldn't reach him. The strap snapped on one of his sandals. Mustapha leaned against the maple tree, breathing hard and clutching his chest.

"Uncle! Your heart!"

"My heart is fine," Mustapha gasped.

"You must take it easy," Omar said.

Mustapha didn't respond. Gradually, he stood up straight. His breathing returned to normal.

"I am concerned about you," Mustapha shouted. "What are you doing in there?"

"Getting what is rightfully mine." Omar tried to catch his breath.

"What is yours rightfully or what is yours rightfully you *think*? Only a fool tries to get back more. I am disappointed in you. What does your papa think right now if he sees you crawling around on your belly like a serpent, begging for favors? Ibrahim is ashamed."

Omar was incensed. What his father would think was none of Mustapha's business.

"A tree that grows in the shade of another will die small," Mustapha continued. "Do not try to fasten your success to your old friend. You must yourself do it."

"I have been trying…"

"Then you are trying not hard enough," Mustapha roared over the sound of the dog barking.

Omar grabbed onto the fence to hoist himself back to a standing position.

"You need to come with me," demanded Mustapha. "We go to planning meeting for City Hall protest. You will stop this folly."

Omar knew he should listen to his uncle, but he didn't want to. "It is late. I have a gig tomorrow, and I must go home to get some rest."

"A gig?" Mustapha spat out the words. "That is all you have. Gigs. Every day. Every night. Gigs. What about Petite Africa? You have no place to lay your head if project goes through."

Omar broke from his uncle and tramped down Liberty Hill Boulevard, the strap of his sandal flapping. He passed by the pawn shop, the ice cream shop, and the bank. Eventually he saw the door to Jake's Tavern and After Hours Club. He grabbed the brass knocker and slammed it against the door repeatedly. He wanted a drink to help him forget about today.

The first thing Omar noticed on entering Jake's was the overpowering smell of cooking oil mixed with sweet syrup, not the type of smell he expected in a bar. He looked around. The place was having a special event in the small dining area. Tables were filled with black American women all wearing the same outfit—a purple skirt and jacket and white blouse with a bow. Waitresses brought them platters of fried chicken wings and waffles. He read the sign in grease pencil on the easel near the hostess station. It welcomed The Gadabouts Social Club in celebration of its thirtieth anniversary. Omar walked to the bar, careful to keep his sandal on his foot. Men turned on their stools to stare. He was fairly certain that few African men walked into Jake's regularly. A man in a *boubou* was something these people probably rarely saw up close.

Omar sat at the far end of the bar near the kitchen. A bartender appeared through the smoky haze and asked him what he wanted. He knew he should eat something. He hadn't had anything since breakfast. But he decided instead to experiment with bourbon and ordered Jack Daniels with ice. He took a sip, then another. His meeting with Hideki had been a disaster. He'd had no intention of asking Hideki for payment for their collaboration. He went to the grand opening to see if The Fierce Warriors would be willing to bring him on as a backup drummer, to tour when he was needed, and in time bring him back into the group fulltime. But Hideki had angered him. His old classmate was still holding a grudge against Omar.

Hideki was dating Natalie when they were at Howard. She found out that he was sleeping around, broke it off, and started dating Omar, who she'd been confiding in about her problems with Hideki. Then Natalie became pregnant. When Hideki found out, he wanted to fight Omar. They were blood enemies after that.

At the grand opening, Omar had felt stung when Hideki made reference to Natalie. In the weeks since she'd left, Omar tried to blot her from his mind. He had sacrificed so much over his love for her, his college education, his friends at Howard, the Wolof Warriors, and the prospect of performing with Duke Ellington. If only Natalie could have been more patient with him while he rebuilt his career. He would have moved them out of Petite Africa. But she didn't give him a chance.

With his glass now empty, Omar ordered a second bourbon, holding his glass up to the bartender to get his attention. It was pointless dwelling on the past. Natalie was gone. He would push ahead with his music.

The bartender slid another drink to him. Omar felt comforted as the liquor filled his empty stomach. Jack Daniels talked to him, whispering that everything would be okay. As he looked around he noticed that everyone seemed to be moving in slow motion, including a large black American man who eased himself onto the stool next to his.

"The name's Sam," the man said, extending his beefy hand. Omar didn't feel like company, but the man wouldn't move his hand away, so Omar felt obliged to shake it. Sam ordered a Scotch on the rocks. After it arrived, he turned toward Omar, sipping his drink. Not being in the mood to talk, Omar continued to look straight ahead at the mirror on the wall behind the bar.

"Shame, ain't it," Sam said. "Those people ain't got a chance."

Omar said nothing, his focus shifting to his drink. He took a long sip and scanned the menu the waiter had brought to him. Chicken and waffles didn't interest him. Neither did any of the burgers listed. Out of the corner of his eye, he saw Sam lean back and unzip his jacket, exposing a large gut. He looked Omar up and down.

"You're an African, ain't you?"

"Senegal." Omar said, regretting that he'd come into an American bar. He was hoping to keep the conversation short. To his relief, the man slid off the stool, tipped away, and squeezed his frame into a phone booth at the other end of the bar. The bartender returned with another drink. Sam returned after Omar emptied his glass.

"You live across the way?" Sam asked, nodding his head in the direction of the door.

"Petite Africa." Omar's tongue felt thick, reminding him of what happened whenever Fama tried to feed him cassava leaves when he was a little boy.

The man grabbed his shoulder and leaned toward Omar so close that Omar smelled his sweet cologne. "Let me be the first to express my condolences."

Omar was puzzled. "I do not understand."

The man raised bushy eyebrows. "They're tearing it down, bit by bit. You know that. They're gonna run you folks out of there. Where y'all gonna move to?"

Omar jerked his shoulder from the man's grip. "They shall not tear it down. There shall still be a Petite Africa."

Sam raised both palms in mock surrender. "Sorry, friend. Didn't mean to offend." He took a sip of his drink, grimacing as he swallowed. "But it's only a matter of time before they take the whole neighborhood and kick you out."

Omar felt dizzy. He held onto the cushioned ledge of the bar. The bartender returned. "Refill?" he asked.

"Yes. No ice this time," Omar said.

"I hear they're gonna fix it up real good, though" Sam asserted. "They're gonna build a marina. I got a boat I can put out there. A fishing boat. Bought it when I took early retirement a couple of years ago. I was with the state thirty-five years, a guard at Concord State Pen."

"They have no right to our homes."

"Huh?"

"They have no right to destroy our community," roared Omar.

Sam threw his head back and laughed. "You must be kidding," he continued. "The city does what the city wants, especially in an election year. Besides that, the place is a dump. I hear you all don't even have indoor plumbing down there. And you're packed twenty to thirty people to an apartment. Might as well be back in Africa, living in one of them shacks."

Isn't that what Natalie had called it, a village of nothing but shacks? Omar swung around with a clenched fist, punched Sam in the chest, and knocked him off his stool. Gasps rose from the social club women. Men at the bar put down their drinks and bottles at the sound of Sam falling to the floor. Sam landed on his back. The seat of his pants had split. He looked up from the floor confused and held up his hands in a pleading gesture.

"Hey, man. Are you crazy?"

Omar leaped on top of him, straddling him. He slammed his fist into the man's face repeatedly. Sam fought back, getting Omar by the throat. Omar grabbed Sam's thick fingers but couldn't break the man's grip. Omar couldn't breathe. He thought he was going to pass out. Then, from behind, someone grabbed the collar of his *boubou* and lifted him off of Sam.

Sam held the side of his face as he looked up at Omar. "What's your problem, man?" he screeched between short breaths.

Omar couldn't see who had him in a choke hold. The person guided him through the bar, grabbed him by his waistband, and pushed him into the street. Omar stumbled and fell on the curb. His *boubou* was ripped down the front to his waist. His pants tore at the knees where he hit the pavement. He rolled over on his side into the fetal position to dodge the kicks aimed at his back and ribs. His head banged into the iron ledge of a storm drain. He smelled the dirty, stagnant water that had pooled in the drain and choked back the vomit rising in his throat. He lay there unable to move and gulped blood that was trickling onto his bottom lip. Sirens wailed in the distance.

CHAPTER 24

SYDNEY ROLLED onto her side and hit the clock radio's snooze button. She was having a hard time motivating herself to get up and slept on and off all day. Della had called earlier, asking to meet at Le Baobab for dinner. Sydney didn't know why Della was so insistent. She could go over to Uncle Mustapha's restaurant for *mafé* when she took Jasmine for her hair appointments. The clock radio came back on. Sydney listened to a report about a hearing at city hall. Three hundred residents had crammed into City Council chambers last night to protest the plan for the city to take over Petite Africa.

The radio report said it was bedlam. At one point, police were called in to quiet the booing and hissing audience and keep people from rushing the seating area for the council members. The outcome was favorable to the residents. Thanks to the protests and legal challenges, the city agreed to let the courts, not city council, determine the legality of taking the properties and weigh the hardship it would put on residents of losing their homes. Sydney thought about how pleased Uncle Mustapha must have been at the result.

Sydney turned off the radio and rolled onto her back. Late afternoon light seeped through the sides of the window shades. The bottoms of her feet ached and her calf muscles were stiff from standing so long yesterday. Foot traffic during the grand opening had been heavy all day. By the time The Fierce Warriors had come on stage, the backyard, porch, and driveway were as packed as Times Square on New Year's Eve. Those who couldn't fit outdoors listened from the kitchen. Later, fans followed the band over to Rhythm and Blues Record Shop, where Kwamé arranged for The Fierce Warriors to autograph copies of their albums for customers.

Malachi decided to keep the bookstore open until midnight. It had paid off. The cash register chimed all night. Malachi took this as a good sign. He figured that if half the number of people who came to the grand opening became regular customers, the store would have a strong chance of surviving. One of the few annoying moments of the day was when Percy showed up with that mangy dog, Bridgette. To Sydney's relief, customers didn't seem to mind the dog and some actually played with her as they came in or out of The Talking Drum.

The phone rang. Sydney hoped it was Della calling to cancel their plans. It was Max. "Great job on those photos, keep it up," he said. "Gonna run them in the next issue. A full spread in the centerfold."

Sydney sat upright. "Glad you liked them." She had taken three rolls during The Fierce Warriors' concert and candid shots after the performance with the musicians and the crowd. Max had sent a courier at the end of the night to pick up the film.

"Can you handle another assignment?" he asked. "I need an article and some photos of Petite Africa. A couple of the holdouts just decided to give up the fight. They want to sell to the city and get out. They don't want to even wait for the court decision. They want O-U-T. If more owners follow suit, we'll have a stampede out of Petite Africa. Man-on-the-street interviews would be good. See how people feel. I know you had a long day yesterday…"

"That's fine, Max. I can get to it today."

"Fine. Just fine. Let's stay on top of this. The day of reckoning is coming for Petite Africa."

"And the people know it. Feelings are raw. I'll be able to get some good quotes for my story."

She told him of her plans to go to Petite Africa for dinner. "Perfect timing," he said. "See what you can get."

After they hung up, she checked the clock. It was almost five. She took a hot shower, letting the spray of water massage her calves and feet. When she got to the first floor, she was surprised to hear the hum of the adding machine. Malachi had left hours earlier to go with Kwamé to a neighborhood improvement association meeting. She had thought he would still be there. But he was back and sitting in the reading room with the cash register drawer on the table next to stacks of cash, checks, and receipts lined up in neat rows.

"What happened to the meeting?"

"Wasn't long." Malachi didn't look up.

He held up a hand as he punched numbers into the adding machine. Once he was done, he ripped a long strip of tape from the machine, looked at it from top to bottom, and frowned. "It's not adding up."

"What do you mean?"

He took his glasses off and squeezed the corners of his bloodshot eyes. "We're one hundred fifty dollars short."

She yanked out a chair and sat down. "Are you sure?"

"I keep coming up with different amounts—first two hundred short, then one hundred and seventy-five. Now one fifty."

She watched him count a stack of cash he had on the table. "Do you want me to stay and help?"

He waved her off. "No. Go on and see Della. I'll figure this out."

She turned to leave but then came back. "Who had access to the drawer?"

Malachi seemed to think this over for a moment. "I rang up most of the sales, and then Lawrence took over while The Fierce Warriors were performing and later when they went over to record shop."

She had a question. She paused to think about it for a moment. Then she went ahead. "Did you have anyone watching

Lawrence? Was he handling the register alone?"

He narrowed his eyes. "Now why would I do that? He was one of my best students. I trust him. He's not like he was before."

Sydney told him about seeing Lawrence stuffing the volumes of *The African and Black American Experience* in his backpack.

"Are you sure that's what you saw?"

"Definitely."

He sat there not saying anything for a while. "Then he must've had a good reason for taking them. Maybe he just borrowed them. Maybe he needs them for a paper he's writing."

He shoved the cash and checks into the slots of the register drawer. "We have to be very careful before we start making accusations." He snapped off the adding machine.

"No accusations. Just telling you what I saw." Sydney was glad that she had someplace to go. She knew Malachi would sit and stew over the situation for hours. She pushed the idea of Lawrence stealing from them out of her mind. He'd done a great job mowing their lawn and organizing groups that could generate customers for The Talking Drum. Already he'd gotten a couple of regular customers to take charge of one of the discussion groups. Cynthia and Renée, a lesbian couple that lived in an apartment above the ice cream shop down the street, had agreed to run the women's employment support group.

Twenty minutes later she walked into Le Baobab. Near the bandstand she spotted Della talking to Omar. When Della saw her, she broke off the conversation and motioned to their booth where two tall glasses of mango ginger lemonade were waiting for them.

"Sorry I'm late," Sydney said as she slid onto the bench opposite Della.

"Girl, no problem." Della gestured toward Omar. "That poor man is having such a hard time."

"The drummer?" Sydney took a closer look at him. His face looked puffy. One cheek was swollen, and the area under his left eye was purple. He had a long scab coming down the center of his forehead shaped like a crooked teardrop.

Omar slapped the face of his *djembe*. Sydney was relieved that after a few minutes his playing was low enough that she and Della could have a normal conversation.

"He got into a fight last night at Jake's and got the worst of it. The cops showed up, threw him in a squad car, but then let him go."

Sydney thought about the argument she saw Omar having with one of The Fierce Warriors before Malachi threw him out of The Talking Drum.

"So," Della started, as she unfolded her napkin on her lap. "Fill me in. How was the grand opening? When Jasmine got home, she said, 'It was fun, Mommy!'" She mimicked her daughter's high-pitched voice. "But I was looking for a few more details."

Sydney told her, leaving out Jasmine's tantrum, which was set off when Kofi and Anamara had to leave. Jasmine had reacted so badly that she hurled herself on the floor in the middle of the lecture hall. She screamed and kicked her feet at the customers. Sydney had to grab her by the wrists and take her upstairs and make her lie down for a while.

"Glad it went well. If I waited for Kwamé to tell me anything, I wouldn't know nothing about it." Della rolled her eyes.

"What do you mean?"

Della sighed. "He's not really talking to me right now. He thinks me going back to school is a waste of time. He says I don't need no more education. He can't or he won't see that I need to do this for me, and it's not just about trying to advance my career."

"I'm sorry, Della."

Her brow wrinkled. "For what?"

"I'm the one who gave you the idea to go back to school."

"Oh, girl, that was one of the best ideas I heard all year. I'm just dealing with an insecure man."

The kitchen doors swung open. Mustapha went over to the

bandstand with a glass of water and put it on the stool next to Omar and then came over to their booth. "*Mesdames,* what am I today to get for you?"

Mustapha seemed preoccupied, as if his mind was on something else. Sydney guessed that he was exhausted from the demonstration last night at council chambers. She had initially thought today would be the right time to interview him, but she now had second thoughts.

Della handed back her menu. "I'm not that hungry. Couple of appetizers would be fine." She turned to Sydney. "What do you want?"

"That's fine, with me, too, but I thought..."

Della looked up at Mustapha. "How about a couple of orders of *karokoro* and *beignets mboga jenn?*

Mustapha nodded. "All good desires. I will add the surprise at the end, a special dessert." He collected the menus and returned to the kitchen.

Sydney turned to Della. "What happened to the *mafé?* The lamb stew? I thought that's why you wanted to come here."

Della was watching Omar and nodding in time with the beat.

Sydney knocked her knuckles on the table to get her attention. "Am I missing something?"

Della turned back. "What do you mean?"

Sydney looked over at Omar. "What's going on with you and the drummer?"

Della furrowed her brow. "Ain't nothing going on. I told you, he just needs someone to listen to him, that's all. He's probably depressed."

"I think you have a crush on him," Sydney said.

"A crush? Of course not." Della took a sip of her lemonade. "Besides, Kwamé would have a fit if he thought I was looking at another man."

As they ate their appetizers, they talked about Della's school-work, in particular, her library studies class on storytelling. She was learning about the history of storytelling, and in the coming weeks she would learn performance techniques. Sydney invited Della to practice during story time at The Talking Drum. While Della talked, Sydney glanced out the restaurant's front window and saw a rush of flashing red lights and fire trucks. Mustapha served them the surprise dessert, *thiacry*—a thin pudding made with couscous, fruit, and raisins—in a vanilla cream sauce, and then returned to the kitchen. Moments later, a man ran through the front door and dashed into the kitchen.

"I wonder what that's all about?" Della asked.

Mustapha rushed out of the kitchen and yelled something to Omar in Wolof. Then he hurried out the door following the man. Omar stopped drumming and went to each table, clearing dishes, and ringing up customers' checks.

"Something's wrong," Della said and then approached Omar. She returned a few moments later. Sydney could see the anguish on Della's face. "There's a fire up the street. It's the building where Esmé's Africa Wear is. There might be children trapped in the apartment upstairs. They can't find Esmé."

Sydney's stomach tightened at the thought of Esmé trapped in the burning building. She didn't know Esmé but had seen her setting up clothing and jewelry displays on the sidewalk in front of her shop. Sydney unzipped her camera case and pulled out the press pass Max had given her, hanging it around her neck. Then she twisted off the camera lens, switched to a zoom lens, and slid her flash onto the top of the camera.

"Watcha doing?" Della asked.

"I'm not sure yet, but *Inner City Voice* wants me to do some stories about Petite Africa. I don't know if they'll need pictures of the fire, but I'll see if I can get close enough to get something. Are you coming?"

Della shook her head vigorously. "I'm gonna sit right here and pray for them people. I don't want to see no babies burned up. That would break my heart. I don't think I could take it." She looked at her watch. "Besides, I have to get home to Jasmine before long."

Sydney put some bills on the table to cover her share of the check. Outside, she walked briskly, along with the crowd. People were rushing from their buildings, crossing the street and going down a block to Hancock Avenue, toward the sound of the sirens and blowing, grey smoke. Soon, she saw smoke clouds hovering over a three-story building with flames shooting from windows. People were lined up on both sides of the street. Beyond them were three fire trucks and a small, red van parked in front of the burning building. Nearby, a police cruiser was parked on the sidewalk with its back end in the street. Sydney squeezed her way through the crowd, holding her camera high into the air, aimed, and snapped. She made her way to the front of the crowd but could go no further because police were holding people back a safe distance from the building.

She noticed a group of people who looked like a family standing by the fire department van—a man, woman, two kids, and an older woman, a grandmother probably. They had blankets wrapped around them. She trained her camera on them. The mother was screaming that her baby was still inside in the crib. Other people stood by, watching, waiting.

Sydney continued to take pictures, moving about to get the best angles. Two firefighters climbed an aerial ladder extended on the front of the building to the third floor. Sydney took shots of the firefighters making their ascent, and then of the lead firefighter breaking the window with an axe and climbing inside. She swung around and snapped pictures of the front door with smoke billowing out, crowd shots, and then back to the family, getting close-ups of their facial expressions. She whispered a prayer for the baby. From out of the corner of her eye, she saw Uncle Mustapha push past the barriers and run up to the front of the building to the firefighter in a white helmet shouting orders to the others. Mustapha started shouting at the chief as another firefighter grabbed him by the shoulder and pulled him away.

Sydney scanned the crowd. She didn't see Esmé anywhere. She asked a man standing next to her if he knew anything. He told her that Esmé had run back inside her store to save more of her merchandise before firefighters could stop her and hadn't been seen since. That was ten minutes ago.

Suddenly, a hush fell over the crowd. She followed their eyes to the firefighter in the building handing a child through the third-floor window to the other firefighter waiting on the ladder. That firefighter came down the ladder with the child who looked to be about three or four years old. The child's head was bobbing with every step the firefighter took. Sydney couldn't tell if the child was unconscious or dead. On the sidewalk, her mother screamed. Her husband held her back as the firefighter laid the child on the front lawn and administered mouth-to-mouth resuscitation. Several people cried and looked skyward with their palms pressed together, calling for God. After several tries the child's eyes fluttered open. The mother broke away from her husband and ran to the little girl, falling to the ground on her hands and knees near her. People cheered. Sydney exhaled and quickly looked back at the front door. Paramedics were carrying a woman out on a stretcher. She was badly burned and looked as if she was covered in charcoal. They placed her on a gurney and put an oxygen mask on her face. Then they hoisted her into the back of an ambulance. Sydney didn't recognize her. The man next to her wiped at tears. "That's Esmé," he said.

As the crowd began to disperse, Sydney saw the figure of a short man wearing a bow tie and suspenders approaching—Max. "I hate stories like this," he said. "They sell papers, but they break my heart." He pointed to the camera around her neck. "Get anything good?"

She gave him a rundown of her photos. He looked back at the building. "Esmé Tavernier's been in business seven, eight years. She was just turning a profit. It doesn't look good for her." He glanced at the captain in charge wearing the white helmet and then back at Sydney. "Fire department wants to see your pictures."

"They're confiscating my pictures?"

He chuckled. "No. This is a good thing. They tell me that you were on the scene here taking photos before anybody else. You might have caught the arsonist in a crowd shot. Sometimes they return to the scene to check out their handiwork."

The fire captain waved him over. Max looked back at Sydney. "I've snagged an interview with the captain. Come on. You're part of this, too. We'll write this story together."

"What happened to you?" Malachi was lying on the living room couch with his feet propped up on the armrest. John Coltrane's "My Favorite Things" was on the stereo. She looked down at herself. She hadn't realized that she had sweat stains on her blouse and that she smelled like smoke. In rapid delivery, she told him about the fire.

He turned off the music. "I hope Esmé will be all right. It doesn't sound good, though."

Exhausted, Sydney responded, "No, it doesn't. I've never seen anybody burned like that before."

He went to her and wrapped his arms around her. "I can tell looking at you that this was a hard thing to see close up. Are you sure you're up for this freelance stuff?"

She pulled away from him and looked in his eyes. "This is what reporters do. It's the job. It's a shock, though when the story affects somebody you know. I'll be fine."

"You sure?"

"I'll be fine, Malachi. You don't have to baby me."

He sniffed her hair.

"I know. The smoke's all in my hair, in my clothes. I'm surprised you want to get close to me."

"It's not that bad." He gave her a peck on the lips.

"What happened with the money? Did it eventually add up?"

He exhaled. "No. We're still short."

"So what next?"

"I'll watch the register like a hawk from now on and keep an eye on Lawrence. I hope he doesn't have sticky fingers."

CHAPTER 25

THE AFRICAN CULTURAL CENTER on Clermont Street in Petite Africa was housed in what used to be Beth Shalom Temple, a cornerstone for the largely Jewish population that dominated the community until they fled in the late 1950s to the suburbs west of Boston. Beth Shalom sold the temple to the Africa Cultural Alliance for one dollar.

The new owners, mostly Petite Africa immigrants, lacked money for basic upkeep. The building desperately needed renovations. As the years passed, exterior bricks began to crumble and shatter on the sidewalk. Rainwater leaked through the roof. The main floor served as a shelter. The Africa Cultural Alliance invited the poor, destitute, and needy African and West Indian immigrants to temporarily move into the sanctuary. They slept on pews and washed up in the bathrooms. Volunteers prepared meals in the kitchen.

Cultural activities were set up in the basement. Classrooms lined the walls on three sides. An elevated stage was at the front. Rooms formerly used for Hebrew, Torah, and Talmud study were replaced with Ethiopian coffee ceremonies, Kenyan pottery workshops, a Ghanaian braiding salon, and Trinidadian Seventh Day Adventist services.

Today, the Senegalese community was preparing for its upcoming fundraiser for the four families and the business owners burned out last month by the fire on Hancock Avenue, one block over from Le Baobab. Esmé Tavernier was still in Bellport

General Hospital's trauma and intensive care unit with burns over sixty-five percent of her body. Mustapha was distraught over his goddaughter's condition. Omar thought the best thing he could do for his uncle would be to volunteer to rehearse the children's troupe that would perform at the fundraiser. Now, he stood at the foot of the stairs leading to the stage where the children waited for him, and counted twenty heads—Kofi and Anamara among them. He had perfect attendance.

Omar pressed a finger to his lips while the children formed a semi-circle around him on stage. They quieted down. As Omar pulled his drums out of the bags, Marie-Claude Agbo stepped out of a classroom. The building owner had purchased the property from the Africa Cultural Alliance and was supporting Uncle Mustapha in his lawsuit against the Bellport Redevelopment Authority. Omar tugged on the strings of his *djembe*, hoping she would assume he was busy and go away. Instead of leaving, she walked onto the stage, clip clopping along in her chunky platform heels. She leaned over him, her red-stained lips close to his ear. Her breasts almost fell out of her blouse.

"You're late, Mr. Bassari." Her voice had an edge to it.

Omar checked his watch. It was three-fifteen. He'd intended on arriving by three but had slept in. The fire that put Esmé in the hospital had him worried about his own safety. He hadn't slept much since it happened. "The children have barely gotten out of school," he responded.

She raised an index finger like a teacher scolding a child. "We are in America, Mr. Bassari. We don't operate on Africa time here. The parents will be here promptly at four-thirty. We need to make sure these children know their routine before they leave here today."

Marie-Claude, a Ghanaian, was starting to remind him of Natalie, the way she insulted his culture. When he first arrived in Petite Africa, Marie-Claude would show up at Fulani Sound performances in her tight dresses and wait for him to come off stage. Omar didn't want Marie-Claude. He had Natalie, who at the time was heavy with his child. Marie-Claude didn't care. She never forgave him for refusing her.

"We're dropping out of the lawsuit," she declared. "If the city wants the property, we'll sell it."

He looked up at her. She had a self-satisfied smirk on her face, most likely because she now had his attention.

"I do not understand."

She inched closer to him. "If the city wants to give us a decent amount for this place, we'll take it."

He continued tightening his drum. "My uncle fought hard to preserve Petite Africa. You are betraying him. You are betraying the property owners in the lawsuit. What about the drumming institute?"

Marie-Claude shook her head. "Your uncle will have to find somewhere else for his little school."

Omar wondered how his uncle would handle the news, if his heart would hold up. Mustapha's nerves already seemed frayed from all that was going on—the lawsuit, the fires, and Esmé. Marie-Claude's change of plans could be too much for him.

He shifted his attention to the stage. "There's no point in this conversation now. The kids are getting restless."

As Marie-Claude turned to leave the stage, Omar pounded on the head of the drum, startling her enough that she turned, stumbled, and almost fell on her fat behind. Omar laughed out loud, but she didn't hear him over the drumming. He created a bass sound, then snapped his hand back as if he was cracking a bullwhip. The boys copied him on their little *djembes*. Then, on the beat, each girl came forward from the semicircle one-by-one to rehearse her dance moves. First, they stamped their feet and thrust their arms into the air. Then they pivoted on one foot and shook their hips. Omar was puzzled. They were awkward, stiff one moment and forced the next. He expected better from them after weeks of rehearsal. He would send them home with instructions to get their mothers to practice with them.

It wasn't until he'd gotten the kids to the second number they would perform that he looked out at the rows of metal folding chairs facing him. The rows were empty except for the last one, where a white man with grey hair and a thick build sat, holding his hat in his hand. When had he come in? Omar had been so distracted by what Marie-Claude said that he hadn't noticed the stranger. What could he possibly want? If he had business about the building, he should go to Marie-Claude. Omar continued drumming, but each time he looked up, the man was still there.

Maybe he was from immigration, looking for expired visas. Well, he was a fool if he thought Omar would give him any information. He hadn't the other times he'd been approached by government men. Omar's stomach began to churn. Could he be a friend of Sam's, that black American idiot at Jake's Tavern? Was the man sent there to get revenge? He regretted that he hadn't listened to Uncle Mustapha that day, that he hadn't gone with his uncle to the lawyer's office after they left the bookstore grand opening. He concentrated on his drumming, striking the center of the drum with the ball of his hand, creating a mellow bass sound, and then hitting the edge of the drum with his fingers to create a sharp sounding tone. He rounded out the rhythm with a series of slaps on the drumhead, his fingers bouncing off the instrument repeatedly, creating a sharp, ringing sound. In his own way, he was speaking to the drum, asking its spirits to protect him from the man in the back of the room.

Omar glanced at Kofi. The child's eyes were glazed over as he slammed his palm against his little drum, his movements robotic. Omar then realized that he had been playing the same rhythm for much too long. The girls were a beat behind, executing their steps lazily. Omar changed the beat, slowed down the tempo.

He looked back at the stranger in the last row. Now a familiar figure walked in and took the chair next to him—Hideki.

What was he doing here? The Fierce Warriors had a couple of shows scheduled in Harlem after the opening of the The Talking Drum. And then, he'd assumed they'd take a break. What was Hideki doing back in town?

Omar was more curious now. He wouldn't be able to have a decent rehearsal until he found out why they were there. He gave the drum a series of quick volleys. Then he raised his hands in the air, the signal that the rhythm was done.

The children skipped off the stage—a little too happy to take a break, Omar thought— and scrambled into the room where Marie-Claude had prepared peanut butter and jelly sandwiches. Before Omar could loosen the strap that held his *djembe* around his waist, Hideki and the man had gotten up from their chairs and were approaching the stage.

"I want to apologize to you, man," Hideki said, stepping onto the stage. He stuck his hand out to Omar. Omar stared at it as if it were a snake.

"Man, I've been doing a lot of thinking," Hideki continued. "Things didn't go right last month. It's been heavy on my mind, know what I'm saying?"

"What do you want?" Omar asked, recovering from his shock.

Hideki let his hand drop to his side. "You were right. If not for you, I would never have gotten into drumming. I'll never forget what you did for me," he paused. "And what happened with Natalie, that's in the past."

"I can think of no words to say right now."

"I understand. I want to start over with a clean slate. That's why I invited Steve to come with me." Hideki gestured toward his companion.

Steve handed Omar a business card that read The Burton Talent Agency. "I run the outfit," Steve said. He had a scratchy voice, as if he'd swallowed sandpaper.

"So what business shall you have with me?" Omar asked.

"Steve's my agent," Hideki said.

Omar couldn't believe what he was hearing. It was surprising enough that Hideki wanted to see him again, but it boggled his mind that Hideki was introducing his agent. Omar pulled out a couple of folding chairs from backstage and invited the two to sit.

Steve leaned back in his chair and crossed one stubby leg over the other. "Hideki has been telling me what a talented musician you are. And from observing you here today I can see that that's true. Your career has not gotten the attention that I think it deserves. You haven't been focused. You need someone to manage you."

"Steve got us our first recording contract," Hideki added, "not long after you left Howard. He's been our manager ever since."

"Do you have a demo tape, something, maybe a reel-to-reel, a cassette of your work?" Steve asked. "I'd like to share what you've got with my associates to get a full evaluation."

Omar tried to remember what he had. Khadim had made some recordings, but if Omar asked for them his friend would figure out that he was stepping out behind his back. "I have not recorded in a while," he said finally.

Hideki looked at Steve. "Can we get studio time?"

Steve pulled out a monthly calendar from the breast pocket of his blazer and flipped through it. He made a notation with a ballpoint pen. "We should be able to get you in the studio."

"There's a studio down at the harbor, not far from here, actually," Hideki explained to Omar. "It used to be a bottle-capping factory; it's a brick building, big billboard on top of it advertising Samsonite Luggage. It's not far from Fisherman's Wharf. We're due to be back in Connecticut tomorrow for some meetings, but we can stay another day."

"Bring your drums around in the morning and I'll record you. Nine o'clock," Steve said. "If I like what I hear, if you think you'd be interested in representation, then we can talk about an agreement."

Omar thought he was in a dream. He tried not to sound over-excited. "How much do you charge for this representation?"

"I get a twenty-five percent cut."

"That much?"

Steve cocked his head to the side. "Think about it. You can be the drummer of Bellport, or sign a recording contract and make a name for yourself. Don't let a few dollars make you miss this opportunity."

"I know you're wondering why I'm doing this," Hideki said. "I'll be straight with you. I'm doing this for selfish reasons. I've been thinking about becoming a producer, grooming my own acts. I help you, and maybe one day you'll be in a position to help me. We both win."

After discussing more details on their agreement, Steve and Hideki shook hands with him and grabbed sandwiches from Marie-Claude on their way out. When rehearsal ended and the kids had left, she stood in the classroom doorway, one hand on her hip, smirking as Omar walked passed.

"You tell your uncle this is nothing personal. I have to do what's best for me."

Omar turned around. "I am not your messenger. You can walk to Le Baobab and tell him yourself."

"So you think you're going to get to the big time, don't you?" she shouted as he walked away. "I hope you break a leg."

He didn't turn around to acknowledge what she'd said. He didn't want to give her that satisfaction and let the door slam behind him.

CHAPTER 26

"I CAN'T BELIEVE my girl here might single handedly bring down an arsonist," said Della.

"I wouldn't go that far," replied Sydney. "It's going take a whole lot more than pictures to solve this case."

"Don't be modest, dear," admonished Inez in a soft voice. "Any clues they get that'll put them one step closer to finding out who's burning down Petite Africa will help a lot of us sleep easier."

The three women stood in the rear of The Talking Drum lecture hall, behind the crowd of seventy-five guests listening to an evening lecture by Amiri Baraka. A dramatist, novelist, and poet, he was reading an essay called "The Legacy of Malcolm X and the Coming of the Black Nation."

A few days after Sydney had handed over to the arson squad her photos from the fire scene on Hancock Avenue, Max had told her that her photos had indeed provided clues to the investigation. Her crowd shots had caught an onlooker in the background who seemed out of place. Max said his source told him that the onlooker was someone who normally wasn't in Petite Africa.

"Are you sure you don't want a chair?" Sydney asked Inez.

"I'm doing just fine, dear." The older woman was leaning hard on her cane. "You know, he was *LeRoi*, not Amiri, when Willie and I used to have dinners with him and his first wife in The Village. LeRoi Jones."

"Must have been some dinners," said Della, "rubbing elbows with all of them intellectuals." She smiled broadly, then stopped abruptly, covering her mouth with her hand.

"It was," replied Inez, her nose tilted slightly upward. "He and Hettie had their own press, publishing all the hip poets and writers—Allen Ginsburg, Jack Kerouac—Hettie and LeRoi were always writing or editing something or putting on a play."

"Wish we could get him here at the library," said Della.

Inez shook her head. "Oh no! LeRoi's on a tight schedule. He's much too busy."

Sydney pulled her camera from around her neck and tucked it back into her camera bag. She felt confident that Max would be pleased with her shots of Baraka. He had said he would use at least one photo with the profile he wanted her to write for *Inner City Voice*.

Sydney turned to Inez. "I want to thank you and Willie for arranging this."

"Willie did most of it," Inez acknowledged, smiling, "calling folks we used to know back then to find out how to get in touch with LeRoi."

Baraka was mesmerizing. He stood up and began pacing back and forth in front of the room as he continued his reading, the audience transfixed and nodding as he spoke.

As Omar strolled back toward The Commonwealth Arms, the anger he felt toward Hideki began to dissolve. He stopped at Le Baobab and called the number on the business card Steve had given him. Burton Talent Agency was legit. His secretary confirmed that Steve was scheduled to be in Bellport through tomorrow afternoon.

If the session went well and Steve signed him to a recording contract, there was a chance he'd get gigs all over the country and maybe overseas. He'd be able to spread the true African culture across the world with his drums, as his father had predicted. Omar decided he would put away his dreams of playing in Duke Ellington's orchestra. If things worked out, he'd do well without the famed musician.

A strong wind coming off Bellport Harbor made his *boubou* flap against his legs. He blinked to keep his eyes from tearing and held onto his kufi cap to keep it from blowing down Clermont Street. He chided himself for not wearing a light coat over his *boubou*. It was mid-November. The air was crisp.

He turned onto King Street. The Commonwealth Arms came into sight. When he got to the building, the wind forced the building's front door to slam behind him. He paused in the lobby a moment to catch his breath. The building seemed different, almost alien, as if he had stepped into a building that closely resembled his, but was in another location altogether. He felt the same way when he climbed the stairs and entered the apartment. Looking around, nothing was out of place. Then he realized what it was: warm air. The heat was on. The maintenance people must have been working on it. It was late enough in the fall that the heat was needed. It was a comfort knowing that it was working. He took off his cap and placed it on the shelf of the front closet. Now that Natalie was gone, it was almost empty, except for a couple of his jackets and a winter coat.

The refrigerator motor came on, gurgled for a while, and then let out a low hum. He opened the door and removed a quart jug of ginger juice, poured himself a glass, and then reached into a cabinet above the sink for the bottle of Jack Daniels he bought after his night at Jake's Tavern.

As he drank, he made *thiou boulletes*, a dish of seasoned fish with spices cooked in stewed tomatoes. As he put the spices away he came across the first jar of Hallima's potion in the back of the cabinet over the stove. Still angry, he imagined hurling the herbs in her face. She was selling products that were useless. He unscrewed the jar and poured most of the contents into the frying pan, thinking they would add some flavor to the dish.

After his meal he showered and then went into the drum room to survey his inventory. He knew he wanted to bring his father's *djembe* with him to the recording session, a couple of *ashkikos,* and one *sabar.* He might take a *dundun.*

Later, Omar settled into bed, feeling slightly woozy from the alcohol. Within minutes his body warmed the sheets. He felt an erection coming on. It must be the love potion, he thought, which Natalie seemed immune to. He fell into a hard sleep and awakened at the feel of the mattress giving slightly and a warm, familiar body easing close to him. It was Natalie.

"Do you think he'll give me an autograph?" Della held up a dog-eared copy of Amiri Baraka's *The Dutchman* she had gotten from a sale at the library. "Some writers don't like to sign old copies of their books."

"LeRoi's not like that, dear," Inez sniffed. "Trust me. He'd be happy to sign it."

The women abruptly stopped their conversation at the sounds of sirens. They turned their heads toward the picture window as a fire truck went roaring past, then another. "That truck is going in the direction of Petite Africa," Della said. "I hope that arsonist isn't at it again."

"That would be just awful," Inez said.

"Maybe it's a false alarm," added Sydney. "Let's hope so."

Once Baraka was finished, Lawrence refreshed the writer's glass of water, and Malachi stacked copies of his book, *Raise Race Rays Raize: Essays Since 1965,* on the table for him to autograph. Customers lined up in an orderly fashion in the parlor as Malachi rang up sales and Lawrence passed the author each book to sign.

"I think I could use that chair right about now," Inez said, grimacing.

"Sure," Sydney replied, letting Inez lead the way to the reading room. "I'll go upstairs and make us some tea."

Della held Sydney back to let Inez walk ahead of them. "You

think she's okay?" she said.

"I don't know," said Sydney. "She's getting around more slowly than usual. Her clothes are hanging off her. I wonder if she's eating."

Della shook her head. "The poor woman. She don't need to get any thinner. She's a skeleton as it is."

"She's been complaining of headaches. I wonder if that's affecting her appetite."

Malachi approached and asked Della to excuse them. He watched Della until she was out of earshot.

"Something wrong?" asked Sydney.

"We have to talk to Lawrence," he answered quietly.

"Why? What's going on?"

"He's up to something. While the reading was going on, he kept slipping out the back door."

"Maybe he just wanted to get some air."

"Five times?"

"Well, that's a lot of air. What do you think it is?"

Malachi looked around to make sure none of the customers was listening. "I've been checking around here. Some things are missing, some of the encyclopedia volumes, a few of the more expensive books."

"I knew you shouldn't have bought those."

He gave her a sharp look. "We'll talk about that later. Anyway, unfortunately, I think Lawrence has gone back to his old ways. I'm going to go out back to see if I can find anything. Lawrence will be on the register until I come back in."

"Are you sure that's a good idea, having him on the register?"

"He's usually on the register off and on for these events, so I don't want him to suspect that we're watching."

Sydney prepared tea upstairs and then carried the teapot and cups downstairs to the reading room on a tray.

"Coming here to Liberty Hill has done so much for my peace of mind," Inez told Della as Sydney walked in. "After my stroke I worried because we were living in the suburbs, way down in Southern Connecticut. It's nice having the best hospitals close by and having Sydney and Malachi right upstairs in case I need them." She placed her hand on Della's wrist, leaned close to her, and spoke in a whisper. "A couple of years ago I fell in the house. Willie was out somewhere. I was on the floor for hours."

"That's just terrible," Della said, recoiling at the image.

"If you need us just call out to us," Sydney said as she set the tray on a reading table. "We should be able to hear you through the dumbwaiter."

"The dumbwaiter?" Della asked, letting out a laugh. "Are you kidding?"

"You'd be surprised at how well sound travels through that thing," Sydney replied.

"That is truly a comfort," said Inez.

As Sydney poured the tea, Inez slowly went over to a bookshelf and pulled out a package in tissue paper. She handed it to Sydney. "I left it in here before we went down the hall to hear LeRoi."

"You didn't have to get me anything," Sydney demurred.

"Just open it, dear. Consider it an early Christmas gift."

Sydney undid the ribbon and carefully tugged at the tissue paper, revealing a leather-bound blank journal with an outline of the African continent embossed on the front. Sydney was overwhelmed. "It's beautiful." She ran her hands over the leather and stitching along the spine.

"Ain't that something," Della exclaimed. "Where'd you find it?"

"Willie and I got that on our travels to Kenya a while back before I got sick. We were both teaching there. Those were some good kids in that village, real attentive, eager to learn."

Sydney opened the journal. It was inscribed with an African proverb: *If you wish to move mountains tomorrow, you must start by lifting stones today.*

"I like that," Sydney said.

"Words to live by, dear," Inez said as she set her tea cup down. Sydney handed Della the journal for her to take a look at it.

"You can write down your thoughts in the journal," Inez added.

"Thank you so much." Sydney gave Inez a peck on the cheek. She felt fortunate that she and Malachi had rented to the Taylors. It made her uncomfortable when she thought how much she had resisted letting them have the apartment. She flipped through the lined, blank pages. "I wonder what I'll write about."

"You can start off about your adventures living in Liberty Hill," Della said.

"It *has* been an adventure," agreed Sydney. "College was an adventure, but nothing like coming here."

Inez's eyes brightened. "I'm sure you'll have plenty of stories to fill the journal." She picked her purse off the table and unzipped it.

"Here, dear." She handed Sydney a thin envelope. "This check will cover the next three months' rent."

"You don't have to pay ahead."

"I insist," Inez stated, settling back in her chair. "Willie and I will be on the road, traveling again soon."

"Is that okay with your health as it is?" Della asked.

"You're a dear to be concerned," Inez said, "but air travel is very comfortable these days and very accommodating. They'll put us in one of those motorized golf carts and zip us around the airport. Willie loves it. We get on the plane before anyone else. While we're in and out of town, we'll stay current on the rent."

"Oh, I have no concerns about that." Sydney turned to the parlor doorway to look at the line of people waiting for autographs. Malachi had rejoined Lawrence at the cash register. She wondered if he'd found any clues to the thefts. "I should get out there and help," she said.

"Go ahead, dear," Inez said. 'I'll sit here with Della."

"I'm not going anywhere," Della said, nodding at Sydney.

"When the line dies down," Inez continued, "we can take LeRoi out for a late dinner, and Della can have him sign her book."

Omar looked over at Natalie. She was naked, except for a silk scarf draped around her waist. Their ritual, before Natalie had turned her back to him so long ago, was for him to take off her undergarments—panties, hose, garters—piece by piece. Now, he tugged on the scarf, but she playfully smacked his hand away. She straddled him and held him by the shoulders, forcing him to lie back on the mattress. This was something new. He had always been the aggressor. Omar watched Natalie's eyes flare with excitement.

"Natalie, I..."

She shushed him, pressing a finger to his lips. He decided to surrender to Natalie's touch. The smell of cocoa butter on her skin filled him up and aroused him more. Her braids fell in his face, the cowrie shells tickling his cheeks. She rode him. He came within seconds, the manic force, bursting forth uncontrollably.

Natalie giggled, planting wet kisses all over his face, neck, and shoulders. She teased his ear lobes with the tip of her tongue, the most sensitive spot on his body. He sucked on her bottom lip and then plunged his tongue into her mouth all the way to the back of her throat. He was hard all over again. This time he was floating. Every touch heightened his arousal. He felt like a wild animal with no conscience or inhibitions. His heart was thumping fast. The room turned dark red. He began wailing and had to press his eyes shut and grip the mattress on both sides to hang on for the ride. He cursed himself for not being able to hold on longer. When it was over, he was embarrassed at his loss of composure.

He watched Natalie ease herself off of him. She lay on her stomach and tucked herself part way underneath him. "I've missed you," she purred. He wanted to respond but was spent. He felt as if he was free-falling in a tunnel, losing consciousness as he tumbled.

Omar shut his eyes. He dreamed that he was in Senegal. It was the morning of his twelfth birthday. Ibrahim presented him with his very own full-sized *djembe*, newly strung. The head was made out of soft goat skin, the intricately carved body made from a hollowed-out Lenge tree.

"Take care of this drum," Ibrahim stated. "It is a sacred object. Believe in its power to heal. Respect the goat that was used to make the drum head and the tree from which it came."

Omar listened to his father, spending the rest of the morning pulling on the rows of ropes, tightening and knotting them to tune the drumhead to the perfect pitch. Then he began to play. After a while, his palms were throbbing, but he kept on. People began to respond. Women in the village left their chores and gathered in the center of the *ker*, jerking their bodies to the beat, whirling around, swinging their heads back and forth. Ibrahim joined Omar, singing as he drummed about kings and chiefs and others who made contributions to the life of the village.

As his dream continued, the women in his village fired up the forge for a big feast in celebration of Omar's first day with his *djembe*. He was standing under a palaver tree with other boys his age, but a force he couldn't stop willed him to move closer and closer to the forge until the heat felt as if it would burn through his skin. He tore at his clothes and covered his face with his hands to shield himself from the heat, yet he drew closer to the flames. The women of the village stood around him talking to each other but not reacting to his distress. They didn't seem to feel the heat from the flames. The dream was so upsetting that Omar forced himself to wake up.

He opened his eyes to pitch black. The bedroom felt like a furnace. Rivulets of sweat tickled his chest. His sheets and blankets were soaked. He reached for Natalie, but her side of the bed was untouched. Half asleep, Omar struggled to make sense of what was going on. He heard the crackling sound of what he thought was a campfire. He tried to yell for help but something caught in his throat, making him cough. He heard sirens and sat up ramrod straight.

He jumped out of bed too quickly, catching his foot in the tangle of sheets and blankets and stumbled and fell, hitting his forehead on the nightstand. He slammed his ankle on a chair by the bed.

"Natalie!" he said between coughs, but got no response. His ankle throbbed. Sirens got louder. He managed to stumble into the living room.

"Omar! Omar! Get out of there, my brother."

It was Khadim shouting from the street. Omar called for Natalie again. Nothing. He heard car horns, walkie-talkies. From the kitchen window he saw fire trucks and a ladder being extended from a fire truck.

Popping sounds like gunshots and fireworks exploded in the air. Windows shattered. Now unable to put weight on his swelling ankle, Omar crawled toward the front door of his apartment. But the drumbeats wouldn't let him continue. They were coming from the drum room. He had to turn back.

On hands and knees he got to the drum room door and pushed it open. As he entered the smoky room, the drumbeat got louder. It was the spirits of the villagers who cut down the trees to carve the drums compelling him to rescue the drums, to not leave them to burn up in the fire. The drumbeat got so loud he thought it would burst his eardrums. He felt a tickling sensation on his upper lip as blood ran out of his nose. He felt his way to the drums, pushed open the window and grabbed the most important one, his father's *djembe,* which Ibrahim gave him when he left Senegal. As a firefighter yelled at him from the ladder, he tossed the drum at the small patch of grass in front of the building, hoping to save it from splitting open as it hit the ground six floors down. Omar tossed his drums one-by-one out of the window, as he did, the drumbeat quieted down. "Are you crazy, man? Get out of there!" he heard Khadim shouting.

Omar had gotten most of them out when he remembered the framed autographed pictures of him with Duke Ellington and the one with Duke Ellington and his orchestra. He wanted to save them, too. He felt along the wall and managed to touch the glass of one of the framed pictures, but it was so hot it felt as if his fingertips were being singed. Bracing himself, he grabbed one photo and then another. His palms hurt so badly he wanted to scream. He tossed the photos out the window. All at once, the door to the drum room burst open. Before he could turn to see what was happening, something heavy fell onto his back. His knees buckled and he crumpled to the floor. He reached behind him and felt the wooden blades of the ceiling fan pinning him down.

Omar tried to get up but couldn't and lay there spitting out lint and other debris. He prayed to the spirit of his ancestor, Maguette Bassari, that he wouldn't die.

Moments later he felt himself being lifted off the floor. It was a firefighter. The firefighter carried him over to the window where the other firefighter was waiting outside on the ladder against the building. As the second firefighter brought him down the ladder, Omar gulped in the bitingly cold air and tasted blood that had trickled into his mouth. The firefighter placed him on a gurney. A cone was strapped over his nose. The pain was becoming unbearable. He felt as if a hot knife was stabbing him in the arms, legs, and shoulder.

From the flashing lights of the fire trucks and police cars, Omar could make out the figure of a large-framed man holding a leash attached to a German shepherd that wouldn't stop barking and kept leaping up. Who was he? Omar knew he had seen him before but couldn't remember where. He wondered why the man wouldn't make the dog heel. Then Khadim's fuzzy face came into view. He was standing over Omar, yelling, wiping at his eyes with the backs of his hands. What was wrong with

Khadim? Couldn't he see that he was okay? He tried to ask Khadim about Natalie, but his friend apparently couldn't hear his words through the cone. Then he noticed Uncle Mustapha nearby. Uncle seemed hysterical, pacing back and forth in front of Omar, his arms flailing as he yelled at one paramedic and then the other. Omar couldn't hear what he was saying. He wished he could calm both men down.

He felt the sensation of moving through the air as he was lifted into an ambulance. Pain came and went in crashing waves, until he had the peace of feeling nothing at all.

After Amiri Baraka autographed the last book for a customer he got his coat and joined Della and Inez in the foyer. Sydney opened the door for the trio as an ambulance went speeding by. She told them she would try to join them at The Bell Tower Steakhouse a little later. Malachi ushered Lawrence into the reading room. Lawrence sat on one side of the long table and Malachi and Sydney on the other.

"What's this about?" asked Lawrence.

Malachi pulled his chair closer to the table. "I'm not sure where to start."

Lawrence looked from Malachi to Sydney. "Well, y'all got to say something."

"You kept going in and out the back door while Mr. Baraka was talking," Sydney added. She felt like an attorney in a courtroom.

Lawrence shot Sydney a look. "Yeah. I took the trash out."

"But you took the trash out at least four or five times," Malachi added.

Lawrence sat up straight and turned to Malachi. "I didn't think it was a problem. Everything was already set up. I put the tablecloth out, arranged the chairs, got the pens and a stack of books ready. I stepped outside to take a smoke. That's all."

"A smoke?" asked Malachi.

Lawrence narrowed his eyes. "I know I told you a while

back that I quit, but I started up again. It's a habit, you know. It's kind of hard to break."

Malachi leaned across the table. "I don't care about your smoking. But just be straight with me, man."

Lawrence threw up his hands. "You be straight with *me*."

Malachi went over to a large box at the end of the table. He pulled out a framed Bridgewaters painting called "The Potter," which depicted an old black man sitting at a potter's wheel while his grandson looked over his shoulder.

"What you bringing that out for?" asked Lawrence.

"We found these in the trash bin," Malachi replied, pulling out three smaller Bridgewaters paintings.

"What were they doing there?"

Malachi said nothing.

Lawrence pushed his chair back. "Aw man, you can't be accusing me of taking those. That's ridiculous. What would I do with them?"

Malachi shrugged. "They're worth a couple thousand on the street."

Lawrence stood up. "Fencing? You're crazy man. All this time I thought you were looking out for me. And you go and accuse me of something like this."

Malachi eyed Sydney, then continued. "We saw you take some books out of here."

"Huh?"

"People saw you stuffing books in your backpack, *The African and Black American Experience* during the grand opening. The three volumes," Sydney said.

Lawrence paused before answering. "The old man wanted those books."

"What?" asked Sydney.

"The old man downstairs. You rent to him and his wife? He wanted to see those. He told me you all said it was okay."

"Willie never said anything to me about borrowing those books," Malachi countered.

"Well, that's what he told me."

"What about the cash?" asked Sydney.

"What cash?" Lawrence snapped.

Malachi stood up. "There's money missing. We were short one hundred and fifty dollars the night of the grand opening. And we are still coming up short some nights. Sometimes I count the drawer and it's twenty-five dollars missing, sometimes fifty, sometimes even more. And it happens every time you're working."

"Don't try to pin that on me. I'm not a thief. I wouldn't steal from you."

"Besides Syd and me, you're the only one with access to the cash register."

Lawrence got up and brushed past Malachi as he strode toward the door. "Like I said, I don't know nothing about that. You've got a thief running around here, and it ain't me."

"Okay then, help us figure out who is stealing from us," Sydney offered.

Lawrence turned back around to face them, red-eyed and frowning. "You must take me for a damn fool. Call the cops." He went behind the front counter and snatched his backpack. He slammed the door on his way out.

They sat there for a while. "I hope we didn't make a mistake," Sydney said eventually.

Malachi sighed heavily. "I know, but I didn't see any other way around it. We had to talk to him. We couldn't just let it go."

Sydney looked toward the front door. "I just hope we did the right thing."

CHAPTER 27

OMAR HAD KNOWN pain before. When he was eight years old he was taken one day from his village outside of Bakel before sunrise and sent with other boys his age to the bush where they underwent a series of exercises and tests to build courage and learn responsibility. Omar didn't flinch when it was his turn to have the *pakka*, the knife, slice through the foreskin of his penis. He pushed back the tears that rushed to his eyes as the pain intensified. He shouted in Wolof, "*leiguii gor la*" or "I am a man!" with the other boys as his blood dripped into the dirt.

But his becoming a *njulli*, a circumcised man, did not prepare him for the pain he felt now. After the fire, he spent two weeks in the burn unit of Bellport General Hospital. He was discharged with no place to go. Bulldozers had flattened what was left of The Commonwealth Arms. So he moved into the cellar of Uncle Mustapha's restaurant. Khadim had offered him his sofa bed, but it was in the living room where his kids normally watched television. Uncle Mustapha's apartments above the restaurant were all occupied. That only left the basement.

He was growing tired of lying on his stomach but it was the only way to keep his back and shoulders from rubbing onto the mattress surface. His second-degree burns had blistered and oozed while he was in the hospital. Now the skin was stiff and crusted with scabs. Pressure or irritation could scrape the scabs off. If he lay face up the mattress would feel like a bed of nails. The nurses had given him a tube of ointment to put on his burns when he was discharged, but he felt uncomfortable having Uncle Mustapha apply it.

Omar replayed in his head what the nurses had told him. A firefighter had gotten to him just minutes before the building was engulfed. Fifteen families lost all of their belongings. The bulldozers were hired by the building owner, James Fullerton, to flatten the building.

The doctors had told him that the burns on his back and shoulders should heal within three to four months. He was more worried about the second-degree burns on his palms. They would take longer to heal—six months or more. He hoped the doctors were right. There was no way he could play the drums with damaged palms. He would be of no use to anyone if his hands didn't eventually heal well enough for him to perform.

Omar instinctively reached for his neck to touch his *gris gris*, forgetting that it wasn't there. He would miss it. It was a reminder of the last few days he spent in Bakel before leaving for America and a special time that he shared with Fama. He was sure the *gris gris* burned up with everything else in the apartment or snapped off in the chaos of his rescue.

A long scab across his shoulder blade began to itch. The sensation was so intense that he turned his attention to his surroundings to distract himself. His cot was up against the wall directly underneath the kitchen of Le Baobab. He was tired of staring at the tiny holes in the cement wall. He flipped onto his other side, keeping his back off the mattress, and faced the room. His blanket, issued by the Bellport Rescue Society, was scratchy and stiff. He kicked it off, preferring to feel a chill from the drafty cellar than the chafing of the wool.

The room was small and unventilated. To make matters more oppressive, Omar could smell burned flesh—his flesh mixed with the medicated lotion that had been applied before he left the hospital. The smell made him nauseous. There was no getting away from it. Omar stared at the narrow cellar window near the ceiling, wishing he could open it enough to get some air. Bits of sunlight shone through the dirty glass. He had enough light to see at the far end of the cellar opposite him, two rows of cots with bare mattresses and pillows. He could make out the chunky form of a woman curled into the fetal position. She rocked back and forth and sobbed into a blanket. He recognized her from Petite Africa and was pretty sure she was Senegalese. A child, who Omar guessed to be about seven or eight, sat on a cot near the woman, looking at the ceiling, swinging his legs back and forth.

Omar didn't know the time. He calculated that lunch was over because he heard no more noise coming from the kitchen overhead. It must be two-thirty or three, he thought. It wasn't time yet for the kitchen staff to start preparing for dinner.

Omar dozed a while but was jarred awake by the sound of the cellar door creaking open. He sat up. His stomach had been growling for hours. Uncle Mustapha's rubber-soled sandals descended the stairs. Uncle's face was drawn, his shoulders slumped more than usual. Omar thought back on the meals his uncle had brought him over the past several days, ground-nut stew when he first got out of the hospital, then gradually heavier meals like *thiebou djeun*, the Senegalese national dish of stewed fish, rice, and vegetables. Omar hoped his uncle wasn't spending all of his time taking care of him and neglecting his health. The aroma of black-eyed pea fritters, one of his favorite dishes, filled the cellar.

"Happy Thanksgiving," Mustapha announced weakly.

"I am thankful, Uncle," he said, wiping away tears with the back of a bandaged hand, "thankful that you take care of me."

"I come down this morning with provisions," Mustapha said. "I try to rouse you, but you are hard sleeping." He set the tray on a small table at the foot of the bed and handed Omar a glass of *bissap* juice. Omar was parched. He carefully took the glass between bandaged hands and pressed it to his lips.

"I help you." Mustapha reached for the glass.

Omar shook his head. "I can do it. I shall not want to be treated like a child." He drank the juice without stopping.

Mustapha went upstairs and brought back a refilled glass. Omar drank it halfway down. Then Mustapha placed the food tray on Omar's lap.

"Who is she?" Omar asked, referring to the woman across the room.

Mustapha sat down on the cot across from Omar. "She is living in building on same block as you," he whispered loudly. "The fire brigade is working on your building, and hers catches fire. Her husband burn up in there. He does not have a chance." He glanced over his shoulder. "That is her son. I think he is having shock. After they get out of hospital they have no place to go, so they staying here. I have five cots here from Bellport Rescue Society. When more people are discharged, they give me more."

"Do they know what happened?"

"A building with no people go up first, then yours. Everyone else run out. You were only one left in the building they rescue. Then three more fires. Very bad. Some say it is so windy, after your building is on fire, the wind is blowing the fire to every building on the block. I think something is suspect. A rotten fish pollutes the whole kitchen."

"You think it was the arsonist?"

"Your landlord, Fullerton, owns one of the other buildings that burned. Fullerton wants to get insurance money before the city takes the properties. I am sure of it."

Omar took a bite of his fritter while pondering what his uncle was telling him. "I thought he wanted to make things better for us. Instead, you say, he kills people to get the insurance money?"

Uncle Mustapha looked at the floor. "My Esmé pass away soon because of them. The hospital has her on machine until her family gets here from Dakar."

Omar felt a deep pang of sadness at the news about Esmé.

He thought about her family coming to America to bury her and for Uncle to have to say goodbye to his goddaughter.

He put his half-eaten fritter back on the plate. "When shall your renters upstairs be leaving town? I can move there soon? You will need this cot for others."

Mustapha shook his head. "They are booked until after Christmas. But you are welcome to stay here in the cellar as long as you are needing to."

The woman began wailing. It grew louder and echoed off the cement walls. Her son edged closer to hug her, but she pushed him away.

"She is grieving her husband," Mustapha said. "Nothing comfort her, not even her son. She cry until she exhausts."

"Fullerton is a bastard," Omar said.

Eventually, the woman's sobs subsided. She muffled her whimpers in her blanket.

"She will eat nothing?" Omar asked.

Mustapha shook his head. "She is here four days. I think that in time she eats. Maybe some of the other victims keep her company when they getting here. They take her mind off her troubles when..."

Mustapha stopped mid-sentence and craned his neck at the window even though there didn't appear to be anything visible through the caked dirt. Omar waited for him to finish his thought, but he didn't. He got Uncle's attention back by tossing his napkin on top of his food. Then Mustapha looked at his shirt pocket and pulled out an envelope. Omar recognized the handwriting. It was Ndeye's, the woman in his village who transcribes letters for his mother.

"Fama send me this," Mustapha scolded. "She say she never hear from you for not seven months."

Omar didn't want to tell his mother the news about Natalie abandoning him and the lack of progress with his drumming career. She would tell Ibrahim. His father would be disappointed, so he'd stopped writing.

"You did not write to her, did you?" Omar asked. "You did not tell her about the fire?"

Mustapha's eyebrows bunched into a knot. "Of course I do not tell her these things. That is up to you."

"I do not know what to say to her."

Mustapha glanced at his bandages. "You cannot write right now. Tell me what to say, and I write down for you when you are ready."

Mustapha put the tray back on the table at the end of the bed. "I have some news for you, and it is not good," he said, his voice breaking.

Omar sat up.

"The court dismiss our lawsuit. They say we do not have a case, that city give us plenty options where to live. We cannot stand in the way of eminent domain."

"I'm sorry."

Mustapha blinked back tears. "There is nothing I can do. Petite Africa will be no more. Condemnation beginning soon."

"But they will give you something for your property?"

"They settle with me, yes."

They sat in silence for a while.

"I must find a place to live," Omar said. "When do you have to leave?"

"They give me a few weeks. I leave early next year."

Mustapha looked around the room. "This place is my life. I sleep here, I eat here, I run restaurant here, I live with my wife, your Aunt Samir, here. We raise Ansa here. Now I have nothing."

After Mustapha left, Omar lay back down on his side. Since the fire, he had a hard time staying awake more than a couple of hours at a time. The room was getting cooler. He carefully pulled the blanket back over him so it wouldn't rub up against his scabs. He dozed off thinking about how defeated Uncle Mustapha seemed.

He was roused later by intense itching from a scab just above the temple near his hairline. His temple ached for days while he was in the hospital; apparently he had bumped up against something during the fire. He tried to rub it with his bandages.

"That ain't a good idea. You might get an infection."

He opened his eyes. It was Della.

"Your uncle said it was okay for me to come down. I hope I'm not disturbing you." Her eyes swept him and then focused on the floor. She seemed uncomfortable. He figured it was because of his injuries.

Omar pulled himself up to a sitting position.

"I came to the hospital to see you," she continued, "but they said only immediate family members were allowed."

"Why? Why did you come see me?" Omar cleared his throat. "I am almost a stranger to you."

"Strangers need friends, don't they?"

Omar held up his bandaged hands.

"They will heal," she reassured him.

"I hope that you are right."

"It's good to see you. When I heard that you were in that fire..." she shook her head, her eyes watering. "I was thinking the worst." Her attention shifted to the tube of ointment. "What is this for?"

He explained.

"Are you using it?"

He shifted around to get more comfortable. "I have been too tired to be bothered."

"Can I sit?"

Omar shifted over to give Della room to sit beside him.

She scooted up close to him. He couldn't help smiling.

"You have to use the ointment. If you don't, you won't heal right." She unscrewed the cap. "Where did the doctor say you should put it?"

"My back, my hands."

"Can I help you?"

He nodded.

Della unbuttoned his nightshirt and let it drop around his waist. She dabbed the ointment on her fingertips and then moved behind him to apply it to his back. He braced himself to feel the sting, but the ointment was soothing, her hands soft and gentle.

"Have you been doing your exercises?" she asked.

Omar shrugged.

"Then you will do them now."

Della undid Omar's bandages and gently applied lotion to his hands. She took hold of his wrists and made Omar bend his fingers back and forth in an exaggerated motion. Omar wanted to cry out in pain, but he thought it would look unmanly in front of Della. "The nurses told me to do this several times a day so my skin shall not get tight," he said.

"Right. You don't want to get scar tissue."

"I am surprised you do not run away seeing me like this."

Della chuckled. "I used to be a candy striper."

"What is a candy stripper?"

"A candy *striper*, silly."

They both laughed.

"I used to volunteer at a hospital back when I lived in Arkansas," she continued. "I volunteered to cheer up the patients. Sometimes the nurses let me come in the rooms when they were tending patients who got burned. They bent the rules for me, letting me in like that. I saw a lot."

She helped him back into his shirt, and carefully wrapped the bandages back around his hands.

He began to feel sleepy but wanted to stay awake. He was enjoying Della's visit and didn't want her to leave.

She reached for the glass of remaining *bissap* juice and held it to his mouth. As he drank, some dribbled down the corner of his mouth. She wiped it gently with a napkin, bringing her face close to his. He leaned forward, turned his head slightly and gave her a quick peck on the lips. She pulled back, looking surprised, and then smiled. Their eyes locked. She leaned forward and kissed him full on the mouth. Then she gave him wet kisses on his cheeks and his nose before returning to his mouth. Their tongues met and did a gentle tango.

"I need to go," she said quietly. "I know you need your rest."

He lay back down, his eyes fluttering shut as he watched her climb the stairs. Later, he opened his eyes to see Khadim standing over him. Omar sat up slowly. "*As salaamaalekum!* How long have you been here?"

"*Maalekum salaam!* Happy Thanksgiving, my brother! Long enough to hear you snoring like a warthog," Khadim laughed. "I hope I didn't disturb you. I'm just glad to hear you breathing. When they pulled you out of that building I thought you were dead. I thought you were crazy when I saw you throwing your drums out the window. But then I understood. You heard the spirits?"

"Yes. There was no mistake. They told me I had to save the drums."

"Of course. You had no choice."

"But did you catch them?"

Khadim sat down hard on the cot across from Omar. "I did what I could, but some of them exploded. They were like mangoes smashing on the sidewalk. The ones I was able to save I took to my home. When you are better we can take a trip to New York to see Baladugu," he said, referring to the well-known drum importer. "You can buy replacements."

"Which ones did you save?" Omar asked. "The *djembe* from Papa? The *dunduns*?"

Khadim breathed out heavily. "I do not know, my brother, a couple of *djembes*, one or two *dunduns*, a couple of *tamas*. The *tamas* bounced off the sidewalk and were still in one piece, I guess because they are small."

Omar told him about the meeting he was supposed to have with Steve.

Khadim said nothing for a moment. "So you were booking studio time behind my back?"

"I have no words to say about this."

Khadim shook his head. "We will talk about that later."

Omar looked over at the woman who had been crying earlier to see if Khadim's loud voice was disturbing her. She had stopped rocking and was looking in their direction. Maybe he and Khadim were a distraction for her.

"I tried to find Natalie. I called out to her. She did not respond."

Khadim grimaced. "Natalie? Are you crazy, man? She left months ago. You know this."

"I know. But she came back." He described their lovemaking.

Khadim chortled. "You do the *boom boom* with your imagination, my brother. I think the fire roasted your brain."

Omar thought this over for a while, and knew it was likely true. After all the time he had waited for Natalie to share their bed again, he wished the dream had not happened. The pleasure it had given him was so cruel. He vowed to push Natalie out of his mind.

Khadim picked up the tube of cream and read the label. "Is it time for your treatment?"

Omar explained that Della had applied it already.

Khadim let out a hearty laugh. "Your American girlfriend came here and helped you out."

"She is not my girlfriend. She is a friend."

"An American woman would not come here for friendship. She comes here for the *boom boom*. That is all."

"Your mind is on one thing, my friend. Besides, she does not live alone."

Khadim moved to the edge of the cot "Who is it?"

Omar told him about Kwamé.

Khadim's eyes got wide. "She is shacking up with the big man that everybody knows, the man who smiles for the TV news cameras?"

Omar felt that he had told Khadim too much.

"If he finds out, you will have to fight for your woman. You must heal quick to get ready," Khadim declared, pointing at Omar's bandaged hands.

"I think it would be good for me to get some fresh air," Omar said finally.

"Why do you say this?"

"Walk around, get some air, maybe I can stop thinking about these." He held up his bandaged hands. "But Uncle says that I am not ready. I need to rest."

Khadim glanced at the cellar door. "Mustapha is treating you like his big baby. We can leave for a few minutes, walk up the block, and get back before he brings down dinner. He will not even notice."

A walk would be good. Omar recalled how the nurses encouraged him to work on building his strength. After he got into the coat that had been donated to him, Khadim supported him with one arm and pushed open the bulkhead with the other. Bright sunshine blinded Omar momentarily. He gasped at first as he inhaled the cold air that rushed into his lungs. Gradually, he got used to it. His legs wobbled at first, but grew stronger as they walked. They were on Garfield Avenue, blocks away from Le Baobab, but still a good distance from his apartment building.

"We will go back to Mustapha's," Khadim said. "There is nothing to see. It is the same everywhere."

Khadim turned back. Omar ignored his friend and pushed forward in the direction of The Commonwealth Arms. He was stunned by what he saw. Façades of buildings stood with missing walls and windows. He walked further and watched neighbors and business owners crawling onto piles of bricks covered in ice, a few weeks later still sifting through the debris, attempting to find something to salvage.

Khadim caught up to him, but Omar walked ahead to the corner of Pleasant and Garfield avenues. The fire and demolition had erased every trace of The Commonwealth Arms except for the crumbling front steps and some furnishings.

"I told you, there is nothing here," Khadim shouted, walking away.

"You do not know that," Omar shouted back. He walked behind the asphalt steps careful not to lose his footing. A refrigerator with the door missing lay on its side. He was pretty sure it was from his and Natalie's apartment. A seagull perched on its frame fluttered away. He stepped around the refrigerator and walked several yards until he got to a pile of bricks. He thought maybe he'd find some items from home, maybe the box of letters he kept from his mother, Fama, but there was nothing to salvage.

"Come on, my brother. We need to get out of here," Khadim said, slipping on icy piles of bricks to reach Omar.

"Someone needs to pay for this," Omar said. "They had no business destroying our neighborhood, our homes."

Omar picked up a brick, flung it as far as he could, and felt the skin tightening along his burned back. He felt weak. He collapsed in the rubble and began to weep.

CHAPTER 28

LYING BACK in the recliner while watching a love scene on her favorite soap opera, *Somerset,* Della thought of the one regret she had about her visit to Omar last week—the kiss. She enjoyed it and kept reliving it in her mind, but she knew it was wrong. She had no business kissing another man. She was still Kwamé's woman, even if her feelings for him were fading. He was closer to a frog than a prince, but he was good to Jasmine.

Della knew that Sydney sensed that Della was attracted to Omar. She was right. Omar was a sweet, sensitive man not to mention handsome and well built with those muscular biceps that she longed to run her hands up and down. Since the day at Le Baobab when he sent the drink to her table, she'd fantasized about him. Her fantasies intensified with every conversation. Of course nothing would come of their chit chat. Her life was with Kwamé.

The front door slammed shut. Kwamé whistled as he tossed his keys on the hallway table. It was unusual for him to be home in the middle of the afternoon, especially in light of his boastful talk that Christmas sales would make up for the lack of much business all year. Kwamé walked into the living room with a beer. Odd. He never drank beer this early in the afternoon.

"Who's running the shop?" she asked.

"Nobody." He sat down on the couch. "Didn't open yet."

She hit the lever on the recliner and sat upright. She thought it would be better to have both feet planted on the floor for the coming conversation. "What happened?" she asked, trying to sound casual. "You hit the number?"

He popped open the beer and took a long swig and then plopped the can on the coffee table. She wished he'd use a coaster.

"How'd you like to move to D.C.?" he asked.

She sat for a moment trying to process the question. She wondered if it was a joke. "Now, why would I want to do that?"

He grinned, looking pleased with himself. "I've got me a job interview lined up."

She aimed the remote at the TV and clicked it off. "You never mentioned wanting to go to D.C."

He cocked his head to the side. "Hadn't thought about it until recently. But you get to know the right people, and opportunities open up."

She started to say something, but he held up a finger to stop her. "And not the way you're thinking neither. This ain't about no woman." He lit a Viceroy, took a long puff, and blew the smoke out of the side of his mouth. "The mayor's been working on this for a while. He's the one who lined this up. I paid my dues with all I've done to build up Liberty Hill, to get people in here, businesses in here."

She tossed the remote on the couch. "You're dreaming. It's just an interview. You might not even get the job."

"Oh, I'll *get* it. The mayor says the interview is just a formality."

"And *if* you get it, what would this job he got for you entail?"

"Housing."

"Can you be more specific?"

"Department of Housing and Urban Development—I'm being offered a staff position."

"Doing what?"

He shrugged. "I'll be an assistant to one of the directors. It pays eight thousand dollars to start. I can work my way up to more."

"How come this never came up before?"

He set the cigarette down in an ashtray. "How could it? I haven't seen you to tell you what's been going on. Seems like you're always out with Miss Sydney and Inez or sashaying out to a study group or in some class."

Some class. Kwamé's insensitivity angered Della, but she let it pass. Why did he continue to trivialize what she was doing? "Our life is right here in Bellport. It wouldn't make no sense to move. My job is going well. I'm a property owner. Tenants pay rent on time. And I'm working on my degree. I'm staying put."

He stood up. "Exactly. *Your* job is going fine. *Your* life is going well. *Your* tenants are paying on time. Can't you think of nobody besides yourself?"

"And Jasmine, she hasn't been acting up near what she used to. She's doing better in school now. The teachers haven't called me in weeks. You would want me to pull her out and take her to a place where she don't know nobody? For some political job that could be gone as soon as a new administration comes in?"

He took another sip of beer and put the can back on the table, creating another wet ring. "Here I thought you would support me. But I shouldn't be surprised. It's all about Della."

She stood up and moved just inches from his face. "I *have* been supporting you. I'm the one who bought this building that you live in. I'm the one who doesn't charge you rent to run that half-assed record shop that don't make no money. I'm the one who lets you borrow money to do those renovations on rundown shacks you can't seem to make a profit on when you try to sell them. Since when have I not been supportive?"

"I'll tell you this," he said, brushing past her on his way back to the kitchen. "As soon as I get that job, I'm going to Washington. You and Jasmine can stay up here, or you can come with me. It's up to you."

Della watched him walk away. Who was he to treat her like this, like she was some kind of rag doll he could drag around anyway he wanted? What made him think that he could lord it over her and make decisions that could hurt both her and Jasmine? For all the time she had known Kwamé, she had deferred to him. He was worldly, city bred. She was country, backwoods Arkansas. But Kwamé was a selfish, skirt-chasing jackass who cared for one person—Kwamé. She walked into the kitchen. He was bent over, reaching into the refrigerator to grab another beer. She measured him with her eyes, angry enough to kick him in his flat behind. He was nothing but a pathetic, weak man, hiding behind all of his hip manner and talk.

She grabbed him by the arm and spun him around.

"Woman, what you think you're doing?" he yelled.

"You can do what you want. Go on down there to Washington. Do whatever you want. I have to look out for myself and Jasmine."

She saw a flicker of his unguarded self. His eyes got big, almost teary, like those of a child in a panic because he'd become separated from his parents at the carnival. But quickly he regained his composure, putting on his self-assured game face and pulling out another beer. "You say that now, but you don't mean it."

"Oh? Try me. I'll even help you pack."

He stared at her, his eyes narrowing into slits. "You're talking crazy." He took his beer and left the room.

Della didn't really care if he left without her. She'd had it. She was sick and tired of relationships that weren't worth her time, like her marriage to Tucker.

She went back into the living room. Kwamé was now sitting in the recliner, *her* recliner, staring into the television screen with the remote in his hand. He didn't acknowledge that she'd come back in the room. She grabbed her car keys and left. She needed to get some air.

CHAPTER 29

IT WAS HARD for Sydney to accept that the Petite Africa she had come to know—a vibrant place full of life—was a neighborhood on its death bed. Groundbreaking for the Harborview Project was scheduled for the beginning of April. It was three months away. She felt a deep sadness as she processed prints in her darkroom. The images were searing. Seeing the devastation of a dying neighborhood isolated in an eight-by-ten photograph pained her in a way it hadn't on the scene.

Sydney had pitched an idea to Max. She would spend some time in Petite Africa taking pictures for a photo spread and article about the after-effects of the fire that destroyed The Commonwealth Arms and the other buildings. It was a tough assignment. Before the fire, Sydney had spent time getting to know the shopkeepers, mothers, and children in the neighborhood, winning their trust. They seemed to appreciate that she was documenting their lives, telling their stories. Sometimes they came from behind their street carts and out of their stores to give her a hug and get her to autograph copies of *Inner City Voice*. One of Max's carriers began leaving free copies of the newspaper at Petite Africa businesses.

Out of all of the rolls she developed, she was most disturbed by the photo of an old woman standing knee-deep in the crumbled and charred remains of her home. Her face was expressionless. When Sydney was there taking the pictures, the woman hadn't seemed to notice her. Sydney had watched the woman dig her hand into the rubble and pull out the head of a doll. The woman held up her treasure and her lined face broke into a smile. She took close-ups of the woman with the doll and kept the rubble in the background out of focus, adding texture to the frames. Sydney wondered how the woman could find joy enough to smile when she had lost everything. Sydney hung the picture to dry along with the others.

She heard Malachi coming up the stairs. He waited until she completed developing her photos before coming into the darkroom.

"We've got a problem downstairs," he said, turning to the stairway. "Please, come with me."

When they got downstairs, Malachi went behind the front counter, opened the cash register drawer, and pulled out two handfuls of cash and checks. Next to the cash register with its motor humming was the adding machine. "I keep coming up two hundred dollars short, and I don't know why," he said.

"Maybe you should go through it again, make sure."

"I have. Twice."

"Maybe a fresh pair of eyes would be helpful."

"Sure," Malachi threw up his hands. "Why not?"

They switched places. Malachi paced the floor as Sydney painstakingly punched numbers into the adding machine and checked off figures.

"I come up with a different amount," Sydney said finally. "By my count, you are actually two hundred and sixty short. That's a lot of money. This can't be bad bookkeeping There's got to be something more."

Malachi and Sydney switched places again, and Malachi put the money and receipts back in the drawer. He put on his glasses. "Let's check the safe."

She followed him into the locked storage room where they had the safe hidden under the industrial-sized sink. "You did make the night deposit, didn't you?" she asked.

His shoulders slumped. "You know I can't get to the bank

every night." He crouched down, his hand trembling as he worked the combination.

The dial on the safe clicked as Malachi turned it to the last number. He turned the crank and pulled open the door. Sydney was relieved to see that the burlap money bag was there, bulging. "At least we can relax about this," he gave a sigh of relief and handed her the bag.

But it seemed lighter in weight than she was used to. She rationalized that it must have less money in it than it had other times she'd handled it. She unzipped it and upturned its contents. She was stunned. Yellow strips of construction paper fell to the counter.

"What the hell is that?" Malachi asked, staggering to his feet.

"Who would do this?" Sydney demanded.

"I don't know."

When they met eyes, Sydney was certain they were both thinking the same thing. Malachi leaned against the sink. "Maybe Lawrence was telling the truth."

"Poor Lawrence."

"Now I wonder about those paintings we thought he took."

They said nothing for a while.

"But what about the books that he took?" Sydney mused. "The ones I saw him take at the grand opening. Lawrence claimed that Willie wanted to see them, and later, when I asked Willie, he told me he didn't know anything about them."

Malachi ran his hand over his thick Afro. "All I know is that I should have believed Lawrence until I had absolute proof that he was lying. Here I was trying to mentor him. Instead I kicked him out, accused him of a crime he probably didn't commit. I blamed Lawrence when the real crook was probably somebody else."

They stood there looking at the slips of yellow paper. Then Malachi said, "It has to be a professional, someone who could figure out the combination to the safe."

"We've had a lot of customers passing through."

"You think somebody's been casing the place?"

Sydney thought for a few moments. "Who knows?"

Officer Wilson Stribling flipped to a fresh page on a small white notepad as he looked over the spot in the hallway where a Ronald Bridgewaters painting had been. He had already jotted down a list of the cash, books, and personal effects that were missing. "This could be an inside job," he said.

"How can you tell?" asked Malachi.

"No signs of anyone breaking in here. It's as if the person who robbed you knew exactly what he wanted, took those items, and left."

Malachi led the way down the hall to the storage room where the safe was kept. "I'll have the door of the safe dusted and let you know if we come up with anything," Stribling stated. "We'll check out the alarm system, too."

"That's it?" Sydney asked.

The officer grinned. "Mrs. Stallworth, you've had too many people in this place to dust anywhere else and come up with anything we could use."

"How could somebody get into the safe?" Malachi asked. "Syd and I are the only ones with the combination."

"And my parents," added Sydney. "But, of course they wouldn't be suspects."

"It could be someone who is here often enough to get to know the building, where things are," the officer said. He examined the burlap money bag. "How come you didn't call us the first time, when the drawer was short?"

"I thought I'd added things up wrong. Then we thought it was one of our employees," Malachi explained. He continued that he and Sydney thought that letting Lawrence quit had taken care of the problem.

Stribling flipped to a new page, "Who's in here on a regular basis?"

"Kwamé," Malachi replied.

The officer looked up from his notepad. "Kwamé Rodriguez?"

"Yes," Malachi continued. "He's a buddy of mine. I trust him."

The officer jotted something down on the pad.

"Kwamé's wife. I trust her," Sydney said.

"What about those tenants in the basement?" asked Stribling.

"The Taylors?" Sydney laughed. "They're an elderly couple. Mrs. Taylor can barely get around. She's frail. They take little walks around the neighborhood, but other than that I don't even know that they're there. I don't think there's any reason to be concerned about them."

Stribling maintained a blank expression. "Do they have access to the main level of the house?"

"No," answered Malachi. "They can't enter the main floor from the basement. It's a separate apartment. We keep the door to the basement locked on our side. The only way they could come in is if they went outside from the basement and came through the front door."

"When the store is closed for the evening we put the alarm on," added Sydney. "So we'd hear them if they tried to come in. And the alarm has a motion detector on it."

Officer Stribling led the way up the hall. "We have to at least talk to them, see if they've noticed anything suspicious."

"But they wouldn't know anything," Sydney said. "They've been in and out of town for the past several weeks."

"Who has keys?" Stribling asked.

Malachi went upstairs to get the spare set. When he came back, he undid the bolt lock leading to the basement.

"Is it okay that we're doing this?" asked Sydney as the three of them walked down the steps.

"Syd, we're the landlords." Malachi responded sharply. "We have the right to go in." He got no response when he knocked on the Taylors' door.

"Try it again," the officer said.

After more knocking, Malachi put the key in the lock. When

the door swung open Sydney was stunned. The living room was empty except for Inez's silver tea service on the serving cart. All the furnishings were gone, the kitchen table, chairs, the living room furniture.

"Any idea what's going on here?" asked the officer.

"This is strange," Malachi said, his eyes sweeping the living room.

"They never said they were moving out," Sydney wondered. "Why would they do this to us?"

"Why? They're low-life thieves. That's why," Malachi replied.

Sydney walked into the kitchen where she found an empty box of Earl Grey tea bags. The album cover of Handel's *Water Music* was lying on a front stove burner.

Stribling pushed aside the translucent beads in the living room doorway and went down the hall. "I found something in here," he called out a few minutes later from the bedroom. The room was empty except for an open suitcase.

Sydney knelt down to examine the contents: a crystal vase and picture frames she and Malachi had been given as wedding presents, a charm bracelet, and miniature ceramic knick knacks from her grandmother and the leather journal Inez had given her. She saw something sticking out of the flap of the suitcase. It was her savings bank passbook. Sydney's eyes began to ache in their sockets as she flipped through the passbook. Her name was forged for several withdrawals. The Taylors had taken all but one dollar from the account, removing several thousand that Sydney had put away over the years. She felt dizzy as she looked up at the officer. "How did they get onto the third floor?" she wondered.

"They could be professional criminals," he responded.

"But she had a stroke," Sydney felt her voice go up an octave but couldn't stop it.

"I don't know about that." The officer crossed the room and reached behind the closet door. He held up Inez's silver-handled cane.

"You mean all this time she was faking?" asked Sydney. She began to feel like a fool for trusting the woman.

They followed Officer Stribling into the kitchen. "I think I know how your tenants did this," he said. He slid open the compartment on the dumbwaiter. "It's the perfect size."

"For what?" asked Malachi.

"To fit a little old lady and send her upstairs," Officer Stribling responded. "She had her own elevator service. She could get to any floor and take only a few steps out to grab small paintings and whatever else she wanted. She didn't weigh that much, so that's how she got around setting off the motion detector. She went up and down in the dumbwaiter while her husband, assuming he is her husband, operated the pulley system from here in the basement."

The dumbwaiter made a screeching sound as the officer tugged on the rope. "Every so often I heard a sound like that," Sydney said. "Sometimes it was in the middle of the night. I could never figure out where it was coming from."

"They were probably practicing, doing test runs," Malachi said.

"You think they were lying about being a married couple, too?" Sydney asked.

"I wouldn't trust a word that came from their mouths," answered Stribling. "They're criminals and criminals lie."

Sydney felt dizzy. She sucked in deep breaths to keep the room from spinning. She couldn't believe what they were seeing. All this time, they had been manipulated by the Taylors. Every little thing the Taylors had done for them, for their shop, had been a smokescreen, a way to gain their absolute trust so they could be robbed right under their own noses.

"Every time Inez and Willie were on the merchandise floor they must've been casing the place," reasoned Malachi, "figuring out how to beat the system."

"But how did they get things out of here?" asked Sydney. "They didn't have a car."

The officer flipped back a few pages on his notepad. "You mentioned that they liked to take walks around the neighborhood. Did you ever follow them?"

"Why would we?" she asked.

"We were always busy with customers when they went out," Malachi explained. He paused for a moment. "They must have planned that."

The officer nodded. "They were probably walking around the block when you were too busy to notice. I bet one of their partners was waiting in a car to haul away the goods. Did the lady carry a pocketbook?"

"Yes," replied Sydney. "A very large one, like a small suitcase. I wondered why she needed one so big."

She thought about the check Inez had given her for the three months' rent. Only days ago, the bank told her it had bounced. Sydney had planned to talk to Inez about it, but the couple had been out of town so much that she wasn't able to schedule time to see them. She then realized what was going on. The Taylors had lived off of them rent free for months.

A disturbing yowl came from the bathroom. Sydney followed Stribling and stood back as he opened the door. A powerful odor hit them like a punch. A small, furry, orange ball uncoiled in the bathtub. It was Pumpkin. The quilt Sydney had let Inez borrow was on the floor, wedged between the tub and the toilet, urine-stained, covered in kitten poop, and clawed into shreds. Sydney was horrified.

The officer excused himself and barked something into his walkie-talkie as he went outside. Pumpkin hopped out of the tub and ran down the hall. Malachi and Sydney followed her into the living room where she ran behind the tea service.

"I'll call the bank, although I don't know how much good it will do," Sydney said, flipping through her passbook.

"I'm so sorry, baby," Malachi apologized, pulling Sydney into his arms. "I don't know what to say, but we'll get to the bottom of this."

Sydney buried her face into Malachi's chest. "I can't believe this. Who knows what else they took."

She felt Malachi become tense.

"You need to leave. Get out now, or I'll have the officer take you out," he shouted over her shoulder. She turned around. Kwamé was standing in the doorway.

"What you talking about, man? I just thought I'd check on you two," Kwamé said. "I see Strib out there. What's happening?" he asked, looking around. "Where's Inez and Willie? They move out?"

Malachi's eyes shone like burning embers. He brushed past Sydney and charged toward Kwamé. "You are the one who got me to rent to those people! They've been all through our home. They stole our money, our paintings, and lots of other stuff, but maybe you know that already."

Kwamé slowly backed up with both palms in the air. "Get off my back, man," he shouted. "I didn't have nothing to do with this."

"We're out of a lot of money because of them," Malachi said.

"It's not my problem."

"Not your problem? You need to fix this."

"Fix what?" Kwamé asked. "You're the one who rented to them. You should have checked them out."

Malachi snatched the cane leaning against the wall and held it like a baseball bat. Then he turned to rush Kwamé. "I'll check you out, motherfucker!"

He charged at Kwamé, who stepped back and held his arms up to shield himself from the blow.

Sydney screamed. Stribling hurried back into the apartment. Sydney had never seen Malachi so enraged. As Malachi reared back with the cane to swing, Stribling grabbed it from behind, taking it out of Malachi's hand. Malachi charged into Kwamé with his bare hands. Both men crashed to the floor in a tangle of swinging fists.

Sydney's heart pounded. She heard fabric rip and buttons pop off and land in the shag carpeting. Stribling waded in between the men, pulling them apart.

Kwamé got off the floor and made his way toward the door leading outside.

"Get out of here," Malachi growled at Kwamé. "Get out of my face. Those people, your friends, may have ruined us. You brought them to us and you swore they were good people."

Kwamé turned back and said, "Look, man. I didn't know they were thieves and I didn't know they would rip you off." He slammed the door as he left.

Malachi turned back to face Sydney and Officer Stribling. "All this time I thought Kwamé was doing us a favor, introducing us to good people. I thought he had our backs," he said. "I'll never make that mistake again."

"We'll do what we can to find the Taylors," Stribling stated. "I'm moving over to the detective division. If they don't turn up soon, maybe I'll get assigned the case. If these people have done this in other places, and my hunch is that they have, other jurisdictions will need to get involved."

CHAPTER 30

THE WEEK BEFORE her wedding, Sydney had obsessed about the weather. Heavy rain had been forecast for all week through Friday—the night before the ceremony—and a mixture of rain and clouds on her wedding day. However, the tropical storm blew out to sea, causing heavy rain in the Boston area and North Shore that October weekend, sparing western Massachusetts. The sky was bright and clear over Old Prescott that morning.

From the second floor window in the bridal suite of Hamilton Estate Mansion, Sydney watched cars pull into the long, circular drive as guests arrived. With half an hour to go before her big moment, she relished her time alone. Throughout the morning the makeup artist had insisted on playing Sly and the Family Stone over and over on the 8-track tape player while she worked on the bridal party. Sydney had heard enough "Hot Fun in the Summertime" to last her until the next autumn. She would have preferred Handel's *Water Music*.

Sydney smiled at her reflection in the full-length mirror. Her gown was simple and understated, sleeveless with a scoop neck and lace sash at the waist, crinoline underneath the skirt to give it volume—traditional white. She didn't want to draw any more attention to herself than was necessary.

Her mother tapped on the door. Sydney assumed Bernadine wanted to give her some last-minute motherly advice before her walk down the aisle, but Bernadine had something else in mind. "I don't want to upset you," Bernadine said, gently taking Sydney's hands, "I just want to make sure you really want to do this."

Sydney wished she hadn't let Bernadine in. "Mother, haven't we been over this fifty times?"

"Weddings have been stopped before, Syd."

Sydney yanked her hands away and returned to the full-length mirror. She adjusted the strap on her dress to hide a wayward bra strap. She was growing weary of what had become a continuous loop of conversation. "Mother, I've told you I want to do this. I want to marry Malachi. What's more, I'm *going* to marry Malachi."

"I know, I know, but once you walk down that aisle, there's no turning back. I wouldn't feel right if I didn't discuss this with you one more time, just to make sure. You're making one of the biggest decisions of your life today. If you hold off, you can finish law school, get with a firm, and *then* consider getting married to someone."

"*Someone?*"

"Yes. 'Someone.' There are a lot of choices out there. Who did you date? There was that boy in high school."

"Jeff."

"Yes. Jeff. And then Malachi. You really haven't given yourself a chance."

"Mother, you used to call Malachi 'a good catch.' Remember? You said you liked his ambition. You said it didn't matter that I hadn't dated much."

"But that was before he walked away from the university. Who gets a PhD and then decides to quit academia when things get difficult? He could have reapplied for tenure, or gone to another university. I'm seeing red flags, Syd."

"What it tells me is that he's being pragmatic and investing in our future," Sydney countered.

Bernadine took a deep breath. "I don't know, Sydney. Marriages are hard enough, even in the best of circumstances. He's an academic. What does he know about retail? What if this business doesn't work out? How will he support you?"

Now, with the classical music station playing in the background, she sat on the bed with her album of wedding photos in her lap and Pumpkin, having been fed, was resting her head lazily on her knee. Sydney wondered if she should have taken her mother's concerns into account that day. She could have finished law school.

It had been two months since the Taylors fled with the artwork, rare volumes, and cash. Detective Stribling said the police still had no clues as to their whereabouts. Sydney and Malachi had slept in separate bedrooms since then and rarely spoke to each other, except when they were on the merchandise floor. Malachi apologized to her but that had not quelled her anger because it was he who had gone along with Kwamé and rented to the Taylors without checking them out as Sydney had insisted. Malachi let himself be swayed by his best friend's opinions over hers. That, coupled with his spending more than twenty thousand dollars buying stock and supplies for The Talking Drum without consulting her, his rightful business partner, didn't help.

Now they had shelves stacked with academic texts and political booklets that weren't selling. They probably couldn't give the stuff away if they wanted to. Malachi was a professor without an academy. He was trying to make The Talking Drum into his university. But he had not understood that customers couldn't be his students.

She turned off the radio, tired of listening to it. Pumpkin got up and sniffed the knobs, then climbed into her lap.

Renting to the Taylors had resulted in a financial nightmare. Officer Stribling had discovered that Willie had forged checks from the Stallworths' business account. Willie made checks payable to himself then cashed them with his signature. They were thousands of dollars in debt and had to beg their creditors to extend their payment due dates. Their creditors had agreed but were charging them interest.

In a weak moment, Sydney called her mother. A few days later, there was a check in the mailbox from Bernadine and Martin that would cover half of their losses. Sydney was embarrassed that she and Malachi needed the money, but she was glad she would be able to catch up on some bills. However, Malachi stopped her, stating that while he appreciated the gesture, they could take care of their own problems. This led to a blistering argument, with flailing arms, hot words, slammed doors, and tears.

She turned to her favorite photo in the wedding album—Malachi and her standing in the mansion ballroom at the marble fireplace facing each other underneath the chandelier as they held hands and exchanged vows. The photographer had positioned himself at the ballroom entrance, just inside the French doors, framing the shot so that the elegant, fluted columns on each side of the ballroom were in the foreground and the ceiling friezes were in frame. Sunlight streaming through the old-fashioned pane windows gave the room a warm glow.

She wished she could go back to that moment in the picture when she and Malachi were just starting their married lives together, when their relationship was relatively easy and new.

She heard Malachi coming up the stairs. Her heart shifted. Maybe he was ready to talk about what happened again so they could begin the work of rebuilding the relationship. She shut the album as he entered the bedroom.

"We have guests downstairs," he announced curtly, then turned on his heels and quickly went back downstairs. She was disappointed at his flat tone of voice and quick retreat. She eased Pumpkin off her lap. The kitten chirped at the interruption of her nap, strolled to the end of the bed and then startled Sydney by charging back to her, grabbing her by the wrist with her teeth, grazing Sydney's skin but not breaking it.

"You stop that, Pumpkin!" Sydney smacked the animal

across the face. Pumpkin bolted and scurried away behind the dresser. Sydney didn't understand the cat's change in mood. She could be so sweet one second and a spoiled brat the next.

When she got downstairs, Uncle Mustapha was standing in the foyer, smiling.

"*Olele! Olele!*" shouted Mustapha as he hugged her. "How is my favorite husband-and-wife team doing?"

"I'll know when I figure out how much we made today," Malachi replied. He led the way to the front room parlor where the adding machine was humming. "It's not looking that great."

"Some days are slow for me, too, my first years in business," explained Mustapha, "but you must hang in the game."

"Running a business is a little harder than we imagined," Sydney said, glancing at Malachi. He kept his eyes trained on Mustapha.

Mustapha raised his eyebrows. "I have special treat for you." He looked toward the door and clapped his hands slowly, three times.

Sydney glanced again at Malachi. He seemed to be as puzzled as she. Moments later a burst of sound came from the porch. It was a rapid drumbeat. Mustapha's nephew, the drummer, came inside. He was wearing a winter jacket over his *boubou*. He nodded to the couple, not missing a beat as he slapped the drum with his palms and fingers.

Whatever the rhythm was, it was catchy. Malachi patted the counter to the beat and without realizing it, Sydney started tapping her foot. Then, the drummer gave his instrument a series of rapid slaps and raised his hands in the air.

"To you I present my nephew, Omar Bassari," Mustapha said like an emcee at a show.

Malachi shook Omar's hand. The drummer winced. Then Omar gently took Sydney's hand and kissed it. She caught a whiff of alcohol.

"Good to meet you on better terms, brother," Malachi said. Omar and Mustapha stared at him blankly. Both had apparently forgotten about Malachi's role in breaking up the incident on stage with Hideki Baruka at the grand opening.

Up until this moment, Sydney had only seen Omar from a distance. Now, standing closer to him, she noticed his muscular build and emerald, green eyes, unusual in a black person.

"I've heard you play at Le Baobab," Sydney said. "You're very good."

"Thank you, *madame*," replied Omar. "We have just come from the Zenobia Club, where The Fulani Sound, my group, performed."

Sydney enjoyed his French accent. It was different from Uncle Mustapha's, whose accent sounded more African with its speech pattern and cadence.

"My nephew try to get back onstage after the fire wipe out his home," Mustapha explained.

"We were so sorry about that," Malachi replied.

"We collected food and clothing for you and your neighbors," Sydney said to Omar. "I hope it helped."

"I am appreciative of everything the people of Liberty Hill do for us," Omar answered.

Mustapha turned to Malachi. "We get here just in time."

"How's that, sir?" asked Malachi.

"My nephew is walking out of nightclub and realize he has to use flush toilet."

Omar unfastened the drum from his waist and started playfully jogging in place." Would that be okay, *madame*?"

"Of course." Sydney pointed him down the hall.

Once Omar left the room Mustapha motioned for Sydney and Malachi to come closer. "I guess you hear the news about my building."

"We're sorry to hear about that. Real sorry." Malachi said.

"I get letter in the mail from city three weeks ago. They give me small time to close up my restaurant, my building. I must be out in one month's time. They have check ready to send me. My block is the last one they tear down. Where do I go?"

"What're you going to do?" she asked.

"Uncle Mustapha will survive," he said, his voice quivering. "But I worry about my nephew. When the wrecking ball comes through he has no place to go. He is depressing. His wife abandon him a while before."

"Can't he go with you?" Sydney asked.

"I don't know where Uncle Mustapha go. But my first business is to protect my nephew. He is my blood. Is your basement still open?"

"Do you mean, is it available for rent?" Sydney clarified.

"You tell me about it before," reminded Mustapha. "That size fit my nephew."

"Sorry sir." Malachi stepped from behind the counter and put an arm around Sydney. "It's not available."

Mustapha's eyes narrowed. "Why? Is somebody occupied there?"

Omar returned, his smile dissolving as he sensed the mood of the conversation.

"We had tenants a few months ago," explained Sydney, "but they didn't work out."

"Why? They tear up the place?" asked Mustapha.

"No," Sydney replied, looking at Malachi for help with an explanation.

"But nobody there now?" Mustapha held his palms face up in a pleading gesture.

"We're not renting to anyone else," Malachi asserted. "The other people stole from us, our money, our artwork, our books."

"Then you need a renter to replenish your money back," Mustapha offered.

"We're just tired right now," Sydney explained.

Mustapha slammed his hand on the counter, startling Sydney. "You do not tell me truth!" he thundered. "You think my nephew is common criminal."

Omar gently took his uncle by the shoulder. "That's not what they say, Uncle."

Mustapha yanked away from his grip. "This is what they exactly say."

"With all due respect, you've got it wrong, sir," said Malachi. "We just need a break…"

"I know how you Americans are!" Mustapha thundered. "You say one thing, and you mean the other thing."

"Uncle!" Omar shouted, but Mustapha did not let up.

"I show you the burns on the back of my nephew! I show you to them right now!"

"We're sorry, *monsieur, madame,*" Omar apologized.

"You Americans give us bags of cereal and socks when our buildings burn down, but the real need you turn your back on," Mustapha fumed.

"Maybe we can help you find housing somewhere else," Sydney said. "There are other people up the street who rent…"

"Never mind you," howled Mustapha, shaking a bony finger at Malachi. "I will not forget this. The Wolof people have long memories." Mustapha turned and walked out, leaving Omar behind.

"I am sorry about my Uncle," Omar said.

"No, man. You don't have to apologize for anything," Malachi argued. "We just don't have it in us to rent right now after what we went through. It really shook us up."

"You do not have to explain. My uncle is upset. He thinks he shall lose everything. He does not know what to do. After the city takes the building he says he shall go back to Senegal. Then he says he shall dare them to take his building and chain himself to the front door. He is scared and desperate, but he does not want to say it. He is grieving the death of his dream."

CHAPTER 31

OMAR ROLLED OFF the cot and onto his feet, inadvertently kicking an empty bottle of Jim Beam across the cellar floor.

He was living on liquor, pushing away the food that his uncle cooked him. He hadn't gotten any gigs since The Fulani Sound performed at the Zenobia Club a month ago. His drumming hadn't roused the crowd at all. He was being too careful, not putting enough power into his technique because he knew he would pay for it later. After performing, his palms ached for hours. He was sure that he was getting a reputation for his dull performances. Khadim had been taking bookings as a solo artist. It seemed that The Fulani Sound was dissolving.

Omar shuffled across Le Baobab's basement floor, until he found the liquor bottle. He held it up to the sliver of light coming through the dirty window, then tipped it to his mouth, draining the last drop. He had a thirst for more but he'd have to go to the liquor store to get it.

The city was scheduled to take over the building today, March 30, 1973, and Uncle Mustapha had to vacate. All week long, Omar had heard Uncle Mustapha upstairs on the phone, asking people to come to Le Baobab for a protest rally. Omar felt sorry for his uncle. The loss of Le Baobab would shatter him, as had his wife's death. Omar had tried unsuccessfully to talk Mustapha into considering another type of work to replace running the restaurant and renting the apartments, but Mustapha would talk over him, shouting that he was too busy to think about such things.

Omar had rented a room at the Bellport YMCA, but he was afraid to leave Uncle by himself considering his emotional state.

His head throbbed like it was being jack hammered. He remembered someone telling him about a home remedy for hangovers—raw eggs and vinegar mixed in a blender. Simply thinking about it made him feel sick, but Omar was desperate enough to try anything. He put on his sandals and walked upstairs into the restaurant. He was stunned. It was packed with three times the number of people who'd come for meals when the restaurant was operating.

All of the tables had been removed. Only the booths along the perimeter remained. People were standing in clusters, some from Petite Africa, others from elsewhere. They were all shouting to be heard over the din. Some were practicing chants. Omar stepped onto the bandstand to look for Mustapha. Moments later, a hand gripped his shoulder. It was Khadim.

"You look terrible, my friend. Are you growing a beard?" Khadim sniffed the air and grimaced. "When was the last time you washed?"

Omar pulled away from him. "I don't want to talk about it."

He watched people come and go. Several held picket signs that read, *No Permis de Demolition*, *Sauvegardez Petite Africa*, *We Hate You Mayor*, and *Harborview Scum*. They went outside with the signs and formed a line that marched down the block and back again.

"Where did all of these people come from?" Omar asked.

"All over, my friend. A bus came from New York. It picked up people in Connecticut and Rhode Island. All of Mustapha's customers are back."

"Where is he?"

Khadim raised his eyebrows as he looked over Omar's shoulder.

The kitchen doors swung open. Clutching a megaphone,

Uncle Mustapha strode past him and out the front door. Omar followed him.

The protesters spilled onto Garfield Avenue near two police cruisers. A reporter for television news station WBLP and a cameraman snaked their way to the front of the crowd.

Mustapha raised the megaphone to his lips, aiming it toward the police "*Yow bujul! Yow bujul! You go to hell,*" he screamed. Immediately, the crowd took up the taunt, yelling at the police in Wolof.

Two cops jumped out of their vehicles and talked into their radios. Mustapha rushed back inside. Omar followed him. "Uncle, where are you going?" he asked.

Mustapha turned in his direction with an unfocused, faraway look in his eyes. He swung back around and headed through the double doors into the kitchen. When Omar caught up with him, he heard the *pong, pong, pong* sound of sandals on the fire escape. He scrambled up the fire escape to the roof as Mustapha lifted his megaphone and shouted at the crowd below. Omar wished he had grabbed a coat. It was bitterly cold on the roof because it was early spring and windy. One of the cops shouted through his bullhorn, "Come down from there, sir, or we'll have to arrest you."

"On what grounds?" Mustapha yelled, switching to English. "You have no arresting rights on me."

"Provoking public disorder," the cop shouted.

Omar grabbed his uncle by the arm. He was amazed that Mustapha didn't seem fazed by the cold. "Uncle, you must listen to them. It is over. There is nothing to be done."

Mustapha turned to face Omar, his eyes wild. "You want me to have dialogue with police!" he shouted.

"Yes, Uncle."

"Okay. I am."

He shuffled to the edge of the roof, the wind flapping his shirt like a flag against his frail body. Omar went to grab him, fearing the wind would blow him over, but Mustapha backed away from the ledge and went back to the fire escape.

Once inside the restaurant dining room, Mustapha grabbed the framed photo of President Senghor off the wall, held it to his chest, and looked around as if wondering what to do with it. He flung the picture onto the bar. Then he collapsed into Omar's arms. "They do not arrest me. They do not take my home," he cried.

Omar pleaded with his uncle. "It is not your home anymore. They paid you. You can get a new home."

"But then they destroy my restaurant, my building." Mustapha wailed. "They destroy all that I have. They give me money for my building but it is little, and not fair market value."

"But you agreed to this!" Omar shouted.

"I don't know why I sign those papers!" Mustapha shouted back.

Omar had never seen his uncle in such a state. He tried to think of a way to calm him down. "You can start over, start over someplace new. I shall help you. Khadim shall help you. Look at the people out there. They shall help you get a new restaurant."

Mustapha pulled himself up and looked toward the front door. Then his shoulders slumped. "I am a seventy-two-year-old man. I cannot start over," he sighed.

"Think about all of the people who showed up for you today, Uncle. They love you. They will want another Le Baobab, even if it is a mouse hole in the wall."

Mustapha became quiet. He seemed to be calming down. Omar loosened his hold on him. But then Mustapha pushed passed Omar, knocking over decorative gourds that were still on the bar and bumping into a table stacked with leftover picket signs. The signs went crashing to the floor.

"I am tired," his uncle said weakly, as he made his way to the back of the restaurant to the staircase leading to his apartment on the second floor. Omar followed him. Sweat streamed down the back of his uncle's neck. His shirt was wet and sticking to him. When they got to the second floor landing, Mustapha surged ahead and shut himself in his apartment.

"Uncle," Omar shouted. He got no response. He stood there catching his breath, trying to decide what to do next. Maybe his uncle needed a moment alone. Omar decided to go back downstairs and check on the activity of the protesters. When he got outside, he couldn't believe how much the crowd had grown. It had spilled onto the next block.

Three more police cruisers had arrived. All of the cops stood outside of their cars talking into their walkie talkies. He heard sirens in the distance, probably more cop cars on the way.

"Mr. Bassari? Mr. Bassari?"

Omar looked around at the sound of his name being called. It was the female TV reporter for the local station, petite, wearing a lot of makeup, with hair that didn't move.

"Why did your uncle organize this protest?" she asked. "The city said it paid him fair market value."

Omar stared at the microphone the reporter had shoved in his face. Out of the corner of his eye he saw the cameraman focusing his lens on him.

"I shall not speak for my uncle. You must speak to him directly."

The reporter lost her balance as she was jostled by the crowd. In a moment, she regained it.

"Where is he?" she asked. "We want to get his side of the story."

Omar brushed past her and went back inside. He wanted to check on Uncle to make sure he was all right. Maybe he could convince his uncle to be reasonable, to call off the protesters and leave the building so the city could begin demolition. Surely uncle could stay with his daughter Ansa or any number of friends until he decided where he wanted to live.

Omar was surprised to find the door to the apartment un-locked. The place was dark with the curtains drawn. He called out to his uncle but got no response. Mustapha's bedroom door was cracked open. Omar went inside. The sparsely furnished room was bathed in late afternoon sunlight. The sound of the protestors could be heard through the window. Mustapha was on the bed, lying very still. His eyes were shut, his skin ashen. Omar went over to him.

"Uncle?"

Mustapha's eyes fluttered open.

Omar exhaled. He had thought his uncle was dead. "Are you okay?"

"Just a little tired," Mustapha whispered. He lifted his hand slightly off the bed.

Omar took it between both of his and sat next to him on the bed. "You want me to call someone? An ambulance?"

Mustapha shook his head weakly.

A photo on the dresser got Omar's attention. It was the only adornment in the room. It was a framed picture of Mustapha's wife, Samir. Uncle didn't talk about her much, but Omar knew he missed her dearly.

"Nephew, we win, right?" asked Mustapha.

"What do you mean, Uncle?"

"We win?" he asked again, his voice barely audible.

Omar was confused by the question. Then he noticed that Uncle was smiling and looking in the direction of the window, apparently hearing the protesters.

"Yes, Uncle. You did good. We won."

Omar laid his head on his uncle's chest and listened for a long time until his heart was stilled. Then he kissed his uncle on the forehead.

"I shall miss you, Uncle," he said. He began crying uncontrollably.

CHAPTER 32

"GLAD YOU WERE ABLE to come in on such short notice."
Max gestured for Sydney to sit down in the chair opposite him. "I know you've got the bookstore and all, but this
is big." Max's secretary had called Sydney in for an important
meeting. It was Sydney's day off from The Talking Drum. She'd
spent the morning filling out paperwork to extend her leave
from law school for one more year.

"It sounded important," Sydney replied, "so I'm here."

"I appreciate that." He took off his glasses. "Got a couple
of things." He reached into a folder on his desk and pulled out
several black-and-white photos. Sydney recognized her work.
She had taken the photos at the scene of the fire at Esmé's
Africa Wear last October, after their grand opening. She felt
sick as she relived the moment she saw Esmé burned beyond
recognition and wheeled out of her shop on a stretcher. Max
took a grease pencil, and circled an oblong, grainy figure in
the background of one of the pictures.

"One of my best sources left the department so it took me
months to find out that the police had your photos blown up.
They now know who this person is."

Sydney looked closer to study a silhouette in the background.
She had no idea who it was but the person appeared to be a
man with a chunky build. "And they think he's the arsonist?"

"They are pretty damn sure." He took the photo back. "You
did a great job."

"I was just shooting all over the place."

He held up a hand. "Take credit when credit is given. In the newspaper business, it doesn't come too often. We normally only get attention when we get something wrong."

"Has this been on the news yet?"

"Five o'clock—TV and radio. We'll have a special press run and your photos will be featured. Have it on the streets within the hour."

He put the folder back in his desk, along with the grease pencil. "You can expect to hear from the *Globe*."

"Why?"

He smiled. "They want you to work for them as a stringer."

She didn't know what to think. "*The Boston Globe*? You're kidding me, right?"

"A lot of fill-in work, covering municipal meetings in Bellport that their staff reporters can't get to, taking photos, covering some breaking news when they're short-handed."

"Sounds like scut work."

He leaned forward in his seat. "It's called 'paying your dues'. That's how I got started."

She had enjoyed filing stories and taking photos for *Inner City Voice*, but they were the kinds of stories she had wanted to write. Then she had to think about her responsibilities at The Talking Drum. Malachi had made her schedule flexible so she could complete the occasional newspaper assignments, but she doubted he would go along with her spending more time away from the bookstore. She shared her reservations with Max.

He leaned back in his chair, his hands folded steeple-like under his chin. "Think it over, Mrs. Stallworth. This would be an avenue to work your way up in journalism. *The Boston Globe* is one of the top newspapers in the country, a black woman with credentials like yours at a white newspaper like the *Globe*, you'd be a pioneer of sorts."

"But I haven't ruled out going back to law school," she said.

"Women have been fighting for years to get into the newsroom as reporters instead of clerks and secretaries."

"I know, but that's not a reason to take the position."

"You're right." He exhaled, impatient. "At least talk to them when they call. Meet with them."

The phone rang. As Max listened, his grip on the receiver tightened. Sydney couldn't tell what was going on, but she knew it was serious. "That was one of my sources." Max explained when he hung up. "Something's happened to the old man, the activist."

"Uncle Mustapha?" Sydney started wringing her hands. "What is it?"

She started to feel ill. The look on Max's face had already given her the answer to her question.

CHAPTER 33

BELLPORT GAZETTE

Bellport Police have made an arrest in connection with a series of suspicious fires this past year and a half in the South End of the city, commonly known as "Petite Africa." Lawrence Briggs, 25, of Bellport, was taken into custody last night. He confessed that he started a series of fires in unoccupied and abandoned buildings throughout Petite Africa.

Bellport arson investigators report that more arrests are expected, as they look for Brigg's accomplices. He was ordered held on cash-only bail and will be arraigned in circuit court next week.

Sydney snapped off the clock radio. So Lawrence had hung around the scene of the fires he'd set. And she was lucky enough to catch him in the frame of one of the shots she took at the fire at Esmé's Africa Wear. She rolled over to the empty side of the bed and listened as Malachi came up the stairs.

He slowly cracked open the bedroom door and stuck his head inside. Then he returned his pillows to his side of the bed as he had been doing for the past few months since their troubles. "I went down to the jail," he said, sounding tired.

"Why?" Sydney asked. "Why would he do that?"

Malachi let out a heavy sigh. "I don't know. Greed. Money."

They said nothing for a while.

"He poured gasoline in old milk jugs, stuffed rags in the neck, and then lit the rags with a lighter." Malachi shook his head. "He's angry. He's lashing out. He said because I made him quit when I accused him of stealing from us, he didn't have enough money for school. Someone had been after him for months to help burn down some buildings, and because of me he finally agreed. He said burning down those buildings was the only way he could cover his tuition."

"That's bull," she shouted.

He sat down at the foot of the bed and faced her.

"Is it?"

She propped herself up. "Malachi, what are you saying?"

He shrugged. "I don't know, Syd. I was his mentor and I let him down. I assumed he was stealing from us and he wasn't."

"Lawrence seemed suspicious when those things went missing. Anyone else would have questioned him, too. Don't let him mess with your head."

"I can't help but wonder if I went wrong somewhere. Maybe I didn't spend enough time with him after he got out of reform school."

"Malachi," Sydney leaned over and took him by the hand, "stop doing this to yourself. You got him into Whittington University, for heaven's sake!"

"I was so caught up in being, 'Mr. Professor,' trying to get tenure. I should have been thinking of somebody other than myself."

Sydney knew Malachi wasn't being rational, yet she tried to reason with him.

"What do you mean? You were so generous with your time. What about all the hours you volunteered with the kids in the Black Student Union? And think about how you got Lawrence involved in the drama department, making sets and props. That was a beautiful thing."

The phone rang, startling them both.

"We're going to have to take it off the hook," Sydney

sighed. "I made the mistake of answering it earlier, and it was a reporter from *The Bellport Gazette* asking for a quote from me about Lawrence. She badgered me so much that I had to hang up on her."

"I know what you mean. Two TV reporters were camped out in front of the jail and got in my face on my way out this morning. They followed me all the way to the car."

Sydney peeked out of the window. Percy, wearing his usual snorkel jacket permanently discolored by filth, was walking by with Bridgette. He made a prolonged stop in front of the house as the dog squatted on the sidewalk. He continued down the block without scooping up the dog's business. Down the street she saw two television news vans. "Seems they followed you here."

"Not surprised."

"We'll have to wait it out. They can't stay out there forever."

She lay back down in the bed. "So what's Lawrence going to do for a defense?"

"I heard that the congregation at Nehemiah Baptist is raising some money to hire a good lawyer."

"At least he'll have that."

Malachi pressed his thumbs against his closed eyelids for a moment to push back tears. "Lawrence said he had no intention of anyone being hurt in the fires, let alone dying."

"He did a stupid thing."

"I know, Sydney. Not only was it stupid. He's ruined his life and the lives of a bunch of other people too."

CHAPTER 34

FOR THE FIRST TIME in his life, Omar was completely alone. Uncle Mustapha was gone. Khadim had moved to Rhode Island. When he had gone to City Hall to apply for a housing voucher, Khadim was told that there were none left. Then Khadim asked about apartments in Chelsea and Malden advertised in the newspaper. But when he went to see them, he was told that the apartments had been rented. Omar had heard stories from other Petite Africa residents of being turned away by landlords who didn't want to rent to them and suspected that his friend was receiving the same treatment.

Khadim resorted to moving two hours away from Bellport to East Warwick, Rhode Island, where he had a distant cousin, Aziz, who owned apartments.

Omar had been living in the YMCA in downtown Bellport for the past two months since his uncle died. He had a two-burner hotplate that he never bothered to use. When he got hungry he'd go to the waterfront and order food from the canteen that served the construction crews. The Harborview Redevelopment Project was on schedule. Groundbreaking was a month ago, April 1st.

He spent his days wandering around the perimeter of what used to be his neighborhood and recalled his friends, Bamba Toukou, who loved to call him "drummer man," and Junio Ortiz whose bakery ovens sweetened the neighborhood. He wondered where they had gone. He wiped away tears as he approached the spot where Esmé's Africa Wear Shop used to be. Esmé, who was long dead now. If the fire hadn't happened, Esmé would have been searching for another location to sell her racks of clothing, souvenirs, and knick knacks.

Now, back at the YMCA after another walk on the waterfront, he heard a knock on his door. It was Della, who he hadn't seen in a week. She was dressed for church, wearing a wide-brimmed hat, flowing dress, and high heels. She was carrying a large shopping bag, which she plopped onto the bed. She reached in and pulled out a sleeping bag. "I went and got this from the Army/Navy Store. "It's got a built-in pillow in it," she said.

He had forgotten that he'd complained to her about his cot's thin mattress.

"I shall make good use of it." He unrolled the sleeping bag on top of the mattress. "Thank you *ma chère*," he said, taking her in his arms and giving her three quick kisses on the lips. She didn't resist, which encouraged him to kiss her again, this time longer.

Then she pulled away.

"No, Omar. You're going too fast."

"But you want to."

She shook her head. "I know, but let's take it slow. No rush. Okay?"

"Very well then." Omar smiled and let go of her.

Della looked around the room. "You ought to get a TV in here. At least a radio. You been following the news about the fires?"

He shook his head.

She reached into the shopping bag and handed him the day's edition of *The Bellport Gazette*. On the front page was a story about the continuing investigation into the set fires. It included a file photo of Lawrence Briggs under arrest in March. Omar read to the end of the article.

"That should be a load off your mind, shouldn't it?" she inquired.

"It is progress."

Della balled up the shopping bag and crammed it into the room's tiny waste-paper basket. "I hear the 'but' in there, but you ain't saying it."

"Uncle Mustapha thought that Fullerton was burning down buildings for insurance money."

"James Fullerton? The landlord? As much property as he owns in this town, why would he?" Della checked her watch. "I have to get over to church. I'll see you at the book factory this afternoon?"

"I will be there."

Just thinking about the memorial service for Uncle Mustapha made him feel empty. Uncle's death was still felt fresh. Omar had put himself in charge of the service. He'd rehearsed his remarks, which he would keep simple. It had taken him weeks to track down Petite Africa people who'd been displaced by the fires and eminent domain. Because the mosque in Petite Africa was demolished with everything else, the memorial service would be held at the former Nathaniel Hawthorne Boot Factory. Uncle would like that. The factory was on the banks of the Bellport River, facing what used to be Petite Africa, the cafetorium spare, without decoration. The only music performed would be a drumming interlude by Khadim.

Omar climbed into his sleeping bag. He regretted not spending more time with his uncle in the months before his death instead of running around playing at drumming gigs. He didn't realize how much the fires and the fight to save Petite Africa were damaging Uncle's health.

If he had been paying better attention he would have encouraged Uncle to take a vacation, to relax. But then Omar realized how unrealistic this would have been. Uncle never slowed down. Not ever. Petite Africa and Le Baobab were his life, particularly after Aunt Samir had died.

Hours later, he stood in the lobby of the former boot factory, shaking the hands of attendees of the memorial service as they left. He was pleased at attendance. The cafetorium had been filled. Extra folding chairs had to be brought in from the storage room.

Malachi and Sydney approached him. He shook hands with the couple. "This was a lovely service," Sydney said. "Your remarks were so touching."

"I thank you," Omar responded.

"Your uncle did so much for us, putting up fliers about our grand opening, giving his customers discounts to shop with us," Malachi said.

"Yes, he was a good friend," added Sydney.

Malachi cleared his throat. "Your uncle caught us at a bad time when he asked us to rent to you."

"You do not have to explain," interrupted Omar.

"Please," said Malachi, "let me finish. Your uncle meant so much to us. We want to be there for you. We want you to move into our apartment."

"Where are you living now?" asked Sydney.

Omar told them about his room at the "Y."

"Please consider staying with us," Sydney said. "We'd love to have you."

Omar watched Sydney and Malachi as they walked to their car. For the first time since Uncle's death, he began to feel happy.

CHAPTER 35

IT HAD BEEN a tough season, Sydney thought, as she sat at her desk, looking over a brochure for Suffolk University Law School. She and Malachi endured more tension than she imagined this early in their marriage. Her mother had told her that the honeymoon period for her and Sydney's father lasted four or five years. For Sydney and Malachi, it had only lasted a few months.

They were beginning the work to repair their relationship in light of the robbery by the Taylors, Malachi's mistakes in running the bookstore, and his hiring of Lawrence, who turned out to be an arsonist. If Sydney had listened to her mother and not married Malachi, she'd be almost done with law school by now and preparing to sit for the bar exam, but she wouldn't have been at her husband's side as he launched the business.

Malachi put his hands on her shoulders and massaged them gently. "Still looking that over, I see."

He spoke softly. They'd agreed to babysit Jasmine for Della. The child was asleep in the back of the apartment. She tossed the brochure onto her desk. "I've been reading about the concentration in civil rights law. I could go to work for a nonprofit, an advocacy group, work on discrimination cases. After watching what happened to Petite Africa, Uncle Mustapha, and Omar, I feel I can actually help people and feel good about what I'm doing rather than work in some corporation."

"You could do the same concentration at Whittington University. Suffolk is not in the same league as Whittington. It would be a big step down. "

"I know, but Suffolk is so close. It's just down the road in Boston, about thirty minutes away."

He took her by the hand and led her over to the couch. "Syd, don't do this because of me. Do what you want to do. You put your career on hold for me, and I love you for that, but now it's your turn. Besides, The Talking Drum is doing just fine. We'll be fine, even if you're on the other side of the state for a year and a half. We'll deal with it."

"But things are finally getting better between us," she said. "I don't want anything to interfere with that."

"It won't. Trust me. Go back to Whittington if that's what you want. It's ranked as one of the top five law schools in the country, and it accepted *you* and gave you a fellowship. Do you know how many people wish they could even make the waiting list there?"

She sat there and thought about it for a while. "Maybe you're right. Maybe I'll call the dean."

"Do that. I'll work it out on this end, hire some part-time help, and drive out every other weekend. When you have a long weekend or semester break, you can take the train out here."

The doorbell rang. "Must be Della," Sydney said and looked at her watch. "Jasmine's been napping for just over an hour. She should be waking up any time now."

"I'll let Della up on my way out," Malachi replied.

Della sat down on the living room couch and kicked off her shoes. "I've been on my feet all day," she shouted to Sydney, who was in the kitchen when she arrived upstairs, "re-shelving books, checking out patrons at the circulation desk. We were short on staff today, so I had to take up the slack."

"How're your classes going?"

"Ain't bad. We've been studying archiving. There's a lot more to it than I thought."

Sydney rolled the tea service into the living room.

"How's your new tenant doing?" asked Della, smiling.

"Maybe I should ask *you* that."

Della chuckled.

"He pays on time, and keeps to himself," said Sydney.

"Sounds like it's working out."

Sydney poured Earl Grey from a silver teapot. "It's working out very well. Uncle Mustapha would be happy."

"I still can't believe he's gone," said Della.

"I know," Sydney said, blinking back tears. "The only time I hear anything from downstairs is when Omar's practicing his drumming. He plays during the day. Never in the evenings. The customers enjoy it."

Della took a sip of her tea. "He's playing that loud?"

"They can hear him through the dumbwaiter. The sound goes right up the shaft. Customers walk around the shop bopping their heads to the beat. I think they like that better than what The Young Turk plays on the radio station."

Sydney sat down across from Della. As they sipped their tea, Pumpkin, now full grown and pudgy for a cat, leaped onto the back of the sofa and nuzzled Della's neck.

"What a sweet cat," Della said. "That's the one silver lining to renting to those awful people."

Mention of the Taylors brought Sydney back to that day when she and Malachi realized that the Taylors were brazen thieves, not the genteel couple they had pretended to be.

"You can have her if you want her. I don't understand why she can never sit still. She's always leaping on something, scratching at something, digging up my African Violets. They're half-dead now."

Della chuckled. "She's just being a cat, Sydney."

"I wish those crooks had taken her with them when they took off. If I had known she'd be like this, I would have dropped her off at the shelter right after the Taylors skipped town."

Della put her teacup down. "You still can, you know."

"It's too late. Malachi would never allow it. He adores Pumpkin. It seems to be mutual. She follows him all over the house, curls up next to him while he's watching TV. She even sits on the vanity while he's brushing his teeth."

Della laughed. "So I guess you're stuck."

Pumpkin jumped off the couch and landed next to the tea service. She stood on her back legs and stuck her snout on the second shelf where Sydney had put a plate of blueberry muffins. Sydney swatted at Pumpkin with a dish cloth, but the cat kept dodging the cloth and never got touched. Sydney moved the plate to the coffee table. "See what I mean?"

Pumpkin crept up to the arm of the couch and stared at Della. Then she sauntered up next to her and sniffed at the muffin in her hand.

"Pumpkin, get down!" Sydney cried out before rolling the cloth into a ball. She threw it at the cat and missed.

"It's okay," Della said, chuckling. "Pumpkin is a nice distraction. She takes my mind off things."

"I'm sorry," Sydney apologized. "I meant to ask how things were."

After several months and three interviews, Kwamé had been offered the job. He'd agreed to take it.

Della vowed to stay in Bellport.

"Kwamé still thinks when he moves down there, I'll cave in and move too, but he's wrong. I'm not leaving."

"What's going to happen?"

"I guess we'll split up. I'm not following him."

They both turned at the sound of the creaky hinges of the bedroom door down the hall.

Della gave a crooked smile. "I guess my little angel's done with her nap."

Jasmine came running into the room, and flopped on the couch next to her mother. Pumpkin sauntered over to the couch armrest, sat on her haunches, and licked one of her paws as she stared at them both.

"Miss Sydney told me you two had a lot of fun today," Della said to Jasmine. The child didn't respond.

"I was telling your mother about the hook rug we were working on," Sydney said.

Jasmine was quiet with a blank look on her face.

"Well," Della said when she finished her tea, "I guess we best get going so I can start dinner. Kwamé claims he'll be home at a decent hour this evening."

Jasmine sat up. "I don't want to go. I want to stay here with Aunt Syd."

Della stood up and grabbed her daughter's arm, but Jasmine pulled in the other direction. They were locked that way like two square dancers frozen in time. Finally, Della let go. Jasmine pulled away with such force that she stumbled, but she regained her footing and ran up the stairs to the third-floor photo studio.

"We need to get her out of there," Sydney said.

"I know," Della agreed wearily.

Della brought Jasmine downstairs, clutching her shoulders. She kicked wildly, but Della was able to dodge her kicks. She hissed a firm whisper in the child's ear, "Now you behave."

Jasmine calmed down and stopped resisting. Sydney followed the two down the stairs to the front porch. Then tears welled in the child's eyes, and she clung to her mother.

"Baby, what's the matter?" Della asked and then turned to Sydney, "I'm sorry about this."

"There's nothing to apologize for," Sydney assured.

Jasmine muttered to herself and tried repeatedly to pull away from her mother as they walked down the porch steps, but Della maintained a firm grip on Jasmine. Just then, Omar came through the front gate carrying a bag of groceries, his shoulders slumped. He stood up straight and smiled when he saw Della and Jasmine approaching.

"What do we have here, the talented drummer?" he asked and crouched down so that he was at eye level with Jasmine.

She rubbed at her eyes and nodded.

He looked up at Sydney and Della. "How about all of you come downstairs. I would like to welcome you to my place."

"Can I play the drums, Mommy? Please can I play them?" Jasmine peered up at her mother.

Della let out a sigh. "I guess it'll be okay. But we can't stay long."

Omar was grinning. "We shall all play the drums." He took them to the side entrance leading to the basement apartment. It was spare and simple, with a couch and high-backed chair in the living room and a small, four-seater table in the kitchen. Folding chairs were stacked in the hall. One wall in the living room was lined with drums arranged by height. Some measured only a foot high. The tallest stood four feet and had a drumhead the size of a hubcap. Sydney had never seen a drum that large. Della seemed interested in the *djembe*. She ran her hand along the intricate carvings in the wood.

"Reminds me of a pitcher," Della said.

Posters and framed pictures hung on the walls, including one of The Fulani Sound. Omar and Khadim were pictured side-by-side, their hands a blur. Sydney recalled the drumming duel she watched between the two at Uncle Mustapha's restaurant. There was another framed picture with a crack running across the glass of Duke Ellington and Omar, autographed by Duke Ellington.

"Do you know him?" Della asked.

"We met a long time ago," Omar replied. "He is my musical hero."

"I've never seen so many drums," Della declared.

"After the fire, drummers gave them to me," he said proudly. "A few I was able to save from my own collection—the *djembe* my papa gave me and some others—but most are donations." He went back into the kitchen.

The drum that most fascinated Sydney was the *dundun*. It stood about two feet with a cowbell attached to it. She picked up the mallet and lightly tapped the cowbell.

Omar brought out a platter of monkey bread and guava juice and placed it on a TV tray. Then he arranged the folding chairs in a semi-circle with his chair facing theirs.

"Sit," he commanded everyone, and then placed a *djembe* in front of each of them. He sat across from them, propping his *djembe* between his knees. Omar closed his eyes and started striking the face, alternating with his full palms, his fingers, and fingertips. He produced some high-pitched, sharp sounds and, at other moments, low, deep, round, and full sounds. As he played, his eyelids drooped and his mouth puckered as if he was in a trance. His head tilted from left to right on its own beat.

Sydney and Della watched as Jasmine started tapping her feet.

He opened his eyes and paused from playing. "Did you know that the African drum shall talk to you?" he asked Jasmine.

She started giggling. "A drum can't talk."

"It shall talk," he stated. "Even the smallest drum can talk, like the one you are holding."

He told the three of them to wedge the drums between their knees, tilt them at an angle as he was doing, and strike the center of the drumhead with an open palm. "This is a *djembe*," he shouting over his playing. "You must never play this drum with sticks."

"Why?" Jasmine shouted back.

"Because the drum will turn into a lion and bite you on the nose!"

Jasmine shrieked as she laughed, bouncing up and down in her chair.

Every so often Omar had to stop playing to correct Sydney and Della's hand positioning, but Jasmine needed no coaching. She played properly and maintained the beat.

"What is the drum saying to you, little Jasmine?" he shouted.

The child looked down at her hands as she hit the drum. "It's saying that I must smile."

"You are right. Do you know why it's saying that to you?"

She shrugged. Omar turned to Sydney for a response. Sydney looked at Della, who shook her head as she played.

"Because you are playing *Fanga*, the welcoming rhythm," he explained.

Omar dropped the palm of one hand on the middle of the drum face, creating a bass sound, and then slapped the face and snapped his hand back like the end of a crackling bullwhip. After several beats, he gave the drum a volley of quick strikes, a hard slap, and then raised his arms. Following his lead, the others stopped playing.

"I must congratulate you," he said to them all. "You have just completed your first drumming lesson. Now we can eat."

CHAPTER 36

BELLPORT GAZETTE

May 20, 1973. Federal authorities have made another arrest in connection with a series of fires in the South End of the city, the area commonly known as "Petite Africa." James Fullerton, owner of several properties in the immigrant community, has been arrested on arson charges. His arraignment is scheduled for next week. Bellport resident Lawrence Briggs was arrested five months ago on charges that he set fires in Petite Africa. An ongoing investigation by the Bellport Arson Squad revealed that Lawrence was on Fullerton's payroll to do upkeep and repairs at some of his properties. Fullerton also allegedly hired Lawrence to set some of the buildings on fire. Fullerton, who lives in the luxury waterfront community of Swift Moore Estates twenty miles north of Bellport, has become known for raising rents unannounced, planting spies at tenant union meetings, and letting his buildings fall into disrepair.

Two people have died and twenty-four others have suffered serious injuries in a spate of fires that began in Petite Africa two and a half years ago. Seven buildings burned down, resulting in four and half million dollars in property losses.

There's no word on whether additional arrests will be made.

In October 1973, Bellport Mayor Chauncey McShane stood on the temporary stage that had been erected on the brick-surfaced plaza in front of the Civic Center Arena. He held up a pair of oversized scissors and cut a symbolic red ribbon draped across the main entrance. Nearby were influential politicians, business leaders, and VIPs from the Harborview Redevelopment Authority.

"This is a new day in Bellport," McShane declared into the microphone. Lights from cameras flashed in his face. A news photographer positioned on a platform facing the stage had his video camera hooked onto a giant tripod. He zoomed in on the scene. "Our Harborview project will transform our fair city into the crown jewel of New England," McShane continued.

People rose from their folding chairs and applauded.

"After we lost Bell Manufacturing, Nathaniel Hawthorne Boot Factory, Bellport Tool and Die, people outside of the state wrote us off. They said Bellport would become a ghost town. But we didn't listen to them, did we? We believed in ourselves, and look at us now."

The applause was thunderous. People whistled and cheered. The ribbon cutting took on the feel of a political rally. Word had leaked from city hall that the mayor had ordered the ribbon cutting months before the interior was completed, hoping the ceremony would help boost his poll numbers among voters. He was counting on the Harborview Redevelopment Project to buoy his campaign. When the applause quieted, he glanced over his shoulder at the VIPs behind him. "I want to bring someone up here. My good friend Kwamé Rodriguez has some remarks. You all know Kwamé."

The crowd cheered. A few people thrust their fists in the air in the Black Power salute as Kwamé mounted the stage.

"We look forward to the prosperity this project will bring, not just to Bellport, but to Liberty Hill," Kwamé shouted. "For too long, people have hit the accelerator when they crossed into Liberty Hill and didn't ease up until they got to the next town. This arena complex and the expressway ramp will rebuild and renew our communities."

"I have heard enough," Omar grumbled to Khadim in Wolof. They were standing next to the platform, waiting their cue to take the stage for their performance. There were still several people to speak, then the Bellport High School marching band would perform.

"Your uncle would spin around in his coffin if he could see this right now," Khadim said.

"I was not going to do this gig until you convinced me," Omar responded. "We are standing in the spot of the gazebo, where Uncle held his rallies and protested against the project."

"And the plaza goes all the way back to Garfield Avenue where Le Baobab was. Your uncle would demand that the city tear up this plaza and rebuild his restaurant for him. He would not rest until they did."

Omar focused his gaze on the glass-brick tower on the front of the arena to keep the tears away. "It is a shame this day has come. Uncle fought for the people of Petite Africa until his last breath."

A state senator was now at the podium speaking.

"I wonder what your uncle would say about your former landlord's arrest."

"It is not what he would say. It is what he would do. He would go to the jail and spit in the man's face. Because of Fullerton, Esmé died. I almost died, too."

Khadim shook his head. "I hope they let Fullerton rot in his jail cell."

Later, as the marching band began the first verse of "America the Beautiful," the men loosened the ropes of their drums, patted the drumheads, and adjusted the tension to set them to the proper pitch.

Omar heard a dog barking. In the distance, near the plaza's edge, he saw a bald-headed man wearing a snorkel jacket, in spite of the warm fall day. He was being pulled along by a grey German shepherd. They seemed familiar, but Omar could not place them.

"After Uncle died, I thought you were gone forever, like the rest of the people of Petite Africa," Omar said.

"I thought so, too, my brother." Khadim put his *djembe* to the side and clutched his *tama* under his arm, patting it lightly. "But driving taxi in Rhode Island is not enough. Benata is having another baby. I need cash. If the city has more gigs like this, I'll take the train up every weekend."

"The drumming institute is not as big as the institute that Uncle and I wanted at the African Cultural Center, but it is a start," Omar said. "I wish he could be here to see it."

Since moving into the Stallworths' basement apartment, Omar had negotiated an agreement to open a drumming school in the bookstore reading room, called the "Mustapha Mendy Drumming Institute." In return, Omar got a break on his rent. Della and Jasmine were the first to enroll, along with Kofi and Anarama.

"But it is nothing to cough at, my brother. Nothing to cough at."

"Someday I will move the drumming institute to its own building. Then I will open drumming institutes all over the country," Omar said.

"Crawl first, then walk, my friend."

Omar laughed. "If you help me, I will soon run."

Khadim cocked his head to the side. "What is your meaning?"

"You must join me. The opportunity that Allah sends does not wake those that are asleep. I have more kids than classes right now. I need another teacher.

Khadim grinned. "How much does it pay?"

"More per day than a weekend driving taxi."

An assistant to the mayor came up to them and flashed two fingers. "Two minutes," he said. They picked up their drums and climbed the stairs at the side of the stage, waiting for the high school band to finish. Khadim turned to Omar. "You give me something to think about."

CHAPTER 37

IN THE TIME since Kwamé took the job in Washington, he and Della had become more distant, barely talking to each other. Kwamé flew home some weekends, and when he did, he spent most of his time at the record shop. When he was home, he never left the television.

Tonight, he was in the recliner, watching *The Streets of San Francisco* with a beer in his hand and four empties crushed on the coffee table. Della peeked in, not wanting to say anything that would rile him. He had been so testy lately. "I'm going across the street," she said.

He said nothing. She waited. Then he burped into his fist.

"Did you hear me?"

He turned his head an inch in her direction. "What you doing that for?"

"I'm going to Syd and Malachi's." She held her breath, hoping he would simply nod and turn back to Karl Malden and Michael Douglas on the screen.

Kwamé took a swig and then set the beer down on the tray table. "Do whatever you want, Dell. Take your classes, go see your friends, but when I have an opportunity I've worked for years to get, you can't support me."

His self-pity made her feel sick. "Kwamé, I…"

He shifted around in the recliner. "You're selfish, Dell. That's the only way to look at it."

Instead of letting Kwamé bait her, she backed out of the

room, grabbed her keys and purse, and stepped out the door. She breathed in deeply when she got outside, catching a cool whiff of air. A light rain fell. She began to realize how stifling it was to be around Kwamé.

She had lied. She wasn't going to the Stallworths. She was going to see Omar. He had invited her over because he said he had news he wanted to share with her. She thought that while she was there, she'd tell him about an opportunity to teach a drumming class at one of the alternative schools, which was expanding its music program.

"*Olele!* Welcome. Come in," Omar said as he opened the basement door. His smile dissolved as he met eyes with her. "You do not look happy, *ma chère.*"

She gave him an update on her troubles with Kwamé. He put his arm around her and led her to the couch. He poured them glasses of wine and sat down next to her.

"So what is your exciting news?" Della asked after they both had taken a sip.

"Uncle Mustapha's estate has been settled. He left his daughter, Ansa, and me, in good shape. I shall have enough money to rent this apartment and have food in the fridge for many years."

Della sat there a moment, thinking about what he had said. Omar had been through so much, with the divorce, the fire. He was finally getting a break.

"Congratulations," she said, lifting her glass to his so they could clink them in a toast.

"You can do better than this, right?" he took both glasses and set them on the coffee table.

Della pulled back. "What do you mean?"

He gave her a playful peck on the mouth, then a longer kiss. She was warmed at the feel of his full, smooth lips and kissed him back forcefully. They sat there a while, holding each other's hands and kissing deeply. Her whole body began to relax.

After a while, she reached for her glass of wine. "I have something I want to tell you, too."

He raised an eyebrow. "What is that?"

"How would you like to teach at..." She stopped at the sound of someone knocking at the door.

"I am not expecting visitors," Omar stared at the door.

After a pause, the knocking resumed. Two seconds later, a heavy fist pounded the door. Omar stood up.

"Are you sure you should answer it?" Della whispered.

"It is my door. I shall answer it."

Omar opened the door. Standing there under the floodlight over the doorway was Kwamé. Della was shocked. Kwamé's eyes shifted from Omar to Della on the couch and back to Omar.

"What are you doing with my woman?" Kwamé snapped.

After a pause, Omar said, "I am doing nothing. We are just talking."

"Bullshit!" Kwamé knocked shoulders with Omar as he shoved past him through the doorway, putting Omar off balance. Omar had to grab onto the wall to steady himself. Kwamé marched into the living room and stood over Della, his eyes bulging, nostrils flared. "You need to come home. I knew I couldn't trust you. " He slurred his words. "You never went to Malachi and Sydney's. They told me."

Della had not anticipated that Kwamé would check up on her and regretted not considering that.

"*No me jodas*, Dell. You lied to me. Why?"

She sat there, staring up at him, still shaken by his sudden appearance at Omar's apartment. "Where's Jasmine?" she asked finally.

"Never mind about Jasmine." He talked through gritted teeth. "I'm talking about you."

"Where is my daughter?" she demanded.

"Upstairs with the friends you claimed you were with."

She hated the sarcasm in his voice. "I don't know what you think you're doing here, Dell, but we're going home and taking care of it."

She stood up. "We were just talking, Kwamé. I came over to

tell Omar about a position in the school system."

"Hmm. You couldn't tell him over the phone?" He pointed at the wine glasses on the coffee table. "And what about these?"

"Okay. Let's go." Della got up and walked toward the door.

"*Ma chère,* are you okay?" Omar asked.

Kwamé spun around at Omar. "You think I don't understand that *je ne sais quoi,* that French bullshit? Who you think you're talking to? You don't talk to Della that way." Kwamé grabbed Della by the wrist and squeezed it so hard she wanted to cry out. Omar stood in the middle of the living room speechless.

Kwamé pulled Della outside. It was beginning to rain heavily. They crossed the street in silence, stepping around puddles. When they got to the front of the record shop, Kwamé let go of her hand.

"Dell, I don't understand what's going on with you anymore. You're playing me for a chump, you and your little drummer man."

Della wanted to explain why she was drawn to Omar, a simple man who she found comfort in, and who respected her. She wanted Kwamé to understand how much he had damaged their relationship with his many women, his big talk, and his indifference to her dreams. She'd put up with him, but leaving her and Jasmine for that job in Washington, D.C., was too much. She could put up with no more. Their relationship had become so strained that they'd become nothing more than roommates. She didn't see the point of explaining how she felt to Kwamé. He was too selfish, insecure, and driven by his ego to listen. Yet, she told herself, she should try.

"Omar's just a friend, that's it. You know what happened to him in the fire. I told you his uncle died. He needs friends right now."

Kwamé shook his head. "There's no reason for my woman to be at some dude's apartment alone."

"Your woman? You're barely even here. I don't know what we are anymore."

"It's not right, Dell. That's how things get started, a couple of glasses of wine, a little conversation, a little kissing, and then you're in the bed."

By the light of the lamp post she could see the vein in his neck twitching "Is that how it started with you and those tramps you chase up and down the streets?"

A light flickered from a window in the building. She looked up and saw one of her tenants on the third floor looking down at them. "I'm not gonna stand out here and argue about this. We can take this inside, or you can stay out here by yourself!"

As she turned to go inside, he grabbed her arm and jerked it hard to force her to stay. She lost her balance and slipped on the wet sidewalk. Her head smacked into a utility pole as she fell. Pain shot from the back of Della's head down her neck. Despite that, she managed to prop herself up on her elbows.

"Dell! Dell!" Kwamé shouted as he stood over her. "Can you get up?" He held out his hand.

She felt the back of her head and looked at her hand in the light from the streetlamp. "I'm bleeding."

They both turned at the sight of a dark sedan with flashing lights pull to the curb. Detective Wilson Stribling got out, along with another plainclothes officer.

"Kwamé," Stribling said.

"Strib, man. Good to see you," Kwamé said. "We were just having a little argument. It ain't nothing, but Della needs to see a doctor."

Della glanced from Stribling to the other officer. "I just slipped on the pavement. It's not his fault. It was an accident."

Kwamé helped her back to her feet.

"That's not why we're here," Stribling said and shifted his attention to Kwamé. "We need you to come down to the station to answer some questions."

"Questions?" asked Della.

"Would you mind stepping into the car?" the second officer asked Kwamé. "Otherwise, we'll have to cuff you."

Two police squad cars pulled up behind the first vehicle.

"I'll come. No need for cuffs," Kwamé said in a barely audible voice. "I'll get in the car."

Della's heart was racing. Kwamé seemed to know what they wanted. "Kwamé, what is going on?" she pleaded. "What's this all about?"

Kwamé looked off in the distance.

"Kwamé?" she asked louder.

"You can tell her," he said to Stribling.

"We're taking him down for questioning about the Petite Africa fires," the detective responded.

"What?" Della couldn't believe what she was hearing. "Arson? Why would they want to talk to you about that?"

Kwamé looked away. Stribling put him in the back of one of the squad cars. "Take him to the station," he said to one of the uniformed police officers.

"Call Bobby," Kwamé shouted to Della before the door shut, referring to Robert Jameson, the attorney who had represented Della when she bought the building. "He knows the kind of attorney I need."

Della stood in the rain as all three cars drove off. On shaky legs, she crossed the street to the Stallworths to get Jasmine.

CHAPTER 38

THE NEXT NIGHT, Sydney unfolded a copy of the late edition of *Inner City Voice* and laid it on the kitchen table in front of Malachi. She'd picked up the paper on her way out of the newsroom after an exhausting day spent at news conferences, interviewing police, city officials, and Bellport residents about the arsons and Kwamé's arrest. Max worked the phones interviewing his contacts. Officials stated that they were confident that with the arrest of Kwamé, they had all of the individuals involved in the arson ring.

The headline at the top of the page read, *Bellport Activist Arrested in String of Arsons*. The byline: *By Sydney Stallworth*. The story, which took up the entire front page and continued inside, included a head and shoulders shot of Kwamé and photos from the fires.

"You've done a great job," Malachi said after reading the article. "I'm proud of you, Syd. I just wish it wasn't Kwamé. He's the last person I'd expect to be caught up in something like this."

"I know," she said. "I haven't been able to eat all day knowing that Kwamé was responsible for ruining people's lives and causing some people to die."

Malachi shook his head. "He had no business getting Lawrence involved."

Through her interview with Detective Stribling, she found out that when the fires first started a couple of years ago, James

Fullerton had hired Kwamé to burn out the residents so that he could collect the insurance money and rebuild later under a city contract as part of the redevelopment project. But as the deadline loomed to get the residents out, so that Petite Africa could be leveled for the rebuilding to begin, Fullerton told Kwamé to pick up the pace, and to set more fires. Facing pressure, Kwamé hired Lawrence.

"So, now we know why Kwamé took that job in Washington," Malachi said, pointing to a paragraph in the article.

"Right. He had two reasons, actually. The job with HUD was a political favor from the mayor for helping to revive Liberty Hill, for bringing people like you and me here to open up businesses. But Kwamé was only half interested, that is until Esmé Tavernier died after the fire at her shop, and the man who died in the fire that put Omar in the hospital. Then Kwamé started getting nervous. He thought if he left town, the police would be less likely to tie him to the arsons. It's interesting that initially Lawrence gave up Fullerton, but not Kwamé. It took police a while to get Lawrence to admit that Kwamé had hired him."

"I wonder why?"

"Stribling wouldn't tell me. He said off-the-record that he made it clear to Lawrence that it was in his best interest to tell them who the middleman was."

"Maybe they dangled a reduced sentence in front of Lawrence."

"That's what I suspect."

"This whole thing blows my mind," Malachi said, handing the paper back to Sydney. "And the dude never did go to 'Nam."

"Nope. He never set foot in Vietnam. He was at Oxbridge Correctional Center. He served two years there for armed robbery and passing bad checks."

"You think you know somebody. You grow up together, he's got your back, you've got his back, but you really don't know them."

Sydney walked into the living room and looked down at the

street from the picture window. Two news vans were parked in front of Rhythm and Blues. A couple of reporters were standing in front of the building, one holding a microphone, the other with a notebook and pen.

"She's been holed up in there all day," she said in reference to Della. "It must be awful."

"I'm sure she's in shock," Malachi said.

She continued to watch as Omar left the basement apartment and walked across the street to Della's building. At least Della and Jasmine would have a little company at this awful time. Omar waved off the reporters as he entered the building.

When Sydney returned to the kitchen, Malachi had buried his head in his hands.

"Sydney, I'm so sorry. I feel I've failed you as a husband. I changed our plans for the future after I didn't get tenure, then you agreed to leave law school to support me opening up The Talking Drum, and then I forced the Taylors on you and didn't check their references, even though you insisted. I hired an intern who turned out to be an arsonist. Over and over again, I listened to Kwamé's advice over yours and on top of that, he turned out to be an arsonist too. I wouldn't blame you, if you wanted to leave me."

Sydney sat back down across from him. "I thought about it. I thought about leaving. But I thought about my parents' marriage. Back when my father was still alive I was too young to know what was going on, but they had some awful arguments. They'd go on for hours. But at some point things got better. They hung in there and worked it out. I remember them being very happy for a good while until my father got sick with cancer. With you and me, I think we're both learning how to be married to each other and it takes a while. I had faith that if I hung in there with you it would get better. And it has."

He reached across the table and took her hand. "Sydney, thank you."

CHAPTER 39

SYDNEY TURNED OFF the adding machine and skipped down the stairs to the main floor to tell Malachi the news. For the first time since they'd been in business, she was able to write checks covering all of The Talking Drum's bills for the month. This was encouraging.

It was February 1974, two months shy of their second anniversary in the house and she was making preparations to go back to law school at Whittington University. She could concentrate on her studies and not worry so much about the business. When she got to the parlor, Pumpkin was pacing back and forth along the front counter as if guarding Malachi like a dignitary as he read a flyer.

"It seems that someone's trying to give us some competition. Why don't we go check this place out?" He handed her the notice about a grand opening a week ago at Prologue, a bookstore on their street, three blocks down.

She decided that now was not the time to tell him her good news. She would wait until after they had visited their competition. They bundled up in their winter jackets and when they reached the sidewalk, they were met by Omar and Della, who had come from the basement apartment.

"*Olele*, my friends," Omar said.

"How're you holding up?" Sydney asked Della.

It had been four months since Kwamé's arrest. Days ago, he was found guilty of involuntary manslaughter in the deaths associated with the fires. His sentencing was scheduled for the end of March.

Della gave them a crooked smile. "I have my good days and my bad days. Omar has been there for me. He's given me a shoulder to cry on."

Omar squeezed her hand.

"How's Jasmine doing?" asked Malachi.

Della sighed. "She's okay. She still has her episodes, considering the situation."

"She is a strong little girl," Omar said.

Della nodded. "I have her seeing a psychologist."

"That's really good, Della." Sydney said.

"She told me something interesting. She thinks the reason Jasmine likes the drumming so much is because she's using it as therapy."

"Therapy?" questioned Malachi.

"Believe it or not, there are clinics for that. Patients hit the drum to calm their nerves. It's called 'drum therapy'," Della explained.

"It is good that we have little Jasmine in the drumming institute," said Omar. "She talks to the psychologist and she plays her drums. She shall be good as new in no time."

"I'm taking the semester off," Della said. "I want to put my attention on getting my little girl better." She smiled broadly, revealing a mouth filled with metal.

"You got braces!" Sydney exclaimed.

"Girl, yes I did. I want to get my smile straight. My classmate's father is doing this for me. He's fixing me up real good at a discount."

Omar looked down the street. "We are going to the ice cream shop. Shall you join us?"

Malachi told them about the new bookstore, which was in the opposite direction.

"You think they'll be okay, her and Jasmine?" Sydney asked Malachi after the couples parted ways.

"I think they'll be fine."

On their way down the street, they passed one, and then another young white couple pushing a baby in a stroller.

"Where are they coming from?" Sydney asked.

Malachi shrugged. "Don't know."

In the months leading up to completion of the Harborview project, Sydney and Malachi had watched as one business after another closed up on Liberty Hill Boulevard. Some establishments would shut down in the middle of the night with the proprietor leaving town without a word. Building owners were hiking the rents, leaving many of the retailers with no choice but to shut down. Jake's Tavern and After-Hours Club was gone, replaced by a fine-dining restaurant popular for its martini bar and humidor. Sydney had heard that it was nearly impossible to get a reservation.

Malachi stopped short when they were half a block from Prologue. Puzzled, Sydney searched his face. He nodded in the direction of the bookshop. Cynthia and Renée, customers who'd organized The Talking Drum's women's employment support group not long after the bookstore opened, were coming out of the store. Cynthia was clutching a shopping bag that looked overfilled.

"We haven't seen them in a while," Malachi said.

"I know. It's been months."

"Hello ladies!" Malachi shouted at the couple as they walked across the street. Both turned around, waved furiously at Sydney and Malachi, and then continued on their way.

A wind chime cut the air as they walked into Prologue Bookstore and Café. Sydney could smell coffee brewing and freshly baked pastries.

"Welcome to Prologue," a red-haired, freckled woman called from behind the front counter. Her earth shoes were partially hidden beneath her bell-bottom jeans. "May I offer you two a complimentary carrot juice shake?"

"I'm not sure," Sydney said.

"It's fresh," the woman replied. "Still in the blender."

"Okay," Sydney agreed, "I'll try one."

The Stallworths looked around the store. It had about the same square footage as The Talking Drum. Round tables were set up in one section with a coffee station. Beyond it was an elevated stage with a curtain. The woman returned with what looked like a pale orange milk shake.

"What's the stage for?" Sydney asked.

"It will do double duty. We'll have puppet shows during the weekends for the kids, and then playwrights and actors can try out their works in progress before an audience on weekday nights." The woman led them to the café area. "We're just getting started, but eventually we'll have someone back here making sandwiches and desserts along with the coffee and the health drinks. This is my husband's dream," she continued. "We finally made it happen."

"Sounds familiar," Sydney said and exchanged a smile with Malachi.

"Are you two tourists?" the woman asked.

"No, we live right down the street," replied Malachi. "We own the bookstore and cultural center three blocks up, The Talking Drum."

The woman shook her head. "Never heard of it. Must be a small place."

"No, it's just as large as yours," Sydney countered. "We've been in business almost two years."

"Well," the woman said, tacking on a smile. "Welcome again. Please come back to Prologue any time." She turned and walked away.

"That was strange," Sydney mused as they left the store. "She just got here, and we've been here for years, and she's acting like we're outsiders."

"Doesn't surprise me at all," Malachi said. "People get territorial quick. How do you like that carrot shake she gave you?"

Sydney turned up her nose. "Tastes like grass." She tossed

the cup in a trash can on the sidewalk.

They walked past Deborah's, an upscale art gallery that had just opened where Paradise Pawn Shop used to be. They turned around at the sound of the front door opening. Officer Robertson, the police officer who was Detective Stribling's partner when he was a rookie, walked down the stairs and waved.

"I wonder what the trouble is," she asked.

"There's no trouble," Malachi answered. "One of the police captains came to the Neighborhood Improvement Association meeting the other day and announced that the city is stepping up the police presence in the neighborhood. Walking patrols are a part of that."

"I have noticed more squad cars on the streets lately," she sighed. "The neighborhood is changing."

Malachi nodded. "I know."

"The black businesses are closing shop."

"Not all of them," he said. "In most cases it's the ones who were renting. It's a good thing we bought our place."

They arrived back home and sat on the front porch. A robin poked its head out of the bird house hanging from the sugar maple tree, chirped and then flew away.

"Do you think we'll survive?" she asked.

He looked at her, eyes narrowed. "What do you mean?"

"Prologue is doing a lot of the things we're doing."

He put his arm around her. "Doesn't matter what kind of bookstore they put in this neighborhood. They're never going to have what we offer. They're not going to sell books by us or put books about us on the shelves. People who want to read black authors, if they want to meet black poets, playwrights, and novelists, will have to come to us."

Sydney thought this over for a while. "But what about Cynthia and Renée? They used to shop with us all the time. Now they're over at Prologue. If they go over there enough and spend enough money, the owners will start stocking what they want and give them no reason to come back here."

He smiled. "Sydney, you're getting ahead of yourself. They'll be back. Prologue is new. They're just curious about it."

"But did you see that shopping bag Cynthia had? It was so full she had to carry it with both hands. Given more choices, black people will shop wherever they want. They'll forget all about the black businesses."

"I believe that black people will support their own. That's not going to change."

She wondered if he believed what he was saying or was refusing to admit to himself the distinct possibility that in time, The Talking Drum Bookstore and Cultural Center would lose its customer base. If that happened, they could end up in debt, Malachi would have to give up his dream, probably leaving him bitter, and the marriage would suffer more than it already had, assuming it survived. Her thoughts made her shudder.

"And don't forget about what the arena and the expressway ramp are doing," Malachi continued. "It's happening slowly but we're starting to see some additional foot traffic in the store."

"I hadn't noticed."

"You weren't there, but just the other day we had some people stop in who said they were coming from the basketball game at the arena. We're going to see a whole new clientele coming into The Talking Drum."

She wanted to respond that one party of customers was no indication of a pickup in business, but decided not to. She was growing tired of being the skeptic.

"Don't forget, Sydney," he continued, "the research center is still part of the plan. Besides out regular customers we'll have scholars coming in, making The Talking Drum a landmark."

Sydney rested her head on Malachi's shoulder. She had married an optimist and a dreamer. She was beginning to realize that now. The bookstore was financially stable for the moment. Maybe it wouldn't falter as she feared.

"Maybe you're right about the future of The Talking Drum,"

she said and told him the news about being able to cover the bookstore's bills for the month.

"See Syd?" he kissed her on the temple. "Things are looking up. Give it time. Just give it some time."

ACKNOWLEDGEMENTS

Writing a novel had been my dream since I developed a love for reading in the first grade. As a six-year-old, I had no idea that becoming a novelist wouldn't happen until many decades later, and that it would be one of the most challenging, yet rewarding experiences of my life. It is heartwarming that when I finally began this project, I wasn't alone. I journeyed through the years with family, friends, and a community supporting me along the way.

This book exists because of my parents. Julian and Elizabeth Braxton owned and operated a men's clothing store in an urban community in Bridgeport, Connecticut, beginning in the late 1960s until well into the 2000s and saw their livelihood and community affected by urban redevelopment, much like my characters in *The Talking Drum*.

I am grateful to my sister, Sylvia Braxton Lee, who reads the first draft of just about everything I write for publication and gives me encouragement and suggestions. She believed in *The Talking Drum* from the beginning, when all I had was a seven-page scene between a man and woman in a bookstore. Thank you to my niece and nephew, Raven Sofia Lee and Julian David Lee, who were playing with Fisher Price toys when I began the manuscript. They cheered me on, with, "You GO, Aunt Lisa!" throughout the years. Raven is now well into her high school years and Julian has his sights set on college. My brother-in-law, Aron "Teo" Lee, a fellow artist, urged me not to give up as I struggled in the later stages to find a publisher. Thank you to the pastor, ministerial leaders and congregation of Myrtle Baptist Church, West Newton, Massachusetts, for your spiritual and emotional support, as well as your enthusiasm in celebrating my publishing accomplishments. The ladies of the Myrtle Book Club gave me an invaluable critique and encouragement during the early stages of *The Talking Drum* and I will always be grateful to them: Jacquelyn Arrington, Melinda Brown, Monique Brown, Carolyn Davis, Barbara Fox, Roberta James, Mary Lightfoot, Maria Manning, Rosalyn Pierce, Susan Perry, Imelda Price, Claire Rosser, Maxine Thomas Smith, Denise Willis Turner, and Sandra Wright. Additionally, thank you to former English teacher, Reverend Inez Dover, for your critique of the manuscript.

For technical advice I thank Alan Tauber, owner of Drum-Connection, a Boston hand-drumming school, for the classes in which I learned both the complexity and simplicity of African drumming, Mamady Keita grandmaster of the *djembe* and one of the world's best-known *djembe* players, Ernest Grant, PhD, burn nurse clinician, and Paul LeBlanc, formerly of the National Fire Protection Association Fire Analysis and Research Division.

Marie Claude Mendy, formerly owner of Teranga Restaurant in Boston, not only introduced me to Senegalese cuisine, but arranged a gathering of her friends from the Boston Senegalese community to help me learn about Senegalese culture. Thank you for the generosity of your time.

A special thanks to the Mountainview Low-Residency MFA faculty of Southern New Hampshire University who shepherded me along on my first draft of what was to become *The*

Talking Drum: Robert Begiebing, Diane Les Becquets, Rick Carey, Katherine Towler, Gretchen Legler, and Merle Drown.

Additionally, I would like to thank my writing community: Grub Street, one of the nation's leading writing centers, Women's National Book Association, National Writers Union-Boston, Boston Women Communicators, the South Shore Scribes, and the Kimbilio Fiction Writers Fellows.

For making "the big dance" leading up to publication so much fun I thank my fellow Debs of The Debutante Ball blog: Amy Klein, Karen Osborne, Kathleen West, and Yodassa Williams.

Thank you to my editor, Luciana Ricciutelli, of Inanna Publications, for her enthusiasm for this story and her commitment to bringing diverse perspectives to the reading audience.

And to my husband, Alexander Reid, who spent many nights reading and re-reading the manuscript, helping me to sharpen my story line-by-line. When I was feeling discouraged you told me that you had no doubt that this work would be published. Alex, I couldn't have done this without you.

Photo: Adrienne Albrecht

Lisa Braxton is an Emmy-nominated former television journalist, a former newspaper reporter, an essayist, short story writer, and novelist. She is a fellow of the Kimbilio Fiction Writers Program and was a finalist in the William Faulkner-William Wisdom Creative Writing Competition. She earned her MFA in creative writing from Southern New Hampshire University, her M.S. in journalism from Northwestern University, and her B.A. in mass media from Hampton University. Her short fiction has been published in anthologies and literary journals across North America. She lives in the Boston, Massachusetts area.